MEDICI HEIST

CAITLIN SCHNEIDERHAN

ATOM

First published in the United States in 2024 by Feiwel and Friends
First published in Great Britain in 2024 by Atom
This paperback edition published in 2025

1 3 5 7 9 10 8 6 4 2

Copyright © Caitlin Schneiderhan, 2024

The moral right of the author has been asserted.

A CIP catalogue record for this book
is available from the British Library.

ISBN: 978-0-3491-2540-4

Printed and bound in Great Britain by Clays Ltd, Elcograf S.p.A.

Papers used by Atom are from well-managed forests
and other responsible sources.

MIX
Paper | Supporting
responsible forestry
FSC® C104740

Atom
An imprint of
Little, Brown Book Group
Carmelite House
50 Victoria Embankment
London EC4Y 0DZ

The authorised representative
in the EEA is
Hachette Ireland
8 Castlecourt Centre
Dublin 15, D15 XTP3, Ireland
(email: info@hbgi.ie)

An Hachette UK Company
www.hachette.co.uk

www.littlebrown.co.uk

Caitlin Schneiderhan, author of *Medici Heist*, is a genre-loving writer on the hit Netflix show *Stranger Things*. Originally hailing from Silver Spring, Maryland, Caitlin hatched from a cocoon of Terry Pratchett novels when she was 13. She spent her teenage years scribbling stories during class instead of paying attention (you can't prove she wasn't just taking notes). Eventually, she decided to chase that storytelling bug all the way out to sunny Los Angeles, where she spent a few years scribbling scripts at assistant jobs instead of paying attention (you can't prove she wasn't just taking notes). She has been named one of *MovieMaker Magazine*'s '25 Screenwriters to Watch', and has projects in development with multiple production companies around Hollywood.

Praise for *Medici Heist*

'I can't remember the last time I had as much fun with a book as I did with *Medici Heist*. Caitlin Schneiderhan takes readers on a wild, sumptuous tour of historical Florence, packed with cinematic action and helmed by a gang of lovable misfits and outsiders who come together to pull off an impossible heist. I couldn't put this down!'
Mackenzi Lee, *New York Times* bestselling author of
The Gentleman's Guide to Vice and Virtue

'If you've ever wanted to hold a fun, daring, historically rich heist movie in the palm of your hands – pick up this book'
Ngozi Ukazu, author of *Check, Please!*

'[A] brilliantly plotted adventure! *Medici Heist* is a fun, rollicking escapade through Renaissance Florence that will leave you wanting more'
Adriana Mather, *New York Times* bestselling
author of *How to Hang a Witch*

'A riotously readable YA historical fantasy caper'
Guardian

TO MY PARENTS,
FOR SHOWING ME FLORENCE
AND GIVING ME THE WORLD

- PART I -

THE DAVID

FLORENCE, 1517

The mud was from the banks of the Arno river. But also, it was from the banks of the Arno river *inside* the city walls, so it was probably not entirely mud. It really *stank* like not-entirely-mud in Cat's hand. But she'd touched worse in her life. And anyway, Gio had dared her.

She followed the carriage.

They'd entered the city through the Porta Romana, which Cat thought was silly. It was a big, fancy carriage, covered in gold and paint and stuff like that, and it was supposed to be full of fancy people too. Shouldn't fancy people know that the Porta Romana was one long snarl of people and carts at this time of day? Or maybe they were too rich to care about that sort of thing.

They weren't too rich not to care about *everything*, though. Cat hung in the shadows as the carriage paused in front of Signore Bruno's bakery, the one that sold the ciambelle that Gio sometimes stole. It was a two-story shop front, and Signore Bruno was perched on a ladder outside. He had a chisel and a bucket of soapy water, and he was scraping at the printed paper that had been pasted to his wall. Cat shrank further back when she saw the two City Guards at the base of Signore Bruno's ladder, keeping careful watch on him.

The carriage's velvet curtain twitched aside. The hand that pulled it sparkled in the sunlight, just as shiny as the carriage. Cat caught a glimpse of a stormy frown before the curtain settled back. A moment later, two of the Medici Guardsmen strode toward the City Guards. Someone inside the carriage thumped on the roof, and the driver urged the horses forward. Cat hurried to keep up as, behind her, an argument broke out between the two sets of uniformed men.

There was still one last scrap of paper clinging to the wall despite Signore Bruno's scrubbing. And Cat was picking up some letters these days. *Reppublica.* That's what it said.

Cat grinned and forged onward.

They were headed into the Piazza della Signoria, a giant plaza in the center of Florence. It was one of Cat's favorite parts of the city. She liked the way the cobblestones sprawled in every direction. She liked the sweeping arches of the Loggia dei Lanzi. And she *loved* the gleaming white marble of the statue of *David*, which towered before the Palazzo Vecchio's front entrance.

The murmurs began as the carriage rolled out into the Piazza. In ones and twos, and then in bigger groups, the crowd turned their faces toward the crest on the carriage doors. "*The Medici?*" Cat heard them whisper as she passed. "*Has the Pope returned?*"

Almost as though they'd heard the question, the curtains of the fancy carriage opened, pulled back by that same bejeweled hand. There were no troubled frowns now—just a man draped in purples and golds, with beneficent eyes and an indulgent smile.

"But you said he was a Medici," Cat had protested earlier that day. "How can he be the Pope if he's also a Medici?"

The look Gio had given her said quite clearly that only babies asked stupid questions like that, and that ten-year-olds like Gio didn't have time for babies.

"My beloved Florence!" Pope Leo X—or maybe Giovanni de' Medici—declared. His voice carried. "I am home!"

The reaction was immediate. The Piazza burst into cheers, pushing forward to get a better look at the carriage. Cat let herself be swept along, taking advantage of the path that the stink emanating from her right hand carved for her.

Guards in Medici blue had sprung into action by the time Cat made it to the front of the mob, shoving people away from the horses. They didn't pay much mind to Cat. Who would notice a little girl in a crowd of grasping adults?

"I am gratified by your warmth and love," the Pope said. His voice carried across the Piazza. "My dear cousin had assured me of your welcome, but it is quite another thing to witness it in person! Would you greet your people, Giulio?"

There was a spindly silhouette in the carriage at the Pope's shoulder. He did not move forward into the sunlight. The Pope rolled his eyes. "That is Cardinal de' Medici for you."

An old woman in a gray shawl had managed to get to the carriage window. "Your Holiness!" she croaked, reaching for the Pope's hand. Cat saw the man shoot a disgusted glance back into the carriage, toward his angular companion. He pulled back out of her reach, sketching a quick sign of the cross over her head.

"Thank you," the old woman called. She fell back from the window, a few tears rolling down her cheek.

"Bless this city," called the Pope. "And bless every soul within it!"

Cat threw shit at him.

She did not have the best aim. The ball of muck hit the edge of the window. But it exploded with a gratifying splatter all across the shiny robes, and the Pope staggered back into his fancy carriage with a "Jesus Christ!" that would have gotten Cat's ears boxed.

"Who threw that?" thundered the captain of the Medici Guard. He wheeled his horse between the carriage and the crowd. But even his bellows weren't loud enough to drown out the "*Look* at me, Giulio, I'm covered in *filth*!" that caterwauled out from the carriage window.

Shock rippled through the crowd, murmurs that grew and grew. Someone shoved Cat back, until the carriage was blocked from sight behind a set of broad shoulders.

"I want them caught! I want them flogged!" the Medici Pope was wailing. But it was harder and harder to hear him over the growing shouts of the crowd. People were no longer cheering, or at least not all of them were.

"Long live the Republic!" The chant rang from every corner of the Piazza until it was deafening. "Long live the Republic!"

It occurred to Cat that she maybe hadn't thought about how to get away. This was especially a problem because of the men in Medici blue who were starting to thread through the crowd, shoving past onlookers. Looking for someone.

Looking for her.

Cat gulped and turned. But the current that had bobbed her all the way to the Medici carriage was working against her now. It was like the Piazza had become a wall of legs and torsos, and nobody seemed eager to budge for the girl with the smelly hands. Not when the guards were closing in. Not until—

A path opened. Just for a moment. And, at the end of it, Cat saw a lifeline.

Without hesitating, she dove into the chaos of Florence and let herself be saved.

2

ROSA

As far as naked men went, Rosa Cellini supposed that this one was impressive. Muscular. Tall enough, certainly. Her neck hurt from craning. But no matter how long she stood by his feet, David's gaze did not creak down to meet hers.

That was alright. He was a statue, after all.

She fanned her skirts, settling comfortably against the statue's plinth. It was a careful maneuver—she had to be cautious not to disturb any of the flowers, the fruit, and the . . . less-savory offerings that had been strewn about the base. Despite her best efforts, a small roll of paper fluttered loose from where it had been pinned down by a pigeon-pecked roll. Rosa scooped it up, doing her best to ignore whatever pleas or prayers or dreams were scribbled on it in blotched ink—but as she did so, something on the cobbles caught her eye: a scrap of paper bearing a few fragments of printed words.

"REPPUBLICA FIORENTINA," it read. The ink was smeared.

Rosa nudged it aside with her toe and managed to find an undisturbed seat. Fishing out a deck of well-worn cards, she began to shuffle, scanning the crowd with reserved interest.

The Piazza was clearing, the chaos of the last ten minutes quieting. Medici Guards were still making the rounds, interrogating bystanders, searching for whoever had been brave enough to lob what had looked to be a handful of pig shit at the head of the Church.

It had been a beautiful carriage. And that muddy projectile had hit smack in the middle of the triple fleur-de-lis Medici crest adorning the front door.

Rosa dealt out three cards and waited.

Florence, for all that it had been built on Roman ruins, had been brought to wealth and prominence by the money and machinations of the Medici bankers. For years upon years, men wearing a veneer of proletariat humility over deep, deep pockets of wealth had transformed the city from a huddle of hovels on the banks of the Arno river into the sprawling metropolis that it was today.

It was almost refreshing, Rosa thought, to see the gilding and the metalwork of the Pope's carriage. This particular Medici scion was not one who would pretend to be one of the common folk. He advertised his fortune. A palate-cleanser. And after six years of avoiding the city like the plague, Rosa had walked through the gates at nearly the same hour he had.

"What are you hanging around here for?"

Rosa smiled up at the two guards across the wooden board balanced on her knees. She could imagine the picture she presented. A short young woman with wild dark hair and dark eyes and a deceptive softness all over. Her red woolen kirtle was heavily travel-stained, and the leather satchel at her side was patched in some places and in need of patching in others.

Not a threat. Not remarkable in any way.

"Good afternoon!" she chirped, flipping the three playing cards to display their faces. *Knave. Six. Queen.* "What a blessed day! Can you believe our good fortune? To have such a man in our midst? Well, of course *you* can—you probably see him all the time—"

One guard was blushing. The other was not. These were odds Rosa could work with.

"Did you see a young girl?" the unblushing guard demanded. The other was fixated on the cards under Rosa's hands.

"A girl? I've seen plenty of girls today. Find the Lady?"

This last was directed to the fascinated guard, who met her eyes, startled. He was younger than his partner, perhaps even of age to match Rosa's own seventeen years. Flustered by the sudden attention, he stammered, "I—uh—I don't—"

"I'll show you how to play," said Rosa. She flipped the cards over again and began to shuffle them, spinning them over and around each other on the board.

"She would be about this tall," the other guard said, ignoring this. He held his hand as high as his waist. "Filthy. Shabby clothes."

Rosa gasped. "Is this the person who attacked His Holiness?" Her hands were still moving, a blur that the younger guard watched, hypnotized. "I haven't seen anyone like that," she said. "But it was all so horrible. So *exciting*. Is His Holiness unharmed?"

"You're certain you haven't seen anyone who fits that description?" the terse guard said.

Rosa shook her head, lifting her hands. The cards lay in a razor-straight line. "On His Holiness's life, I swear I haven't seen *anyone* like that. Now. Can you find the Lady? Where is that queen hiding?"

Seemingly without thinking, the younger guard tapped the middle card. "Ricci," barked his partner, but Rosa was already turning it over to reveal the Queen of Cups' impassive face.

"Well done, signore," she said. "You're a natural."

The other guardsman had reached the end of his patience. "She's a charlatan, you rube," he snapped. "Get your head on straight. We're wasting our time." Without another word, he turned and marched across the Piazza, headed for the lingering crowds inside the Loggia dei Lanzi. Ricci, suitably chastened, moved to follow.

"Signore," Rosa said, carefully removing the board and rising. "Here." She held out the Queen. "For you."

He had already taken it when his brain caught up. "Don't you need this?"

"Some things are worth a little sacrifice," she told him. The chilly breeze off the Arno was whipping color into her cheeks. She winked at Ricci, plucked the card back from him, and tucked it into his belt. "Lovely to meet you," she said.

Rosa may as well have axed him between the eyes. He blinked, empty-headed, until—

"Ricci!" The grumpy guard looked about ready to spit nails. With an anxious jolt, the young man turned on his heel and hurried after his partner, tripping over his feet in his haste to catch up. Rosa continued to shuffle her cards as she watched the two of them go, Ricci cowering from his partner's scolding.

"Are they gone?"

The voice was muffled by layers of Rosa's woolen skirts and the wooden board she had propped up against the statue's plinth. Rosa didn't chance a look at the girl crouched behind her. She could tell by the smell that the girl hadn't taken advantage of Rosa's waterskin to clean the mud and God-knew-what-else off her hands.

"Shh," she said. Ricci had managed to distract his partner away from berating him and toward interrogating more of the throng thrumming through the Loggia dei Lanzi. Their sights set on some other poor bastard, they finally disappeared from view. "Yes," she said. "But don't you come back out here until you've washed those hands." Water immediately began splashing onto the cobblestones, and Rosa bit back a smile.

It had been a matter of course to hide the girl when she'd darted out of the crowd, hands filthy and face wild with terror. She couldn't have been more than eight years old, and Rosa had plenty of memories of similar scrapes at that age (though none that involved the Pope).

Now the girl emerged, empty waterskin in hand and a sheepish look on her face. She handed it back with a little bob of the head. "Thank you, signorina."

"Don't mention it," Rosa said, wiping the skin discreetly on her skirts before fastening it once again to her bag. There was a commotion over by the Loggia dei Lanzi. *Someone*—perhaps a young guard in the uniform of one of Florence's most preeminent noble houses—seemed to have mislaid his purse. Rosa shouldered her pack. "Come on," she said. "Time to go."

"Are you in trouble, signorina?" The girl followed on Rosa's heels as she strode out onto one of the many side streets. "They didn't see you hide me."

"They didn't see me lift that guard's money either. But it will only be a matter of time before they decide to circle back."

"You let him win that hand, didn't you?"

The girl's eyes were sharp as she watched Rosa, cleverness honed by necessity. "Of course," Rosa told her. "You always let a mark win the first hand of Find the Lady. Maybe even the first few hands."

"Why?"

"So they think they're in control," she told her. "When that happens, you can ask them to wager whatever you want, and they'll say yes. Then all you have to do is take it from them." She nudged the girl. "Wouldn't you rather walk away with a gold florin than a single lire?"

"Hm," the girl hummed. "But that man seemed nice." She didn't sound upset about it.

"Maybe he was," Rosa said. "Now he's nice and poor. At least he still has his job."

"Nice people don't last long with the Medici family."

"Sounds like that will be very hard on him." Rosa paused, looking around. Their hurried pace had taken them several streets away from the Piazza della Signoria, and the crowds had thinned to a more manageable stream of well-to-do pedestrians and shopkeepers. It was a good part of town, but most things this side of the Arno were the good part of town. Rosa scanned the unfamiliar buildings and cursed herself for avoiding this city for so long.

She knew where she was. She *knew* that she knew where she was. Six years ago, she would have been able to walk these streets blindfolded. Florence had been a second home, a school, a place of business, *everything*. But now, Rosa squinted at the storefronts and the banks and the churches, frowning as they tripped at her memory.

"What's your name?" she asked the girl, who was still lurking in her shadow, apparently unsure of whether or not she was allowed to leave. The girl hesitated, her street smarts showing. "Fine, then what do I call you?"

"You can—call me Cat," she said.

"Cat. I'll trade two lire for directions."

Cat's eyes bugged out of her face. "Directions to where?" she asked, still cautious.

"Do you know where the apothecary is?"

Her face twisted in confusion. "Apothe . . ."

"Agata de Rosso. Do you know where Agata de Rosso's shop is?"

Cat brightened, all at once. "Oh!" she said. "You're looking for the witch!"

Two lire was apparently overpaying for mere directions, so Cat took it upon herself to personally guide Rosa through the bustling streets of central Florence, chattering a tour guide's monologue that, with any luck, was about half-accurate.

Rosa focused on tuning out Cat's local flavor in favor of refamiliarizing herself with the patterns of streets and piazzas. It was a mental trick she'd done countless times—first as a tiresome exercise administered by her mother, and then later, once she'd struck out on her own, as a reflex. The map of the city sketched into view in her mind, coming together in rough strokes and finer details, the haze of memory infusing with the grime and grit of reality.

"It's all about making the intangible *tangible*," her mother had told her before she was old enough to understand what those words even meant. They had been leaning over a candle in the drafty attic, whispering in the depths of the night. There was no reason to keep quiet—they were painfully alone in the house, ever since Rosa's father's funeral. But neither of them had been all that good at sleeping, and so they had begun to find one another beneath the creaking beams of the attic when the sun was a distant memory, nowhere near either horizon.

She could still picture the way Lena Cellini's dark eyes had sparkled in candlelight, wicked and sad. "We learn a place the same way we learn people," she had said, and Rosa had nodded as though she knew what her mother was talking about. "When we first meet them, or when we first meet a place—it's a chalk outline. Just a little paper cutout. Nothing to fill it inside the edges." She'd grabbed her daughter and tickled her sides, and Rosa had squealed, forgetting to be quiet. "But then we get to know them, and those blank spaces get filled in with memories. Instead of just any person, you see the baker's wife who laughs like a goose. Instead of just any street, you see the place where you skinned your knee. But there's a trick to it."

Rosa's eyes must have been as wide as her entire face. "What's the trick?"

Lena's expression turned solemn, watching Rosa in their sanctuary. Alone together. "Would you like to learn?" she'd asked, but she'd meant more than that. She'd meant *everything*.

Now, following a little girl who was fool enough to throw shit at the Pope, Rosa filled in the edges of Florence. And what Florence was filled with was the Medici family.

For a century, the family's wealth and influence had held Florence in its sway, sculpting it (sometimes literally) in their image. Sculptors, painters, architects—they could all credit their success to the patronage of the Medici. Lorenzo de' Medici, one of the last patriarchs, had been especially prolific in this field, his generosity earning himself the title of Lorenzo il Magnifico—Lorenzo the Magnificent—and a legacy of cultural works that were known the world over.

Of course, that legacy could not protect the family forever. After Lorenzo's death, mounting military losses had resulted in the exiles of the nineteen-year-old Giovanni de' Medici, Lorenzo's son, and his sixteen-year-old cousin Giulio—two of the last scions of the Medici clan. For decades they had been barred from the city they saw as their birthright, their righteous indignation growing with every passing year. Meanwhile, Florence had found peace and prosperity without them, coming into its own as a free and democratic Repubblica Fiorentina. It turned out that the city did not need the Medici to be great.

But the banished Medici cousins had not been content to accept this new reality. Together, they had schemed up a way to retake the city in their family's name. By the time this plan had come into fruition, Giovanni had earned the scarlet vestments of a cardinal. And five years ago, with the might of the Church behind them, he and his cousin had gathered together an army and set out once again to bend Florence to their will.

It had not been a bloodless transition, though Florence itself had been spared the worst of it. The honor of setting a harsh and savage example for the city had fallen on . . . other luckless shoulders. Why, after all, would the Medici want to break the plaything they'd plotted so intricately to reclaim? And so Florence had been cowed into accepting their prodigal patriarchs back with open arms. Giovanni had shelved his Medici name in favor of the appropriately papal Pope Leo X, and Giulio had stepped into the cardinal role his cousin had vacated. But if the angry bills on the walls and the smear on the Pope's carriage were anything to go by, the Medici's return to power was far from universally welcome.

Rosa shivered. The last time she'd been in Florence had been the days of the Republic. Now she could feel the cold fingers of that memory brushing the back of her neck as she followed in Cat's wake, passing the alley where Lena had beaten bank clerks at just the right number of dice games before they got angry; the Church of Santa Maria Maggiore, where her mother had spent a very enjoyable few days telling ghost stories about the poor woman buried in the walls while Rosa had made off with her audience's money; the tavern where Rosa had stolen a sip of gin and vomited on the steps outside.

Ghosts and ghosts. But she had been expecting that. She could take it in stride. And, thankfully, they were fewer and further between as Cat led her away from the city's center, finally drawing to a stop before a shop front tucked between a greengrocer and a saddler's shop.

"The Witch," Cat intoned, pointing. Rosa tossed the kid an extra lire for the performance.

"Stay away from the Medici," Rosa told her. "Unless you've got an escape plan."

"I will," Cat said, obviously lying. "Good luck with your card tricks!"

Then she was gone, pelting down the street with a speed that had Rosa checking for her purse. Reassured it had not been stolen, she turned her attention back to The Witch.

In contrast to the unfamiliar chaos of central Florence, Agata de Rosso's shop was a timeless landmark. Even the sign was unchanged—though granted, the last time she'd seen it she'd been . . . ten? Eleven? Young enough to have forgotten important details. But the lettering was the same, the designs were the same, the colors were the same . . .

APOTHECARY, it read. Someone must have repainted it recently. Rosa doubted that Agata had been the artist, but then again, Agata had always had a deep stable of folks who owed her for all manner of things. The list of reasons why a person might need an apothecary was long and humiliating—intimate ailments, unwanted pregnancies, potions and powders . . . It would be easy to coerce one of her clients to spend an afternoon sprucing things up, especially if it meant that someone close to the spruce-er didn't learn a sensitive piece of information . . .

Rosa was on the verge of thinking something cliché about *playing with fire* when a small explosion inside the shop did the work for her. Without hesitating, Rosa barged inside, dimly registering the faint chime of a bell as the door slammed shut behind her.

The interior of the apothecary was a mass of smoke and shadow, so dark that Rosa didn't see the long wood counter until her hip banged hard into the edge. She bit back a curse and squinted, coughing, through the gloom. She could make out a mess of shelves and baskets lining the wall behind the counter—the source of the strange, earthy, herbal scent she could just detect through the overwhelming acrid stench of chemical burning.

Something clanged in the back of the shop. "Agata?" Rosa called. "Are you still alive?"

"Don't ask foolish questions" was the creaking, irritable response from the depths of the smoke. "Stop coughing. So dramatic. I'm coming, I'm coming. And don't open the door."

Rosa wiped at her streaming eyes with her sleeve. "*Don't* open the door?"

There was a small, hunched figure moving in the gloom, shuffling toward Rosa. Slowly, an old woman emerged, stepping into the afternoon light.

Just as the outside of the shop was frozen in time, so was Agata de Rosso. She looked just as Rosa remembered—in her seventies, with frizzing gray hair and sprigs of an unidentified herb stuck behind her ears. A pair of thick spectacles perched on her nose, rimmed with durable black metal. Her gown, while finely made, was covered in soot and burn marks, a testament to the appreciation of her clients and the way that Agata appreciated that appreciation.

"That's right," she said, scanning Rosa in a way that made Rosa fidget. "The neighbors get all worked up about smoke. They threaten to call the City Guards on me."

"I doubt very much that there's a guard in Florence who'd dare take *you* in, Signora de Rosso."

"Mm. Charming." Agata nestled her spectacles in her hair. "You sound like your mother."

Rosa smiled. "You remember me?"

"People don't change, Signorina Rosa," Agata said. "They just get taller and fatter. Get that box. It's too heavy for my old bones."

Agata's old bones looked more than capable, but in the name of self-preservation, Rosa did not comment. She followed the apothecary, carefully lugging the large wooden box Agata had indicated and listening to whatever was inside tinkle ominously.

"Put it there." Agata pointed to the stone-topped table that was set against the wall, and Rosa settled the box as gingerly as she could. "Don't be so cautious, girl, it won't bite. Open it, open it—*ach*—" Unsatisfied with Rosa's speed, Agata shuffled her to the side and pried the lid back herself. Inside, rows of glass vials winked in the firelight. "Take them in pairs, like this—" Agata demonstrated, plucking two vials at random. "Bind them together with twine, and then pass them to me. Can you manage that?"

"Yes," said Rosa, not quite sure how she had come to be enlisted in Agata's service, but not ready to push back for fear of another explosion.

"Good." Agata bustled back to the trestle table beside the hearth and snatched up a mortar and pestle. She ground them into one another, scraping granite against granite hard enough to set Rosa's teeth on edge. "And while you're doing that, you can remind me how long it's been since I've seen you. Five years?"

"Six." Rosa tied a knot in a piece of twine and set the paired vials aside.

"Six years and you didn't come by," Agata said. "Is that how your mother taught you to behave?"

"You'll have to ask her when you see her. She's tied up in Verona right now," Rosa said. "There was a job and then there was a man. But even before Verona, we'd been working separately for a while."

"Oh?" Agata inspected Rosa closely. There was a long pause before she spoke again. "That's good. A woman should be able to make her own way in the world. Still. The next time you see her, you remind her that she owes me ten florins and that it's not my fault she doesn't know how to cheat at bassetta."

Rosa set aside another set of vials. "I love my mother, signora, but you'd have better luck climbing Monte Pisano with no legs." She plucked up the completed pairs, holding them out to Agata. "What are these for?"

Agata's grin had too many teeth. "Oh, those are my Specials," she said.

"But what are they *for*?" Rosa asked.

"Emergencies. Put them on the trestle when you're done with them—for God's sake, don't *touch* anything—"

"I'm not, I'm not—" The vials were safely deposited without any incendiary incidents, and Rosa looked up to find Agata watching her, hawk-eyed. The pestle continued to grind in her hands without her active attention. "What?"

"Don't you 'what' me," Agata said. "Lena Cellini's girl shows up after who-knows-how-long just to pay a visit to some old lady?"

"To my mother's dear, dear friend."

Agata's laugh was like old leather. "I've been alive too long to believe that sack of horseshit. Are you going to keep wasting my time? Why are you here?"

"I'm looking for Sarra."

Agata must have been expecting this because she didn't react. "She's not here," she said, her oversized gesture taking in every smoky corner of the apothecary.

"Do you know where she is?"

The old apothecary scraped the contents of her mortar—some gray-green paste that made Rosa sneeze—onto the table. "What are you up to, girl? You reek of trouble."

"You'll know soon enough. I promise. I wouldn't be asking if it wasn't important." There was a light *clink* as Rosa set the shining gold piece on the marble table next to Agata's pestle. "A partial payment on my mother's debt," Rosa said.

Agata's hands stilled, just for a moment, at the sight of the coin, but they were moving again, dipping into sacks of herbs and powders, flicking pinches into the now-empty mortar. She didn't look at Rosa as she worked. She certainly didn't look at her as she spoke.

"I heard you and Lena had settled in Prato," she said.

Rosa's jaw clenched down around her smile. She inched the gold closer to Agata. "Please, signora."

There was a long, quiet beat. Then, almost too fast for Rosa's eye to follow, the gold piece was gone, disappeared into Agata's purse. "Oltrarno," Agata finally said. "But you won't find her there right now." *Flick* went something green and piney into the bowl.

"Agata."

"The word is—lately—she's been . . . running with a bad crowd." *Splash* went a dash from Agata's waterskin. She picked up the pestle and began grinding once more.

Rosa raised a wry eyebrow. "Surely a Nepi would not associate with *criminals*."

The glare Agata shot her was eviscerating. "Of course it's *criminals*," she said in a tone that could flay the bark off a tree. "It's the wrong sort of criminals."

"Violent?"

"Worse," Agata said, with a particularly vicious twist of the pestle. "Stupid."

3

SARRA

"I could take his head off from here."

Sarra could feel the throb in her temples growing.

"I could shoot him right through the *eyeball*."

"A bit quieter, Master Spinelli?" Sarra asked. "If you would be so kind?"

But Alberto Spinelli had never met a piece of good advice that he hadn't ignored. He leaned further off the rooftop, crossbow sight pressed to his eye socket. In the building across the street, the subject of his fascination—a guard—yawned against a wall. "Where do you come *up* with this stuff?"

He was going to fall to his death. Or he'd get them spotted and maybe stabbed, shot or hanged for good measure, and Sarra would have a hell of a time explaining that to Pietro. This really wasn't how tonight was supposed to go. Sarra gingerly reclaimed her crossbow from Alberto. "Please, Master Spinelli. If we could concentrate on the task at hand . . . ?"

Alberto did not concentrate. "When this is done, do you think I could borrow that? 'Cuz my wife said it's not because of that Modena peddler she kicked me out, but—"

She took a steadying breath and checked over the crossbow, on the chance that his clumsy handling had done some irreparable damage. At her side, Alberto kept up a steady stream of nonsense, muttering about everything from his wife's infidelity to his new wagon to his mounting tavern bill. There was no point in shushing him. This was

Alberto's job—his mark, his plan, his team. All Sarra could do was jump when she was told.

"Do you see the guard?" Alberto hissed.

"Just a moment." She lined up the sights. Sure enough, there was the guard . . . taking a piss off the edge of the opposite building. The Pazzi family should invest in better security.

Conventional wisdom said that sixteen-year-old Sarra Nepi should not be anywhere near this damp, chilly rooftop. She certainly should not have been wearing an ill-fitting set of her brother's castoffs with her fiery hair braided up and shoved under the ugliest cap she could find. And she *definitely* should not have been consorting with Alberto Spinelli, a thief so notoriously awful that his claim to fame was how few people agreed to work with him a second time.

No, Sarra Nepi should not be here. She was the virtuous younger sister of a respectable and educated printer. She was a good girl. She was not a criminal.

Sarra the Tinkerer, though—*she* was a different story. For two years, her inventions had paved roads into the lawless underbelly of Tuscany, lining her purse along the way. *Half for the Tinkerer,* she told herself, a mantra. *Half for the press. And Pietro never needs to know.*

A flash of movement from behind the pissing guard on the Pazzi's rooftop caught her attention. Sarra reached for her belt-kit, a handmade contraption designed to resemble a folded knife. But when she flicked it open, no blade sprung forth. Instead, a set of tinkerer's tools spread out like a fan, each hinging from the oak handle. Sarra selected the tiny screwdriver, folding the other tools back into the hilt, and used it to twist the small brass dials on the telescopic crossbow sight. Somewhere inside the sight, gears and levers shifted and whirred, and the picture in the sight grew closer and clearer. Now Sarra could make out a black-garbed figure pulling itself onto the roof. The figure—a man, maybe a little too round in the gut to be making such a climb—staggered and slouched, panting for breath.

"Vittorio's in position," she muttered out of the corner of her mouth.

"See!" Alberto crowed. "I told you he could handle it!"

She kept her gaze pinned to the clumsy black-clad figure across the street. There was something in the way Vittorio was swaying that made her frown. "Is he *drunk*?"

"Vittorio always has a pint or two before jobs," Alberto said. "It calms his nerves."

That explained why Vittorio was the only person Sarra had ever met who'd agreed to work with Alberto more than once. Shifting the crossbow, Sarra watched through the sights as the limestone brickwork of the Pazzi mansion blurred.

"Do you have it yet?" Alberto asked. His voice was, as ever, far too loud.

"Patience, Master Spinelli," Sarra said, proud at how little frustration seeped into her words. Years of lying to her brother's face had been a boot camp in inscrutability, and Alberto Spinelli's boorishness had nothing on Pietro Nepi's gruff insight. The crossbow sight whirred and clicked as she twisted the dials, coaxing a blurry mash of bright and dark into—

There.

The image resolved, clear and brilliant, bringing the ground floor dining room of the Palazzo Pazzi into focus. Through the stained glass windows, Sarra could make out the heavy oak table, the high-backed upholstered dining chairs, a few marble busts . . .

And, of course, the massive chandelier dangling from the ceiling.

It was impressive even to Sarra, who had engineered more than her fair share of impressive things. The wrought iron branches each held three white beeswax candles. Crystals dripped from every twist in the iron, catching and refracting the dim light from the street outside. It was blinding even when the candles were dark. Sarra could only imagine how dazzling it must be when it was lit.

Too bad. They should have tied it to the ceiling with something stronger than rope.

"Ready," she said, once the woven length of hemp was in her sights. "Vittorio should move in three . . . two . . ."

"Who are we robbing?"

The world tilted. And then—

Sarra was nine again. She was nine and willing herself older, her shoulders barely level with the sticky tavern table. Matteo Nepi had been a solid warmth next to her, slouched as he was over his untouched tankard, and Sarra had leaned into her father's side, trying to absorb some of his secret sadness.

"It's certainly quieter with him gone." Across the table, Lena Cellini had perched sideways on her bench, her eyes on the other tavern goers. "And you can't tell me you don't miss him." She'd nudged Matteo's tankard with her own.

The small girl beside her was Lena's double, watching the world with a scrutiny that laid it bare. It was a rougher, more unpracticed copy of the way Lena had about her, but she'd kept it up even as her hands moved like lightning, flipping three cards back and forth across the tabletop so quickly that they became a blur. When she finally stopped, it was to look up at Sarra with a quirked eyebrow, cleverness buried under cool passivity that had dared Sarra—dared *anyone*—to underestimate her.

Find the Lady . . . Find the Lady . . .

"If that boy had stuck around one more day, I think we'd have shouted the house down," Matteo had grumbled. "He's better off at university." A surge of empty sadness had welled up inside Sarra at that, and she'd moved closer to her father. Without looking down at her, he'd squeezed Sarra around the shoulders. "And it's not like I've been left alone to waste away."

Bolstered by this, Sarra had reached across the table to pick a card. It was flipped with that same viper-speed. *The Ace of Swords.* "You cheated!" Sarra had exploded.

"My little grifter!" Lena had said, wrapping both arms around her daughter in an exaggerated embrace. The girl had disappeared into Lena's sleeves and hair with a squeak and a giggle. "You remember this, Sarra," Lena had said over the top of her daughter's head. "The secret to Find the Lady—you never watch the dealer's hands. If you want the slightest chance of winning, you watch their *face*." Sarra had nodded, her frustration quickly dwindling under the onslaught of Lena's teasing, Rosa's half-hearted protestations, and her father's proximity. Together, they dulled the loneliness in her stomach, reminding her that, though Pietro might be away, Sarra still had family around her.

Lena must have read all this on Sarra's face, because she had leaned across the table toward her. "You'll tell me if your father languishes, won't you?" she asked in a loud, conspiratorial whisper. "We can break your brother out of that stuffy school in half a second."

"Enough of that." Matteo had flicked a stray crumb at her. "I'm fine. Don't we have work to do?"

And Lena had straightened. "Again," she'd told her daughter, and the cards once again began to dance. Sarra fixed her gaze stubbornly on the girl's face as Lena's warm smile sharpened.

Who are we robbing?

Now, seven years and a lifetime later, Sarra's finger loosened on the trigger. She did not look up from her crossbow, in fear that her memory was lying to her and that it wasn't the second coming of Lena Cellini slouched next to her on the tiled rooftop.

"Francesco Pazzi," Sarra said.

"What the hell is this?" said Alberto.

Sarra sensed, rather than saw, Rosa Cellini arch an eyebrow. "Interesting."

"Who are you?" said Alberto.

"You're taking out the chandelier?" Rosa asked.

Sarra bit back a hysterical laugh. "A distraction."

"For the house guards?"

"That was the idea. Draw everyone in earshot downstairs. Break in upstairs."

"It's a bit flashy."

Sarra nodded toward Alberto. "He likes flashy."

"*Who* the *hell* are *you*?" Alberto said again.

"Ah," Rosa said. "I can see what you mean."

On the roof of the Palazzo Pazzi, Vittorio had been forced into a tipsy game of hide-and-seek with the still-unwitting guard. As Sarra watched, the thief tripped into the shadow of a gable just as the guard's rounds brought him around the corner, barely staying out of view.

It was almost too much to hope, but—"Are you—back?" Sarra asked, trying not to sound as pathetic as she felt.

"I thought I'd offer you a job."

This wasn't the answer to Sarra's question. "A job?" she echoed, finally looking up at Rosa. "After—how many years? You don't come to Papa's funeral, but you show up when you want to offer me a *job*?"

"Hey!" Alberto forced himself between the girls. With a wince, Sarra pushed herself up to her knees, feeling every ridge of the roof tiles through her hose. "She's already *on* a job."

Rosa just peered around his legs at Sarra. "What do you say?" she asked.

Find the Lady.

Sarra was no longer nine, but that did not mean she'd forgotten Lena's advice. Crouched on the rooftop, she studied Rosa's face, picking apart the layers of carelessness and nonchalance. The childish rough edges were gone, sanded smooth. So, Sarra noted, were the warmth and giddiness. Instead, Rosa seemed to have built herself on a foundation of icy calm, a glacier frozen around . . . flashes of what looked, to Sarra's eye, like white-hot *anger*.

All of that packed down and held in place by Lena's smile. Sarra felt a little chilled.

"Why me?" she asked. "I'm nobody. Unless this is for family's sake—"

"If you're nobody, then that must be a different Sarra the Tinkerer I've been hearing stories of for two years."

Sarra was being played. She knew she was being played. Still: to be offered work by a Cellini, someone who could put together more than brain-dead smash-and-grabs, someone Sarra could work *with* instead of *for* . . .

Someone who knew Sarra the printer's sister *and* Sarra the Tinkerer. Someone whose familiar presence warmed some of the lonely depths that had only grown deeper these last years . . .

"How big's the job?" Sarra asked.

Rosa's smile widened. "Big enough to fund your brother's print shop until the Second Coming. Biggest of your life."

"What's the target?"

"Hey!" That was Alberto again, this time whining because Rosa had shoved his knees so hard that he'd been forced to stagger back a few paces or risk toppling over the edge of the roof. Wordlessly, she held out a hand and, without hesitation, Sarra handed over the crossbow.

"It's local," Rosa explained as she held the sight up to her eye. The cogs inside whirred as she focused it on some distant point. "No need to spend money on room or board."

"Mm-hm." *Find the Lady*, Sarra thought.

"And like I said—massive payout."

"What's. The. Target."

"Hold your horses. Here—" She shuffled back so Sarra could take her place, squinting through the crossbow sight toward—

No.

"You did say massive," Sarra said faintly.

The Palazzo Medici had always been one of the more imposing buildings in Florence, gobbling up an entire block of the city with looming walls and blazing lights. It reeked of power and wealth and *danger*, and every ounce of saliva in Sarra's mouth dried up just at the sight of it.

"Yes," Rosa agreed.

"Rosa, this is suicide!"

"It'll be suicide if you don't stop *chatting* and *get off my roof.*"

Alberto had finally had enough of their exchange. He paced toward Rosa, drawing a dagger from his belt. From this distance, Sarra could tell that the metalwork was cheap, though the blade glinted sharply enough. Even so, Rosa watched Alberto's approach with disinterest.

"I'm sorry, who are you?"

"That's what I've been asking *you* for *five goddamn minutes*," said Alberto.

"This is Alberto," said Sarra, keeping her eyes on Rosa's face.

"Flashy Alberto. Nice to meet you." Rosa rose. "Now I don't mean to critique, especially since we've just been introduced . . . and I see that you have the Pazzi's security covered—" she said, as Vittorio slipped on a loose tile and nearly crashed through a skylight. "But I don't suppose you've noticed the increased street patrols?" There was a moment of silence as Alberto's expression shuttered between fury and confusion. "No?" Rosa said. "It's just, with His Holiness returned to Florence, something flashy like, say, a chandelier in a well-to-do house inexplicably crashing down in the middle of the night? Would have the block swarming with guards in a matter of moments. There wouldn't be time enough for you to get off this roof, much less for your man over there to grab anything of value and get clear." She shrugged. "Just a thought."

Sarra stared at Alberto. "You hadn't considered this?"

Alberto shrank where he stood. "I . . ."

A distant shout echoed across the cobblestones. Alberto and Sarra both glanced over to see the Pazzi Guard finally—*finally*—spot Vittorio. He grabbed the alarm bell off his belt and swung it, filling the night with an echoing *clang-clang-clang*. In a panic, Vittorio lurched over to grab him by the collar, and the two men staggered into a half-drunk grapple, stumbling across the rooftops, struggling for control of the guard's bell—

And true to Rosa's word, the street below was coming to life. City Guards swarmed the wealthy neighborhood, drawn by the alarm. In the blink of an eye, the block was flocked with men in Florence red, each one of them with a sharp sword and the intent to use it.

"They'll search every house in the area," Rosa said. She was still smiling pleasantly at Alberto. "We're trapped up here. Unless you have a way to distract them?"

Alberto just stared, transfixed by the scene, by the sight of his immaculate plan falling to pieces around his ears, by the sound of the Pazzi Guard's muffled protests as Vittorio clamped a hand over his mouth. And still, the City Guard was closing in.

"For heaven's sake—" Sarra snapped. Her crossbow was still resting against the roof ledge. She pressed her eye to the sight and refocused her target.

"What—what are you doing?" Alberto stammered. "We have to—We have to—"

Sarra pulled the trigger.

Across the street, the hemp rope holding the Pazzi chandelier snapped as an iron bolt zipped through it. The wondrous contraption hit the tiled floor below with a crash loud enough to wake the dead, and Sarra felt a pang of contrition for destroying the work of a fellow tinkerer.

"There!" one of the City Guardsmen shouted, and to a man, the flood of Florentine red ebbed through the Pazzi front gates, stampeding for the ballroom. For a moment, at least, the street below was clearing.

Rosa's eyes were crinkled in laughter when Sarra looked at her again. "I did say 'draw everyone in earshot,'" Sarra said.

"Flashy," Rosa replied. "Shall we?"

"Please," Sarra said.

"Who *are* you?" Alberto asked, still looking glassy. But Rosa just sidestepped him, moving toward the open trapdoor in the roof. Snatching up her bag, Sarra followed, only pausing long enough to roll her eyes at the gape-mouthed Alberto.

"You'll catch flies with that thing," she said.

They were off the roof and out of the building before Alberto could bully his lonely brain cell into responding.

The Palazzo Pazzi was still a mill of City Guards when Sarra and Rosa slipped out the back of the mansion across the street. Sarra kept pace with Rosa easily as they set off together—Rosa had always been shorter, despite the year she had on Sarra.

"Did you have to go that hard on Alberto?" Sarra asked, struggling to wrangle her crossbow into her satchel as they walked.

"It was a matter of professional pride. And common sense."

"Rosa."

"What? He's an idiot."

"He was paying me."

"With what money?" Rosa asked. "He didn't have any on him. And when you all got arrested, there wouldn't even have been a cut to give Pietro."

The mention of her brother sent a chill of guilt through Sarra's stomach. "Would you slow down?" she hissed. "Some of us are carrying very delicate equipment."

"Some of us don't want to *look* like we're carrying very delicate equipment," Rosa shot back, but she slowed as they approached the mouth of the alley. Beyond, in the narrow Piazza degli Antinori, two guards in Florence colors rushed by. Sarra and Rosa froze, half-lit by the moonlight filtering between the tall buildings around them.

But the guards' pace didn't falter as they passed, thundering across the cobblestones and down the next street. Silence stretched as Sarra listened to the distant commotion of men descending on the site of her would-be robbery. She finally managed to cinch her bag shut.

"I wasn't sure you'd ever come back," she said. Rosa kept her eyes pinned on the guards' retreat. "I missed you. We both did." There was no sign that Rosa had heard her. "Rosa."

Rosa's eyes flicked to her, just for a half-second. "It's good to see you too," she said.

It felt like a moment for an embrace. Sarra was certainly poised for one—to welcome back the girl she'd thought of as a sister for her entire life. But Rosa was focused only on the Piazza, and Sarra capitulated with a sigh, shifting her satchel on her shoulder. "So," she said. "The Medici family."

This, at least, garnered a reaction. "They're as good a target as any," Rosa said, casual innocence dripping from every syllable.

"They're not as good," Sarra said. "They're worse. They're *the* worst."

Rosa's eyes were black pools in the dark. "If you don't want in, I'll understand."

"I never said that."

"Good," Rosa said. "Because you've been following me across Tuscany for two years. Everywhere I went, everyone I talked to, it was *Sarra the Tinkerer, Sarra the Tinkerer*. Apparently, you're the best there is. And that's considering that you've been stuck working jobs for numbskulls like Alberto." She cocked her head. "Your brother must be proud."

Sarra's chest went tight. "He—doesn't know."

"What—seriously?"

"And he wouldn't be happy knowing you've come to me with a suicide mission." Adrenaline sang in Sarra's veins. "Because that's what this is."

Rosa's expression was a mask of ice, glacial in a way that only happened over centuries. "I know this job will be dangerous," she said. "But we can pull it off, and even live to spend our money afterward. I just . . ." She sighed. "I need you."

"You've thought about this."

"For five years," Rosa said. "Are you in?"

Yes! shouted every thump of Sarra's heart. But there was a dour rhythm beating counterpoint to that thrumming exaltation. *Find the Lady. Find the Lady.*

"I'm in," Sarra said. "On one condition."

"What's that?"

"Swear this is just about the money," Sarra said. "A job this big can't be about anything more. The moment things get personal is the moment we doom ourselves."

Rosa met Sarra's stare straight-on. "Money only," she said. "I promise."

Sarra listened to the distant shouts of the City Guard descending on the Palazzo Pazzi and took a deep breath of night air. It filled her lungs, cool and crisp, and she suddenly felt lighter than she had in longer than she could remember.

"Very well," she said. "Let's rob the Medici family."

4

ROSA

S unlight painted the inside of Rosa's eyelids pink. She grumbled, squirming back into her pillow and yanking the blanket over her head.

"Rosa."

Something nudged at her side. It felt like the toe of a shoe, and with a start, Rosa remembered where she was. In a surge, she sat up, pushing wild hair out of her face and squinting into the bearded, solemn face of Pietro Nepi.

She stared at him. He stared at her.

"Upstairs," he finally commanded in a low, rumbling voice. Then he was gone, tromping up the staircase before she could respond, the steps above Rosa's head creaking ominously. With a groan, she hauled herself to her feet, taking in her surroundings in the morning light.

The vanguard of Sarra's personal corner of Florence was a wooden sign that declared NEPI PRINTING for those who could read, and the pictograph of a printing press for those who could not. It was a beacon of respectability amidst the narrow alleys and shabby storefronts of the Oltrarno quarter, which lurked just across the river from the wide streets and sprawling piazzas of Florence proper. Those who inhabited the warren of the Oltrarno were artisans and laborers, who jammed the neighborhood with life and energy, even at this early-morning hour.

Their muffled shouts and laughter were the accompaniment to Rosa's quest for a water pitcher, in the hopes that washing her face might make her feel a bit more human. She wound through the shop's interior, bypassing the single table, the two chairs . . . and the hulking printing press that dominated the remaining space. It was a monster of unvarnished wood and iron, as tall as it was long. A wide bed of solid oak lay beneath an equally solid framework, upon which dangled what was essentially a heavy, massive stamp. The handle protruding from the side was unwieldy, but someone—Rosa suspected Sarra—had fixed it with a hinge, allowing it to rotate upright for storage once the day's work was finished. An open cabinet filled with trays and trays of etched metal letters and more punctuation than Rosa even knew the names for had been left beside the press. She gave one of the trays a curious poke, sifting through its contents—

"Rosa!"

Pietro's bellow shook the ceiling as capably as his footsteps, and Rosa snatched her hand back. Feeling suddenly a great deal more awake, she spotted a pitcher beneath the front window, splashed a handful of freezing water across her eyes, and darted up the stairs before Pietro's temper could worsen.

The rooms above the print shop were small but well cared for, and as Rosa slunk in through the front door, she found herself attempting to smooth her hair into a low knot to match the general atmosphere of tidiness. Every chair, every table, every wall hanging had all been tended with an attention to detail, down to the oiled hinges on the doors. Most eye-catching of all was the sturdy set of shelves set against the wall, loaded with so many books and scrolls that Rosa expected to hear the wood groaning under the weight. It was a collection that she would venture surpassed all others this side of the Arno river—a collection whose value outstripped everything else in this room.

It was also a collection that had notoriously been missing from the University of Pisa's library for three long years. Rosa did not remark upon this as she passed.

Sarra was busying herself by the hearth, hose and jerkin abandoned in favor of a dark blue dress and a woolen shawl. Her copper hair gleamed in the early-morning light as she poked and prodded something over the fire. Her brother slumped at the kitchen table, sullen and sleepy, barely glancing up as Rosa came through the door.

"Come sit," Sarra said, oozing forced enthusiasm. She was carrying a skillet of spitting-hot eggs, which she plunked onto a thick stack of rags in front of Pietro. "Did you sleep well?"

Whatever the brewing storm between Sarra and her brother was, Rosa absolutely did not want to ask about it. Abandoning her hair for a lost cause, she perched on the chair next to Pietro. "Best sleep of my life."

Pietro just shook his head, shoveled the majority of the eggs onto a plate, and pushed it in front of Rosa. "You don't have to—" she began.

"You are a thoughtless chicken, Sarra Nepi," Pietro said, putting the rest of the food on his own plate and tucking in.

Pietro Nepi had been less of a stalwart of Rosa's childhood than Sarra, the upright scholar to Sarra's aspiring grifter, the perpetually exasperated older brother. To remember him was to remember the smell of leather bookbinding and dusty paper and drying ink. Sitting next to him now, Rosa saw that this, at least, had not changed.

Rosa shoved a bite into her mouth. "This is wonderful."

"There would have been more for dinner last night," Pietro said, pointedly not looking at Sarra. "If you had *come upstairs*."

"I was quite comfortable in the shop, signore—"

"'Signore.'" Pietro pushed back from the table with a frustrated *tch* and snatched the poker out of his sister's hand. "You sit. Eat. Stop buzzing. You're giving me a headache."

Whatever Sarra hissed back to him was too low for Rosa to catch, but it made Pietro scoff and clatter pots together as Sarra sank into the chair he'd vacated. "He's happy you're here," Sarra said. "Really. I'm in trouble because I made you sleep downstairs last night."

"I did not want to wake you with puttering about, Signore Nepi."

Sarra scoffed. "I *told* him this and yet—"

"When family comes home from traveling, you wake to greet them," Pietro said without turning around. "And if my father was alive, he'd laugh you out of the house to hear you calling me *signore.*"

Rosa picked at a slice of bread. "You are too kind to me," she said, and meant it.

"Pietro doesn't like to remember that he's old now," Sarra said, rolling her eyes.

"Pietro might be *old*, but he can still throw this dishrag at you," retorted Pietro from the lofty peak of his twenty-one years. Rosa sat back from the table, ill at ease with this familiar, familial bickering.

It was possible that Pietro picked up on this because he was already in motion, tugging on his shoes. "I'm off to the shop," he said. "If you're staying another night, move your things upstairs, for God's sake."

"Thank you, Pietro," Rosa said. Pietro gave her a decisive nod, and then the door was swinging shut behind him.

By unspoken consensus, Sarra and Rosa waited until the printing press began to clatter downstairs before clearing the breakfast dishes. Sarra dumped the rough clay plates into a bucket as Rosa hauled her bag up onto the table. "He knew about Matteo, didn't he?" Rosa asked, nodding toward the front door and the shop below. "Why not tell him about this job?"

"I promised Papa," Sarra said, wiping her hands on the scorched rag hanging by the hearth. "On his deathbed, even. He said, 'Don't drag your brother into this business,' and I couldn't exactly refuse him."

"It wasn't just the rooftop last night? Pietro doesn't know about the Tinkerer at all?"

"It's probably for the best," Sarra said, but she didn't sound happy. "You remember how much he hated this work. He and Papa screamed themselves hoarse over every job Papa took." She turned back to Rosa, face set. "I don't know, Rosa. Pietro didn't inherit the Nepi love of chaos, and it's as simple as that. Sometimes I think that the only good thing that came out of Papa's death was that Pietro left university and gave up all that politicking. He lives and breathes for this place." Rosa pointedly did not glance at the tiny purloined library as Sarra took a breath, shaking her shoulders loose. "I promised he wouldn't find out, so he won't find out. Anyway. You said there were details. Or are we going in blind?"

"Have a little faith." Rosa flipped open her pack to retrieve her most treasured possession: a nondescript cylinder of paper wrapped in waterproof waxed canvas. With both hands and a fair amount of reverence, she laid it on the table.

Sarra lifted the corner with a careful finger. Her eyebrows shot immediately toward her hairline. "Where in the heavens did you get these?" Rosa unrolled the paper enough to reveal a signature along the bottom edge. Sarra's eyebrows, if possible, climbed even higher. "You didn't," she said.

"I did."

"You walked into the architect's house and, what? Just asked him for the blueprints?"

"Don't be foolish," Rosa said. "Michelozzo died decades ago. I walked into his house and asked his *granddaughter* for the blueprints."

Sarra just stared at her for a quiet moment. "She just *gave* them to you?"

"Maybe she wouldn't have handed them over to Rosa Cellini,"

Rosa said. "But she was only too happy to give them to the daughter of an old, old family friend."

"Or as near to her as you could approximate, I wager," Sarra muttered. She let the corner of the blueprints roll back to join the rest. "So what's the approach? We could try the Twin Doves, but on a target this big . . ."

"I've been thinking . . . this calls for something new," Rosa said. "You're right—it's too big for the two of us to take on alone." She worried at her lip. "We'll need a Trojan Horse."

Sarra laughed. "Right." Then she caught Rosa's expression. "You're serious?"

"Yes."

"Those are hard to come by in the easiest of jobs. And you want—with *this*—"

Her tone dug at Rosa. "If you're having second thoughts—"

"These aren't second thoughts, Rosa, this is collaboration. Don't you remember how it was when we were children? Papa pushed. Lena pushed. Papa pushed harder. Lena punched him in the arm. Then they'd move on. That was their process."

Rosa grimaced. "I'm not going to punch you in the arm."

"I'm counting on it."

"And I have someone in mind for the Trojan Horse."

"You—*really*? Who?"

"I will tell you," Rosa said. "But I can't just yet. I have to think about it. The approach is going to be . . ."

"Tricky?"

"At least."

"Well, aside from this magical Trojan Horse," Sarra said, and Rosa reconsidered the promise not to punch her in the arm, "how many?"

This was an answer she could give with the weight of five years of obsession. "Three."

"Mm. A hitter, definitely."

"Yes. And a player. And . . . an alchemist."

Sarra nodded, considering. "Henrik Novak? He did that job with all the dyes in Lyon—"

"Poisoned," Rosa said. "Himself. Accident. Eight months ago."

"Oswald Albrecht? With the . . . demolition kits—"

"Blown up."

"Alchemists," Sarra sighed. "Well, if you've already got someone in mind—"

"Agata," Rosa said.

"Agata *de Rosso*?" Sarra stared at her. "She's over *seventy years old*."

"And still alive." Rosa shrugged.

"Witches are hard to kill," Sarra muttered. "Fine. Do I have to guess who you have in mind for the other two openings as well? Because you know as well as I do that there's really only one hitter who's up for this kind of job."

"Oh yes," Rosa said, smiling. "But I left Genoa on . . . bad terms last time. How do *you* feel about checking in on Khalid?"

Sarra groaned. "Genoa's a four-day ride. Pietro is going to have questions."

"You're the one who can get past Traverio with her head still attached to her body."

"Fine. *Fine*. I'll talk to Khalid." Sarra scrubbed a hand over her face. "So that's two. Who's the player?"

Rosa winced. "You're not going to like it."

A long moment stretched between them as Sarra studied her face. Then the penny dropped. She surged to her feet, pacing to the other side of the room. "No."

"We need him—" Rosa protested.

"He's *crazy*—"

"He's not *crazy*—"

"We can't rely on him—"

"We can if there's enough money involved—"

"There are a thousand other players out there who aren't—"

"But they're not Giacomo," Rosa said. "Which means they're not the best."

Which was how Rosa came to find herself in the countryside outside of Modigliana a few days later, watching a sappy-eyed young couple who had definitely already abandoned chastity in some secluded hay bale pledge themselves to one another before the eyes of God, their families, the town, and a bushy-browed, beneficent priest.

It was a pretty little church and a pretty little ceremony, all things considered. The bride and groom looked about two seconds away from ripping one another's clothes off, propriety be damned, but Rosa could think of worse ways to begin a marriage. The priest was blithely oblivious to the radiating waves of cheerful lust, smiling kindly as he intoned familiar, sonorous, *unending* phrases in Latin. Rosa, perched at the end of the last pew, dug her fingernails into her thigh to keep herself from falling asleep.

Finally, when it seemed as though either the young couple would say to hell with marriage and go find that hay bale again, or the entire town would nod off, the priest dipped his fingers into the dais's gleaming, golden chalice, painted an anointed sign of the cross in the air, and switched out of Latin. "The vows," he creaked. "My son?"

The young man clutched his beloved's hands close to his chest. "Lucia," he said. "I give myself to you in holy matrimony."

The young woman stared up at him with limpid eyes. "I receive you," she said, in a voice that made it clear that she was very eager to do so. Somewhere in a pew near the front, an older woman who shared the bride's hair color and eyes made a disapproving sound.

None of this registered on young Lucia, who was watching her groom slide a golden band onto her finger as though he was gifting her the keys to the Garden of Eden.

"And now, my daughter?" the priest prompted.

Lucia drew out her own golden band. "I give myself to you," she said, slipping it onto the groom's finger.

"I receive you," he replied.

"Then by the power granted to me by our Lord," intoned the priest, "I pronounce you . . . husband and wife. You may—well!"

It had taken Lucia launching herself at her new husband's face for the priest to realize what had been bubbling beneath the surface throughout the ceremony. He stumbled back, shocked, as the rest of the assembly burst into a mix of rowdy cheers and appalled scoldings and Lucia attempted to excavate her husband's tonsils with her tongue.

It was a chaotic moment before the young couple separated, red-cheeked and beaming, at which point two things became evident almost simultaneously. The first was the notable empty space where the kindly priest had been. And the second was the notable empty space on the dais where the church's prized golden chalice had stood.

The speed with which the wedding party transformed into a mob was a credit to the town, and to Lucia's fearsome direction. The girl's pleased flush had dipped into a furious tomato-red, deepened by the awful fact that some thief had tainted her wedding day, and she had wasted no time in commanding her guests into groups to search out the village's far-flung corners. Determined not to miss any of the action, when Rosa saw Lucia, the groom, and a few weather-beaten farmers setting out together, she sidled up to join the search party.

"It was a lovely ceremony," she offered. "Before—you know. Down to the last detail, the most wonderful wedding I've attended. Those rings!"

"Aren't they wonderful?" Lucia gushed, her militance cracking. "Papa paid *two florins* for them, you know."

"Thank you for coming," the groom said, with an edge of confusion. "Signorina . . ."

"Oh, come now, cousin!" Rosa exclaimed. "I know it's an eventful day, but a person should always remember family!" She leaned in to Lucia. "This is why it's good he has you now, to keep track of things."

A spark of affection blazed across Lucia's face. "Federigo would forget which direction he was walking if he didn't have his toes to point the way."

"He's always been so. It's a family trait, I'm afraid—our aunt was the same."

"Of course I remember," Federigo said, desperate to change the subject. "Those summers running around Aunt Emilia's garden?"

"Her poppies!" Rosa exclaimed, hitting her stride. "I've never met a woman more proud of—"

One of the farmers, a middle-aged man with dirt ground into his fingernails and a graying mustache, slapped the boy across his shoulder. "Don't you have better things to do on your wedding day than talk to a woman you aren't married to?"

"But—I—" Federigo stammered.

"Don't you worry about me, signore," Rosa chirped. "I'm only here to track down this awful thief before he can strike again."

"Hmph," the farmer grumbled, studying her with a shaded gaze.

"Look!" Lucia, bored by this exchange, had been scanning the environment with a detective's gaze. Now she pointed toward a sloping house that rambled into the surrounding countryside . . .

And at the church's golden chalice, which perched atop a barrel by the door, glinting in a direct beam of sunlight.

To a man, the search party stopped in their tracks, staring at the missing chalice. "He just . . . left it?" Federigo asked.

"Maybe he got frightened," Rosa offered. "So many honorable people hunting you—it'll turn your stomach inside out."

"Go and tell Signora Boriardo this pantomime is finished," the mustached farmer instructed his fellows. "We'll be at the house for the wedding feast soon enough." The other farmers departed with a nod as the mustached man stomped forward, plucking up the cup. "Come here," he instructed the newlyweds. They stepped forward together. "Hands," he snapped, and they hastened to obey, not resisting as he wrapped both of their fingers around the chalice, squeezing them tight. "Take this back to the church," he said. "Don't let go 'til you get there. And then we can put this silly episode behind us and get on with the celebration."

Lucia's eyebrows were furrowed. "But what if he's still—"

"Come on," Federigo muttered to his wife. "Your mother spent all day toiling over this dinner. We'll be in for it if we miss it."

"I'll have a look around for the thief," Rosa assured Lucia. "Go have fun. Enjoy your wedding."

This finally seemed to be enough. Lucia allowed Federigo to drag her back toward the center of town, where the sounds of music and revelry were already kicking up. Soon, it was just Rosa and the farmer here, on the outskirts. Alone.

She watched him. He watched her.

"Strange, that a rogue would just abandon his prize like that," she said.

"Strange," the farmer agreed.

"That chalice must be worth at least a few florins. All that gold."

The farmer's mouth twisted beneath his mustache. "Unless it was just gilding."

"Of course," Rosa said. "Then it wouldn't be worth much at all."

"Mm."

"Except as a lure."

A pause. "Mm."

Rosa cocked her head. "Where'd you put the rings?"

The farmer's face broke into a wide grin. It was a strange expression, pulling at his features in unsettling ways while simultaneously making him appear much younger than his forty-plus years. "I don't have the slightest idea what you're implying," he said happily. There was something similarly altered in his voice now, the inflection lighter and more refined.

Rosa snatched the hat from his head. Curls tumbled down around his ears, gray and wild. "Hey!" he said, but Rosa was already darting backward, running a finger beneath the hatband. A moment later, the newlyweds' two gold rings—*two florins*, Lucia had said—were hooked around Rosa's finger, glinting in the sun.

"How do you always *know*?" asked the farmer.

"A lady has her secrets," Rosa said. "Ah—!" This undignified sound was the result of the farmer having swept her into a bear hug, lifting her off her feet. "Put me down!" Rosa demanded, tapping at Giacomo's shoulders.

"No," he said, voice muffled in her shoulder. "My lady, my queen, the light of my life, you cannot imagine the balm it is to my soul to lay eyes upon you once more—"

"Yes, yes, I missed you too, Giacomo. Put me *down*, your hair is getting on my clothes."

"Damn—" Giacomo san Giacomo dropped Rosa back on her feet so quickly that she rocked in place. Sure enough, streaks of the same gray color as his hair were smeared across Rosa's kirtle.

"This stuff comes out, right?"

"Yes, look—" He ducked his head upside down, rustling the curls with his fingers. White clouds of powder plumed up. "I've been working on the formula," he explained, still upside down, "but it either rubs off too easily, or it sticks in my hair like tree sap."

"Take off the rest of that getup," she said. "I need to talk to you about something."

Giacomo straightened, pressing a hand to his chest. "Surely you aren't implying—"

"Giacomo."

"You are taking advantage of an unprotected and innocent young man!"

"Let me know if you see one and I'll apologize. Come *on*, Giacomo."

Giacomo shucked his rough-spun coat and began tugging his shirt over his head. "As my lady commands, I shall hasten to perform—damn—" The hem of the shirt had snagged on the priest's cassock he was still wearing underneath. "Could you—"

Rosa deftly unsnarled the garments. When she stepped back, the priest from the church—now slightly ruffled—was smiling back at her, fingers making light work of his own buttons. "Was all that business really necessary?" she asked.

"I see a couple in need of a holy union, I grant a holy union," Giacomo said. The cassock fell from his shoulders, leaving him bare-chested. "Would you be so kind as to return my shirt to me? Or would you prefer to keep me at a disadvantage?"

There was a mark on one of his shoulder blades—a burn or a scar or—but it was none of her business. Rolling her eyes, Rosa tossed the shirt at him, hitting him in the face. "I didn't see the lift in the church," she said. "How'd you do it?"

"Kiss, kiss, cheer, cheer," Giacomo singsonged as his head emerged from the neck of his chemise. "Clasp their hands and disappear. Nobody looks to the priest. Where the devil is my jerkin? Oh." With wild energy, he pushed aside the house's ramshackle front door, emerging with a satchel. A flourish produced a brown leather jerkin that looked too fine to be anything he could have afforded by legitimate means.

"Are you finished?" she said.

"Nearly." And then Giacomo peeled off his own nose.

It stretched as it came loose, pulling at the skin of his cheeks, elongating and then reforming as it snapped free of his face. Beneath it lay another nose, perfectly normal, but without the wide nostrils and reddish tint of the discarded one. Looking at the flesh-colored putty, Rosa couldn't help but feel a little queasy.

With two little tugs, Giacomo yanked away the priest's bushy eyebrows and the farmer's mustache. Where once had stood a middle-aged farmer—and before that, an elderly priest—now stood a young man of nineteen, handsome and curly haired, with bright brown eyes and tanned olive skin. He rubbed the skin around his nose with both hands. "It always itches when I do that," he said. "Now. This conversation you are so intent on."

Rosa crossed her arms. "A job offer."

Giacomo's mouth curled in an easy smile. "Fascinating. What job?"

"I can't tell you here."

That smile widened. "Even *more* fascinating. And you're playing lieutenant?"

"It's my job. I'm putting the whole thing together."

"Rosa Cellini!" Giacomo exclaimed. "You conniving, adorable little snake!"

"Don't call me adorable."

"Will there be money?"

"More than you can imagine. Come to Florence," she said. "Two weeks' time. We can talk details there."

"Rosa," Giacomo said. Rosa managed to dodge back in time so he wasn't able to scoop her up into his arms again.

"If you pick me up, I'll kick you," she told him.

He managed to snare one of her hands in both of his. "I," he said, "will see you there."

"Wonderful—" She tried to tug her hand away, but he held on tight.

"And I shall dream of you every night until we are reunited."

"Don't be ridiculous."

"Every night, signorina," he told her, and pressed a light kiss to the top of her hand.

"Don't make me regret this."

He winked again. "Two weeks shall stand as an eternity between us—"

"Ugh." Finally, Rosa was able to tug her hand out of his. She strode out onto the country road, leaving Giacomo san Giacomo to monologue alone to the air.

It wasn't until she and her horse were a kilometer away that she realized the wedding rings she had stashed in her sleeve were missing. The feeling of Giacomo's fingers on her hand—on her wrist—flared briefly in her memory.

Rosa gave in to the urge to laugh. *Nobody looks to the priest.*

KHALID

Khalid al-Sarraj had long ago mastered the art of the purposeful lean. Without words, it conveyed to anyone watching that the burly man in the patched green jerkin would only be moved at the expense of someone else's internal organs. Even in this warehouse, a run-down, abandoned thing on the Genoa docks that was packed to the gills with life-hardened men, Khalid's flat glare bought him a wide berth.

"Where's Cibo?"

Khalid didn't bother to look down at the ropy little gambler. He kept his eyes on the circle of shouting onlookers at the center of the room. "Not here."

The man shifted. "He always handles my wagers—"

"Not tonight." Khalid spared the man a glance. "If you would like to place a bet, I am the one to speak to." In the ring of spectators, Khalid heard rather than saw Marino take another punch on the jaw. When he hit the packed earth floor, he didn't move for five long seconds. He was barely breathing. Blood seeped from his ripped mouth, his swollen nose, his cracked teeth, mixing with the dirt. "On the sooner side, signore," Khalid told the gambler. "I believe this fight is nearly finished."

Marino's opponent, a giant of a Spaniard named Salazar, was not courteous in victory. He paced the boundaries of the painted-out boxing ring, shaking his arms over his head. Around him, the crowd roared and cheered for their champion.

As planned, Khalid thought, from a distance. *Signore Traverio will be pleased*. He wondered if it was possible to hear the ocean from here.

He wondered what he would have for dinner. He wondered how long it would take the fish to eat Cibo's body once the waves closed over his head.

Perhaps the gambler read some of this in Khalid's face. He did not even bother with a muttered excuse before he retreated. The crowd swallowed him whole, surging as Salazar led them in a Spanish drinking song. The men laughed and shouted along with him, even if they did not understand the words.

But Khalid was not here tonight to keep an eye on Salazar. He was here to keep an eye on the bloodied man lying in the dirt next to Salazar's feet.

And Marino was stirring.

"He is a bad idea," Khalid had told Signore Traverio earlier that day. He had been proud that his voice remained steady, even as a man gurgled his last breaths on Signore Traverio's mosaic floor. "He is erratic. He cannot be trusted."

Signore Traverio, the Weever of Genoa, had just wiped his stiletto dagger clean on the curtains. Khalid watched the blade all the while. On the surface, Signore Traverio was not an imposing man. Decades of easy living had given him a certain padding. They had softened his muscles and added lines around his eyes and mouth. He was unassuming, just like the Genoan fish that had given him his nickname.

But weever fish were more than shoal-dwelling lurkers; they were venomous, storing toxin in the spines that ran along their backs. And they struck when their targets were most unprepared.

Signore Traverio had no need for venom. His dagger and his quick, cutthroat mind had bought him control of Genoa and beyond. Bookies and brothels from Ifriqiya to Bavaria owed him cuts of their profits. Sometimes Khalid felt as though there was not a man alive who did not work for the Weever of Genoa.

His treacherous dagger clean, Signore Traverio had clapped

Khalid on the shoulder. "Stick to brawling, not worrying," he had said. "That's where your talents lie. Marino knows what's good for him. Unlike this halfwit." The toe of Signore Traverio's boot had squeezed another surge of crimson blood from the unfortunate Cibo. "He'll stay down if he's paid to stay down."

Well. Marino had been paid to stay down. And now he was standing up.

Any dreams of dinner or an early night or the ocean evaporated. Khalid could only watch as Marino tapped Salazar on the shoulder. He was swaying on his feet. But only a fool would fall for that.

Apparently, Salazar was a fool. "You want more?" he laughed.

Marino spat a broken tooth in his face.

Wonderful, Khalid thought. If he concentrated hard enough, he could imagine the sting of a weever spine piercing the sole of his foot.

The crowd had only grown more excited with Marino's unexpected resurrection. The majority were jeering at Salazar to turn Marino into pulp. A hopeful few, always ready to root for the underdog, were encouraging Marino to do the same to Salazar. Altogether, it was an overwhelming din. And through it all, Marino was smiling.

If Khalid had been allowed, he would have stepped in to end the match. But doing so would reflect poorly on Signore Traverio. It might suggest that the outcomes of such bouts were ... not *quite* determined by the capabilities of the fighters.

Khalid resolutely did not think the word "rigged." There was always the off chance that, somewhere in Genoa, Signore Traverio would be able to hear it. Cibo the bookie had not been so careful. He had thought to advertise the true nature of these bouts by selling tips to gamblers. And worse than that, he had neglected to cut Signore Traverio in on the proceedings. Now there was a hole where his throat should be. Which meant that all Khalid could do was cross his arms, listen to the ocean, and watch.

Salazar was cocky. He paid more attention to the cheers of the crowd and the shouts of his supporters than he did the wiry scrapper in front of him. With much fanfare, Salazar drew a fist back. His blow bowled toward Marino's side, gathering strength and speed like a boulder rolling downhill.

It was a nightmare of bad form and bad execution. Khalid played out the next few seconds. With frustrated clarity, he could see how Marino would dodge. He could see the way Marino would jab in—one punch to the kidney and one to the shoulder. He could see how Salazar would stagger. How Marino would bring his foot down against Salazar's knee. How the crowd, so recently cheering for Salazar's victory, would be screaming their joy in his defeat.

Khalid walked out of the warehouse.

He emerged onto a rotting boardwalk, propped up on posts over the lapping, gray waves of the Ligurian Sea. The flimsy warehouse doors shut behind him, cutting off the warm glow of the uncovered lanterns and leaving him alone in the cold moonlight. To his right, the steady beam of the Lanterna di Genova shone over the open waters, a distant warning and a welcoming beacon to sailors and merchants.

He still remembered his first time seeing it, from the deck of a ship sailing into the Lanterna's safe harbor. Tunis had boasted more than its fair share of towers—elegant and intricate and sun-drenched. This lighthouse had seemed so alien in contrast. It was solid in every aspect, square and unmoving. He had not realized that his mouth was open as he watched it grow closer until Signore Traverio had clapped his shoulder, laughing at him.

"She's a beauty, isn't she?" Signore Traverio had said.

Khalid had nodded, absorbing the sight. Only weeks before, his world had seemed made of dead ends. He would never escape the streets of his childhood. He would take over Baba's textile shop and work there until he passed it on to his own son.

Or at least he was supposed to. But Baba had never had much of a head for business. He had taken out loans with Diego de Ávila, a Castilian dyemaker who had followed the royal army into Granada, and had continued south without them once he'd discovered that the weather of northern Ifriqiya agreed with him far more than that of his home country. At first, his arrangement with Baba had been amiable, Diego was a neighbor and, for the sake of their working relationship, he had been happy with Baba's small, sporadic payments.

Then things had changed. Suddenly Diego was no longer neighborly. He charged brutal interest, and their door rang with pounding as he demanded payment on a punishing schedule.

It had been Khalid's idea to venture to the funduq—the inn where Genoan traders and merchants conducted their business in Tunis—in order to seek work. Baba had decreed it too dangerous—everyone knew that places like the funduq were riddled with pirates. Besides: *It is not a boy's responsibility to handle the debts of his father.*

Khalid had gone anyway. He was no longer a boy, and if saving his father's business was what proved it, then that's what he would do.

He had thought himself blessed when Signore Traverio, the mysterious Genoan businessman, had offered Khalid a job. A job that paid enough to keep Diego at bay, at least. And the best part of all was that, in accepting Signore Traverio's offer, Khalid would get to see the world. No more dead ends. Khalid had accepted in an instant. Why would he think twice? He'd been granted a future, one his entire family could benefit from—one that glittered like the lantern atop the lighthouse tower.

He'd been as foolish as Salazar. Khalid knew that now. The Lanterna di Genova was no more magical than any other lump of rock in this claustrophobic world. Since laying eyes on it, the dead ends had only closed in tighter, tight enough to suffocate. And there was no glitter in his future, only blood—the destiny of a naive boy who had jumped at the first opportunity to cross his path without asking questions.

Somewhere inside the warehouse came a crack and a pained scream in a voice too deep and loud to be Marino's. Khalid turned his back on the Lanterna and gazed out at the ocean.

In his head, he counted down from fifty.

The warehouse door burst outward at twenty-three, which was sooner than he had anticipated. The roar of the onlookers inside swelled, bloodthirsty men surging onto the docks.

Khalid sighed. He rolled his shoulders. He faced the crowd.

Someone had propped the warehouse door open. Golden lamplight spilled out into the chilly night. Khalid could see the faces of the men surrounding him, bright with excitement and drink. He could not find Salazar.

But Marino was front and center, grinning at Khalid. His face was still streaked with blood, and he had a bruise blossoming across his collarbone, but he did not seem to notice any of his injuries. His firelit eyes were fixed on Khalid.

Behind Khalid, the ocean swelled. "You are making a mistake."

Marino just scoffed. "I'm just here to collect my winnings. Isn't that right, boys?"

The crowd's answering cheer hurt Khalid's ears. He did not blink. "You do not want to make an enemy here, Marino."

"I want my money," Marino said.

"Then you should have lost that fight," Khalid said, his voice pitched below the hubbub of their audience. "If you think either of us is being paid after tonight, you are mistaken."

Marino scowled. "If the Weever wants me to take a dive, he better start paying me per bruise. I saw you collecting wagers. Traverio won't pay me out? Then you will."

"You are making a mistake," Khalid repeated.

Marino turned a fat-lipped grin back on the crowd. "What do you think? Should I make Traverio's guard dog pay up?"

His audience roared. The boardwalk rocked with every rough ocean wave. Khalid took a measured breath of salty air. He stepped to the right.

Marino's fist whistled past his face.

It would have been misguidedly poetic to say that fighting, to Khalid, was like the ocean. Fighting was like fighting. It was the contraction and the release of muscles, the strategic exploitation of strengths and weaknesses. It was contact and pain. It was bruises. It was blood.

But even so, Khalid breathed in time with the waves as his feet traced patterns on the boardwalk. He shifted, inhaling the sea, as he led Marino around in a circle. Here, standing his ground like this, he kept his back to the light of the warehouse, leaving Marino illuminated and his own face in shadow. He dipped left, exhaling the sea, allowing Marino's swing to pass by.

The Lanterna di Genova loomed over Marino's right shoulder. In Khalid's starved imagination, the brilliant light at the top flared, burst into flames, taking the whole goddamned tower down with it.

Khalid glared at it. Then he glared at Marino. Then he unleashed a deceptively powerful elbow to the spot on Marino's temple where a bruise had already formed.

The connection was jarring. Shocking. It always was. Marino stumbled to one knee, but only for a moment. He was up again in half a moment, feet slipping on the damp boards, his glare narrowing to a fuzzy squint.

"This is your last chance," Khalid told him.

Marino caught a glancing blow across Khalid's chin.

Khalid broke Marino's wrist and his nose, fractured two ribs, and shoved him off the boardwalk into the surf.

He was surprised to find that he was angry. His heart hammered in his chest. The pay he should have received for the night's work—the money that should have gone to Baba's bottomless debt—was dust in the wind, scattered by a greedy, selfish moron. He wanted to scream. But the crowd was still watching. They were silent, for the first time all night. They had gotten their blood, but they didn't know what to make of their champion.

"We are done here," Khalid told them. "Those with wagers can settle up in the morning." A few men looked as though they'd like to protest, but he fixed them with his flattest stare. "If anyone has a problem, they are welcome to take it up with the Weever."

That name was enough to disperse the crowd. Khalid stood his ground, his back to the ocean, listening to the waves crash as—in groups or pairs or all alone—the men trickled down the boardwalk and back into town. They were grumbling, shooting looks back over their shoulder at Khalid as they left. This was not going to be the last Khalid heard of tonight. His bad luck was accumulating interest.

So it did not surprise him nearly as much as it should have when he realized that there was one member of the crowd hanging back. The man stood at his ease in the slant of light from the open warehouse door. He was tall and slim. His hands were shoved casually in his belt. He was watching Khalid. Though he was backlit, Khalid thought he might be smiling.

Khalid sighed and rolled his shoulders. He didn't want to end his night by beating another grin off someone's face, but if the situation called for it—

"I didn't come all this way to get punched, Khalid," the man said, stepping out of the doorway. And now Khalid could make out his face: the hairless chin, the wide-set eyes, the stray strands of copper hair. Not a man at all.

Sarra the Tinkerer held out a hand. "Good to see you. That was very impressive."

Khalid clasped the girl's hand in return. He felt a small amount of tension run out of him, for the first time all evening. "Good to see you too, signorina."

Despite her strange clothes, Khalid had always liked Sarra. They had only crossed paths twice, but from what he could tell, she took small jobs and didn't complain. She had an understanding of the criminal landscape that came from a lifetime of watching and listening. And she was not an idiot.

Yes, Khalid liked Sarra the Tinkerer. He also did not trust her. This was a compliment. He liked so few people, after all, and the mistrust was professional courtesy. Anyone Khalid had met on Signore Traverio's payroll—which was everyone he'd met since setting foot on that ship back in Tunis—was at least a little bit crooked. Khalid included himself in that generalization. A person could not exist in Signore Traverio's orbit and claim morality.

And Khalid's mistrust for the redheaded girl was born from respect, not apprehension. He knew that, despite her age, she was capable of many impossible things. He had seen some of the contraptions that emerged from her workshop. This brand of genius, the clockwork brain inside her head—a man could never guess at what Sarra was thinking at any given moment.

"Acquaintance of yours?" She nodded toward the edge of the boardwalk. Marino could still be heard moaning and cursing as he hauled himself up the beach below.

"Business associate," said Khalid, prodding at a growing bruise on his chin.

"Business seems tetchy."

Khalid's politeness had long since floated out to sea. "He deserved what he got."

"I know about working with fools like that," Sarra said. "Come on. Dinner's on me."

There was no world in which Sarra the Tinkerer materialized out of the darkness, watched Khalid beat seven kinds of hell out of someone, and then offered to buy him dinner out of the kindness of her heart. But Khalid's stomach was growling. If she had an ulterior motive—an offer or a question or an assassination attempt—she could try it over a plate of fish.

Khalid led her to a small dockside tavern where the owner, a leathery-faced woman called Flora, plopped full platters in front of them without being asked. Flora had five sons, she had told Khalid once, all of them sailors, all of them years gone around the world. Khalid apparently reminded her of her middle son, the one who had been gone the longest. "He barely says two words in a stretch," she had told him, "but he can eat more than my other boys put together." Khalid, at a loss, had just nodded, which made her face scrunch up in a mass of smiling wrinkles. She'd been giving him extra helpings at no cost ever since.

He didn't bother asking why Sarra was in Genoa. She would tell him when she was ready. Instead, he concentrated on the spirals of steam rising from his plate.

"This is a nice setup," the girl said around a mouthful of bass. In her rough-spun woolen jacket and shallow-brimmed cap, she could have been a particularly slight dockworker. "The sea views, the steady work. Not to mention the food." She raised her cider tankard to Flora, who was watching, hawk-like, from her post by the kitchen door. Flora glared in response, untrusting of outsiders as usual.

This cool reception didn't throw Sarra off. She shoveled another bite into her mouth. "Weever still keeping you busy?" she asked.

Khalid very thoughtfully did not point out that this was a stupid question. "Yes."

"That man," Sarra said. "He's always got something going on."

"Does he know you are in Genoa?"

"No, no," Sarra said, banishing the question with a wave of her knife. "He doesn't care about nobodies like me. I don't want to waste his time. Anyway, I won't be here long."

She might as well have struck an alarm bell over Khalid's head. Genoa was Signore Traverio's home. Nothing happened within the city's walls and especially by the docks without him being informed. And while Sarra might not be notorious, she had a history and a reputation. For her to even pass *near* Genoa without sending Signore Traverio respectful notice—

It was the recipe for an unpleasant interaction. Khalid had a nauseating flash of Cibo's wetly smiling throat. He set down his knife. "How long?" he asked.

"Long enough to extend a congratulations," Sarra said. She took another sip of her cider.

"To me?"

"Mhm."

Khalid tamped down his growing frustration. If Sarra was going to stick to nonanswers, they would be here all night. "I do not like to play games, Tinkerer."

Sarra sighed, putting down her drink. "Nor do I," she said. "But we are short-staffed at the moment, and so here I am." She looked up again, fixing Khalid with a straightforward gaze. "I'm here to congratulate you on the impending birth of your brother's child."

For a moment, Khalid almost believed himself back on the ship. The world tilted beneath his feet like ocean waves. "My—brother—?"

"Your brother."

Khalid tried again. "Yusuf . . . has a child?"

"His wife," Sarra clarified, "is about five months along."

If Khalid fainted at the table and created a fuss, then Flora surely would have something to say about it. The last time he'd seen his brother, Yusuf had been fourteen years old, gangly, dusty, and laughing with his friends. Khalid had not said goodbye as he followed Signore Traverio to the docks. He'd been too excited. He'd just rolled his eyes at Yusuf's guileless glee as he fled the tedious safety of his father's house for something greater.

And now . . . Yusuf was *married*. He had a child on the way. And Khalid hadn't known—

Well, whose fault is that? "How . . ." Khalid forced through the choking wall of self-recrimination.

Sarra was watching him over the rim of her tankard. "I believe you know Rosa Cellini."

The fog of confusion in Khalid's mind parted briefly to admit the image of a young woman's dark eyes, sharp and clever. "She passed through a few years back."

"And made an impression on Traverio, I understand."

She had. As Khalid recalled, Signore Traverio had tried to recruit her with gold at first, and then by force. But the young woman had not been nearly as naive as Khalid. She had slipped through the Weever's best efforts and disappeared into the night. "Yes," he said.

"She has been in contact with your brother," Sarra said.

"She wrote to him? She had no right," Khalid bit out. "My family is none of her concern."

"Yusuf passed along a message," Sarra said. "He wanted to be sure that you knew—just because you left doesn't mean you can't return." She cocked her head. "He wants his child to know their uncle."

The sun-washed street—his childhood home—his brother's face—they danced before his eyes, so real he felt he could almost touch them. Every moment of homesickness, of distance, every kilometer that stretched between Genoa and Tunis, everything he had tamped down and refused to allow himself to feel for three years—they all welled up at once, and threatened to drag him under.

But reality was a sharp blade. It stabbed between his ribs, cutting that golden vision short. "It is impossible," he said. His voice was gravelly. He took a sip, swallowing his emotions with his water.

Sarra was still watching him. "Because of your employer."

"Because I made a promise," Khalid said. "My payments barely keep the creditors from knocking in my father's door as it is. I cannot return home until I have made enough money to wipe his accounts clean."

"Promises to fathers. They'll get you every time. How's yours going?"

Khalid did not dignify this with a response. The job he had been offered back in Tunis had been a fantasy. The reality was bloody, mindless mundanity, a life of underpaid, paranoid purgatory. And what were the alternatives? No one else dared offer him work here in Genoa, not unless they wanted to bring the Weever's wrath down on them. There were no options in Tuscany for a Tunisian far from home.

Traverio's guard dog. That was what Marino had called him. He would be Traverio's guard dog until he died.

His silence was enough of a reply for Sarra. "Ah," she said. "I see."

Of course she saw. It was the reason she was in Genoa. It certainly was the reason she was in Genoa without alerting Signore Traverio. Khalid took the bait. "What do you want."

"I want to give you a job."

This startled a dry laugh out of Khalid. "Signore Traverio would not be happy to hear you say this."

"Who's telling him?" Sarra asked. "There is a chance here for you to make more money than you can even dream of. Two months. One job. You'll walk out with enough to buy first-class passage to Tunis, save your father's business, and set yourself and your entire growing family up well enough to live out the rest of your days in comfort. You'll never have to think about Genoa ever again."

Khalid had been fool enough to blindly accept employment once in his life. He would not make the same mistake again. "And the catch?"

"Giacomo's on the team."

A phantom laugh tickled Khalid's ears. He groaned, sitting back. "That madman?"

"I said the same thing, but he's the best. So are you. It's why we want you."

"'We'. You and the Cellini girl."

Sarra finished the last of her cider. "We don't need an answer now. Come to Florence with me. Hear Rosa out and you can make your decision then."

"Signore Traverio will not let me leave Genoa."

"He will. Because there's an upstart in Florence with designs on the Genoa harbor."

"Is there," Khalid deadpanned.

"Oh yes. He's daring. He's scary. And surprise of all surprises, he is from Ifriqiya."

"I have never heard of such a mastermind."

"Well, the Weever has. He got word about it—very trustworthy information—just this afternoon. I hear it rattled him quite a bit."

Which it would. Signore Traverio had always been paranoid. News like this, of an up-and-comer he had never heard of . . . it would shake him. He would want someone to investigate. And who better to root out the truth behind rumors of an Ifriqiyan challenger than—

"Do you trust her?" Khalid asked

Sarra didn't need to ask who he meant. "I trust that she's a better chance than that idiot who took a swing at you earlier."

"Mm." It was exactly the kind of answer Khalid would have expected from someone like Sarra. Yusuf's face flickered in Khalid's mind again, and for once, he didn't push the image away. Maybe there was a glimmer of hope in the world. Maybe his fortunes could change—enough to pay for passage home to Tunis, to settle with Diego de Ávila, to save his family once and for all. Maybe the world was not so full of dead ends as he had feared.

And if Signore Traverio never found out, then he wouldn't even wind up like Cibo, for his troubles.

"The rest of the team," Khalid said. "You, Signorina Cellini, the mad player . . ."

"Agata de Rosso," Sarra said.

"Is that all?" It seemed a small team, if the job was as large as Sarra was promising.

She grimaced, looking uncomfortable for the first time since she'd approached Khalid on the docks. "There is one more," she said. "Though he is still . . . to be decided."

"Who is he?"

Sarra sighed. "A liability."

6

DOMINIC

I t was a disaster. There was nothing to salvage. It was a complete catastrophe, and it was all his fault, and he was hopeless, and he might as well just give up forever.

The paintbrush handle was creaking in the clench of Dominic's fist. *Lightly, lightly,* his mother whispered in his head, and he forced his fingers to loosen. But there were not enough light, free brushstrokes in the world to save this canvas from himself. To save it from *him*.

He reached for his pallet and only succeeded in smearing himself with verdigris from fingertip to palm. With a huff, he let the brush drop and scrubbed his clean hand over his face.

It was the toga. That was the problem. He'd rendered it well, he knew he had. It was identical to the image in his head, down to the minute folds in the left sleeve. But somewhere between conceiving it and putting it on canvas, something had gone wrong. It just didn't fit—none of it did, not the toga, not the woman wearing it, not the swoop of Santa Maria del Fiore that loomed in the background. Together they had turned his painting into a puzzlingly confrontational riot of color. *Again*.

On paper, Dominic Fontana was a boy bound straight for the top. At fifteen, he had mastered the intricacies of countless painting techniques, able to duplicate from memory the sketchy lines of da Vinci, the romantic curves of Botticelli, the clean colors of Bellini. It had been enough to land him an apprenticeship at one of the most competitive workshops in Florence, where he would presumably go on to win patronage from any number of wealthy, culturally-minded nobles and make a name for himself that would stand the test of time.

And yet. Three years later, Dominic was realizing that the mastery of other men's art did not necessarily translate to the creation of his own. Which did *not* make sense, because if he copied it precisely, then a toga in his piece should be *just* as good as the original by—

"Da Carpi?"

For a moment, Dominic thought that his mother was whispering in his head again. But no—that had come from just over his shoulder, muttered in the gloom of the workshop. Dominic yelped, one flailing arm scrabbling for his discarded paintbrush and knocking over his palette, paint knives, and oils in the process. He whirled, holding the brush out like a weapon. If he was to be murdered by an art critic, he would not go down without a fight.

Instead, he found himself face-to-*very-close-face* with a girl. She stood a few inches shorter than Dominic's own unimpressive height, and was staring up at him from under a wild crop of curls. A cloak hung around her shoulders, already growing gray with the marble dust that hung ever-present in the air.

Her eyes were wide and surprised, somehow dark and bright at the same time. Dominic's grip on the paintbrush tightened.

"Who—" he finally said, once he'd regained the power of speech. "What—"

"Sorry, sorry—" The girl stumbled back a few steps, enough to put a discreet distance between Dominic and her magnetic gaze.

"What?" he said again, the only word he could think of.

"I said 'I'm sorry'—" the girl repeated, but Dominic was blinking back to himself now, reacquainting himself with his surroundings. There was no clatter of chisel on stone, no cheery banter from the older apprentices. The workshop—a massive, open space—was dark, its jumble of rough tables, chunks of marble, and sheets of canvas swallowed by the night.

"Oh no," he said through welling dread. "What's the time?"

"At least three hours past sundown, signore," the girl said.

Dominic groaned. He'd promised to clear out when the other apprentices did tonight, but he'd been so absorbed in his terrible painting that he'd lost track of time. "Damn. *Damn.*" As though the devil himself was cracking a whip behind him, he began scraping together everything he'd upended at the girl's sudden appearance, dumping it all on the rickety trestle that also held his lone candle. The girl retrieved an errant paint knife that had skidded to a stop against her foot.

"It's a fine painting," she offered, sidling around him to get a closer look at the signature scribbled across the bottom of the canvas. She smelled like citrus. "Dominic . . . Fontana?"

This lie, even more than her inexplicable presence, irked him. He snatched the paint knife from her fingers. "It's late," he said. "We're closed to visitors."

"Oh, I'm not a visitor," she said, her face lighting up with a bright smile. The sight of it and its practiced perfection ratcheted his irritation up higher. He frowned. "I'm meeting someone," she went on. "Da Carpi?"

Dominic blinked. "Who? No—" He tossed the paint knife onto the trestle table with its fellows. "He's not even in Florence."

"I'm aware. But this figure. Here." Her finger hovered above the toga that had been giving him so much grief. "I've seen her before. In one of Ugo da Carpi's woodcuts, back in Venice. The cobblestones are familiar as well. Pietro Perugino. It's well done, practically indistinguishable from Perugino's original. But it's definitely Perugino."

She was right. He'd copied—*been inspired*—by both artists. But that didn't mean Dominic was happy to be found out. He snatched the sheet from the floor, draping it over the canvas in one quick motion. "You have to leave. Come back in the morning, if you must."

"I didn't think artists were supposed to sign their work until it was completed," the girl said, leaning against the bookshelf Dominic used to block his space from the rest of the workshop. "Isn't it bad luck or something?"

Derivative. Even days later, Dominic could still feel goose bumps from his master's criticism. "It was supposed to *be* completed," he muttered, and then wished he hadn't.

"Really?"

"You have to leave," he repeated.

"I told you," she said. "I'm waiting for someone. I have an appointment."

Dominic's gesture took in the empty workshop. "I think you've been stood up."

"I can wait," the girl chirped. "I don't have anywhere to be. Why are you still working on your painting if it's supposed to be done?"

His eyes narrowed against the glare of her grin. "Who are you waiting for?"

"I asked you first."

"You're in *my* workshop."

"I'm in your *master's* workshop. Waiting for your *master.*"

His eyes went even narrower. "Why?"

"I told you. I have an appointment. He's expecting me." She leaned closer. He backed up. "It's a *personal matter.*"

His back was to the wall, but he risked blinding to study her radiant smile. Something about her unsettled him. He couldn't quite put a finger on it.

"Do I have something on my face, Signore Fontana?" the girl asked, and Dominic realized that she was studying him in return, those dark eyes sharp. "You'll have to tell me if I do."

Suddenly it all made sense. Her late arrival, her artistic knowledge, her supposed appointment with his master. "Oh, I *see*," he said. "I know why you're here."

Her eyebrow quirked, and Dominic had the nonsensical idea that this was the first real expression he'd seen cross her face since she'd startled herself by startling him. "Is that so?"

"We get a few of you every week." He shook his head, beginning once again to tidy his workspace. "He won't sign anything for you. He has no words of encouragement for . . . whatever artistic aspirations you may harbor." The words were bitter in his mouth. "So you might as well leave now and save yourself the disappointment."

True delight broke over the girl's face. "Do you think I'm here because—do you think I'm a *fan*?"

"You could pick out da Carpi and Perugino from across the room," Dominic said.

"Because you *copied them exactly*."

"I—no, I—"

"Botticelli too. Don't think I didn't notice. I don't have 'aspirations' but I'm not *blind*."

"Who *are* you?"

"Is that why you're still working on it?" the girl asked, flicking at the easel. "Trying to turn this into something more than a mishmash of other men's art?"

It stung more than it should have, coming from a strange girl he'd only met minutes ago. His fists clenched. "Get. *Out*."

"*Fontana*."

His name became a whip, barked in that low, gravelly voice. Dominic felt the blood drain from his face so fast that he had the fleeting worry he was about to faint, and he lurched into something approaching military attention as he whirled around.

"She—she was just leaving," he stammered into the ever-scowling face of his master, "Master Michelangelo."

7

ROSA

The man standing in front of Rosa was made of compressed intensity. The arms folded across his chest were so solid that Rosa could believe he had sprouted, arboreal, from the flagstones. She pegged him at somewhere around his mid-forties, with the strength of someone who worked with his nicked and scarred hands. Marble dust coated his curling hair and beard, thick enough to be baked onto him. He watched Rosa with a sharp-eyed focus that took her in piecemeal, cataloguing every centimeter of skin, every joint, organ, and vein . . .

"Why are you here?" the artist—Michelangelo—Michelangelo *Buonarroti*—*Il Divino himself*—said, chillingly displeased.

It took Rosa a moment to realize that the question was not directed at her. Young Signore Fontana suffered no such confusion. "I was painting," he floundered, suppressed panic in his gray-blue eyes, "and I—lost track of the hour—"

"Hm" was Michelangelo's only response. The syllable conveyed everything he thought about Dominic, his work, and painting as a general concept. Dominic deflated accordingly.

Rosa might have pitied him if he hadn't been such an ass. She stepped forward before Michelangelo could finish reducing his apprentice to a heap of smoldering ashes. "Good evening," she said, dropping into a curtsy. "I believe you were expecting me."

"Do you really think you should be going by yourself?" Sarra had asked the night before she'd left for Genoa. They had been huddled over the Nepi's kitchen table, chopping onions for their dinner and listening to the creak of Pietro's footsteps in the shop below.

"I don't want to gang up on him," Rosa had said.

"He could have the City Guard waiting."

"He won't."

"You don't *know* that." In the candlelight, Rosa wondered if Sarra was seeing her or her mother.

But Rosa did not have time for ghosts. "We're going to have to take some risks sometime, right?"

She'd been especially glad to be alone as she'd made her way through the upscale neighborhood of San Niccolo earlier that evening. The doubts had begun to creep in as the workshops and shopfronts of Santo Spirito gave way to their upscale counterparts. She'd nearly missed the long, dusty building sulking in the shadows of its more impressive neighbors. It had only been the ground-in blanket of marble dust carpeting the cobbles in front of the wide oak double doors that had clued her in. Shoving her misgivings down, Rosa had squared her shoulders and slipped inside.

The combative apprentice and his eyelashes had been a surprise, but Rosa couldn't let that shake her. Now as Michelangelo's piercing gaze continued to size her up, moving past the physical and on to her spirit, Rosa kept still and let him tally. Her smile did not budge. She could hold it. She'd smiled at worse people for longer than this.

"Hm," he finally said, that sound again containing entire reams of meaning. Then, instead of elaborating, he turned his back on Rosa and his chastised apprentice and stalked away.

He hadn't kicked her out and he hadn't called the City Guard. That would have to do.

"Pleasure meeting you, Signore Fontana," Rosa shot over her shoulder, hurrying after the retreating Michelangelo. Dominic barely spared her a glance, wrapped up as he was in wrestling the canvas off the easel with white-knuckled hands. If Rosa was a betting woman, she would wager that canvas would be in the river by sunup.

Michelangelo Buonarroti, the manifestation of the muses walking on earth, the God-touched artist, worked in a tiny corner of his own workshop, hidden from the prying eyes of worshipful apprentices and fascinated patrons by a few lengths of tacked-up cloth. The sheets billowed in the breeze from the back door, painted in ethereal shades by the moonlight filtering through the shutters. Rosa pulled one of these curtains aside to find the sculptor crouched at the base of a marble slab, chisel in one hand. The other hand was pressed to the stone, tracing every line with a care that made Rosa feel as though she should look away.

He did not say anything. This was fine. Two could play at that game, and Rosa would not be the first to break the silence.

"You've got some nerve, sending me a message like that," Michelangelo finally said. A moment later, a muffled *thwack* split the quiet night. Rosa jumped. She'd barely seen him move, but Michelangelo's chisel was now embedded in the implacable surface of the marble. It must have taken an incredible amount of strength. Michelangelo didn't look at her as he lifted a mallet, poising it over the end of the chisel. "What business could a girl like you have with me?"

"If you were truly uninterested in the answer, you would not have waited for me tonight."

"Hm," he said. She was beginning to think that sound made up half the man's vocabulary.

"As for 'business,'" she said, "mine lies in wealth redistribution."

"Oh yes?" A bitter laugh colored his words. "Is that supposed to mean something?"

"Asked like a high-minded artist," she said. "For some of us, wealth redistribution is a way of life."

The man snorted. "You're good at weaving words."

"Thank you."

"But what you're saying is that you're a thief."

"Hm," Rosa said, throwing his favorite syllable right back at him. "Of course, *your* wealth is perfectly safe—"

"I don't give two shits about *my* money." Michelangelo tapped the end of the chisel once—twice— "Here—girl—what's your name?"

"You can call me Rosa."

"Rosa. You think you're very clever. But I know why you're here."

"Oh?"

"You have your eye on the Medici." Fragments of marble the size of a man's thumb shattered to the floor.

"Il Divino lives up to his title," Rosa said. "Such insight."

"How's this for insight? You're out of your mind. I should call the guard on you."

"So why don't you?"

He looked up at her, eyes sharp. "The Medici set me up in this place."

"It's very nice."

"They provide me with the best materials. They come to me with incredible projects. They *pay my commissions.*"

"Oh? I thought you couldn't give two shits about that," Rosa remarked mildly.

"Everyone knows, signorina," he said, a touch of bitterness coloring his words. "My whole life, I owe them. They gave me my start. Plucked me out of obscurity. Lorenzo de' Medici practically raised me as his own son." His shoulders twisted, wiry muscles coiling and releasing, and in another one of those uncanny split seconds, the chisel was embedded back in the marble again. "For God's sake," Michelangelo said. "They even gave my idiot apprentice a job repairing that hideous fresco of theirs."

Some of Dominic's paint-focused angst shook itself into focus in Rosa's mind. "I understand your concerns," she said.

"Do you?" Michelangelo said. His mallet crashed down on the chisel, unleashing a chunk of marble the size of Rosa's fist. It smashed to the ground, a puff of dust painting the hem of her skirts white. "Do you understand that you are in *Florence*? Do you understand that the Medici own this city? Do you understand what happens to those who are stupid enough to cross them?"

Beneath her ribs, that icy flame flared. "Can I ask you a question, Master Michelangelo?" she asked. "If we have a few minutes before you call the City Guard to haul me away?" Michelangelo's grip on his chisel did not loosen, but he also did not plunge it into her eye socket, so she counted that as permission to go ahead. "On my arrival to the city, I passed by the Palazzo Vecchio. I couldn't help but notice the striking statue standing outside. The David."

Michelangelo was watching her closely. "Yes."

"You carved it."

"With four years of my blood and sweat."

"So evocative. But here is my question. What does that statue mean to you?" He blinked at her, the first crack in his gruff armor showing. "The people of this city leave offerings at its feet. Flowers, sweets. Love letters. Hate letters. They smear it with mud. It is not just a work of art to them. It means something more. And if it means that much more to the huddled masses, then what must it mean to Il Divino, the genius who created it?"

Michelangelo's face was a mask of conflicted frustration. He said nothing. "I'll tell you what I think it means," Rosa said, pressing her advantage. "I think that for years, Florence was a Republic. It flourished as a Republic, free from the rule of the Medici family. And in those years, you set your chisel to marble and created something extraordinary. Something to celebrate. David, the conqueror of Goliath, cradling the weapon of victory. I think that you carved a symbol of democratic liberty, something you loved. And then . . ."

"Prato." The name slipped from Michelangelo on a breath, heavy with fear and grief. "The Medici burned Prato."

Rosa's approachable smile did not falter. "Only a fool would try to sway you to their cause with promises of gold or power," she said. "You have enough of both. So I come to you with the memory of the Republic and ask ... if there was a chance to make even a crack in the armor of the family that stole it from you, wouldn't you take it?" Maybe she was laying it on a little thick, but she only had one shot at this. "I've seen the bills on the walls. The graffiti. Florence remembers the Republic. And since the *David* did not simply appear from thin air, I would wager that you do as well."

The silence was overwhelming. It pressed in like a cotton bubble around them, muffling everything inside the flimsy cloth walls. Here, in the workspace of the greatest artist in Florence, time stretched, moments flowing into minutes flowing into hours. Rosa realized she was holding her breath and released it, slowly enough that it would not make a sound.

Michelangelo had put down his chisel in some space between the inspirational hyperboles. Now he stood with both hands pressed to the marble slab, eyes closed, drawing strength from the promise of the stone. With his shoulders slumped and his arms outstretched, it was painfully obvious how small a man he was.

"They're too powerful," he said finally, but he looked up as he spoke. Was it hope sparking inside that fiery gaze? "Too wealthy. Too well-armed. It's useless to rise against them."

"Who said anything about well-armed?" Rosa said. "I'm taking my cue from their family motto. *Festina lente*. Make haste slowly. I don't need an army. All I need is an introduction."

"But how could that possibly be enough?"

"Ah, Master Michelangelo," she said. "I think an artist like yourself will understand more than anyone. You don't need more than a stone to conquer Goliath."

8

GIACOMO

I n Giacomo's experience, Florence was an upbeat town, glowing with a prosperous, festival atmosphere. And perhaps it was his own fault for going so long between visits, but he was frankly *shocked* by the undercurrent of tension that ran through the city as he walked through the gates. It was written on the faces of the shopkeepers and the panhandlers and the guards in Medici and City colors that patrolled up and down the narrow streets. It was written on the *walls*, for Heaven's sake. This Florence was a city primed for . . . something. On the verge of *something*.

Giacomo couldn't wait to figure out what.

He arrived at the millhouse on the outskirts of the city just as the sun was beginning to set. It was an old building, slumped along the shores of the Arno river as though someone had spilled it there, and Giacomo regarded it doubtfully for a long minute before the rumble in his stomach reminded him that he had not had more than a bite to eat today, and if the smell wafting through the open window was anything to go off of, the odds were better than good that there was food waiting somewhere inside. It was an easy decision, then, to stick his hands into his belt and shove through the door.

He had expected the rustic furnishings, the fire crackling in the hearth, the packed earth floor. He had even expected the spread of bread and cheese, fruit and wine on the long table.

He had *not* expected to see Khalid al-Sarraj's grimly handsome face snapping around to glare at him.

"Khalid?" The name burst out of him before he could check it. "What in Heaven's name are you doing *here*?"

If there was one thing that the past three years of their friendship—acquaintance—*tense mutual enmity*—had taught Giacomo, it was that only the Devil himself could pry Khalid out of Genoa and that gangster Traverio's hands. The sight of him here, in Florence, crumbling a piece of Pecorino into dust, was almost too strange to be believed.

"Same as you," Khalid said, radiating dark displeasure across the room.

"Well, I *must* say," Giacomo said, sidling toward the food, "if Rosa had led with the fact that *you* were considering this job, then I would have jumped at the opportunity *much* sooner." He popped a few grapes into his mouth, grinning as Khalid continued to glare. "You look quite distressed, Signore al-Sarraj. How about this: if you'd like to hit me, let's get that out of the way up top. I only ask that you aim for my stomach instead of my face."

The silence that followed was not encouraging and Giacomo rolled his eyes because *really*, opportunities like this did not simply come around every day. "I won't even hold it against you," he said. "I'd actually prefer it, because looking at your sour frown and wondering *when* and *what* and *how* is going to drive me *absolutely* out of my gourd."

"You are already out of your gourd," said Khalid.

"Right," said Giacomo. "So if you're going to do something about that, do it now please." He shut his eyes. "I'm ready."

The only response was an annoyed exhale of breath. Giacomo cracked one eyelid. "No? The last time we met, you told me you'd flatten my nose if you ever saw me again."

"Because you stole two gold pendants out of the *Viola*'s hold and I had to answer to Signore Traverio over it."

Giacomo gasped. "I never!"

"Then you knocked my lunch into the ocean."

"Then what are you waiting for? This is your last shot, Signore al-Sarraj. If you try to swing at me later, I will take it *personally*."

Khalid did not move, but Giacomo would never give up hope. He would get Khalid to crack if he had to drop every one of Khalid's lunches into the sea for the next twenty years.

But such a thing was not in the cards today. The door swung open, admitting a column of red, dying sunlight and the crooked silhouette of an elderly woman.

Khalid immediately straightened. "Signora de Rosso!"

"Ah, Khalid, there's my handsome boy," the old woman said, stepping nimbly between the dusty fragments of furniture that cluttered the mill. "And Signore san Giacomo, I presume."

This could be none other than Agata de Rosso, one of the best working apothecaries in the world. "That a lady like yourself would know of me is the greatest flattery in all the world, Signora," Giacomo said. He dipped into a low bow, his mind racing all the while.

He had already been harboring suspicions as to the scale of this job—why else would Rosa seek him out personally? But it was one thing to make a quick journey to Modigliana. It was another to brave the displeasure of Giuseppe Traverio and steal his most prized enforcer out from under his nose. And it was yet another to enlist the help of the Witch of Florence.

All of which was to say, with talent like this involved, then this promised to be an even more intriguing opportunity than he'd previously hoped.

"Allow me to assist you." Giacomo swept his arm out to Signora de Rosso. "Please consider me at your disposal. No whim is too small. I am your humble servant."

"*Humble*?" Khalid muttered.

Giacomo ignored him, guiding Signora de Rosso through the

jumbled room and toward the large walnut table in the center. "Wine?" he offered, settling her on one of the only functioning chairs.

"There's a dear."

Giacomo poured a generous glug and presented it to Signora de Rosso. She watched him, eyes sharp, over the rim of her cup. "You're the one who did that sapphire job, up in Milan."

"That might have been me."

"And the jewelry heist in Genoa."

Khalid's glare drilled into the side of Giacomo's face. Giacomo smiled. "Who's to say?"

"The violin scam down in Grosseto?" Signora de Rosso asked.

Giacomo's shoulder blade itched. "I'm afraid I've never been to Grosseto."

"Mm." Signora de Rosso turned her attention back to her wine. But when Giacomo glanced over, he found Khalid still watching him, studying Giacomo like a puzzle to be solved.

The door opened again. "Oh good," said Rosa. "We're all here."

She stepped inside, followed by lanky Sarra the Tinkerer, who nodded her greetings to Khalid and Signora de Rosso, and frowned at Giacomo, which Giacomo personally considered unwarranted and *rude* since they hadn't exchanged so much as a single word in a *year*.

The third person to enter was a wiry man with a dark beard matched only in wildness by the mop of curls sprouting from the top of his head. Despite the curious looks of Giacomo, Khalid, and Signora de Rosso, he refused to meet anyone's eyes. Nonetheless, there was something familiar about him . . .

"Il Divino?" Giacomo said. The man's face snapped up with a glare that could rival Khalid's. "You *are*! You *are* Il Divino!"

"Giacomo," Sarra cautioned.

"Rosa, why is *Michelangelo Buonarroti* here?"

Rosa stepped forward, putting herself between Il Divino and Giacomo's onslaught of enthusiasm. "All in time. If we're ready?"

She looked different here, though perhaps that was due to the slant of the dusty daylight. She still wore a smile—Rosa Cellini always wore a smile, was always open and approachable, because that was how you reeled people in. But there was something honed beneath it all. Something wicked and blade-thin sheathed beneath that grifter's mask, leaking ice and frost.

Giacomo shivered, just a little, as he gathered around the table with the others.

"You already know why you're here," Rosa said. "The basics. And some of you have traveled quite a distance to hear me out, so I won't waste any more of your time. I would like to hire you for a job. Possibly the most dangerous job that any of us have ever pulled. But if we manage it—and I think we can—it will be the greatest windfall that any of us have ever seen."

The promise of fortune sucked at Giacomo like a riptide, and going off the faces of the others, he was not alone in that. Even Il Divino was affected, though he kept his eyes to the floor.

"If all this sounds a bit too rich for your blood," Rosa continued, "then now is the time to walk out. No judgment, no questions from any of us. You will have my blessing if you choose to go, and I hope that our paths may cross sometime in the future." She paused, long enough to make careful eye contact with each of them in turn. "Anyone?"

It was Khalid who broke the weighty quiet first. "How big a windfall?"

For such a short woman, Rosa managed to unfurl the oversized roll of parchment with a flourish that Giacomo viewed with professional appreciation and perhaps a degree of envy. He gave a quick round of applause.

"Quit that and get the corners," Sarra said, busy pinning down the curling edges with cups and plates.

Any thoughts of a retort withered and died in Giacomo's throat the moment he set his eyes on the unrolled paper. *Blueprints*, Giacomo realized, leaning closer to take in the details. Blueprints of a large, square building. There was the arched entry—there, the wide courtyard—there, windows and doors leading to the interior—

He recognized that building. He had passed it earlier that day. "Forgive me if I'm mistaken, signorina," Giacomo said. "Surely—surely this isn't the Palazzo Medici?"

Rosa smoothed out a crease in the edge of the blueprints. "It's our target," she said.

Giacomo laughed, because this was all a very good joke—an excellent ploy to get him all the way to Florence for the *real* job Rosa was running, whatever that was. But his mirth lasted only a second in the face of Il Divino and Sarra's serious expressions. Across the room, Khalid's solid arms had dropped to his sides. He stared at Rosa as though she'd grown a second head.

And Signora de Rosso, who by all appearances had seen and done pretty much everything there was for a person to see and do on God's green earth, clenched her fingers around her wine cup so tightly Giacomo worried it might shatter. "Rob the *Medici family*?" she asked. Her eyes were curiously bright.

What was truly insane was that Rosa was *nodding*. "I'm sure you've heard by now, but the Pope has returned to Florence," she said. She didn't look like a maniac with a death wish, but Giacomo had been wrong about people before. "While in town, he is staying at the Palazzo Medici with his cousin, Cardinal Giulio de' Medici."

"If you want to rob the Palazzo," Khalid said, "then would it not be more prudent to wait until the Pope has returned to Rome?"

"You'd think that," Sarra said. "But that's not where the real money is."

Rosa tapped the blueprints, right in the center of the courtyard. "Normally, the Palazzo Medici contains no more gold than any other wealthy house in Florence. Not *nothing*, certainly, but not anything to write home about."

"And not enough to risk our necks," Giacomo muttered.

"*However,*" Rosa said, and threw something onto the table.

What winked at them from the center of the parchment was a velvet bag embroidered with a glinting golden cross. Giacomo had not been gone from the orthodox path for so long that he could not recognize a church's purse when he saw one. He'd seen more than his fair share of coin tipped into similar such bags.

Click-click, went the wooden beads in his memory. He shoved the echo aside.

"I see," said Signora de Rosso, leaning over the table. "That's rather clever, girl."

"What is it?" Khalid asked.

"Indulgences."

It took Giacomo a moment to track that voice back to the speaker. Il Divino hadn't moved since Rosa had unrolled the blueprints, but his attention was glued to the parchment, riveted with an artist's focus. Recollection brushed at the back of Giacomo's mind—hadn't Michelangelo Buonarroti gotten his start beneath the sheltering wing of the Medici family?

"Indulgences, yes," Rosa said. "Across the Christian world, the faithful dump money into the hands of the church in order to save their immortal souls. Wrath, lust, envy, pride . . . any of these sins would be enough to damn a person to eternal torment, which the Church is only too happy to remind them every Sunday and most weekday mornings. But lucky for the believers—and for us—the Church is also willing to offer absolution . . . for the price of a few gold florins and a prostration before any of the Pope's emissaries."

"A bargain," said Sarra.

"On both ends," Rosa said. "The believers are saved. And the Church gets rich."

"So the Vatican is sitting on a mountain of gold," Giacomo said. "Is this news?"

Rosa planted both hands on the blueprints, palms framing the front entrance of the Palazzo Medici. "Are you so certain of those riches? As a rule, being the mouthpiece of the Lord is pricey business. And even by those standards, Pope Leo X has run up quite a tab. There are cathedrals to be built and outfitted. Then of course there's the church's nasty warfare habit. And finally, there's the personal expenses. His Holiness has quite a few personal expenses."

"I've heard he has an elephant," Signora de Rosso said.

Giacomo was agog. "What, really?"

"Long story short," Rosa said, "the Church coffers are dry as a bone. There's no mountain of gold to speak of." She traced the cross on the velvet purse. "So he's building one. Over the next weeks, Medici Guards will be collecting those indulgences from churches all over Tuscany in order to transport them back to Rome with the Pope. If my calculations are accurate, then before they leave . . . this will amount to something approaching *ten thousand gold florins.*"

If the silence that had blanketed the shed upon the blueprints' unveiling had been palpable, then this silence was crushing. It had weight. It had *wealth.*

"Lord above . . . ," Signora de Rosso muttered.

"The people who pay these indulgences do so out of desperation," Khalid said. "Is this not taking advantage?"

"The Church has already done that," Rosa said. "And at any rate, isn't it the act of giving money that saves the soul?"

Khalid didn't look entirely convinced. "I suppose . . ."

"Well then. The money has been given. The soul has been saved. What happens to the money after *that* should have no bearing on the giver. It has served its holy purpose."

"Morally and theologically gray at best, signorina," Giacomo chipped in.

Rosa turned that bladed smile on him. "As I have already indicated, if you have an issue, the door is behind you."

Ten thousand gold florins. Giacomo backed up, hands waving. "You misconstrue me. I absolutely *adore* a theological quandary and would do *anything* to be a part of one myself."

Rosa nodded to Sarra, who stepped up beside her. "In six weeks, the Medici will be hosting a banquet to send the Pope back to Rome in a style that befits his position," Sarra said. "Influential families all across Tuscany will descend on this city. The Este, the Sforza, the Borghese . . ."

Cold trickled down Giacomo's spine. "Influential families?"

Rosa nodded. "They will seek an audience with the Pope. To give confession. To gain the Vatican's favor, or Medici favor."

"This is why you have enlisted Michelangelo," Khalid said. The rumble of his words came to Giacomo over the leagues that *influential families* had transported him. "If anyone is to receive such an invitation, it would be him."

"Hmph," Il Divino grumbled, an affirming grunt.

Rosa's gaze slanted sideways toward the artist. "Has the invitation arrived?"

He glowered. "Days ago."

"Have you answered it?"

"I was getting around to it."

"Don't," she said. "Let it sit." She turned her attention back to the room at large. "Each private audience with the Medici will come with a hefty price tag. One that could as much as *double* that ten thousand flowing in from the countryside. And all that money will be tucked away in the vault beneath the Palazzo Medici until the Pope's departure the day after the banquet. So the only question is: How do we access it?"

It was a meaty dilemma. The Palazzo Medici was built like a fortress, and it looked like one as well, at least from the outside. The blueprints did nothing to belie that impression. Even to Giacomo's untrained eye, the thick walls, winding corridors, the massive open courtyard—they screamed of a job that would take a miracle to pull off.

"We start with the facts," Sarra said. "The Pope is paranoid. So is the rest of the Medici family. And they've made themselves enough enemies that their paranoia is not unfounded. However many guards you think he'll have at his disposal? Double it."

"The walls may look rough and rustic," Rosa said, sketching her fingers along the perimeter of the Palazzo, "but they are crafted from the finest limestone money and power can buy. Attempting to breach them would be impossible. The only ways in are through the front and back gates, which are manned at all hours. And if you do manage to slip through, you'll find yourself in the courtyard"—and here she finally snatched up the purple velvet church purse—"at the very center of the Palazzo."

"Surrounded by windows," said Sarra. "And servants. And guards. And crossbows."

The courtyard, rendered with graceful arches, pillars, and walk-ways, suddenly took on a much more ominous cast. "If you manage to run that gauntlet," Rosa continued, her voice echoing in Giacomo's panicking ears, "then there's still the vault itself to deal with." She traced a path from the courtyard into one of the rooms that bordered the walkway.

That end of the blueprints was closer to Khalid. He squinted at the tiny script that bled into the parchment. "It says 'chapel,'" he said. "Not 'vault.'"

"The Magi Chapel," Rosa said. "One of the jewels of the Palazzo. Frescoes, statues, tapestries . . . it's their pride and joy. And *also*"— she tapped a door set into the edge of the chapel—"at the end of this unremarkable back passage? Is the Medici's personal vault. Now I know what you're all thinking: This sounds far too simple." Giacomo and Khalid let out twin sounds of disbelief, and Giacomo caught a mischievous smile at the corner of Rosa's mouth. "Well, you'd be right," she said, her eyes dancing. *Was she* enjoying *this?* "This corridor looks innocent, but the flagstones hold all kinds of nasty surprises. Da Vinci rigged it to hell and back, so unless you—"

"*Who* rigged it?" Il Divino's gaze was pure acid, boring straight through Rosa.

Her face was all innocence. "They hired Leonardo da Vinci to design a series of mechanical traps, hidden beneath the floor. Are you feeling well, Master Michelangelo?"

Master Michelangelo, in fact, looked on the verge of having an apoplexy. "They went. To that *hack*. They hired that woolen-brained *fool*—to—"

"I appear to have upset you, Master Michelangelo."

"I'm fine," Il Divino bit out, but his white-knuckled grip on the edge of the table had Giacomo worried he'd tear a chunk off.

"Well. If you're certain," Rosa Cellini, master grifter and manipulator, said. "I'll just—where was I?"

"The passage," Sarra supplied helpfully, picking up the cue.

"Right," Rosa said. "The traps. They're tricky. Unless you know exactly where to step, you'll find yourself with a spike through the foot or worse. I couldn't find diagrams, but there are reports of apprentices and servants losing fingers, eyes, or hands. If you trigger the wrong flagstone, you'll find yourself bleeding out in front of the vault door, and none the richer for it."

"The vault door," Sarra said, "which is fitted with a Henlein lock. Latest from Germany, made personally as a favor to Lucrezia de' Medici. Very advanced, very complicated."

"So you can't pick it," Giacomo said.

"Every lock can be sprung one way or another," Sarra said. "You could pick this one in . . . two days?"

"We won't have two days," said Rosa.

"No, no, of course," said Giacomo, feeling a little bit like the top of his head was on fire. "Why would we want *time* to get past an army of guards into a heavily protected private chapel, down a corridor that could murder us, and through a door that can't be opened?"

"Once you get into the vault, it's easy," said Rosa, as though Giacomo hadn't spoken. "There are no locks or traps guarding the gold. Just a slab of stone about the same size as this." She slapped the *massive, solid* table they were all gathered around. "So once that's gone, you hand out a few hundred pounds of coin, transport it out of the city, and you're home free." She straightened up. "Any thoughts?"

The look on Khalid's face was inscrutable. "It is impossible."

"This whole thing stinks like a Nepi-and-Cellini job," Signora de Rosso said. Giacomo didn't miss the way Sarra bloomed with the comment, a pleased flush rising in her pale cheeks. Rosa's reaction, on the other hand, was entirely understated. The only sign she'd heard Signora de Rosso at all was the minute flicker of her eyes as her gaze blinked to Sarra and then back again.

"There's nothing 'impossible' in this world," Rosa said. "There are only things that very clever people have not done yet." Giacomo snorted. "Theological quandaries aside . . . are you in or are you out?"

Khalid nodded, with a lack of hesitation that Giacomo envied. "In," he said.

"Agata?"

The apothecary picked up her wine cup. "To take a swipe at the Medici family? You only have to ask."

Rosa turned her barbed cheerfulness to Giacomo. "Signore?"

The blueprints looked impassible. The target was unbreachable. Khalid was glaring daggers at him from across the table.

But *ten thousand florins*. And Giacomo san Giacomo was a madman, wasn't he?

He grinned. "The more harebrained, the better, my lady," he said. "Just let me get a drink, and you can tell me how we begin."

- PART II -

9

ROSA

"The Medici Pope would have us believe that the Lord's forgiveness can be purchased, as a length of broadcloth or a loaf of bread."

Rosa speared a piece of catfish onto her plate. "Where'd she find this one?" she muttered across the low table to Giacomo.

"*He would have us turn out our purses in the name of eternal salvation,*" Sarra went on, wrestling with the oversized parchment as she read. "*But here he shows himself for what he truly is: not a man of God, but the latest in a long line of bankers.*"

Giacomo hadn't so much as blinked at Rosa's question, transfixed as he was by Sarra's recitation. His knife was poised halfway to his mouth, a piece of fish dangling precariously off of it. "*Giacomo,*" Rosa hissed, kicking the player beneath the table.

He jolted, his catfish splattering to his plate. "Pasted to the wall outside the Palazzo gates, if you would believe it," he said.

Rosa's eyebrows shot upward. "The Palazzo *Medici* gates?"

"Half the Santa Croce quarter is papered over with bills," Khalid observed from the bench next to Giacomo.

"Whoever's behind this is the maddest person in Florence," Sarra said. "Madder even than you, Giacomo."

Seditious bills aside, it had been two deceptively quiet days since Rosa had first gathered her team in the millhouse on the banks of the Arno. Khalid and Giacomo had settled into their new living space with minimal bickering, and Rosa had attempted to hide the wave of relief she felt as she retrieved her belongings from the Nepi's print shop to do the same.

"I just thought you'd want to stay with us," Sarra had said, a frown creasing her forehead.

"And it's kind of you to offer," Rosa had replied, shouldering her pack. "But I should be with everyone else. This way, if something goes wrong, I'll be nearby to deal with it. And it would be hard to move nimbly with Pietro around."

The mention of her brother only etched Sarra's frown deeper, but she'd stopped protesting. And so Rosa had taken herself off to the mill and staked out a pallet near the hearth. She'd made her own home before she was co-opted into someone else's, and it wasn't as though she was cutting Sarra off—the girl had turned up at the mill-house every evening to partake in what Giacomo had gleefully begun to call "family dinner."

"No matter who this writer is," Rosa said, plucking the bill from Sarra's fingers, "we owe them our thanks. The more eyes looking for them"—she tossed the parchment into the hearth—"the fewer looking for us. And anything that helps us avoid notice, I can only welcome."

Which was when the millhouse door flung open and Agata de Rosso stormed inside, smelling of acrid fireworks and sooty to the eyebrows. "Well, dearheart," she said, by way of a greeting. "I'm afraid I've blown up."

The detonation had been minor, Agata insisted, but it had also been the third such incident inside of a month. And between the episode in the Piazza della Signoria, the sabotage of a certain chandelier, and the increasingly proliferous bills papering the walls across Florence, the City Guard had decided to *take an interest*.

It's over. The words skittered through Rosa's mind once Agata had finished telling her tale, hope and breath leaving her in the same rush. *It's all gone wrong, and we haven't even started yet. I'm finished.*

No. Rosa shook her shoulders loose and stood as straight as she could, watching Agata drain the contents of a waterskin. First thoughts were rarely best thoughts, and she would not let herself be fooled into listening to them. She'd moved into this millhouse in order to be able to deal with situations like this, and so that is what she would do.

She could not lose access to her apothecary, and her apothecary could not lose access to her tools. Which meant that both would need to be relocated without delay.

"Dinner's over, my friends," she announced to the room. "We've got work to do."

She had hoped the task might be completed quickly, but this soon proved to be a fool's dream. It was not until the small hours of the morning that, with Agata's goading and Sarra, Rosa, and Khalid's efforts, all contents of the apothecary's still-smoking shop were salvaged and relocated, piled onto a pair of mule-drawn vegetable carts. The result was a couple of precarious and combustible mountains, which loomed tall and ominous in the moonlight.

"Are you finished?" The anxious whisper grated across Rosa's nerves. She locked away her irritation as she turned to smile at the middle-aged man in City Guard red peering at them out the apothecary's rear door.

"Nearly, signore," she chirped, unfurling a rough blanket over the pile of sachets and crates in the second wagon.

"The others will be here any moment," he said. "I don't know how much more time I can buy."

"Stop fretting, Pip," Agata ordered, with the same general's authority she had commanded them with all night. "You didn't worry near so much when you had that sore in your—"

"Thank you, yes, signora, I'll be—" The man's crimson face was a blur as he fled back into the shop. Agata cackled and followed, possibly to torment the poor man some more and possibly to do one final sweep for any overlooked potions or poisons.

"What in the world is she going to do with all of this?" Sarra whispered. She had climbed into the wagon bed with Rosa and was carefully tucking the blanket in.

"Do you want to know the answer?" Giacomo asked. He was already lounging on the driver's bench in the first wagon, having somehow sidestepped lifting so much as a single packet of herbs all evening.

"You better go before she hears you talking like that," Rosa said. "Khalid?"

Khalid nodded, jumping up beside Giacomo, and a moment later, he and the player and half of Agata's belongings were rolling down the street and toward the city gates.

Sarra, however, did not seem to notice their departure. She was frowning, lost in thought, focused on the wagon bed beneath her feet. Rosa watched as Sarra jumped, drawing an irritated flick of the ears from the long-suffering mules, and Rosa bit back a yelp as something jingled in one of the mounded boxes.

"Ten thousand . . . ," Sarra muttered.

"Sarra?"

Agata emerged from the rear of the shop, moving fast. "Time to go," she hissed. "We've got a patrol headed this way, and Pip doesn't have the brains to distract them any longer." She squinted at Sarra, who had one foot on the edge of a box. "Are you a tumbler, girl? Stop mountaineering all over my things and *drive*."

With a flick of the reins, they were trundling down the street, Agata deposited on the front bench next to Sarra. Rosa, by dint of being neither the oldest nor the tallest, was forced to tuck herself into the aromatic wagon bed and breathe through her mouth.

She caught the edge of City Guard red as Sarra directed them onto the next street. But the patrol was marching for the painted apothecary sign and did not notice the wagon and its bulging cargo as they slipped into the current of Florence traffic. Rosa sagged against the side of the wagon as the men slipped from view, eyelids sinking with relief.

"Do you remember the Doges Palace job?"

Rosa didn't open her eyes. "What?"

"The Doges Palace job Lena and Papa ran," Sarra said. "They lost half their haul because the rowboat sank under the weight."

"What are you talking about?" The invocation of her mother had sent something zinging down her spine, igniting sparks of temper.

"You said our take could exceed ten thousand florins."

"It might even double that, with all the nobles swarming this city."

Agata gave a low whistle, but Sarra didn't seem to share her appreciation. "That's my worry. Five thousand florins, we'd be able to transport in any wagon. We'd be able to use *this* wagon. But double that? Quadruple it? We'll be running into broken axles or splintered wagon beds."

"Then you'll just have to build one yourself," Rosa said.

Sarra laughed, but only for a moment. "You're serious. Rosa, it's not that simple. The materials that build would require . . . I'm talking Rimini maple, or even walnut; you'd need the Pope's own carriage to manage it!"

"Then assuming the Pope's carriage is not an option, you will have to come up with an alternative." She could only make out Sarra's profile from her place in the wagon bed, but it was a stubborn one, her chin set in frustration. "Sarra," Rosa tried again, gentler this time—

And tumbled forward, ribs colliding with the wagon edge as Sarra yanked the reins so abruptly that the mules practically skidded to a stop.

"What is *wrong* with—" Rosa yelped from somewhere near the wagon floor. But her jaw snapped shut when she saw Sarra's hand waving frantically behind her back. Cautiously, Rosa pushed up to a seat, peering between Sarra and Agata to the street beyond . . .

. . . and to the patrol of Medici Guard uniforms barring their path.

Rosa allowed herself one small moment of dizzying confusion. There was no reason why the Medici Guard should be making the rounds so close to the city gates. Their jurisdiction extended to the Palazzo and to the Medici family's immediate presence. Had the City Guard enlisted them in their raid on Agata's apothecary? Because if that was the case . . . then their little wagon was in more trouble than Rosa had bargained for.

"Good, uh, evening, signori," Sarra stammered. Her fingers were white-knuckled around the reins, and Rosa cursed internally. Sarra was no player—she had no skill for dissembling, especially not when faced with so many swords.

Placing a calming hand on the other girl's back, Rosa stood, her brightest smile fixed in place. "Can we be of service in any way?" she asked.

One of the guards stepped forward. "What is your business out so late?" he demanded.

He could be as curt as he wished. Rosa would not be shaken by someone so arbitrary. "As you can see," she said, "we are moving our elderly grandmother into her new living quarters."

"Hm?" Agata squawked from the driver's bench. "What was that? Who's speaking?"

"Poor, dear Granny," Rosa said, patting Agata on the head.

The guard did not appear convinced. "What's under the blanket?"

"Only my grandmother's belongings."

"Who are you?" Agata quavered up at Rosa.

"Show me."

Sarra jolted in her seat, a protest rising in her throat. Rosa's hand flew to the other girl's shoulder, heading the objection off before it could meet the air.

Because something had caught Rosa's eye: a scrap of paper clinging to the guard's sleeve. There was something written on it—printed lettering, part of a longer word that had been torn to bits in (Rosa studied the guard's expression) a fit of pique.

"Of course!" Rosa said, cheerful as ever. And in one fluid move, she whipped the blanket aside, unveiling Agata's apothecary for all to see.

"Rosa!" Sarra hissed, but Rosa's focus was trained on the Medici Guards, who circled the wagon, peering close at its contents.

Because there was no recognition on any of their faces. No spark of victory. None of them had been sent after the combusting apothecary. No, these men were on a very different mission tonight.

"Well?" the lead guard demanded.

One of the others shook his head. "Nothing."

"Perhaps if we knew what you were seeking," Rosa said, "we might be able to point you in the right direction?"

But the guards ignored her as they jostled in closer. One reached out an entitled hand, shifting one of the trunks heedlessly.

"*Don't touch that.*"

Agata was iron-eyed, her doddering act abandoned. And this warning was nothing like the playful cautions she'd peppered Rosa and her band with as they'd cleared her shop. This was bitter and angry—sharp enough to have the young man yanking his fingers back as though he'd been bitten.

"Ag—Granny?" Sarra whispered, leaning in close to the older woman. But Agata just sat straight as a board, glaring down the men in Medici blue as though she'd like to do to each of them what she'd done to her apothecary.

Rosa cleared her throat. "Well. It's late and, as you can see, my grandmother does not do well when she's tired."

The lead guard was a little off-balance in the face of Agata's glower. "Move along," he mumbled, waving his men back. Sarra snapped the mules' reins and they were off, trundling down the street as though nothing had happened.

"So near the gates," Sarra muttered over the clattering of their wheels. "Why are the Medici patrolling so near the gates?"

Rosa settled carefully back into the wagon bed. "The bills. They're looking for the culprits." Agata's shoulders had not relaxed, even with the streets they put between themselves and the guards. "Agata?"

Agata did not look back at her. "I'm alright, dearie."

"They're long gone now."

The apothecary's voice was hard as diamonds. "The Medici are never *gone*."

"They're pushing the boundaries of their authority," Sarra said. "We'll never know where to expect them."

Rosa closed her eyes, letting the chilly river wind cool the adrenaline in her veins. "Yes we will."

"They could turn up anywhere."

"Which is why," Rosa said, "we're going to have a man on the inside."

10

KHALID

The alcove where Khalid had taken refuge was starting to flood. He could feel the water seeping through his shoes. If he had any sense, he would stop rolling these stupid dice and find more substantial shelter from the torrential downpour.

"Nice weather we're having."

There was barely room for one in here, but the rotund baker made a space for himself anyway, shoving his way onto the cramped, empty stool that sat across from Khalid. Khalid barely batted an eyelash as the man made himself comfortable. He rolled the dice. *Eight.*

"No hello?" the baker asked. He scooped the dice up and rolled them before Khalid could react. "So rude. Ooh, an eight!" The lire Khalid had only just placed onto the board was gone in a flash.

Khalid gritted his teeth. Weather like this always set him on edge. The pounding of the rain and the rising humidity sent him back— back to his earliest days on Genoan soil, back to the moment he'd realized that he was a trusting fool.

The first twenty-four hours Khalid spent in Genoa had gone like this:

He had awoken before the sun in a small garret room above one of Signore Traverio's many pleasure houses. It had been a restless night. His body had still been accustomed to the days it had spent aboard the ship, and the steadiness of land disagreed with him. This, in addition to the raucous business below and the drumming rain on the roof, had meant that the sleep Khalid managed to snatch had been spotty and plagued by strange dreams. He had done his prayers through an upset stomach and a throbbing head, and his day had not improved from there.

Khalid had been summoned to Signore Traverio's offices, a set of sunlit rooms just off the harbor. Signore Traverio had laughed at his green face when he arrived. "You'll soon get your bearings, my boy." Khalid had not possessed the courage to voice his doubt. He had nodded his thanks as his generous new employer pressed bread and cheese into his hands and conjured up a man with a scarred eyebrow to act as Khalid's guide. And with that, Khalid had been turned loose on Genoa for the first time.

It was a close city. The walls and buildings and streets were narrow and dark, shoving in around him. The stench of rotting fish followed wherever he went, not dampened at all by the hazy, steady rain. He had thought his grasp on the language was solid enough, but the local dialect made his ears ring. The experience had been dizzying and dour, nothing near the wide, sparkling adventures Signore Traverio had described back in Tunis. But it was only the first day, Khalid had reassured himself. Surely things would improve.

They had shown no sign of it by the time he was tossed his first assignment. The sticky crush of day had been sliding into evening when Khalid's guide had told him in as few words as possible that Khalid was to be a bouncer at one of Signore Traverio's gambling halls. What he had not told Khalid was that the gambling hall was not a "hall" in the traditional sense. Signore Traverio had purchased several ancient ships from various drink-addled old captains—junkers not up to another sea voyage, but perfectly capable of floating just far enough offshore that they were too much of a nuisance for the local guards to reach. There, the citizens of Genoa who craved an evening of losing their money to Signore Traverio's dealers were free to do so and be welcome to it.

His responsibilities were simple, his guide had told him. Stand. Glare. And if anyone got too rowdy, throw them into the ocean.

He hadn't been exaggerating. Khalid had spent the night standing and glaring, just as the man had promised that he would. He hadn't needed to throw anyone into the ocean, but he had broken up two fights. For the most part, though—

For the most part, Khalid just listened to the waves.

It was something he hadn't realized he'd been missing until he'd heard them again. For days, the waves had been a constant lull, filling his ears and calming his racing heart whenever panic rose up to suffocate him. They had been familiar, an echo of Tunis. Steady. Soothing. They smoothed the jagged edges of his mind with cool green water. They promised peace, a refuge from the chaos of Genoa.

Dawn was breaking over the horizon by the time Khalid was released from duty. He had not slept for twenty-four hours, but he felt energized, revitalized by his time on the water. If all his work for Signore Traverio was like this, then perhaps he had not made a mistake in leaving Tunis after all. And so Khalid easily accepted the two sacks of coins—the night's take—from the hall's overseer and rowed back to shore to deliver the money to Signore Traverio's offices.

It had been quiet as Khalid began the winding path off the docks, so he had not heard the approaching messenger rounding the corner until it was too late. They had collided, the edge of the oversized wooden box the boy was carrying plowing into Khalid's side with bruising force. Then the messenger was sprawling backward, his speed bouncing him off the stone wall of Khalid al-Sarraj. He tumbled to the ground with a loud thump, his crate spilling out of his hands.

"*Christ*," the messenger said, the swear forced out of him along with most of his breath.

Khalid took a moment to line the words up in his head before speaking. "Are you hurt?"

The messenger was a boy of about Khalid's age, barely into his late teens. He was clutching at his ribs with one hand. His breath was coming in shallow wheezes, but he cracked his right eye open to look up at Khalid. It was warm and brown. Khalid thought it was interesting, as far as eyes went.

"I'm fine, I'm fine," the messenger said. "You just knocked the air out of me, is all. What are you made of, granite?" The interesting brown eye slid from Khalid's boots up to the top of his head and then settled on his face. "Maybe you are, at that."

Khalid was fairly certain that the messenger was not being serious. He was *definitely* certain that he was not comfortable under the traveling gaze. A tightness was spreading over his skin. He didn't like it. "You should be more careful," he said, extending a hand.

The messenger reached out to take it, revealing a flash of bright liquid red. Sometime between hitting Khalid and hitting the ground, he had managed to scour a long strip off the edge of one of his palms. "Oh!" he'd said, sounding genuinely surprised. "That's obnoxious. How long do you think it'll take to heal? I need my hands, you see." This all had come on a single breath, swirling through Khalid's ears. Then the messenger was taking Khalid's hand and hauling himself to his feet. The tightness of Khalid's skin got worse. It was all he could do to nod along with the other boy's words, because everyone needed their hands, and that was the only thing he had said that Khalid had really managed to process. He also, of course, kept one eye on the messenger's fingers as he brushed himself off. Khalid might have only been in Genoa for one day, but he had lived in a busy city his entire life. He had learned from an early age not to allow a stranger's fingers anywhere near his pockets.

It was because he was so closely monitoring the messenger's

movements that he noticed them falter. "Oh no," the messenger had muttered. "No, no, no . . ." Aches and pains forgotten, he had scrambled toward the wooden crate. It lay cracked open on the street, straw spilling out. "Please no," he had whispered, reaching for the lid with trembling hands. "Please . . ."

Khalid had watched with uncertain dread as the messenger lifted the lid back. Inside, nestled in the straw, was what had up until recently been an oversized ceramic pot. Now, it was seven pieces of an oversized ceramic pot. As the messenger shifted the crate, it became eight.

"I'm dead," the messenger said. "I'm dead. He'll kill me."

He sounded so empty that Khalid could not stop himself from stepping forward. "Is it—what is it?" he asked.

"It's—" The messenger had shot him a watery smile. He was putting on a brave front. Khalid could relate. "It's nothing. I was—my master sent me to pick up this parcel from the *Cecilia* when it docked earlier this evening. He paid a great deal to have it shipped all the way from Constantinople, and he has been waiting on it for many long months, but—" His breath hiccuped in his chest as he looked down at the broken pot again. "Well."

"You will be in trouble?"

"When am I not?" the messenger muttered. "I'll—he has a temper, but. I'll. Be okay. Teach me to watch where I'm going, right?"

It was the quiet devastation that spurred Khalid's decision. Reaching into one of the purses inside his jacket, he withdrew a handful of lire. Surely Signore Traverio wouldn't miss such a small sum? "Here," he said. "Take it."

"What? I can't—"

"It may not be enough for the pot," Khalid said. "But it is something. Perhaps you can leave the city."

The offer had been mundane. But as he made it, Khalid realized that he was putting forth something that he could not take for himself. This boy was free to leave Genoa, should he be that desperate. But Khalid . . .

It had been the first time he'd fully contemplated his new reality. A swell of something binding and awful rose in Khalid's chest. He had beaten it back, but only just. And all the while, the messenger was studying him, his gaze flickering over Khalid's face. Slowly, he had reached out his scraped and battered hand and plucked the coins from Khalid's palm. "Thank you," he'd said. "You are—very kind."

"Good luck to you, signore," Khalid said. And with a firm nod, he had turned and marched away. If he focused on the kindness he had just done, then perhaps he would not have to linger on his life's newly visible prison bars.

It was not until he had finally reached Signore Traverio's office that he learned that there was, in fact, no ship called the *Cecilia*, that there had been a new grifter in town spotted working the docks, and that the money he had co-opted from the gambling galley's winnings was most *definitely* missed.

And that had been how Khalid al-Sarraj had first met Giacomo san Giacomo.

He had run through that encounter countless times in the years that followed. He had dissected it from every angle. He had picked it apart, looking for the seams. It had been a lesson for him. He had learned that nobody he met while under Signore Traverio's employ could ever be trusted. Especially not a chameleon of a player like Giacomo.

Which is why he didn't react when the mustached baker tossed the dice back in Khalid's direction with a bright wink and a wide grin. His eyes were still an interesting brown, three years later, but Khalid was mostly immune to that now.

"You look miserable, signore," Giacomo said. "*Really*, anybody else would think that you didn't want to be here."

Khalid rolled the dice and gave up another lire to the board. "Is it done?"

"You've got a few minutes." Giacomo was streaked with flour from neck to knees. It was caked under his fingernails. "Just enough time to finish this game. Would it absolutely kill you to *pretend* as though you're having a good time? It's a game, it's meant to be fun!"

"Roll the dice."

"One day I'll see you with a smile on your face, Signore al-Sarraj," Giacomo said. He rolled the dice absentmindedly and cleared off the four square. "You mark my words. It's not that hard, I do it all the time! Look—" He pointed at his own face. A brilliant grin beamed from beneath the horrible mustache. "See? No pain at all, you should try it sometime."

Khalid frowned at him. "I do not enjoy it."

"Smiling? I could have told you that."

"No," said Khalid. He picked up the dice and turned them over in his rain-chilled fingers. "Pretending. I do not enjoy it."

"That's just because you're bad at it," Giacomo said, flapping a hand dismissively. "You'd love it if you learned. I could teach you. I have a system, you see."

Khalid managed to retrieve a coin from the nine square. "I do not need lessons."

"Really? From what I remember, your skill set is predominantly showing up where Signore Traverio tells you and flexing your muscles until people piss themselves."

"You would prefer that I pick those peoples' pockets?"

"I never picked your pocket, Signore al-Sarraj." Giacomo cocked his head at Khalid. "Haven't you ever wondered why?"

Khalid had. He would die before admitting this. "No."

"Bad liar." Giacomo frowned in false disapproval. "This is where those lessons would come in handy. How hard are you trying not to punch me?"

"Mm," Khalid said.

"I thought so. Too bad you passed up your chance." Giacomo glanced down at the barrel. "Oh, look! I rolled a twelve!"

Khalid frowned. "You cheated."

"Can't cheat at Playing the Boat," Giacomo said, which was a blatant lie. "Everyone knows that." Khalid watched Giacomo shovel every coin on the board into his purse. He couldn't help but feel like there was something he was missing—like he was back in that Genoa street, watching a young man with scraped hands peel open a crate of broken pottery.

Three men pounded past his narrow shelter, boots splashing muddy water onto Khalid's shins. They came to a stop outside of a narrow, ivy-covered house. One of the men—a muscled black-smith, going off his scorched clothes—grabbed at the doorknob and shook it.

"Lisa!" he roared. "Lisa, you bitch! I know you're in there!"

"Is that him?" Khalid murmured to Giacomo, who was watching this scene with interest.

"That's him," Giacomo said.

One of the second-story windows burst open and a curvaceous woman leaned out. Her hair was disheveled, and her clothes were . . . minimal. "You come home in the middle of the day, shouting in the street like a mad—"

"I know he's in there!" yelled the blacksmith. "I know he's with you!"

"Go to hell!" the woman screamed. She was almost loud enough to drown out the sound of a nearby door banging shut.

"Back door," said one of the blacksmith's friends. As the woman continued to shriek insults, the three men took off for the side of the building.

"Looks like you're up," Giacomo said. Khalid was already on his feet. His quarry had disappeared from view, but the distant crashing and shouting meant that they had not gone far. "Remember to have fun!" Giacomo called after him as he jogged away.

It was a pitiful sight that greeted him as he cleared the corner of the house. The blacksmith and his friends were standing in a huddle around a stocky man, who was sprawled on the wet, dirty cobblestones with his arms over his head. He was in about as much of a state of undress as the woman upstairs, who was continuing to scream epithets at the men from a rear window. The rain did nothing to muffle the cacophony. Everyone in the alley was too absorbed with either shouting, kicking, or being kicked to notice Khalid.

That was fine. That would change.

How's this for a skill set? Khalid thought, and tapped the blacksmith on the shoulder.

The man paused and turned, his boot still planted in the prone man's stomach. "What do you want?" he snarled.

Khalid reciprocated with his usual blank stare. "Leave him alone."

"What are you, some kind of saint?" The blacksmith poked the man on the ground again. "You know this man, Bianci?"

Bianci stared up through an eye that was already starting to swell. "I—uh—"

The blacksmith scoffed. "What about you, Lisa?" he shouted up at the woman. "Are you messing around with him too?"

Khalid just watched him. Behind the blacksmith, one of the other attackers fidgeted in the face of Khalid's stoicism. "Let's leave it," he muttered. "He's had enough."

But the blacksmith was focused on Khalid now, eyes narrowing. "No," he said. "Someone is going to get their neck broken today. If it's not this piece of crap"—he dug his boot heel into Bianci's stomach, lower than before, drawing a panicked squeak from Bianci—"then it's gonna be his guardian angel."

The blow, when it came, was not with a fist or a knee. The blacksmith had produced a length of iron from somewhere on his person. This, he directed toward Khalid's ribs with a fierce jab, aiming to drive the air from Khalid's lungs.

It was a clever move, and cleverer still to surprise him with a weapon. But the blacksmith was more of a brawler than a fighter. He was used to situations where he had friends to back him up. Without the support of his companions, he would be next to useless. Khalid skipped lightly out of the way of the iron bar, feeling it brush the cloth of his sleeve.

The blacksmith stumbled—caught off-guard by Khalid's dexterity or by the fact that he was not running away, it didn't matter. As he reared back for another blow, this one aimed to shatter Khalid's knee, Khalid dipped lightly around him to drive his elbow into one of his friend's faces.

The friend staggered back, blood and rainwater dripping between his fingers. "Jesus Christ!" he shouted, the blasphemy bouncing off the narrow walls. Khalid didn't give him a moment to recover—in the next second, his knee was coming up and in, driving between the man's legs, sending him staggering. The next move was a kick with the same foot, the side of his boot connecting with the man's temple. He slumped to the slimy ground face-first.

One down. Two to go.

Behind him, Khalid heard the blacksmith utter a curse. He barely managed to step aside as the bar came whistling down. It glanced off his shoulder, shocking his left arm with numbing pain but thankfully missing his head. Swinging around, Khalid found the blacksmith and his one remaining friend standing shoulder to shoulder, effectively blocking any path toward escape. In the sheeting rain, there was no sign of the unfortunate Bianci.

"You're going to regret that," the blacksmith gritted. His knuckles were white where they clutched the iron.

Khalid did not give them the chance to charge. He was already in motion, dodging toward the two men. There was a disintegrating wooden crate here, just below Lisa's window. Khalid planted a foot on the slippery surface and vaulted, snatching at the window ledge—his fingers slipping against the moldy stone, scrabbling for purchase—

Latching on—

And he was hanging, swinging, suspended, feet pedaling in the air. Above him, Lisa let out incomprehensible shrieks. Below, her husband let out unintelligible bellows. Khalid wondered if, perhaps, they deserved one another.

He let himself drop. Knees tucked up, bootheels aimed straight for the blacksmith's head, momentum and mass combined to turn Khalid al-Sarraj into a projectile of deadly force. His legs shot forward as he closed in, and Khalid felt the connection of his feet and a soft human body with satisfaction.

He hit the ground and ducked into a roll, coming up in a crouch. The blacksmith was not so lucky. He had been knocked sideways into the wooden crate, which had broken into jagged pieces around him. Now he lay groaning among the wreckage. It did not appear as though he would be rising anytime soon.

Only his friend still stood. Khalid cocked his head at him, bracing against the cobbles in case the man decided to take his chances . . .

Which was when a wooden stave hammered across the back of the man's head. He crumpled, revealing Bianci's bruised face directly behind him.

Bianci stared at Khalid. Khalid stared at Bianci.

"You . . . ," Bianci said. He seemed to have lost his capacity for speech. His stave—part of the destroyed crate—dangled from his fingers. "You . . ."

Khalid dipped his chin. "Are you hurt, signore?"

Bianci stared at him another moment. Then he tipped his head back, unleashing a full-throated laugh. "Am I *hurt*?" he echoed, wiping a tear from his eye. "My God, man! You're incredible. Who *are* you?"

"I heard the commotion," Khalid said. It was not an answer and it was not a lie. Still, he felt as though his face was on fire. How did Giacomo *do* this? "When I saw the numbers that you were facing and the . . . condition you were in, I had no choice but to step in."

If Bianci had been less grateful or less concussed, then perhaps he might have noted Khalid's blatant discomfort. Thankfully, this was not the case. Bianci beamed at him in woozy wonder. "You're an angel, is what you are."

There was a scuffling from the end of the alley. A few moments later, a tall, rangy man appeared, silhouette slim in the rainy fog. "Sergeant?" he called.

"Vieri, you bastard," Bianci said, congenial smile slipping. "You were supposed to be keeping watch!"

"I was!" Vieri protested, slopping through puddles as he drew nearer. "I went to pick up the wine and fruit like you asked."

Bianci frowned. "I didn't ask you to get anything."

"Yes you did," Vieri said. "Signora Lisa's cook told me." At Bianci's blank expression, Vieri pushed on. "The big man? With the mustache?"

"If you want to bugger off for a drink, do it when I'm not getting beat to death," Bianci snapped. "And don't try to lie to me after! If it hadn't been for this gentleman, who knows what would have happened?"

Vieri's gaze slid over Khalid, seemingly for the first time. Khalid did not miss the way he paused on Khalid's travel-worn clothes and his bloody knuckles. "This . . . gentleman?" he said, ladling a mountain of scorn onto that last word.

Khalid bowed. "Yazid bin-Halil," he said. "Of Ferrara."

"All the way from Ferrara, eh?" Bianci asked, turning his back on Vieri. "What brings you to Florence?"

"Looking for work, signore," Khalid said. "I came to Florence because I heard it was plentiful here." Behind Bianci, Vieri snorted. "So far I have been . . . disappointed."

"Work, eh?" Bianci was studying him with a sly light in his eyes. "Well, you certainly can handle yourself in a fight—"

"My love!"

Lisa seemed to have recuperated from the brawl. She leaned out the window, clutching a bundle of cloth. Bianci opened his arms, and she tossed it down to him. He blew her a kiss, which she returned. Then she disappeared back into the house, unaffected by the sight of her husband, still groaning in the alley below.

Bianci stepped into his hose, lacing them up. "Thank God for that," he said. "Would have had a hell of a time stumbling home half-naked. Now—" He tied the laces shut. "It may be as much your lucky day as it is mine, bin-Halil."

"Signore?" Khalid said. He tried to remember how Giacomo had looked in that dark Genoa street the first time they'd crossed paths— the wide innocent eyes, the furrowed brow. He did his best to copy it. He was sure he was making a fool of himself.

"Oh yes," Bianci said. He shook out his jerkin and shrugged it on, buckling it closed across his chest. A family crest was revealed from the folds of the cloth—a triple fleur-de-lis in deep red. The uniform of the Medici family Guard. "I think I know a noble family who would be quite happy to have someone of your talents on their payroll."

SARRA

I t was still dark when Sarra slipped out of bed the next morning, shivering in the early chill. Velvet-soft, she eased open the trunk at the foot of her bed and began to dig.

The first time she'd donned hose and a jerkin to run a job, it had been out of practicality. One night of sprinting across rooftops and fiddling with finicky inventions while wrestling long skirts had been almost enough to kill her grifting dreams stone dead, and so she had stolen a set of castoffs from her brother. But when she had ventured out with her hair tucked up and her shape disguised, the world opened in a way it never had before. She could go anywhere she liked, at any time she liked, without anybody looking at her askance. It was *exhilarating*. And so the jerkin, hose, and doublet had become a uniform, to be worn whenever a job came her way. They didn't fit right—they never would, not even with extensive adjustments—but she felt more like herself in them than she ever had in the kirtle of a respectable printer's sister.

Pietro was a lump of blankets on the pallet near the banked fire when Sarra gently eased the bedroom door open. Creeping gingerly and carrying her change of clothes in both arms, she stepped across the warm floorboards. She had almost made it to the front door when the mountain of quilts gave an almighty shift. Sarra froze on the spot as Pietro shoved himself to a seat, fixing her with bleary eyes. The sounds that came out of his mouth could only generously be called a sentence, but Sarra had sixteen years of experience in translating early-morning Pietro Nepi, and while the layperson might only hear a garble of consonants and vowels, Sarra heard "Why the hell are you awake?"

"Go back to sleep," she whispered. "It's early yet."

He blinked at her, and Sarra realized that he had been up even later than she had the night before—she hadn't even heard him come home. "Where are you going?" he asked, gravelly but in actual words this time.

For a fraction of a second, the echo of solitary emptiness swelled within Sarra—the same emptiness she'd felt when he'd left for university all those years ago. It had been so long since she'd heard her brother ask that question. *Where are you going?* Pietro would ask from behind his stacks of books as their father loaded provisions into a pack, Lena lounging somewhere near the front door.

He would ask, and Matteo would answer, Lena laughing and teasing as she filled in tantalizing details and exciting destinations. Sarra had hovered in Lena's shadow, buoyed by a child's hope that this time they would take her along with them. She never understood why Pietro always frowned at their father's plans, why he would ask Papa to stay behind and stay safe—not when Matteo would return every time hours, days, weeks later, laden with coins and jewels and gold.

He hadn't brought back stories, no matter how Sarra begged for them. She'd had to get those from Lena, the tales of their thrilling escapades and daring escapes. And even though Pietro refused to listen along, choosing instead to sulk in the corner or to cloister himself at university, Sarra had never felt alone. She'd had Rosa to sit with, cross-legged in front of the hearth, as Lena spun her tales, dreaming of the day when they'd be having adventures just like Papa . . . the day they'd be grifters as talented as Lena.

But then—

Promise me—you won't drag your brother into this.

The words had been scraped from Papa's throat by fever, just hours before he'd slipped away. Clinging to his too-warm hand, with Rosa and Lena Cellini long-since disappeared, Sarra had nodded and promised. And then the empty loneliness had started to creep in.

"I told you," she whispered to Pietro. "I picked up a few odd jobs to help us with the bills. I'll be over with the de' Baldis this week."

"The bills?" Pietro's eyes blinked wide at her for a moment before sliding back into half-wakefulness. "Oh. The bills."

She felt a pang at calling out the lack of work, which wasn't at all due to a lack of industry on Pietro's part. But there was nothing that would turn Pietro off this particular line of questioning faster and so . . .

"They needed some help with deliveries," she explained, bundling her jerkin into an unrecognizable wad of cloth. "With the new baby, and all the people coming to town on account of the Pope—"

"Mm," he said, as she shrugged on her cloak.

"Anyway, I'll be in and out, so don't worry about me," she said, closing it with a quick twist of her fingers. "I'll see you when things are a little less chaotic."

"Sarra," he said.

"Pietro," she said, mimicking his serious tone.

His gaze was intense in the gray dawn light, searching her face. She wondered what he saw. Some part of her hoped he'd find the truth, so she could start to melt this mountain of lies . . . but it was not a part she could afford to let overwhelm her.

He was the one who broke first, eyes squinting in a yawn. "Is that all?" she teased. Her heart was hammering in her chest. "Am I dismissed?"

"Hush." He flopped back onto the pallet. "I'm sleeping."

"Of course." She reached for the doorknob. "I'll see you later."

She was out on the landing when she heard the mumble of his reply, so muffled that it was near inaudible. "Please be careful."

She felt the words land somewhere between her shoulder blades, weighted more heavily than words ought to be. They settled across her back like snow—if she stopped in the print shop to change out of her kirtle, she thought she might collapse. So she carried those words, and her jerkin and hose, out of the city and to the millhouse.

It was early yet—the only person on their team who might be awake at this hour was Khalid, and he was working his first night patrol for the Medici family, not expected back 'til midday. Sarra briefly entertained the idea of going inside to see if there was anything to be found in the way of breakfast, but the river was so clear and the sun promised an appearance and if she forced herself into a place with four walls and a roof she might scream. With this in mind, she settled for the second option, which involved wood, rope, a comfortingly heavy hammer, and a sharpened chisel.

By the time Rosa stuck her head out the mill window, Sarra was covered in wood shavings and had tripped over her skirts twice. "Shit," she hissed as a poorly aimed mallet stroke sent her chisel slipping, drawing a thin line of blood from the side of her little finger.

"Rough morning?" Rosa chirped. She had a shawl drawn around her shoulders against the chill, and her breath steamed in the air.

"No," Sarra said, which both was and wasn't true. "I just wanted to get an early start."

"Did it have to be *this* early?" said a grumpy voice from somewhere inside that could only be Giacomo.

"Hush," Rosa told him. "I'm still waiting on your plans for the wine, by the way." Giacomo's grumble was too low for Sarra to make out, answered only by a roll of Rosa's eyes. "I'll be right there," she told Sarra, and closed the shutters. Sarra allowed herself a quiet moment to stick her injured finger in her mouth, thoughts fuzzing to a peaceful lull.

A few minutes passed before there came a thumping at the mill door, and then Rosa was stumbling through it, toeing it open with a bare foot and letting it slam shut behind her. Her arms were full, laden with fine broadcloth, and she had a handkerchief clutched awkwardly in one hand. "Take this," she said. "Before I drop it—"

Sarra did as she was asked. "Is this for me?"

"Breakfast." Unbundling the kerchief, Sarra found a hunk of bread, a piece of cheese, and a bit of honeycomb. "Agata sent the honey. It's for your hand. Not for eating."

"What about that?" Sarra asked through a mouthful of bread and cheese, nodding at the bundle in Rosa's arms. With a sideways smile, Rosa shook it out. What had, upon first glance, appeared to be a shapeless mass of fabric was revealed to be a beautiful gown in bottle-green, edged with yellow ribbon along the neckline and the cuffs. Sarra let out a whistle. "Very fine."

"Only the best for Il Divino's niece," Rosa said with only the barest hint of mockery. "Is this for the wagon?" She somehow managed to study the carpentry chaos and shrug her way into the green dress at the same time, scrabbling for her laces while her sharp eyes flicked over the wooden staves and Sarra's chisels.

"The barrels," Sarra said. "But I've been going over the wagon specs, and Rosa, we really do have a problem. The materials we need, I can't source on our timeline. *But.* There are a few people I can ask to lend us—"

"No," Rosa said. The tone was pleasant, but there was steel beneath.

"You're not listening to me. It's going to be impossible to—"

"Then we will have to figure it out. We're not going outside our circle for something as small as a wagon. I'm not taking that risk." Her fingers flew as she cinched the front of the gown. "Tell me about these barrels."

Sarra was not done with this conversation, but she let Rosa have her change of subject. "They should be ready about eight days after I'm done setting them," she said. "After that, it's all about the internal shell, but that's easy enough. I've got some schematics for sound-proofing that I'll show you. Any word from Khalid?"

"He's in," said Rosa. "I haven't seen him since yesterday, but no news is good news as far as I'm concerned. He'd be able to let us know if anything went south."

The *unlike others* was unspoken. "You're worried about Michel-angelo," Sarra said.

Rosa tucked her laces down the front of her gown. "I've got everything under control."

Sarra let out an exasperated sigh. "He was your idea!" she said. "What if he talks to the wrong person?"

"He won't." Rosa's light smile did not slip as she slid a pin into her hair.

"I know this might be radical to you, Rosa," Sarra said, her chisel moving along the wood in long, even strokes, "considering how we were raised, but some people have to work to keep their jobs secret from those close to them."

"I suppose."

"Is there anyone in your life who *doesn't* know what you do?"

"Are we still talking about Michelangelo?"

Sarra had never had the gift of dissembling that Lena or Rosa or (God forbid) Giacomo had been blessed with. She turned the stave and began working on the other end, keeping her chisel moving so she wouldn't have to meet Rosa's eyes.

"How's Pietro." Rosa's voice was as deadpan as her expression.

"Don't be an ass."

"Did you tell him?"

Sarra snorted. "No. Like I said. I made a promise."

"Very well," Rosa said. "You can't tell him. He doesn't know. What's the problem?"

She didn't understand. The realization hit Sarra like a lightning strike. All of Rosa's cleverness, a lifetime of training under the greatest grifter Sarra had ever known, and she couldn't wrap her head around the situation. Or perhaps she just didn't want to.

Two years. That was how long Sarra had lived alone with the Tinkerer, lying to the last of her family every time she took another job. All so she could do the work she was born to do—and all so Pietro wouldn't ask *where are you going?*, wouldn't stay up late waiting for her, wouldn't worry over her the way he'd worried over Papa.

Two years with that empty loneliness growing in Sarra's belly. And then Rosa had reappeared out of thin air, the sister Sarra thought she'd lost—

But if they were family, then why wouldn't Rosa let Sarra through her coolly smiling mask?

Shhhick. Shhhick. Sarra's chisel didn't falter. The rough pass on this stave was nearly complete. And Sarra realized she was asking Rosa the wrong question.

"Who do you talk to," she said, "when you *don't* talk about your work?"

The moments where she was able to pull one over on Rosa Cellini were so few and far between that Sarra made sure to treasure them. This was one such moment—Rosa blinking at her in the early-morning sun, wide-eyed as a landed carp.

"Come on now, Rosa." The crack in Rosa's armor goaded Sarra into giddy singsong. "You may keep the details of this job close to your chest, but grifting can't be your whole world. What about everything else?"

"I—" Rosa stammered. "Who has time for any of that?"

"Having a life isn't a distraction."

Rosa's gaze flickered to the blood on Sarra's hand and Sarra fought back the urge to hide the injury behind her back. "I have to go," Rosa said, gathering her handkerchief and picking up her shawl. "Let me know how the wagon is progressing when you get the chance." The chastisement was subtle, but it was there, and Sarra tried not to rankle at it. With an exchange of nods, Rosa was striding off down the riverbank in the direction of the city gates. Sarra was alone on the grass in front of the millhouse with stinging pride and a pile of wooden planks.

"Half for the Tinkerer, half for the press," she muttered to herself. "Half for the criminal, half for the sister."

And nothing for me.

With that forlorn thought choking at her, she picked up her chisel and got back to work.

12

GIACOMO

There were two things that Giacomo had known going in about the gatekeeper of the Porta Romano, and one of them was his name. The other was that Captain Santini of the City Guard thought himself a *great* deal more intelligent than he actually was, which was Giacomo's favorite type of person in the entire world and which meant that Giacomo was going to have *fun* with him.

"You can't imagine how miserable it's been, Captain," moaned Giacomo, who was having a wonderful time. "My poor head. It is *throbbing*."

Upon meeting Captain Santini, Giacomo's list of known traits had expanded to include (a) the fact that, though Captain Santini was *ostensibly* a member of the City Guard, he had obviously either cheated or bought his way out of training; and (b) he would bend over backward for a noble family crest, no matter which crest or who was wearing it. Unsurprisingly, he was not popular among the men in his command, whose pride in the City Guard was paramount and who had made their displeasure with their subservient captain known by sending him out of the gatehouse alone to deal with the fainting Medici family barrister and his stoic guard.

"First there was the tension, just *yards* of tension," Giacomo said, dabbing at his forehead. "And then there was the yelling. The cook started throwing things, which was a nightmare, and of course the smell just oozed through—"

"Oozed?" Captain Santini did not look prepared for *oozed*.

"My dear man, you would understand if you were there," Giacomo said. "In all honesty it would have been a delight to get away from it all if it wasn't for . . ." He lowered his voice and jerked a thumb over his shoulder. "*Him.*"

Him was the six-foot-plus wall of Medici blue with crossed arms and shiny buttons and also Khalid al-Sarraj. It was very, *very* difficult for Giacomo not to laugh at the waves of anxiety and envy that smashed across Captain Santini's face as he took in the muscles and the uniform in turn, but Giacomo was a professional, and so he kept wilting against the rough stone wall of the Porta Romana like the delicate flower he was.

"I—can assure you that the City Guard has been more than assiduous in our duties," Captain Santini said, barely managing to avoid a stammer. Khalid really was a champion glower-er; Giacomo would have to ask him for some tips. "We take our posts very seriously here at the Porta Romana."

"And of course I believe you," Giacomo said. "You and I—we're simple men—bean counters, at our hearts. Our greatest joy in life is making certain that the duties entrusted to us are performed smoothly and easily. We are of the same cloth, Captain."

"Hm," said Captain Santini, radiating smugness.

"So when a shipment of fish is delivered to my household a day later than it is expected—at *nighttime*, no less, and left to sit out until the following morning—you understand how that thrown cog undermines the entire clockwork? While the Pope enjoys a bit of trout, he does not like it quite so much when it is perfuming his entire courtyard."

The name-drop was a gong struck in Captain Santini's face. "The Pope?"

Somewhere a few meters back, Giacomo could hear Khalid shifting purposefully. "You can ask Guardsman bin-Halil," he said, flapping a hand at Khalid distractedly. "*I* wasn't privy to His Holiness's reaction, but *he* certainly was. And when we reached out to the deliveryman, he informed us that the shipment was delayed coming through this gate." He leaned forward, and Captain Santini unconsciously mirrored him, two conspirators sorting out a troublesome snarl *together*. "Apparently," Giacomo said, "there was something or the other about a dice game?"

Captain Santini reared back, affronted. "My men do not gamble on the job!"

"Of course not, of course not!" Giacomo said. "I would never *dream* of implying such a thing. No, I think we *both* know that the odds are far more in favor of that shiftless deliveryman getting swept up in some distraction and neglecting his own duties."

"He's trying to pass it off on us," Captain Santini fumed.

"And I would not want your good name besmirched in the eyes of His Holiness," Giacomo said. "Especially with the banquet coming up so soon, which will depend so heavily on the passage of goods through the Porta Romana. If the Medici family knows that they can depend on you and your men, then life will be easier for the both of us, Captain." With a sigh, he knocked his cap aside and ruffled a hand through his hair. "There must be some way to reassure His Holiness that any delay in deliveries is not due to this gate."

Bless the man. Giacomo could almost see his lips moving as he thought. It might have stirred pity, but if Giacomo pitied his marks, then he would not be a good grifter. So instead he frowned and wrinkled his brow and pantomimed *thinking* loud enough for even the thick Captain Santini to hear.

"Why not simply tell him what you want him to do?" Khalid had asked in that plainspoken way of his as they wound toward the Porta Romana an hour earlier.

Giacomo had scoffed. "Be *direct*? I can't believe you, Signore al-Sarraj. A disgusting notion. *How* are we even working the same job?"

"It would save time."

This had startled a laugh out of Giacomo. "Do you have some-place to be that I don't know about? My job is to make people think that they're being clever, when really they are marionettes, dancing to my every whim. I cannot go up to a man and ask him to hand over his purse. That man would knife me in an instant. But I can go up to a man and put on a show and string him along until *he comes up with the idea* to hand over his purse. That way I get the money and I remain un-stabbed, which is a very good outcome for me."

"How?"

The question had caught Giacomo slightly off-guard. "Are you asking for lessons? In pretending?" Khalid hadn't looked at him, which meant that Giacomo had to laugh again to fill the silence. "You will never stop surprising me. *Well*. When I am feeling out how to approach a mark, I consider two components. Vice and voice." This had earned him a quirked eyebrow, and Giacomo's grin had widened. "Catchy, right?"

"Vice and . . . voice?"

"Like this. Let's say you're a mark. Just any old dashingly hand-some man sulking by on the street—yes, exactly like that, don't change a thing, you're a natural. I would spot you, and then the first thing I would try to determine is what you want."

"I do not want anything."

Giacomo had rolled his eyes. "Everybody wants something. It's not always *tangible*, like money or food or shelter or a new pair of boots. Sometimes it's more . . ." He waved his hands, whistling lightly. "Atmospheric. Amorphous. Some people want to feel powerful. Some people want to feel smart. Some people want to feel kind." The memory of an early morning in Genoa, a box of pottery fragments, and a boy's sad eyes had welled up inside him. Giacomo had plowed it into a gutter and kept chattering. "That's vice. And then once you've tackled that, it's all down to the voice. Who does this person think will help them get what they want? You become *that*, and then your mark is putty in your hands. They'll fall over themselves to give you anything."

A stormy cloud had settled over Khalid's face. "I see."

"You don't approve."

Khalid had shrugged, tense and staccato. "I told you before. I don't like pretending."

"You say that, Signore al-Sarraj," Giacomo had said, nudging Khalid's shoulder with his own, "but I think we'll make a player out of you yet."

The exchange was fresh on Giacomo's mind as he watched the gears labor and creak inside Captain Santini's head, which meant that Giacomo had something to prove, which *meant* that when Captain Santini surfaced from whatever sinkhole of thought he'd been drowning in and said "I've got an idea: the record books!" Giacomo had *earned* his swell of smug pride. He resisted the urge to turn to Khalid and gloat because that would give the game away, and also because Khalid would probably only glare and go "Hmph." It had to be enough to relish the *idea* of Khalid's admiration, radiating from somewhere a few meters back, and so Giacomo contented himself with clapping a hand to his forehead and crying, "I can't believe I didn't think of that!"

"There should be a note of the entry time for every arrival in the city," Captain Santini said. His spine was very straight. He looked like he was mentally polishing a Medici fleur-de-lis on his chest. "That driver would have had to check in with one of my men when he arrived."

"We'll have this cleared up in no time!" Giacomo said. Captain Santini downright *beamed*, and Giacomo beamed back. "Lead the way, Captain!"

Captain Santini was only too eager to open the door to the guard-house and usher Khalid and Giacomo inside. The interior was as unassuming as the exterior, and Giacomo had to fight past a moment of claustrophobia as the damp, chilly air pressed in around him. He and Khalid trailed the captain down a short hall, ignoring the scalding glares of City Guardsmen.

"Captain," hissed one of the guards. "You're granting the Medici jurisdiction even in our own guardhouse?"

"I—I don't recall asking for your opinion," Captain Santini blustered. He grimaced apologetically at Giacomo. "The Medici family is of course always welcome here. They are the custodians of this city, after all. Anything you need—anything at all—"

If the man licked Giacomo's boots any more, he was going to make himself sick. "You are a true patriot!"

They paused in front of a rough door. "All our records are kept here," Captain Santini said, pushing inside. "It should be a matter of moments to confirm—"

Giacomo had a split second of worry that the man had inexplicably choked on his own tongue, which resolved once he saw Khalid's hand clamped down around Captain Santini's wrist. "What do you mean by—" the captain managed to squeak out.

"Him first," Khalid rumbled. It was his deepest, most intimidating voice—Giacomo had been subjected to it many times back in Genoa, and he knew how good it was at shaking a man down to his bones.

"Excuse me, Captain," Giacomo said, slipping past him into the office. Somewhere in the corridor behind him, Captain Santini was in the process of recovering himself, but Giacomo didn't waste a glance on him, taking the opportunity to peruse the room while the man spluttered and blustered.

"You must understand our position," Giacomo said. His eyes slid from one wall to the next, noting every inch of the dreary space. It was no wonder that Captain Santini dreamed of working for a noble house, if *these* were his accommodations. The creaking wooden shelves, the rickety table, the single solitary window . . . they whispered something familiar, cold, and damp to Giacomo, something that plucked at long-scarred strings of terror. "His Holiness will want to know that everything in our power was done to ascertain these records are truthful beyond a shadow of a doubt. *I*, of course, trust you, but I have to be able to tell the Medici, when I report back, that I handled this without any . . . outside hands." It was a long and tangled set of sentences, so Giacomo added another "you *must* understand" at the end, just to make sure that the point was driven home.

"Very well," Captain Santini said, sagging against the grip Khalid still had on his arm.

Giacomo smiled foolishly. "Wonderful. These are the records?" He pointed to the green leather-bound book on the desk, splayed open next to an inkpot and quill. There was spindly writing spilling across the unlined pages, and a stack of identical books on the shelves. Captain Santini nodded. "Thank you, Captain," Giacomo said. "We'll be out of your hair in no time."

The chair creaked as he slid into it, pulling the record book into the sunlight. The writing was more legible from this angle, scrawled letters crawling across the paper at an upward slant, almost as though they were trying to escape.

Farmer Lombardi. Poviglio. Mercato Vecchio. 27 bales of hay.
Merchant Strozzi. Carpineti. Palazzo Pazzi. 42 bolts of silk.

It was an account, line by line, of every farmer, merchant, and peddler who entered the city, what their wares were, and where they were planning on offloading them. It was *gold*. Giacomo paged back with eager fingers, hyper-aware of the anxious gatekeeper behind him. He would only be cowed by Khalid's glower for so long before he began kicking up a fuss.

Luck was on Giacomo's side; he found the first sign of his quarry five pages back—a dashed-off scribble in what must be Captain Santini's illegible handwriting.

Vintner Bartolini. Cortine. Palazzo Medici. 22 casks.

Snatching the quill from the inkpot and digging a small booklet out of his belt-purse, Giacomo copied the information down as carefully as possible.

"Is that it? Is that what you need?" Captain Santini asked.

"Almost, Captain, please be patient," Giacomo soothed. Entry after entry tumbled by as he flipped through the pages, pausing only to jot down information whenever he came across the words *Palazzo Medici*. Farmers, weavers, merchants, cheesemongers . . . they all found their way into Giacomo's little notebook, line after line of potential ammunition.

"Really, signore, I must insist—" the captain faltered as Giacomo turned the last pages in the record book.

"And you are absolutely correct to!" Giacomo said. There were no further deliveries listed for the Medici family, and he *supposed* that he could try his hand at one of the older record books, but he was already looking at listings from June and he had a small army of names scribbled down in his own tiny notebook. "We have imposed on your time and good grace for long enough. Bin-Halil!" Khalid released his grip on Captain Santini's arm, and to his credit, the captain did not immediately rub the spot where Khalid's hand had been. "Thank you so much for all your help, Captain," Giacomo said, flipping the record book back open to its most recent entry, with Farmer Lombardi and all his hay bales. "The Medici family is in your—"

He froze, the words drying on his tongue.

He hadn't noticed the entry on the opposite page. He'd been too busy scanning for any mention of the Medici name to take much notice of anything else, and so—

Butcher de Mori. Monteloro. Casa Petrucci. 10 Hogs.

Cold shock ran down Giacomo's spine.

He should have expected this. He really, *really* should have. *Influential families*, Rosa had said, and that should have been his first clue. But he'd been so caught up in the exhilaration of an impossible job, the promise of a mountain of glittering gold, the thrill of *six whole weeks* of pestering Khalid that the thought hadn't even crossed his mind.

Petrucci. He had not let himself so much as *think* that name in—but there it was now, written in this book. They were here, in Florence. Or at least they would be very soon. And even across the chasm of distance and time, Giacomo was shocked by how . . . topsy-turvy he felt.

"Signore?" Captain Santini was watching him, confusion pinching at his eyebrows.

"Debt," Giacomo said, pasting the smile back on his face. "The Medici family is in your debt." He cleared his throat. "Ten hogs, eh? These Petruccis must be a hungry bunch."

Captain Santini gave a nervous little laugh. "I suppose so."

Khalid was glaring at Giacomo. Giacomo ignored this. "Do you have the address?" he asked, tapping the scrawled *Casa Petrucci*. "I should greet them if they're so newly arrived."

The captain was squinting a bit, which was understandable, because not even Giacomo really understood what Giacomo was doing right now. Khalid was a lost cause. Khalid was maybe going to kill him. "No?" Captain Santini said, slow and uncertain. "Am I—should I?"

Giacomo's pulse was thrumming in his skull. "Of course not!" he chuckled. "Just thought I'd ask. I will be sure to put in a good word for you with the Medici." He was sliding by Captain Santini, edging past Khalid out into the corridor. Somewhere behind him he heard Khalid bid a monosyllabic farewell to the hapless gatekeeper before following.

He would have questions, but Giacomo didn't have to have answers for him. He couldn't tell Khalid. He *couldn't*. Because what would Khalid even *do*? Urge caution? Logic? Useless.

He stepped into the sunlight and let it hit him like a battering ram. He felt a little like laughing and a lot like screaming, but all he did was allow himself to think *they're here*.

They're here.

13

ROSA

Every morning, bright and early, Rosa Cellini set off along the riverbank for the westernmost city gate. But it was never Rosa Cellini who arrived.

"I couldn't be asking less of you," she had told Michelangelo. "All you have to do is nothing."

He had grumbled and wrung his hands, but he hadn't raised more than a single eyebrow when Rosa de' Lombardi had shown up at his workshop the next morning, his fresh-faced niece visiting her famous uncle in the big city for the first time in her young life. There had been some gawking from the more socially awkward apprentices, and then a place by the window had been made for Rosa, who had a smile for everyone, an unending supply of mending, and one eye ever-pinned on the front door. It would take an insightful person indeed to spot the patient hunter buried deep inside the sweet, cheery, and somewhat silly facade of Rosa de' Lombardi.

The whole thing had been easy—two weeks of easy. Rosa and her team clicked in and churned, smooth as clockwork. She was beginning to look forward to Khalid's quiet, astute observations over breakfast every morning. She could translate Giacomo's jumbled flow of words, cutting through the noise to discover whatever nugget of truth or information lay at its heart. She could identify some of Agata's concoctions on sight now, which was comforting, and Sarra could always be counted on to one-up whatever task Rosa put on her plate, adding her own twist or flair.

Was it always this way? Rosa wondered as she pulled her needle through the strip of heavy canvas in her lap. She was at her customary post in Michelangelo's workshop, nestled in her chair near the window. *Surely things couldn't always be this—*

"Signorina."

Rosa stabbed her thumb through the canvas.

Dominic Fontana had not been around the workshop much over the last two weeks. Most days he was off-site, scurrying in the direction of the Palazzo Medici. His absence hadn't bothered her—they had only exchanged words once, after all, and tense words at that. But the sight of him practically *skipping* to grovel at the feet of the Medici—

He glared down at her now, hands fisted at his sides. "Signore Fontana!" she exclaimed, abandoning her sewing to dip him a small curtsy, partly for politeness but mostly for the joy of watching Dominic's manners force him to give her a reluctant bow in return. "What a pleasure! I was beginning to think you were avoiding me."

"Not at all." He was already on edge. "I've been—busy."

"You must be the busiest man in Florence! I've scarcely seen you. It really is too bad of you not to come and say hello." She frowned at him. "I've been bored."

"It's not my job to entertain you," he bit out before he could stop himself.

She buried a smile. "Still," she said. "How much does a hello cost?"

He wanted to rise to the bait. *God*, he wanted to, Rosa could tell. He was so close to lashing out with a terse remark and stalking away. Instead, what she was handed was: "I wanted to apologize."

She blinked at him. He was staring at a point somewhere over her left shoulder, avoiding eye contact. "What was that?"

"I wanted," he said, speaking slowly and loudly, as though the workshop clamor had damaged her hearing, "to apologize. That's why I'm here. I'm sorry for what I assumed when we first met. If I had known your relationship to Master Michelangelo, I—never would have said any of those things."

Ah. He was here to apologize to Rosa de' Lombardi. "You mean when you said you get a 'few of me' every week?"

Dominic's cheeks flamed. "Yes."

"Or are you referring to the way that you lost your temper and yelled at me to leave?"

"*You* were the one prying into my work—"

"Oh, I see," she said. "You're worried I've tattled on you to my uncle."

His tongue must have been in tatters, with how he was biting it. "Please accept my heartfelt apology," he said, stiff as a board.

"Don't you fret, Signore Fontana," Rosa assured him. "My lips are sealed. Uncle Michelangelo doesn't need to know." She leaned against the sill with a coy smile. "For now."

He bent so lightly that Rosa was hard pressed to call it a bow at all. "Good afternoon, signorina," he said. Then he was marching back through the workshop.

He didn't like her. Which would be unremarkable except: He didn't like her, and that wasn't something she had done on purpose. Rosa should be worried about this. She *should* be. But she was . . . intrigued. Dominic Fontana was a dead cat bloating in the sun and she had a stick. She wanted to know how someone with so little confidence wound up working under one of the greatest artists of all time. She wanted to know how he wound up working for the Medici family. She wanted to know why he *kept* working for them. She wanted to poke at him until he *exploded*.

Somewhere in the depths of her mind, Sarra asked, *Who do you talk to?* But this was easily ignored because Rosa was winding through the workshop chaos, hot on Dominic's heels. A number of bearded artists who looked like watered-down imitations of Il Divino exchanged amused glances as she passed.

Let them smirk. "Signore Fontana!" she called, rounding into Dominic's sanctuary.

Dominic kept his back turned resolutely toward her. Paintbrushes and palettes and oils disappeared into his satchel, shoved with indiscriminate hands. "Signore Fontana . . . ," she said, singsong. His shoulders grew, if anything, tighter. "I know you can hear me."

He actually *sighed* before turning, which Rosa registered with gleeful offense. *Poke, poke.* "Was there something you wanted to discuss?"

"You didn't let *me* apologize," she said.

"There is no need" was his stiff response.

"Of course there is," she said, injecting as much warm sincerity as possible into her voice. "I should not have critiqued your work, especially not when we had yet to be introduced. You must allow me to make amends."

"Fine," he said. "Apology accepted."

"You don't sound like you mean it."

"What does it matter?" he said. He shouldered his bag, on the verge of bolting past her.

Rosa Cellini was a woman who could sell boots to birds. She had convinced the greatest artist in all Florence to work against his own generous patrons. She would not be resisted by a man as inconsequential as Dominic Fontana. "Uncle Michelangelo tells me you are favored by the Medici family."

The tension did not drain from him, but it did change shape, morphing from frustration into anxiety. He glanced toward Michelangelo's curtained-off workspace. "He did?"

"He spoke very highly of you," she said. "Is that where you're headed? The Palazzo?"

"Master Michelangelo spoke highly of me?" Dominic did not seem to have heard her question.

"Oh yes," she said. "He said you were doing fine work repairing the Medici frescoes."

It should have sent him blushing and stammering, the praise from a difficult-to-impress master. But instead Dominic's gaze just snapped to Rosa and narrowed. "No he didn't."

What fracture was he seeing? What was he picking up on? She wished she could ask him. "Well. He said you were repairing one of their frescoes. I *assumed* it was fine work."

He didn't glance at the shrouded canvas lurking behind him, but Rosa could read awareness of it in every line in his body. "It's an honor to be singled out by the Medici family."

"You don't have to sound so dour! Is this a funeral?"

"Funeral for my career," he muttered. It must have slipped out, because his eyes shot wide, surprised at himself.

She couldn't suppress her laugh. "I didn't know you could joke, Signore Fontana!"

"That wasn't—I didn't—" He stumbled to a stop, his grip loosening on his bag. A sheepish smile broke out over his face, and Rosa found herself . . . not transfixed, because she wasn't a helpless chicken . . . but certainly *invested* in this particular development. "I guess I don't know many people in Florence who encourage it."

"Well," she said, twirling a paintbrush, "if you ever get the impulse to make another joke and find yourself without an audience, please seek me out. I'd love to hear it."

He ducked his head, that smile blossoming into something wider and more genuine. "I'll remember that," he said. "But truly, I shouldn't say such things. The Medici family has given me a wonderful opportunity, and I am very grateful for the chance to work for them."

Rosa bit at the inside of her lip, nodding. "Of course."

His eyes narrowed, that delicate smile disappearing in an instant. "What is it?"

"Hm? Nothing."

He huffed. "Fine. Until another time, Signorina." He stepped around her.

"Can I ask you something?"

He was very close when the question tumbled from Rosa's mouth. Clearing his throat, he took a gentlemanly step backward. "I do have to go to work—"

"Yes, right," she said quickly. What was she doing? "I only— wanted to know if you were aware of the Medici family's history."

"I'd hardly be any good as an apprentice to Michelangelo if I wasn't. Il Duomo. Donatello. Botticelli. You can barely turn a corner in this city without encountering some reminder of their influence."

"That's not what I meant."

"Then what did you mean?" he asked. "Please speak clearly. I don't share your luxury of time."

Cold flared in her chest. She stood a little straighter. "When did you come to Florence?"

"Three years ago."

"Ah."

"'Ah,'" he mimicked. "Do you have a real question for me, or can—"

He might have finished that sentence, but Rosa was no longer listening. Her focus—the focus of everyone in the workshop—had shifted to the double doors at the front. Typically, they stood open to let in sunlight and fresh air and a lifeline to the outside world, but at this moment, that sunlight was nothing but blue shadows, swallowed up by the silhouette of a looming carriage . . . and the dour figure that stepped over the threshold.

He was a thin man, spindly and tall. He might give off the aura of a disapproving spider, but for the blindingly crimson robes that hung from him. A small cap in the same hue perched on top of his balding head. His presence had brought all industry in the shop to a standstill—even Michelangelo had emerged from his cave to greet the arrival of Cardinal Giulio de' Medici.

She couldn't hear the words they exchanged, but her view was clear enough as Michelangelo bent nearly double to kiss the Cardinal's ring. The moment his lips touched the metal, an ocean of rage and grief swelled up within Rosa, so sudden and all-consuming that for an instant, she thought she might drown in it. Her breath froze in her lungs, and burned, and froze again. Her world swam scarlet—the scarlet of the Cardinal's robes.

It had been a dark night the last time she'd seen such robes. That didn't matter. She'd know them anywhere.

"Signorina?" Dominic was watching her. "Are you alright?"

She wondered what her face looked like and immediately fixed it, smoothing her smile back in place. This was the moment she'd been awaiting, the reason she'd been haunting this workshop for two weeks, and she would be damned if her opportunity was betrayed by something as amateur as a lack of control.

Michelangelo was directing Cardinal de' Medici toward his shrouded corner as the awestruck masons looked on. "I wonder if they're thirsty?" Rosa asked. Without a backward look at the apprentice, she bustled after Michelangelo, leaving Dominic to stare after her in dumbfounded confusion.

The sheets that partitioned Michelangelo's workspace from the rest of the shop offered little in the way of actual privacy. The sunlight spilling through the open back doors lit the artist, his visitor, and the emerging marble sculpture in sharp silhouette, and the brisk autumn breeze carried their words. Rosa busied herself at an unoccupied bench, filling a pitcher with wine and arranging a pair of cups on a tray while she listened.

"... whether you would be in attendance," Cardinal de' Medici was saying. Even as the sheets billowed, his profile remained frozen—almost as though he was the sculpture, not Michelangelo's work in process.

Michelangelo was not nearly as composed. The artist was standing, hands clasped behind his back, shifting his weight. Rosa gritted her teeth against the impulse to hiss out a correction.

"I did not know a reply was necessary," Michelangelo said.

"Come now, my friend," the Cardinal said, tone warming almost imperceptibly. "You know we always enjoy hearing from you at the Palazzo."

"Still," Michelangelo said. "I thought that if the Medici request a thing, it is guaranteed."

"In these trying times, displays of support are always appreciated."

"Then I will be there," Michelangelo said. Was he squaring his shoulders? "In support."

"You are too generous with your time."

That was her cue. Tray in one hand and wine pitcher in the other, Rosa shoved the sheet aside, stumbled into Michelangelo's sanctum—and stopped short. "Oh!" she exclaimed, dropping into a deep curtsy. "Your—Your Eminence!"

She looked up to see Cardinal de' Medici turn to Michelangelo with a barely perceptible hint of amusement on his face. "I am surprised," he said. "I did not think that you tolerated ... female companionship. Even in your servants."

Michelangelo was watching Rosa through a haze of panic. She could almost see the fractures beneath his flyaway hair. With the slightest pressure, the artist might shatter, and Rosa would find herself marched out of the workshop and straight to the gallows.

But Michelangelo had carved his democratic dreams into marble and placed them outside the city hall for all to see. "My niece," he said, a heart-stopping lifetime later. "Rosa."

Finally—*finally*—Rosa straightened. "I am honored to meet you, Your Eminence," she said. "Please forgive my forwardness. I saw your carriage and I thought you and my uncle might like some refreshment." She set the tray and pitcher down on Michelangelo's workbench.

Cardinal de' Medici's cool gaze was heavy as she filled the cups with wine. "You never mentioned a niece, Michelangelo."

"My—my sister's daughter," Michelangelo said. "From the country."

"I arrived only this month, Your Eminence," Rosa said with a bright smile. She delivered a cup into the Cardinal's hand before handing Michelangelo his own. "Sadly, Mother and Uncle Michelangelo have never had much of a relationship, but I jumped at the chance to meet him. And to see this city! I've been hearing tales of Florence ever since I was a little girl!"

"Mm." Cardinal de' Medici regarded her over the rim of his cup. She winched her smile even wider. "And what do you think of our fair city so far, signorina?"

Michelangelo was gulping the wine in his cup. Rosa stepped on his foot. "It is unlike anything I have ever *seen*," she gushed. "I had never dreamed there were so many people in the entire world! The churches, the piazzas, the houses—I can scarcely believe my eyes!"

There was a smile curling the edges of Cardinal de' Medici's mouth now. "Has your uncle taken it upon himself to show you around?"

"Well . . . ," Rosa hedged.

"I've been busy," grunted Michelangelo.

"Uncle has had a lot of work," she agreed. "But I've explored the neighborhood a bit."

"Shame, Michelangelo." Cardinal de' Medici set his cup down. "You drag the girl here from the countryside and then you don't even let her leave San Niccolo? She has barely seen Florence at all." He nodded once, all dour decisiveness. "You and your uncle will come to lunch at the Palazzo. Then you will see the real Florence."

Rosa gasped. "The—the Palazzo Medici? Me?"

"I'm sure His Holiness would love to meet you," Cardinal de' Medici said. "I *know* he would like to see you, Michelangelo."

Michelangelo's jaw was clenched so tightly that it was a wonder his teeth didn't shatter. "Of course," he said. "If the Medici request a thing . . ."

"Yes, yes." Cardinal de' Medici stood. "We look forward to having you. Next week?"

"Whenever you wish."

"Lovely. Bless you both. Signorina Rosa—I look forward to meeting you again soon."

She bobbed another curtsy. "*Thank you*, Your Eminence. I am honored."

He nodded graciously. "Michelangelo," he said. "Walk me out." The sheets billowed around him as he swept gracefully onto the main floor, Michelangelo stalking at his heels.

Rosa lingered, watching the Cardinal's scarlet back retreat toward the front doors. She thought about flaming rooftops and unclenched her fists before her fingernails could draw blood.

"*Festina lente*," she whispered. "I'll catch up."

14

KHALID

Glares and glowers crawled over Khalid's skin like fleas. They itched across the nape of his neck and burrowed into his scalp. They *infested*.

It had been like this since his first patrol. The Medici uniform was like a beacon, attracting sneers and muttered curses wherever he went. Shopkeepers, beggars, artisans—it did not matter whose path Khalid crossed, the reception was sure to be curdled.

"It's just because the patrols are new," Sergeant Bianci explained. They were on duty together tonight, meandering through Piazza di Santa Croce. The sergeant did not seem to mind the hostile scowls. "Once the people get used to seeing us, it won't be so much of an issue."

"These patrols are to be permanent?"

"Oh yes," Sergeant Bianci said happily. "We'll be expanding across the northern part of the city by the end of the week. By month's end we may even be in the Oltrarno."

Only Khalid's well-practiced indifference kept the surprise off his face. "Is the rest of Florence not under the authority of the City Guard?"

Sergeant Bianci had the grace to look a bit abashed. "Well. They're not exactly *practicing* that authority, are they? There's a streak of audacity growing in this city. That's what Captain Romano says. I mean—" He pointed to the shadowed depths of an awning. Bills, printed in large lettering, plastered every open centimeter of wall space. "The situation is getting outrageous, and the City Guard—they're either incapable or unwilling to stamp it out. Did you hear about the attack on His Holiness when he first returned to Florence?"

"No."

"He was assaulted in the middle of the Piazza della Signoria. He could very well have been killed. And the City Guard has still not hunted the terrorist down. So in the meantime, we are just trying to lighten the load on their shoulders."

Khalid thought about the venomous glowers he'd received from the City Guardsmen at the Porta Romana. "They must be grateful for the aid," he said.

Sergeant Bianci's wide face twisted. "They are—"

"It's no secret you lapdogs would see the whole city in chains."

The words came in a growl from the next street over. They were followed by the unmistakable sound of a fist hitting flesh. Khalid did not wait for Sergeant Bianci's permission before he was springing into a sprint, racing toward the disturbance.

It was a tumble of activity that he found once he rounded the corner. A gaggle of men thronged in the light of an abandoned lantern, which lay cast aside on the cobbles. The men struggled and shoved, the occasional fist flailing from the muddle to connect again, haphazard.

Raising two fingers to his lips, Khalid gave an ear-splitting whistle. Surprised, the men fell away from one another in factions; two in the homespun of woolworkers, two in the red of the City Guard, and one—one who Khalid recognized.

His stomach sank as he took in Guardsman Vieri's scowl.

"Are you lost, bin-Halil?" Vieri spat. "What the hell do you want?"

The man had never forgiven Khalid for their first meeting. Vieri had been lured away from his post playing lookout for Sergeant Bianci's assignation, and the sergeant held Vieri personally responsible for all of his bruises. Now, even weeks later, Vieri channeled all his frustration onto Khalid. Honor, race, intelligence, talents—nothing was beyond insult for Vieri. He hurled his barbs through a brittle smile.

One day, Khalid would plant his boot in Vieri's gut, and it would not be his fault.

Vieri only stood to attention when Sergeant Bianci panted up. "What in the Lord's name is going on here?" the sergeant grumbled, wiping sweat from his ruddy cheeks.

The City Guardsmen shared a glower. "We don't answer to you," the burlier one said.

"Sergeant," Vieri said, grabbing the collar of one of the wool-workers. The man swayed beneath his hand, obviously intoxicated. "These two men were brawling in the streets. I stepped in to separate them and take them in for—"

"'Take them in'!" the burly City Guardsman exclaimed. "You want to lock them up—"

"*Disturbing the peace,*" Vieri forged ahead. His grin was gritted. "Per the request of the Medici family—"

"That's just Landi and Donati," the smaller City Guardsman protested. "They do this every week, but they only fight each other—"

"Who's disturbing the peace?" one of the woolworkers—Donati, Khalid thought—slurred. "Your man is the one throwing punches—"

Sergeant Bianci frowned at Vieri. "Is this true, Vieri?"

"We have an authority to uphold, Sergeant," Vieri said. "Even bin-Halil over there understands that. Captain's orders."

"'*Captain,*'" the burly City Guardsman spat.

"A challenge to that authority is a challenge to the Medici themselves," Vieri continued.

"We're not trying to *challenge* your *keepers,*" said the smaller guard.

"What did you call them?" Vieri snapped.

"Bark a little louder, lapdog," snickered Donati, dangling from Vieri's grip.

"Yes, run along back to your *palace*," said the burly City Guardsman.

The situation was spiraling. It did not take a genius to see this. But Sergeant Bianci just stood by, watching as faces grew redder and insults more heated. Any moment now there would be another punch thrown. Only this time, the sergeant and Khalid would be required to back Vieri, and the brawl would spread.

Khalid did not want to back Vieri.

He cleared his throat. "If I may offer a suggestion, Sergeant?"

Sergeant Bianci nodded, eager. Vieri scoffed.

"Guardsman Vieri is correct," Khalid said. "If these men are disrupting the peace, then they should not be on the streets."

The burly City Guardsman sneered. "Of course you'd suggest that, you blue-suited—"

"Perhaps the City Guardsman might take them back to the Porta Romana, or another gatehouse," Khalid breezed on. "To sleep it off."

Donati peered through the darkness at Khalid. "Not arrested?"

"Not arrested."

This was apparently satisfactory to the woolworker. He extracted his collar from Vieri's fingers and stumbled toward the City Guards. "Then lead the way, signori!"

"Sergeant—" Vieri protested, but Sergeant Bianci just shook his head.

"You heard the man," he said. "Lead the way, Guardsmen."

The City Guards each grabbed hold of a drunk. With distrustful glowers, as though they thought the Medici Guards might try to snatch their charges, they towed the woolworkers away.

"Sergeant," Vieri tried again as soon as the guardsmen were out of sight. Sergeant Bianci once again shook his head.

"That was good thinking, Guardsman bin-Halil," he said. The words were enunciated, barbed to skewer Vieri. "Only a complete idiot would think to antagonize our comrades in the City Guard."

Khalid nodded his thanks. "We have dealt with similar situations back in Ferrara—"

The rest of the sentence died in his throat. In the wake of the City Guardsmen, Khalid's eyes had landed on a scrawny figure lounging against the limestone wall. From this distance it was difficult to make out their features, but Khalid could see how they cradled their arm to their chest.

He knew that arm. He had broken that arm himself.

In the moonlight, Marino gave Khalid a little wave.

"You forget the language, *Yazid*?" Vieri sneered. It was enough to bring Khalid back to himself, the stab of irritation and anger shocking his thoughts into focus.

"I was—thinking," he said. It came out strangled. "That I should follow up with the City Guard. To make sure all is well. Sergeant?"

"Another good idea. Go, go," Sergeant Bianci urged. He turned a more thunderous glare on Vieri. "You. With me."

"Sergeant . . . ," Vieri whined, but the sergeant had already begun striding back in the direction of the Palazzo Medici. With one final poisonous glare at Khalid, Vieri ducked his head and trailed after. And then Khalid was alone.

Marino had been wise enough to disappear once he had gotten Khalid's attention. He only popped up again when Khalid turned onto the next street, materializing out of the darkness at Khalid's side.

Khalid did not break stride. "Where?" he muttered.

Marino grinned. The bruises on his face had faded, but his nose still looked puffy. "Vite Contorto," he said. "Come on."

The sailor had a good handle on his direction. Khalid struck a line through the impulse to run. If Marino knew the streets this well, the odds were good that he was not in the city alone. Any attempt to flee would be greeted with a knife in the throat.

Khalid kept his head down. He followed.

Marino led him to the Vite Contorto pub on the outskirts of the city. To his surprise, Khalid vaguely recognized the place. It was favored by the guardsmen, more for the prices than for the ambiance. He knew what he would see as he pushed through the warped door: tilting tables, tacky with ale, a few creaking benches, and tallow candles that filled the windowless room with thick black smoke.

What he was not expecting to see was the Weever of Genoa lounging in the corner.

Khalid drew up short at the sight, his feet rooting to the floor. Marino, just a pace ahead of him, let out a cackle. "You're catching on now," he said. "Don't keep him waiting."

Signore Traverio smiled at Khalid's approach. It did nothing to put Khalid at ease. "Khalid!" he said. His voice was as warm as it had been when he had first welcomed Khalid aboard the ship to Genoa. "Sit, sit! Can I get you anything to eat?"

Khalid obediently perched on the splintering bench. "No, thank you."

"Anything to drink? The ale is atrocious, but it is wet."

"No, thank you."

"Suit yourself." Blue eyes, pale as a frozen sky, studied Khalid across the table. Khalid did his best not to fidget. "Do you know why I'm here, Khalid?" Signore Traverio finally said.

Khalid did not reply. There was nothing to say.

Signore Traverio sighed. It came from the disappointed depths of him. Khalid had heard it dozens of times, directed at other people. Usually those people wound up maimed or dead. Sometimes they didn't wind up at all. "Alright," he said, shaking his head. "If you find that question beyond you, let me try another. Do you know why *you're* here?"

Again, Khalid kept his mouth shut. He heard Marino let out a snort, and a moment later Khalid's bench jolted across the floor, propelled by Marino's kick. "Speak up," Marino said.

"Marino!" Signore Traverio barked. His face transformed in a single moment, anger drowning his features. "You talk when I tell you to talk." The sailor subsided, putting a few steps between Khalid's bench and himself. Signore Traverio's expression had smoothed back into bland amiability by the time he turned it back on Khalid. Khalid did not relax.

"I'd like to stop playing games now, Khalid," he said. "I've come a very long way, and I'm tired. And it's all because of you."

"I . . . apologize." The words dragged themselves out of Khalid's throat, scratchy and raw. He was horrified to realize that there was an actual tinge of fear wrapped around them. He had let himself slip these last few weeks. He had stood at Rosa's side. He had watched Sarra's clever fingers. He had studied Michelangelo's work in awe. He had dodged Agata's experiments. He had teased Giacomo. He had felt himself come alive in a way he never had as the dead-eyed right fist of the Weever of Genoa. But if he was a living person again—that meant that he could be afraid.

"You've been playing hooky," Signore Traverio said. "You are meant to be chasing down a challenger, and I find you . . . wearing the uniform of the Medici Guard? And that's not the worst of it. Because Marino here—he tells me that you were spotted with Sarra the Tinkerer in Genoa just one month ago. This information is the only reason he is still enjoying the use of his hands." At Khalid's shoulder, Marino was notably quiet. "Now," Signore Traverio went on, "since the lovely Tinkerer neglected to clear her visit with me, and you have since been spotted in her company here in Florence . . . I have reached a conclusion, Khalid. One that I do not much care for." He put his tankard down with an emphatic thump. "Ask me what that conclusion is."

"What conclusion, Signore Traverio?"

"My conclusion is: Sarra Nepi came to Genoa to offer you a job. And, my dear sweet Khalid, you were foolish enough to take it." He shook his head. "Working for me *and* for the Tinkerer? Genoa *and* Florence? Double-dipping. You know what I do with double-dippers."

Khalid's mouth was dry. "I—" was all he managed to get out before the rest of his words crumbled.

"I know, I know," Signore Traverio said. His eyes bled sympathy. "It's a lot for you. It's always been a lot for you. But that's why you have me. You're a very talented boy, God knows—that's why I plucked you out of that dusty city in the first place. But scheming? It's not your strong suit, Khalid, and we both know that." He patted Khalid's hand. "Things aren't broken yet, though. We can still fix this. *You* can still fix it."

The air in Khalid's lungs was as heavy as lead. "How?"

"Here's my thinking. If Sarra Nepi dragged you all the way from Genoa, that must mean that whatever job she pulled you in on is a big one. The payout must be huge." Signore Traverio settled back into his seat. "I want it."

"You—are welcome to my cut—"

"Not just *your* cut," Signore Traverio snapped. "You're going to bring me everything."

Everything. The entire take. If Signore Traverio expected Khalid to walk away with that, then he must always expect—

"His new friends might get grabby," Marino chipped in.

"Then he will handle them." Signore Traverio's gaze was half-lidded. "Because if you try to satisfy me with a *percentage*, then I will add double the remainder to your father's debt. And then I will call it in."

There was a rushing in Khalid's ears. "You can't do that. Diego de Ávila owns my father's debt."

"He collects on it, certainly. But he hasn't *owned* it for—oh, a little more than three years now. And let me tell you, this current spot of misadventure aside, that purchase has been worth every penny."

Three years. Signore Traverio had bought Baba's debt before he'd hired Khalid. "Why—"

"Don't be so modest."

Khalid's mouth was dry. "You—did this for me."

"I did this because it was mutually beneficial. You wanted a reason to leave. I wanted you working for me. Come now, don't play the coquette and pretend that you took much convincing." Signore Traverio's air of pleasant nonchalance did not crack as he unsheathed his stiletto dagger, inspecting the blade in the smoky candlelight. "How many debts have you collected for me? And you never thought I might be your father's creditor?"

No. He hadn't. It had not once crossed his mind. How was it that he was still finding new depths to his naivety?

"I see." There was laughter glittering in the Weever's icy eyes. "Then I am happy we finally understand one another. It means I can speak plainly." He gave his dagger a spin. "You work for me. So do many dangerous people. If I wish, I can simply say the word and back in Tunis, someone will burn first your father's shop and then his entire life to the ground. I can have Sarra Nepi and whoever else you're working with wiped from the face of the Earth. And I will do all of this if you don't bring me the money as soon as your job is finished. Do you understand me?"

Khalid's fists clenched. "Yes, Signore Traverio."

Signore Traverio's face broke out in a broad grin. "I knew you would."

It was a dismissal, or as much of one as he would get without the Weever's blade in his neck. Khalid stood, shoulders straight. He did not look at Marino as he passed.

"Keep your eyes open, Khalid!" Signore Traverio called, his voice jubilant and boisterous. "We'll be in touch!"

15

GIACOMO

"Paroli, signori, last call, Paroli—"

The cards flipped and danced in Giacomo's hands—only a few of them left now, but still enough to put on a show—a fan, a cascade, a finger-twisting construct flashing tantalizing glimpses of suit and color.

The performance served its purpose, which was, of course, to mesmerize and excite the men huddled around this massive circular table at the center of the smoky, low-ceilinged gambling house. Scars bit deep into the wood, the angry slashes of unlucky gamblers and the initials of their more fortunate counterparts, speaking as much to the history of this establishment as the chatter of the garrulous wagerers did.

Giacomo dealt out the top two cards and listened to the cheers and groans that followed.

"A noble effort!"

"Fifteen and the go is *always* a gamble—"

"Five wins!" Giacomo announced, shaking a curl of dyed red hair out of his eyes. It would never do for him to go out on a job as *himself*, after all. "Knave loses! Collect, signori!" Again, his fingers sprung to life, gathering the coins sullenly rolled to him by the less fortunate players.

There was one player, however, who was accepting more money from Giacomo than he was giving back. This was the man Giacomo kept at the edge of his vision as he worked, watching as he stacked his winnings in careful piles, considering the three cards lying face-up in front of him. The man's face was impassive and smooth, betraying nothing as he rested a single finger on the five of cups.

"Paroli, signori," Giacomo called, and the player bent the corner of his card upright with the flick of a fingernail. Around him, onlookers broke into fascinated and frantic murmurs, assessing this decision between them.

"Pardon me." A barmaid leaned out over Giacomo's shoulder with a tray full of tankards, handing them around to the remaining players. "You all look parched."

There were a few jeers and whistles at that, but they were rote, a scripted response as opposed to a genuine appreciation for the barmaid's rather lanky charms. Still, the appeal of a drink was not to be overestimated, and as the players busied themselves with their first sips, Giacomo had the opportunity to catch the end of the warning glare Sarra Nepi was arrowing between his eyes.

Careful, he read in her expression. *Don't give him too much at once.*

Giacomo resisted the urge to stick his tongue out at her as she retreated to the bar. Didn't *anybody* trust him to do his job? He knew how to keep a mark at a table, *for Heaven's sake.*

But even with that irritation pricking, Giacomo was careful with the next hand he dealt. After all, who knew when they'd get another chance to rob the captain of the Medici Guard?

The issue for *weeks* had been this: above all else, Captain Luigi Romano was *responsible.* An impenetrable fortress of virtue who executed his duties to the Medici family during the day and then marched home to his wife and three children every evening to join them for Vespers. He did not go out drinking. He did not visit brothels. He paged through his Bible for half an hour until the candlelight failed, and then he fell asleep beside his wife and snored until morning.

These were admirable habits in a guard captain. They were also a pain in the ass for those who might be interested in relieving him of any safeguarded objects of a sensitive nature . . . objects such as, for example, the keys to the intricate Henlein lock on the Magi vault.

"I have heard some of the men say he sleeps with the keys under his pillow," Khalid had said, hazy-eyed after a night on guard duty. The group had been gathered for breakfast in the millhouse, early sunlight filtering through the shutters. Only Sarra, of all of them, had been fully awake, and Giacomo was fairly certain this was because she hadn't gone to sleep the night before, inexplicably choosing to stay up all night fiddling with who-knew-what at her worktable instead of going home to her warm bed.

"Wonderful," Sarra had sniped back, picking at the shell of her boiled egg. "At least that's convenient if we need to unlock his dreams."

"If Captain Romano keeps the keys on him at all times, it means that he trusts himself," Rosa had said. "He trusts his judgment and he trusts his instincts."

"And he trusts the personal army under his command," Agata had added.

"This sounds hopeless," Giacomo had moaned. Khalid's shoulder, he'd discovered, was almost as good as a pillow, and so that was where he had slumped, eyes half-mast. "We may as well cut our losses and return to our farms. Signore al-Sarraj can hammer his sword into a plowshare. I'll have to learn how to plant grapes or something."

"Captain Romano keeps the keys on him because he trusts himself," Rosa had repeated, rudely ignoring Giacomo. "So what does he do with the keys when he doesn't trust himself?"

"No man is without vices," Khalid had said, slowly, as though he saw some solution there that Giacomo was blind to. "Not even Captain Romano."

Rosa had reached across the table to poke the top of Giacomo's head. "How good are you at working a deck?"

Gambling. It was cliché in its mundanity. Captain Romano, the untarnished commander of the Medici Guard, was brought low every two weeks by *gambling*, and, now that Giacomo had a moment to consider it, this made an irrefutable sort of sense. If the rest of the captain's life was so virtuous and repressed, then all that recklessness had to go *somewhere*. And where better to put it than into bassetta, a card game *notorious* throughout Florence for shoveling money into the pockets of the house dealers. It was impossible to win and almost as impossible to break even.

Unless, of course, the dealer had a reason to want you to at his table.

"Queens win!" Giacomo announced. "Nines lose!" At his left, Romano tossed over a few coins that had been resting on his upturned nine of cups—a small sacrifice, negligible compared to the building fortune riding on the five of cups. "Paroli, signori!"

"Con-sti-tutes a gross misuse—"

It was the crinkle of paper that drew Giacomo's attention, even in the swelling chaos. Paper wasn't something a person traditionally encountered in gambling halls like this one, and it took Giacomo no time at all to seek out the three men huddled at the edge of the crowd, their heads bent over something flimsy and yellow and folded.

One was sounding out the words printed on the paper in a low voice, unnoticed by the carousing gamblers around him. "'Of power, which has become the'—Christ, this goes on."

"Keep going," his friend muttered, agog.

"It's just more of the same," said the reader. "They're saying the Medici shouldn't be in charge. They're saying . . . we were better off as a Republic."

"Paroli, signori!" Giacomo called, louder this time, flipping through the four remaining cards. It didn't take a genius to figure out what exactly these men were reading, and if Romano caught wind of it—

He caught Sarra's eye at the bar. She gave him a little nod, wiping her hands on her apron, and began wending her way toward him.

"Twos win! Eights lose!" Giacomo announced, drowning out the man with the bill as he said, "Whoever wrote this is asking for a hangman's noose." Giacomo listened to the whoops and bellows that followed his announcement and *prayed* that Romano was too absorbed in the game to notice the idiots across the table.

He was in luck, it seemed, because all Romano did was toss another coin on his five of cups and sit back in his chair, staring into the middle distance and completely ignoring the jeering men who surrounded him, cheering and booing him in turns. "The final hand, signori!" Giacomo announced, brandishing the last two cards. "Paroli!"

The three men with the bill were *still talking*—Giacomo could hear their rumbling voices through the rest of the tumult. It would be only so long before a lull hit . . . and then they would all be in trouble.

Where was Sarra? Giacomo scanned the crowd for her, for any sign of her—and yes, *there,* a current running through the growing mob, making for the table—

But when the current washed up on the shores of the bassetta game, it wasn't Sarra who emerged. Two middle-aged men shouldered their way through, both standing out like peacocks, their embroidered clothes a sharp contrast to the grimy surroundings. One of the men—a gray-bearded fellow in deep blue—had a kerchief to his mouth and nose, his eyes watering. The other, bald head warm beneath a maroon velvet cap, looked more sure of himself, his gaze steady as it landed on the object of his search.

His very familiar gaze.

Giacomo froze.

"Captain Romano!" someone exclaimed, but it was a struggle for Giacomo to identify who it was. He was too busy scrambling for air—light—the ability to move. He couldn't look away from the maroon cap as it bobbed closer to Romano. He was aware, in the back of his head, that this situation was very bad—that Romano had pushed away from the table, that he was watching the noblemen with a mix of shame and embarrassment . . .

He ducked his head, hoping his dyed curls would do enough to hide his face, but that was as much self-preservation as he could muster. *Do something,* he hissed to his malfunctioning limbs. *You knew this might happen. Don't let it send you to pieces.*

"Signore Talliere?" One of the players had grown tired of waiting for the grand finale and was prodding Giacomo. It was all he could do to fumble his numb fingers around the last cards in his deck and flip them over. "Ten wins," he muttered, his tongue clumsy. "Five loses."

Even trapped in conversation with the noblemen, a wince of loss crossed Romano's face. He shoved the stack of money on top of his five of cups toward Giacomo, not paying any mind to the coins that rolled off the table's edge.

Giacomo made no move to catch them. He knew, vaguely, that what had just happened was not what was supposed to happen, and that he had just made a rather large mistake. Sarra, wherever in this crush she was, was most likely calling him every insult she knew. But all Giacomo could do was watch as Romano gave the noblemen a little bow.

"Next week then," Romano said, backing away from the table. "Signore Petrucci. Signore Loredan."

The crowd parted around him as he left, the players already clamoring for another game. Giacomo caught a glimpse of Sarra swerving into Romano's path—asking him some question—struggling to keep him at the tavern, at the table—doing Giacomo's job for him—

"You see? You just have to know how to talk to these people," Petrucci said. He glanced after Romano, eyes sweeping past Giacomo without a hitch of recognition. There were veins of adrenaline suffusing the cloud of shock in his mind, and they were coming to life, sparking like a lightning storm, whispering *maybe maybe maybe*—

Which was when the cobblestone smashed through the window and all hell broke loose.

16

ROSA

What does Captain Romano do with the keys when he doesn't *trust himself?*

The Casa Romano was a humble two stories, with spotless lime-stone walls and a terra-cotta–tiled roof that bore no scrap of rotting autumn foliage. It was the inanimate copy of its owner, neat, controlled, respectable—

It made sense. Romano trusted his most precious belongings only to himself. So while he was cutting loose at the bassetta table, the four walls shaped in his image would stand watch.

Predictable, Rosa thought.

"There will be a guard at the door," Khalid had told them. "Captain Romano is not so foolish as to leave his house unattended. However . . ." He had broken off, pensive, which had delighted Rosa. Of all her team, Khalid was the one with the most aptitude for putting pieces together. Traverio had held him back, but Rosa thought that was because he was frightened of Khalid's potential. Given the space, Khalid was a canny mastermind in his own right.

"The Casa Romano posting is a probation," Khalid had continued. "Every young or unproven guard must spend at least one night standing watch under his eye to prove that they know how to conduct themselves. Captain Romano will not risk assigning someone whose skills are not up to par to patrol the Palazzo Medici. The stakes are too great."

"So he lets them keep the safety of his own family," Sarra had said.

"The longer a guard fails to meet his standards, the longer they must suffer the ignominy of the posting," Khalid had continued. "Guardsman de' Carlo has been confined to the Casa Romano for nearly a month."

A *month* of probation. Now, from the shadows of a cypress tree, Rosa could see why. The young Guardsman de' Carlo had been posted at the Casa Romano's front door for two hours, and he had spent the entirety of that time in a sulk. She had watched him shiver, spit, mutter curses, and frown with increasing venom as the minutes dragged on. Now, as the clock neared midnight, he looked ready to breathe acid at the next person who walked too close.

"Not long now," Rosa whispered. Khalid, at her shoulder, nodded twice. He had been even less talkative than usual this evening, and Rosa missed his succinct observations. The silence was beginning to wear at her.

No sooner had Rosa spoken than the de' Carlo boy shoved himself off the wall, muttering something inaudible and most likely profane. With an irritated yank, he unlatched the front door, disappearing into the warm orange glow inside.

Rosa and Khalid exchanged a glance. *Ahead of schedule.* The guardsman had made a habit of turning in for shift change before he was due, but typically he only dared fifteen minutes leeway at the most—fifteen minutes during which the front door would be unguarded and the majority of the house would be asleep.

"You think you can sneak in, nab the vault keys, and get clear inside of fifteen minutes?" Sarra had asked.

"I think I can do it inside of ten," Rosa had retorted. "The other five are just padding."

The front door of the Casa Romano was locked when Khalid and Rosa reached it, to the young guardsman's credit, but it only took a few twists from Rosa's lockpicks to send it swinging open.

There was no sign of de' Carlo in the front hall—no sign of

anyone, in fact. The only glimmer of light that Rosa could see came from the end of the right-most corridor, shining around the edges of a closed door. *Kitchens*, mouthed Khalid, in response to Rosa's inquisitive eyebrow.

This must be where the young guardsman had taken refuge from the November chill. If Rosa strained her ears, she could make out a conversation filtering through the door. The walls were too thick for her to catch individual words, but the tone was clear enough: whiny rather than alarmed. She'd put good money on de' Carlo complaining about his posting to the cook, whose sleepy grumbles of reply were so noncommittal that they gave Khalid a run for his money.

With the Romano security occupied, Khalid led the way through the house. Together, they padded down undecorated, modest corridors, and then up a set of polished wooden stairs, keeping to the wall so that the steps didn't creak. The house, true to Khalid's prediction, was well and truly asleep, and the second level was even more silent than the first—

"Mama?"

Or at least, it was supposed to be.

The voice, small as it was, had come from somewhere down the hall ahead. Rosa listened as a pair of tiny feet pattered across the stone floor. Something creaked, and for a heart-stopping moment Rosa thought that either she or Khalid had put a foot wrong on the steps. But no—that sound was metallic, the groan of iron hinges opening. The little girl had inched open a door.

"Mama?" she called again.

The voice that answered was thick with sleep. "What are you doing out of bed?"

"I had a bad dream."

"A bad dream?" Signora Romano was not awake enough to comprehend what her daughter was saying. "It's not real. Go back to bed."

"It's too scary in there."

A gusty sigh blew down the corridor. "Come on, then." The little footsteps scurried forward. "And shut the door behind you," Signora Romano added.

The door closed. The latch clicked. The corridor was silent once again.

Khalid and Rosa let the silence breathe for one minute, then two. There were no further signs of life either from Signora Romano or from any of the children. Gingerly, Khalid climbed the final few steps and peered out into the hallway.

Clear, he mouthed back to Rosa.

She followed him onto the second floor and past two identically bland oak doors before stopping outside a third. Trying the knob, Rosa was unsurprised to find it locked. But the front entrance had shown that Captain Romano did not have the same close relationship with Peter Henlein that his employers enjoyed, and the door was soon opening to allow Khalid and Rosa to slip inside. When it shut again behind them, Rosa finally allowed a small amount of tension to leach from her shoulders.

Romano's study was, impossibly, even more unfussy than the rest of the house. Double windows most likely did a good job of lighting the room during the day, under the management of the plain gray curtains that framed them. A single desk sat near the far wall, heavy and well-made. The chair behind it was tucked in with military precision.

A few shelves lined the opposite walls, laden with a notable collection of books—the only obvious sign of wealth in the entire house. These Rosa gave a curious glance as she made a circuit of the space, studying the room's dimensions with a professional's eye. She paused before she crossed the windows, drawing the curtains shut on the off chance that a passerby might catch a glimpse of something they shouldn't.

"What should I look for?" Khalid whispered. It was the most he had said in a run all evening, but the quietly troubled look was not quite gone from his eyes.

"Something that doesn't fit," Rosa said. "It's impossible to make a strongbox entirely invisible. There will be evidence of it—books that don't line up or uneven bits of floor."

They began at opposite ends of the study, tracing their fingertips along running boards and testing the seams between the floorboards. Rosa was just moving to the desk to check the drawers for false bottoms when she heard Khalid make a noise near the left bookcase.

"Rosa," he hissed as, beneath his grip, a single shelf of the bookcase swung open. Behind it, Rosa could pick out the edges of something squat and square.

She grinned. "Good eye." Slipping closer, she could make out the details of what had been revealed: a wrought iron strongbox, set into the wall so neatly that there was no question as to the quality of the workmanship. Romano had wanted no chance of its removal.

"Light," she whispered. Khalid fished a shielded lantern out of his belt-pouch and lit it, directing its concentrated glow away from the curtained windows.

A once-over of the strongbox revealed nothing but a series of iron hobnails, struck into the door at regular intervals. Beginning on the left, Rosa ran her fingertip around each stud, feeling for a gap between the stud and the iron beneath it, searching for a hint of give—

One of the hobnails shifted in its setting. Rosa pressed harder. With a second, louder click, the stud popped out into her palm. In the space that remained lay a tiny keyhole.

Palming her lockpicks, Rosa set to work.

17

SARRA

Shards of glass, scraps of the wooden shutters, and fragments of cobblestone rained down onto the gambling hall floor, shocking the patrons into silence as men and women in varying states of inebriation struggled to piece together what this meant. Captain Romano's jaw was slack. The two noblemen who had accosted him wore matching expressions of absolute shock. Even Giacomo, whose face was still pale, looked rattled.

Then, through the gap where the shutters had been, they heard the shouting.

It wasn't the sporadic exclamation of an overexcited reveler. The noise swamped the gambling hall, a mass of voices that wove together in a crestless wave, swelling and swelling.

When the front door burst in to reveal a man in Medici blue, it was barely a surprise. "Captain!" he called, with obvious relief.

"What the devil is going on?" Romano growled, stalking up to the guard.

"The bills, Captain," the man said, and winced when Romano hissed at him to keep his voice down. Behind Sarra, the hum of activity was picking up again as dealers corralled players back into some vestige of enthusiasm. "The seditious bills. We caught someone with a stack. We were planning on bringing him in, but his friends . . . heard the news."

The trio of men Giacomo had flagged to Sarra exchanged shifty glances. One stuffed a square of paper into his belt-pouch.

"Have the prisoner brought to the Palazzo," Romano ordered. "We'll make an example of him tomorrow—"

"That's the issue, Captain," the guard interjected. "The seditionist . . . he's just a boy. Barely ten years old. And his companions are intent on getting him back. They've blocked the arresting guards in at the Loggia. With all the attention they've drawn, the uproar is spreading through the streets."

"Spreading?"

"West, mostly, through the Santa Maria Novella quarter."

Captain Romano's shoulders stiffened. "My horse," he growled. "Ready my horse."

"Captain?" the guard asked, but Sarra did not share in his confusion. The Santa Maria Novella quarter was home to any number of Florence's wealthy houses, beautiful piazzas, and verdant gardens.

It was also the home of the Casa Romano, which Khalid and Rosa were presumably still ransacking under the noses of Romano's sleeping wife and children. And if Romano roused the household in a panic—

Whatever fate awaited that poor boy in the Loggia dei Lanzi would be nothing compared to what would happen to Rosa and Khalid if they were caught. Sarra had to warn them. But there was no way she would be able to beat Romano home if he was on horseback.

Romano's hapless guard was already wending past the bassetta table as he made for the rear exit and the stables outside. Giacomo made no reaction as he passed, still frozen stiff as a useless statue. He had not even made to collect the shining coins stacked in neat piles in front of the bassetta players.

Sarra's breath caught. *Yes.*

It was easy enough to maneuver to Giacomo's side. The bassetta players were more absorbed in muttering about the stampede outside the broken window than they were in the game. "Giacomo!" Sarra hissed in the player's ear. "What is *wrong* with you?" She was rewarded with a slight twitch, his mind resurfacing from whatever shocky depths had submerged it.

She could not wait for him to wake. Sarra would have to act now. Wedging her knee beneath the tabletop and grabbing hold of one of the legs, Sarra gave an almighty heave—

Florins and lire showered to the ground in a glorious rainfall, scattering against the packed earth floor. They rolled beneath tables and stools, some not stopping until they hit the far wall. The reaction among the gamblers was immediate. Men abandoned their gossip in an instant, diving to their knees to reclaim their lost winnings, elbowing and shoving as they went.

Romano's guard released a pained yelp as somebody's flailing fist caught him in the sternum. He went down in the mill of bodies, swallowed by the chaos.

"*Rendezvous*," Sarra gritted at Giacomo, and dove toward the stable exit before her tenuously clear path could close. Her last sight of the player was of his eyes narrowing with some unknown determination. Then she was through the door and in the fiery night.

Even so close to the city's northern walls, the thoroughfares were crowded, men and women flooding toward the Piazza della Signoria where the Loggia dei Lanzi stood. A seething ripple of anger bubbled through the streets, souring the air. Sarra could feel it in her veins, venomous and . . . familiar.

Five years. That was the last time she had seen Florence in such a state—five years ago, when the newly anointed Pope Leo X and his cousin had led the papal army to the gates of the city and demanded that rule be returned to the Medici family. She had only been a child, but she would never forget the upheaval in the streets and the terrified look on her father's face. He knew what the Medici and their invading army were capable of. All of Tuscany knew. News of Prato had spread throughout the city like a plague, contagious in its anguish and despair. It had been enough to cow the Florentine soldiers into standing aside for the Medici, leaving only those civilians willing to lay down their lives for the Republic to do just that.

Old grief choked Sarra's throat. She battled it back, digging her belt-kit out of her purse and flicking open the screwdriver. She had made a note of Romano's gelding when he'd arrived, and it was easy to find him in the stables now, stomping and huffing at the sounds of the riot.

Romano had kept the saddle buckles polished to a shine. This meant they were easy to spot in the dim light—easy to wedge her driver into, easy to bend out of shape. With a little luck, Romano wouldn't notice the damage until the straps went out from beneath him. With a little *more* luck, this would happen in the middle of a crowd. And with the most luck of all, this would mean that Sarra could beat him to the Casa Romano on foot.

Hanging all her hopes on a damaged bit of steel, Sarra scrambled into Florence's seething streets and *ran*.

18

KHALID

The minutes stretched, unending. Still, Rosa knelt by the strong-box door. The only thing moving was her fingers, twisting the slim lockpicks over and around each other. Khalid's hands ached just watching her.

Finally, after time had lost all meaning, there came a satisfying *pop*. The lock rotated. Rosa sat back with a satisfied grin. "There we go," she whispered, and swung the door back.

The inside of the safe was as organized as the rest of Captain Romano's study. Ledgers were stacked in a neat platform, supporting sheafs of paper, a velvet purse full of coin . . . and two iron keys joined together on a ring.

These Rosa plucked up. "You have the mold?" she asked.

Khalid nodded. Reaching into his belt-purse, he dug out a hinged metal case about the size of a deck of cards and passed it to her. Opening it revealed a spongy putty set into both halves. Rosa separated the keys and laid them in the box. Then, careful not to jostle them, she closed the lid, pressing the keys between the two halves.

"Think of it like plaster," Agata had informed Khalid, shouting to be heard over the grinding of the millstone. "If you press something into it, the plaster keeps that shape even after you take it away." She'd poked the surface of the putty in front of her. When she took her finger away, Khalid could read the ridges of her fingerprints in the indentation. "But unlike plaster, this won't dry out on you."

"How do you manage that?" Khalid had asked.

Agata's eyes had crinkled with a smile as she'd patted his cheek. "Never ask a witch her secrets, sweetling."

Thunk.

The sound of something small colliding with the windowsill was unmistakable. Rosa and Khalid froze. He raised a finger to his lips. "Stay here," he whispered. Rosa nodded, her attention already slipping back to the open strongbox.

Khalid crept toward the window, keeping low to the floor. With only the edge of his hand, he pushed the heavy curtains aside, just far enough to get a glimpse of the street below.

It was busier than it had been when they'd arrived. Men and women scurried past the house, in pairs and in small groups. Some were clutching onto one another as they moved. Others gripped clubs and axes and shovels in a way that did not indicate a workman's intent.

There was no sign of whoever had tossed the rock—not until a flicker of movement caught his eye beneath the awning next door. As Khalid peered through the darkness, someone ducked out from beneath the overhang into the moonlight, just long enough for Khalid to make out their face.

It was Sarra the Tinkerer. And she looked panicked.

"I believe," Khalid muttered, "that it is time for us to go." Sarra waved—*now, now, now.* "Now," Khalid added, dutifully echoing her. "Rosa?"

Rosa did not appear to have heard a single word Khalid said. One of Captain Romano's ledgers was open on her lap. A faint line creased her brow as she turned a page.

"What is that?" he asked.

"It seems as though Romano is growing a sense of paranoia," Rosa said. Khalid peered over her shoulder. The ledger page was full of the small, neat writing that Khalid recognized as that of Captain Romano. "What do you make of this?" Rosa asked.

It still surprised him, every time Rosa asked him such a question. Signore Traverio had never solicited his opinion of anything. Khalid squinted closer at the page. In his careful hand, Captain Romano had recorded a list of names and dates and, strangest of all, areas of the city. "'San Niccolo'?" Khalid read aloud.

"They're patrols," Rosa explained, flipping another page. "Guardsmen, the dates of their employ, and their patrols."

"But San Niccolo is not a neighborhood under Medici jurisdiction."

"These men aren't in the Medici Guard," Rosa said. "San Niccolo . . . Porta Romana . . . Porta Prato. These are the patrol routes of the Florentine City Guard." She squinted closer. "Santini. Wasn't that the Guard Captain who gave Giacomo the vendor list?"

"Yes."

"Looks like he was generous with more than just gate records." She tapped her mouth, eyes distant. "But what would the Medici want with intel on the City Guard?"

We are just trying to lighten the load on their shoulders, Sergeant Bianci had said. But Sarra was frantic below. There wasn't time to unravel this mystery. "We need to go, Rosa."

"Just one more moment," she said, flicking through another page.

Somewhere downstairs, the front door burst inward so hard it hit the wall. *Captain Romano.* "*Rosa*," Khalid hissed.

The sound of heavy footsteps jarred Rosa out of her thoughts.

"*The keys*," she whispered. Khalid hinged the impression box open with gentle fingers. Carefully—*so carefully*—he lifted the keys free. The imprint left behind was clear. Khalid let out a sigh of relief. Rosa plucked the keys out of his hand and slipped them back into the strongbox, swinging the bookshelf back over the safe door.

The City Guard ledger was still clutched to her chest. "Will he not notice that it is gone?"

"Probably," Rosa said. "No harm in pouring a little kerosene on his paranoia." She slipped over to the door, easing it open enough to get a glimpse of the corridor outside.

A pair of feet shuffled nearby. Khalid nearly had a heart attack. Rosa didn't look much better off as she jolted back from the door. "*Caro?*" Signora Romano called, her voice echoing as she moved toward the stairs. "Is that you? Oh—what's happened to you?"

"My damned saddle gave out. Where are the children?" That was unmistakably Captain Romano, brusque and tense.

"Asleep," his wife responded. "What's going on?"

Rosa inched the door closed. "We won't be able to get downstairs without being spotted."

There was nothing else for it. "Then we will not go downstairs."

Sarra was gone when Khalid drew back the curtain. He gingerly released the window latch, allowing the twin panes to swing outward over the street.

"There's a trellis here," Rosa whispered. She was leaning on the window ledge beside Khalid, shoving the ledger down the front of her bodice. "It leads up to the roof next door."

"Go," he hissed. He could hear Captain Romano's heavy footsteps climbing the stairs. If one of them was to be found out, it would be better if it was him. Rosa might still be able to carry off her scheme without Khalid. "I will follow."

She was gone in a flourish of gray skirts, ascending the creaking wooden trellis as though the climb was nothing. One of the struts gave a threatening pop as she clutched the edge of the roof, and a few red-green leaves fluttered to the ground. Still, impossibly, no one seemed to have noticed. Traffic in the streets had only increased since Khalid had opened the curtains. Now there were more people moving toward the city center than away from it. He could vaguely pick out the distant sounds of shouting. It sent the hairs on the back of his neck on end.

". . . out of the city as soon as possible. I'll give you money for the journey—"

Khalid was almost on the ledge when Captain Romano's voice filtered through the office door. Instinctively, he glanced toward the strongbox, recalling the coin purse inside.

His stomach turned over. The bookshelf still stood ajar. The gap could not have been more than a few centimeters and if the room had belonged to anyone but Captain Romano, Khalid would not have hesitated in his escape. But the captain was a man of precision, and if anything in this chamber was out of place . . .

Willing his feet into silence, Khalid raced back across the room. He heard Rosa hiss his name in a panicked whisper, but there was no time to explain himself, to ask her permission. As firmly as he dared, he pressed in on the bookshelf, not stopping until he felt the latch click into place.

He would have to trust that this had done the trick. He sensed rather than heard Captain Romano stop outside the study door. Spinning on his heel, Khalid sped toward the open window. In the hall, a hand landed on the doorknob just as Khalid swung over the windowsill and out onto the ledge. It took every ounce of restraint not to slam the window shut behind him, but he managed to ease the panes closed with sweaty, careful fingertips.

Through the glass, the study door swung open. Khalid ducked out of sight just as Captain Romano stalked inside. He held his breath, watching the captain draw up short just in front of the bookcase, awaiting the dreadful inevitable—

But Captain Romano only swung the bookshelf aside. Then there was the scrape of a key, and the strongbox was creaking open just long enough for the man to grab his coin purse. He slammed the safe closed with far less care than Khalid and Rosa, leaving the bookcase ajar in his haste back into the hallway, to his waiting wife. As soon as he was gone, Khalid, still balanced on the ledge, sagged in relief.

"*Khalid!*" Rosa hissed his name from the next rooftop, her wild-haired head just visible. Khalid scrambled forward in a lurch, grabbing at the rungs of the trellis with both hands. The wood splintered and cracked beneath his weight as he hauled himself upward, losing no more seconds to caution.

One hand grasped the rooftop. Then the other. Then Khalid was heaving himself over the edge and sprawling onto the terra-cotta tiles beside Rosa, trying not to gasp for breath.

"Christ," she muttered. "*Christ.*"

"We have to go," he managed.

"In your own time," she deadpanned. With a burst of effort, he flipped onto his stomach and dragged himself across the roof, Rosa close behind him.

The descent was a much less fraught experience. Soon, Khalid and Rosa were hurrying along the streets of the Santa Maria Novella quarter, lost in the manic energy of the crowds.

"This way," Rosa whispered, veering onto a quieter street lined with well-kept, modest houses and shops. Every window was covered, the shutters closed. No one who lived in this neighborhood wanted anything to do with the unrest brewing in the city center.

"What is all that?" Khalid asked. In the distance, glass shattered.

"I don't know," Rosa said. Her face was troubled. Khalid shared the sentiment.

The rendezvous had been set at a toolshed behind an elderly carpenter's workshop. Sarra was already waiting when they arrived. "Oh, thank the Lord," she muttered as they ducked inside. "What took you so long?" She squinted at the lump in Rosa's dress. "What is that?"

Rosa dug the ledger free. "Just some of Captain Romano's reading material."

"Is that why you almost got caught?"

Even Khalid could see that Rosa bristled under Sarra's scolding tone. "We got the keys," she said, a little defensively.

"Well, thank God for that, at least," Sarra said. She was yanking the laces of her kirtle. Khalid tactfully looked away. "No one is ever getting another shot at Romano. You should have seen him at the gambling den, he's been shamed out of it for *life*—"

The distant shattering of glass sent a pause through all of them. "Do we know . . . what that is?" Rosa asked.

"Those idiots with the anti-Medici bills," Sarra said. She dug a pair of hose out of a flour sack. Khalid did the same with his guard uniform, rushing to swap the shapeless, dark clothes he was wearing for familiar Medici blue. "One got caught. His friends have been whipping the city up in a storm."

"Where is Giacomo?" Khalid asked. The question had been sparking since they'd reached the shed. Now, with all the talk of protests, it surged with urgency. "Did he not leave with you?"

Sarra buttoned her doublet, blowing copper hair out of her eyes. "That's the other thing."

Rosa's eyebrow quirked. "The other thing?"

"The other-other thing. Giacomo was doing fine, running the bassetta table—he had Romano on a leash. But then these two men came in, looking for the captain. Giacomo took one look at them and just froze."

"He froze? Giacomo?"

"Stone-still. He blew the rest of the game. Then the riot started and Romano left. I told him to meet us here, but I haven't seen him. As far as I know, he's still at the gambling den."

Rosa chewed her lip. "Did these men say anything to Giacomo?"

"Not that I could tell," Sarra said. "They were wealthy. And they had business with Romano that Romano didn't want to deal with." She fastened the last button, blue eyes focused. "Loredan was one of them. And . . . Petrucci."

Petrucci. The name conjured up brief images. A stack of green journals. A small, dreary stone-walled office.

Giacomo's face as he grilled the hapless captain of the City Guard.

These Petruccis must be a hungry bunch.

"The city is a nightmare right now," Rosa was saying. "Where could he have gone?"

Khalid unclenched his jaw. "I may have an idea."

19

GIACOMO

This is a mistake.

The thought bobbed through Giacomo's mind like an apple over river rapids. He beat it down as he left the gambling hall, trailing in the wake of Signore Petrucci. He refused it again as he turned onto the worn cobbles of the Mercato Vecchio, watching the maroon velvet cap sidestep the crowds with authoritative ease. And he valiantly drowned the thought once more when the gates of Casa Petrucci loomed in front of him, framed by two guards in eye-searing red-and-white and opening to allow the master of the house inside.

It was only when those gates clanged shut that he allowed the thought a gasp of air.

This is a mistake.

The thing was—the thing *was*—that Giacomo really shouldn't be doing this. He shouldn't be *here*, outside this expensive house on the outskirts of the Mercato Vecchio—and he was aware now, in a distant sort of way, that the atmosphere of the Piazza and its surrounding streets had taken a tangible dive in the hours since he'd arrived at the gambling hall.

However. Reading the name *Petrucci* at the Porta Romano those weeks ago had left Giacomo at odds with himself in a manner to which he was *entirely* unaccustomed. He'd *known* that they were in town somewhere, or at least that they would be very presently. And Giacomo san Giacomo had braved ruffians and miscreants and Khalid al-Sarraj just after he'd destroyed his lunch. So why had he been so panicked by the thought of encountering this house?

He had done everything in his power to avoid the slightest *whiff* of the name Petrucci. And he had been successful, too. Right up until Signore Petrucci had loaded himself onto a platter and served himself up right to Giacomo's bassetta table. *Here I am,* he'd said. *What are you going to do about it?*

It had blown a hole in Giacomo's panicked self-preservation, left him taking on water. And now here he was, exactly where he should not be, because—

He'd done four years of waiting. And now that the door was cracked open, he had to know. He *had to.*

Giacomo's steps did not falter as he strode past the menacing guards and rounded the corner of the Casa Petrucci, ducking into the small alley that bordered the rear of the house.

He had smelled worse things in his life—for God's sake, he'd smelled worse himself—but this back street *reeked,* and when his foot splashed into a puddle of something that was definitely not water, he shuddered. But there was no time to obsess over whatever was soaking his stocking—the servants' entrance was only a few meters away. That door could open at any moment, and Giacomo did not want to have to explain himself to whatever harried maidservant tumbled through. He would have to be smart about this, and perhaps also canny, which was a struggle when every instinct was urging him to yank the door open and storm inside.

Taking a step back, Giacomo pursed his lips and began to whistle.

It was a trick he'd cultivated as a boy running wild through the hills of Grosseto. Even then he had been fascinated by imitation— not yet knitting new personas and personalities, but he'd had to begin somewhere. And for Giacomo, it had begun with birdsong. Imitating their whistles and chirps had been a challenge, one to which he had applied himself until he could mimic them so well the birds would not flee until he was practically beside them.

His family had despaired of this as a tiresome waste of time. They had called him a fool and a layabout and a—

Well. *Most* of his family had called him that.

What emerged from Giacomo's lips was not a human's whistle, but the lively and upbeat song of the mustached warbler, a tiny songbird native to Grosseto. It had been one of his favorites, as cheerful as it was—and it had been one of hers as well, the impression she had requested most from him, especially over the long, cold winter months.

Was he going mad, or had the curtains of the left upstairs window twitched?

Giacomo whistled again, loud enough that any passing birdwatcher would have feared a small bird was being violently murdered. He whistled and whistled, eyes pinned to that curtain, willing it to move, to give any indication that there was someone on the other side who heard him and knew him.

"Hey!"

The birdsong evaporated. Giacomo whipped around. In his fascination with the curtains, he'd forgotten to keep watch on the end of the alley, and now the two red-and-white-striped guards were bearing down on him, scowling and sour. The one on the left, whose wide sideburns covered most of his cheeks, was already grasping his sword.

Giacomo slumped against the wall, ignoring the smear of something organic and brown that transferred to his jacket. "Signore!" he greeted them, as cheerfully as he could manage. "*Two* signori! Or are you two?" He leaned forward, almost toppling onto his face. "I may," he said, whispering too loudly, "have had . . . a few drinks."

"We better get him out of here," the sideburned guard muttered to his friend, "before Master Petrucci hears him."

"Shhh," Giacomo said, stumbling closer. "Don't tell Master Petrucci!"

"Do we need to report this?" the clean-shaven guard asked over Giacomo's head.

Giacomo hiccuped like a man about to puke all over the nearest person's shoes. The sideburned guard stepped out of the line of fire. "Do you *want* to report this?" he said.

Another hiccup sent the clean-shaven guard rolling his eyes. "Come on," he said. "Move it along. Don't let us catch you back here again."

"Such *kindness*! " Giacomo slurred, reaching out to pat the sideburned guard on the shoulder. The guard sidestepped him, sending Giacomo stumbling. "I shall always remember you wonderful men—"

The curtains were open. And like Giacomo had dreamed so many times . . . there she was. Staring down at him with wide eyes.

The last time he had seen her, he had not been Giacomo san Giacomo at all. He had been—well, younger, for starters. Fifteen, and kinder, slower, softer. Happier. Definitely he had been stupider. Until—*until*—

Giulietta Petrucci. He could never mistake the curl of graying chestnut hair that fell over her eyes, or the way her mouth moved as it shaped the question of his name.

He dipped his chin in a nod.

This, of course, was a *dreadful* impulse, and had he been operating with full faculties he would have kicked his own ass from Florence to Naples and back again. Within a moment, the sideburned guard had a grip on Giacomo's collar and was hauling him around. "What was that?" he hissed into Giacomo's face, so close that Giacomo could feel spittle landing on his cheeks.

His stomach turned at the feeling of the man's hammy fist clenched so tightly on his clothes. "What?" The drunken slur came easier now, his tongue turning to cotton in his mouth.

"Giorgio." The clean-shaven guard had his eyes pinned to Giulietta's window. It was empty now, but the curtains were swaying. "Our lady has an admirer."

Guardsman Giorgio tightened his hand on Giacomo's collar, which was strange because Giacomo felt the pressure in his wrists. His hands felt *heavy*. Christ almighty, he was losing it—"Lady?" he gasped. The alley wall was pressing into his back, and a droplet of something cold and wet plummeted from the gutter, straight down his neck. He flinched. In the distance, he could hear the *click* of wood on wood, a familiar, nauseating sound. "Not at all, signore, I was just finding my way home—"

"Finding your way to Signora Petrucci's bedroom window," the clean-shaven guard said, circling around to Giacomo's other side. He was penned in now, a wall at his back and two hulks of muscle surrounding him, and the sound of wood on wood was deafening—

"Ave Maria, gratia plena, Dominus tecum—"

Click-click *went the beads in his fingers—*

Giacomo pressed himself back as far as he could go. "I was not looking at *anyone*, signore, I can *assure* you—"

Pain flashed, hot and fast, before Giacomo even had the chance to process the fact that Giorgio had slammed the hilt of his sword into Giacomo's ribs. He crashed backward, one hand clutching at his side—

"Benedicta tu in mulieribus—"

"Shut up," someone said, their voice coming from so deep underwater that Giacomo could not tell who had spoken. His vision was fuzzing out, blurring and twisting. A hand winched tighter in his collar, and Giacomo tried to bring his arm up to shield his face, but the manacles were back and they weighed him down—

"Et benedictus fructus ventris tui, Iesus—"

"Again," *whispered Father Bernardo.*

"Hold him," ordered one of the red-white blobs, before raising something over his head.

"I will guide you," said Father Bernardo.

And it was all Giacomo could do to close his eyes and murmur "Amen."

20

KHALID

These Petruccis must be a hungry bunch.

Giacomo san Giacomo wore a careful mask of flightiness every moment he was awake. The gatehouse at the Porta Romana—that was the first time Khalid had glimpsed the man underneath. He had a suspicion that anyone who hadn't spent three years making a study of Giacomo and all his mannerisms wouldn't have noticed the fracture. But in that fleeting moment, to Khalid, Giacomo had been an open wound.

Open enough to bleed all over their plans, evidently.

Khalid ran faster.

If the streets near the Casa Romano had been agitated, then those closer to the river were pure chaos. Shouts and crashing rang out on all sides. Every alley Khalid passed revealed a flicker of tumult—men carrying torches and makeshift weapons, guards in Medici and City Guard colors, shrieking women and children.

Khalid's own Medici blue was, perhaps, a liability. He frequently found himself the target of insults and curses as he ran, weaving through the madness. No one had dared to slam an elbow or a club into him, but Khalid thought it was only a matter of time before this changed.

The Mercato Vecchio was deserted when he skidded into it. This was an eerie sight to behold. On a typical day, the Mercato was a filthy, lively Piazza where a person could purchase anything they might desire. Now, the only signs of life were the prowling silhouettes of guardsmen, hunting for trouble.

Khalid kept his distance and moved on.

A curt question to a scuttling peddler pointed him to the Casa

Petrucci, a squat and solid mansion on the east side of the Piazza. It was unmanned when Khalid approached, the gates free of guards despite the nearby cries of protesters. Khalid's unease grew. If the Petrucci family was as wealthy as Sarra had estimated, there was no reason this should be the case.

And that was when he heard the voices.

They were a muddle, too quiet for Khalid to pick out anything more than their direction. He felt for his sword, following the sound past the gates and around the building, toward the gloomy mouth of a small alley where the voices were clearer.

It took Khalid a moment to identify Giacomo's. He had never heard Giacomo speak in that tone before, and he had heard Giacomo put on every persona under the sun. Now, the player's voice had a foreign edge to it, sharp and high and tense. He stuttered the beginning of something that might have been "Please."

A man cut him off, deep and a little gleeful. "Hold him."

Khalid rounded into the alley and solved the mystery of the missing Petrucci Guards. Two men in red-and-white uniforms had a third man pinned up against the alley wall. One was drawing his sword. In a few dozen steps, Khalid was standing behind him just as the man brought the weapon to bear.

"Guardsmen," he said.

Khalid could move quietly when he wanted to. It was a talent he had been born with. His brother had not appreciated it, given that one of Khalid's favorite activities had been sneaking up on him. Signore Traverio *had* appreciated it, because an enforcer who appeared out of thin air was more terrifying than one you could hear coming.

The Petrucci Guardsmen fell more in Yusuf's camp. The swears were ear-scalding. Khalid's expression did not shift.

"Thank you for finding my charge," he said, keeping his gaze pinned to the guards. He could spot the edges of Giacomo in the gap between the guards' shoulders. There was something off about his posture, the way he was slumped against the bricks, but Khalid did not dare examine it closer. Not when the guard had not put down his sword.

It was this guardsman who spoke up first. "This fool is under your care?" he asked, his eyes flicking from the top of Khalid's hat down to his boots and back again. Khalid watched in cool disinterest as the man's Adam's apple bobbed in a gulp.

"He slipped away from me earlier," Khalid said.

"Seems he found a tavern or two in the meantime," the younger guard muttered. Behind them, Giacomo had the presence of mind to unleash a body-shuddering hiccup.

"Cardinal de' Medici will be most displeased to learn he is in such a state." Khalid allowed himself a proper look at Giacomo. He was clutching at his ribs tight enough to turn his knuckles white. But there was something else that sparked an ember of worry within Khalid. Giacomo's eyes were . . . strange. That warm brown gaze, typically so lively, was fuzzed and distant, as though Giacomo was watching something that was not really there.

"Cardinal de' Medici?" The younger guard went green against his uniform.

His partner was not so easily intimidated. "He was harassing the lady of this house," he said. "Master Petrucci is adamant that such trespasses are punished."

Lady? Most of the curtains of the Casa Petrucci were drawn, but there was a window on the second story that stood open, shades flung wide. There was no sign of movement beyond.

"Feel free to petition the Medici for the right to do so," Khalid said. "I trust that you know where they live." Reaching between the guards, he grabbed hold of an unresisting Giacomo by the collar and hauled him forward. "Good evening, Guardsmen."

"So nice to meet you!" Giacomo slurred. His feet were dragging against the cobbles. Khalid realized that he was not focusing on the guards at all. Giacomo's eyes kept sliding to that empty second-story window.

But the window was no longer empty. A small face peered down, tanned and heart-shaped and framed by gray-brown curls. A lady, just as the guards had said. She was watching Khalid and Giacomo with wide eyes. And Giacomo was watching her back.

Irritation swamped Khalid. "Hurry *up*," he hissed, and gave Giacomo a bit of a shove. They emerged onto the Via degli Speziali, and Khalid reeled at the tidal wave of sound and chaos. He had forgotten the riot. He had seen Giacomo on the verge of blowing their entire scheme apart by getting himself stabbed and the ensuing panic had chased the riot from his mind. Now it all came rushing back. He tightened his grip on Giacomo's collar and steered him left, away from the Mercato Vecchio and the Loggia and the uproar, and toward the Arno river.

He wanted to shake Giacomo. He refrained. He wanted to demand to know who the woman in the window was. He refrained from that too. He would be a professional, even if Giacomo would not. He would control himself. He would not *lose his head* over some *random woman*. He kept moving, kept Giacomo stumbling, weaving toward the Ponte Vecchio.

But what could possibly have possessed Giacomo to do such a foolish thing? Khalid had never known him to be careless. He had certainly never known him to be swayed by a pretty face if there was something serious on the line. Maybe Giacomo was madder than Khalid had given him credit for. Maybe it was true, what people said about him.

Maybe Khalid was the foolish one, for thinking too highly of him.

Maybe Signore Traverio had been right, and Khalid should leave insight to the schemers.

They had nearly reached the bridge when Khalid realized that something was wrong. He had kept his grip on the back of Giacomo's collar, partly because he was irritated and partly as a reassurance to himself that Giacomo had not disappeared again. For his part, Giacomo had done well to keep up with Khalid's punishing pace, even as the city surged and swelled around them. But then Khalid's foot slipped on a loose cobble and he wrenched accidentally at Giacomo's collar. And in that split second, he heard a whimper.

It was animalistic, a noise that might be kicked out of a stray dog. But it had come from Giacomo, ripped from his throat. Khalid looked at him, through the haze of worry and frustration. He could see that the dazed cast of Giacomo's gaze had only grown more intense. There was something harrowed about him now. Something hunted.

Khalid stopped in a circle of lamplight outside a boot-maker's shop. Giacomo stopped with him. Now that they were no longer moving, Khalid could feel that the other man was quaking, tremors that ran through his entire body. "Giacomo?" Khalid released his collar, reaching what he hoped was a comforting hand toward Giacomo's wrist.

The flinch took Khalid by surprise. Giacomo snatched his hands away, backing up. "Don't—" he said, a choked, awful word. He squeezed his eyes shut. When he opened them again, Khalid was relieved to see that some of the fuzziness had cleared.

"Hah," Giacomo said. The smile he slid on was brittle. He clasped his hands behind his back, out of Khalid's reach. "For Heaven's sake, Signore al-Sarraj. A modicum of care, please."

There was a clatter behind them. The boot-maker, on edge from the chaos, had slammed his shutters closed and latched them. Khalid ignored him. "Are you alright?"

"Oh, I'm fine," Giacomo said breezily. There was sweat standing out on his forehead. He ran a finger around the collar of his doublet, frowning at whatever he found. "It's this embroidery I'm worried about, I mean *honestly*, do you know how expensive this is? To have that *beast* of a guard manhandling it, and then you? Don't you have appreciation for artistry?" The color was coming back to his cheeks. "You can stop hovering, Signore al-Sarraj, it's not as though I'm going to run. Where on earth would I go?"

Khalid crossed his arms. Giacomo's transition from pale and wobbly to sharp and biting left him wrong-footed. "You would think of something."

"I never would have anticipated such faith from you, I may die of shock—"

"What was that?" Khalid demanded, the intensity surprising even himself.

"Hm?" Giacomo's brown eyes were wide and innocent as he adjusted his collar and cuffs. But when Khalid took a step forward, Giacomo scrambled back again. "Alright, alright, alright—listen to me—just listen for one single solitary moment—"

"I am listening," Khalid said. "You are not saying anything."

"Don't tell Rosa. Please."

Khalid's face must have been a picture. "Those men could have killed you."

"But they didn't."

"You could have been caught by the City Guards."

"I know, but—"

"This plan does not work without you. None of us get paid without you." *Without you, my family is destroyed. Without you, I am doomed.*

"I'm *aware*." Giacomo rolled his eyes at Khalid, an imitation of his normal persona. "I give you my word that it won't happen again. That means I promise. I promise that I won't—"

"I know what it means," Khalid bit back. Giacomo was trying to needle him off-topic.

Giacomo must have noticed that it was working, because he grinned and stepped back into the street. Shoving his hands into his belt, he began to meander toward the Ponte Vecchio. "My word's no good to you?" Khalid grunted and hurried to catch up. "How about this instead? I will give you five percent of my cut if you let this little adventure slide."

Somewhere in Florence, Signore Traverio was laughing at him. *I want it all*, he'd said. And here was Giacomo, bargaining with something he could not keep.

"Come on," Giacomo wheedled. He was too used to Khalid's silences to be suspicious of this one. "What do you say? You're a reasonable man, Signore al-Sarraj, I know that. A reasonable, intelligent, clever, level-headed—"

"How do I trust you?" Khalid asked.

"How can anyone trust anyone?" Giacomo said, with a prayerful sigh. "We are all liars and thieves, doomed to spend our days back-stabbing and squabbling—"

The man was impossible. "What did you want with that woman?"

Giacomo grimaced. "You saw," he said. It wasn't a question, but Khalid nodded anyway. Giacomo's shoulders dropped. "She's—who that woman is—has nothing to do with our job. I *swear*." They were nearly to the Ponte Vecchio, the City Guards posted there watching their approach with suspicion. "That's—all I can say. I'm sorry. Please don't make me lie to you."

It felt more like the truth than anything else Giacomo had said. Khalid inclined his head to the guards, who reluctantly stood aside. He did not miss the sneers they aimed at his uniform.

"You don't lie," Khalid muttered to Giacomo. "You distract."

"Oh?" Giacomo said. They were out of reach of the lamplight

now. Giacomo's face was all silhouette, but mischief dripped from his words. "You want me to distract you?"

Khalid's stomach twisted, sickening and sudden. "No."

"That's what I thought." Giacomo shivered in the cold river wind. "Look, I promise it won't happen again. I am very aware that you won't always be around to bail me out when big strong guards want to punch my teeth in, and I know it's asking a lot, but I really am begging you not to tell Rosa." There was a brush at Khalid's sleeve. Giacomo had pinched the fabric, just a little, just enough to get Khalid to look at him. "You wanted to know how you could trust me, right?" he asked. He was fully back now, the light behind his eyes rekindled. "If I pull something like that again, the odds are excellent that I won't get paid, due to arrest or torture or being dead. And," he continued, "isn't 'trusting' just what we have to do? You could turn me in tomorrow. So could Sarra or Agata. God knows why Il Divino hasn't. But I suppose, if one of us goes down, all of us go down. So. Trust." He spread his hands. "Trust me."

Khalid could not comprehend saying such a thing so easily. But in the moonlight, Giacomo's smile was earnest and his eyes were bright. The picture of an honest man.

"Ten percent," Khalid said, picking up the pace.

Giacomo scrambled to keep up with him. "Of my cut? Do you want to bleed me dry?"

"Ten percent."

"Six," said Giacomo.

"Ten percent."

"You're doing this the wrong way. You're supposed to say nine, and then I'll say seven."

"Ten percent."

"I have *expenses*, Signore al-Sarraj—" Giacomo moaned.

Khalid let himself enjoy the familiar, bickering rhythm. There was only so long he would have it. Sooner or later, Khalid's debt would come due, and after that—

Khalid al-Sarraj did not trust anyone in this business. If Giacomo did not share that mistrust . . . he would by the time the job was done.

21

SARRA

The shouts across the river had diminished, leaving the air heavy with silence as Sarra and Rosa trudged through San Niccolo. The city gates had been barred to contain the chaos that still roiled within, and with their mill out of reach until daylight, Rosa would be spending the night at Michelangelo's workshop.

"There's always the print shop," Sarra offered. "You could sleep there—"

"I have some work to do," Rosa said. It shouldn't have felt like a stinging rejection, but it did. "I don't want to keep you awake." Rosa drummed her fingers on the cover of her ledger, clutching it tightly to her chest as they walked.

That ledger. Rosa had not let it out of her sight since the rendez-vous, and she had not explained it to Sarra with more than enigmatic smiles. And despite the steady stream of empty reassurances, her dark eyes were unfocused, fixed on something far away.

"Giacomo better not have gotten himself killed," Sarra said, searching Rosa's face for some—any—reaction. *Find the Lady.*

"Mm," Rosa hummed, as though Sarra had just pointed out that the sky was blue. Her fingers drummed again. "He won't. Khalid can handle him."

Sarra fought the urge to scream. "How about the riot? Can he handle that, too?"

Rosa's eyes were black marbles. "The riot isn't our concern."

"Those protesters set half the city rabid!" Sarra argued. "I haven't seen Florence like this since I was a child. You weren't here when the Medici retook it, you don't understand—"

"I don't understand?" Rosa asked. Her smile was sharp, its corners edged, jagged enough to set Sarra back a pace. Then it eroded, edges sanding smooth into something more welcoming and familiar. "It's been a long night. Excellent work today—I'm sure you're worried about your brother—"

The mention of Pietro sent a zing through Sarra—she hadn't been able to check on him, and with all the chaos in the streets, who knew what might have happened—

But this frenzied anxiety was what Rosa wanted, and Sarra was getting better at seeing through that practiced smile to what lay beneath. "You remember what you promised me, don't you?" she asked. Rosa just cocked her head. "You promised this job was just about money," Sarra said. "You said it wasn't personal."

"I'm afraid I don't follow."

Sarra ground to a stop. She needed Rosa's full attention for this. "Stealing the keys—that's part of the plan. That's about money. This?" She jabbed at the ledger, damning. "You almost got caught for it."

"But we didn't."

"*Rosa.*" Sarra took a deep breath, fighting down her temper. "What's in the ledger."

"Nothing you need to worry about."

"Nothing? No, don't shut me out," she said, and wished it didn't sound so much like a plea. "I can't help you if you won't show me the full picture. I *want* to help you with whatever it is. It's what our parents would—"

"*We are not our parents.*"

The words snapped out of Rosa. But the fury only lasted long enough for Sarra to blink in surprise. A moment later, Rosa's injured snarl had been replaced by a perfect mask of accommodating, if tired, politeness. "Sorry," Rosa said. "The adrenaline is wearing off. I'd like to get some sleep."

Rosa was not alone in her exhaustion. It gritted Sarra's eyelids and hung weights on her limbs, bearing her down. And she knew a losing battle when she met one. "Whatever you think is best," she said. She and Rosa bid frosty farewells and set off in opposite directions—Sarra toward Nepi Printing, and Rosa to the workshop.

Against all odds, signs of the riot across the river were almost nonexistent in the Oltrarno. Still, it was impossible to ignore the hushed whispers and tense shoulders of the Oltrarno's denizens. Sarra moved as fast as she could without drawing suspicion, trotting through the familiar maze of streets to the print shop.

"Pietro?" she called, unlatching the front door. "Are you awake?"

There was no response.

Anxiety—already a low simmer—rose to a boil in the pit of Sarra's stomach. Pietro was a light sleeper. Even if he had already sacked out for the night, he would have roused to grumble at Sarra for waking him. Not bothering to soften her footsteps, Sarra pounded up the stairs to the second floor. "Pietro?"

The kitchen was dark. The silence was suffocating. And the pallet by the fire was empty and cold.

There was no sign of her brother anywhere.

Her first impulse was to panic. What if he had gotten swept up in the protests? What if he had gotten injured in the crush, trampled or beaten? What if the Medici Guards had taken him for a rioter—Pietro had a kind heart, he might have been helping one of the instigators and been apprehended as a collaborator by mistake—he could have been thrown into a Medici cell—he could have been tossed in a ditch, bruised and broken—

Calm down. Sarra marshaled her breathing into order. There was no sense in getting frantic. There was no logical reason to suspect that Pietro had been anywhere near the riots this evening. No. No, he likely had taken himself to the tavern to gossip with his friends. He would come stumbling home at some small hour, smelling of ale and with a thousand theories about what had happened, courtesy of whatever drunkard had convinced Pietro to buy him a drink.

She changed into her chemise and tucked her jerkin and hose away, but still she could not bring herself to climb into bed. Her nerves would not allow it. Instead, she wrapped a shawl around her shoulders, poured a cup of wine, and plucked up a book, settling herself at the kitchen table. She then proceeded to neither drink the wine nor read the book and spent all her energy staring at the empty second-landing door, willing her brother to appear.

It could have been a lifetime—it *felt* like a lifetime—or it could have been thirty minutes, but just when Sarra was considering raiding every tavern in Florence in search of Pietro, she heard the front door open. Pietro's heavy footsteps were next, tromping across the creaking floorboards and up the steps. She surged to her feet, nearly upending her yet-untouched cup and, to her horror, discovered that there were tears of relief pricking at her eyes.

"Where have you been?" she hissed the moment Pietro reached the landing.

He stared at her. For a moment she thought that his vision was just adjusting to the low candlelight, but when she took a moment to study his face, she could make out the deep circles beneath his eyes and the long rip along the side of his cloak. He seemed to be struggling to place her in the kitchen at all, as though his mind could not wrap itself around her presence. "Pietro?" she ventured, gentler this time.

Pietro shook himself out of the fog. His fingers were sure at the clasp of his cloak. He didn't bother to hide the tear in the cloth as he draped it over the wall peg. "You're back."

"I'm—*you're* back!" Sarra said, irritation flaring. "Didn't you hear what happened?"

"I heard." His heavy steps carried him toward Sarra, but he did not look at her.

"So you decided to go to the pub? You should have told me, I've been worried sick—"

He plucked up Sarra's wine and took a swig. "I would have," he said. "But I haven't had the opportunity to tell you much lately."

It would be so easy to tell him. Every part of her—still stinging from Rosa's walled-off smile and *We are not our parents*—screamed to come clean. But—

"I've been so busy with the deliveries," Sarra said.

Pietro put the cup down. "The de' Baldis must do good business. To keep you so late."

"Mm," Sarra said.

Pietro finally met her eyes. She wished he hadn't. There was sadness there, deep sadness that grew deeper by the second. "Sarra," he said, then stopped.

"What is it?"

He shook his head, turning back to the door. "I'm sleeping downstairs tonight," he said. "In case anyone tries the front door."

"But—"

"Tell the de' Baldis not to worry about keeping you out," he said. "I've learned not to wait for you." He paused in the doorway, just the briefest of hesitations. "Feel free to return the favor."

And then the door closed, shutting Sarra in with her loneliness.

22

ROSA

"Are you going to vomit?"

The jostling of the carriage added a staccato to her words as they bounced across the cobblestones. Despite the fact that, in deference to his gentle artistic temperament and the fact that he was the one most likely to fracture and blow up her entire life, Rosa had allowed Michelangelo the honor of the forward-facing bench, the artist was still green from the tip of his chin to the tops of his bushy eyebrows. "No," he said.

Rosa didn't believe him. Michelangelo had been on the verge of a breakdown ever since the riot, and Rosa had taken to extending her hours in his workshop just to make sure he did not suffer a total collapse and shout their plans at the top of his lungs.

He was your idea! Sarra's words echoed in her mind on a loop, and Rosa fought back the reflexive swell of frustration in her gut. She had spent five long years working her way to where she was, taking jobs with every sort of person under the sun. On no team had she seen the second challenge the leader the way that Sarra challenged her.

Well. That wasn't entirely true. Matteo Nepi and Lena Cellini . . . they had been different. Argumentative, certainly. But also—

Family.

She pushed the thought down. This carriage was not the place to be mulling over that particular issue. Not when there was another problem—a bearded, sulking one—that demanded her immediate attention.

"What," Rosa teased Michelangelo. "Don't tell me you're having second thoughts?"

He glared at her over his crossed arms. "I'm not used to this."

"No one is used to this," she said. "I'm not used to this. I've never met a Pope before. But we've only a few minutes 'til we arrive at the Palazzo, and I am going to need you to look less as though you're going to spew your breakfast. So what can I do to make that happen?"

He turned, if anything, greener. *Easy*, she reminded herself. *Easy*.

"You've already seen Cardinal de' Medici," she said. "The world didn't end. What's different this time?"

Michelangelo's jaw was so tight she could barely make out his response. "The—the Palazzo. I haven't been back. Not since . . . the end of the Republic." His face hardened, and the next words came sharp and vicious. "I know I want no part in whatever future they plan for this city. But—that place—"

Rosa nodded. "I always was taught—we learn places by filling them with memories. And if that place sours, then it rots like an open wound. The memories too." She didn't look out at the street, at the buildings and statues and alleys as they rolled past. "You will step inside that Palazzo, and it will feel for a moment as though you are traveling back in time. Like you're an apprentice again, with all the good and bad that entails." They were nearly to their destination, and she was willing to risk a bit of tough love if it pulled Michelangelo out of his self-reflective mire. "Are you telling me you'll take one look around, then hand me to the guards?"

His chin went up. His cheeks looked a little rosier. "You overestimate the hold the Medici have over me."

"Good," Rosa said, as the carriage swayed to a halt. "Prove it."

They were expected, and so there was a modest honor guard waiting at the Palazzo, two men in blue uniforms lining each side of the gates. Cardinal de' Medici emerged as the carriage rolled to a stop, his gaze cool on the footmen who scurried forward to unlatch the carriage door.

Rosa had walked past the Palazzo countless times over the last weeks, noting every detail—the guard patrols, the eyelines to the windows, the foot traffic at all times of the day. But there was a difference between studying the minutiae and taking in the grandeur of the Palazzo as a whole. Even with her well-practiced professional remove, she only barely saved herself from stumbling as one of the footmen helped her from the carriage.

Amusement shaded the Cardinal's dour face. "Have a care, my child."

She blushed and bobbed a curtsy. "Your Eminence," she said. "It's just so *wonderful*. I've never seen anything like it in my whole life."

Michelangelo stomped down the carriage steps behind her. "The rest is pretty nice too."

"Quite," Cardinal de' Medici said, and swept back through the Palazzo's front gates. Rosa's sideways glance caught Michelangelo's shrug, and so they trailed after the Cardinal, following in the wake of the scarlet robes.

The main courtyard of the Palazzo Medici was as Rosa had seen it in the blueprints. Covered walkways ringed the edges, surrounding an open, tiled space in the center, the overhangs supported by graceful columns. "Lovely," Rosa murmured, just loud enough so that Cardinal de' Medici might hear it.

"All the more lovely for having you here, signorina," the Cardinal responded. "Our humble home is flattered by your presence."

They came to a stop at the far end of the walkway and the Cardinal inclined his head to Rosa in apology. "I must steal your uncle for a few moments," he said. "There are some sensitive matters we must discuss, and I am afraid they would bore a gentle young lady."

Sensitive matters could only refer to the civil unrest, and Rosa felt a momentary pang at being excluded from the conversation. She wanted to know whether the Medici had been set back on their heels by the protests—whether they were nervous or even frightened—

But instead, she was being left to her own devices in the middle of the Palazzo under the assumption that she had every right to be there. This was too sweet a chance to pass up. "Of course, Your Eminence," she glowed. "I'm sure I can find something to entertain myself."

Rosa had noticed the entrance to the Magi Chapel the instant she had entered the courtyard. Now she took a meandering path toward it, stopping every few meters to marvel at a sculpture or to gingerly trace the petals of a flower. There may not have been any servants or guards around, but there was no telling who might be watching from one of the upper windows.

She paused when she reached the chapel, a young woman uncertain what was off-limits in her host's home. But Rosa was thrumming under her tentative facade, buzzing, brimming with lightning. She had seen the chapel so often in two dimensions, had traced the outlined walls over and over—and now, she could open the door and confirm everything she had imagined—

She stepped into the dark.

Blueprints didn't do it justice. What had seemed on paper to be a simple, smallish room was revealed to be a chamber bursting with rich colors and dazzling patterns. The floor was tiled in swirling mosaics the walls draped with velvet, the pews shining a golden-brown in the low lantern light. Even the air smelled decadent, brimming with a sandalwood incense that warmed her lungs with every breath she took.

It was overwhelming. Or at least, it would have been if not for the slapdash skeleton of scaffolding that ate up the far wall, and the boy sprawled upon it, laid out on his stomach. He was clutching a paintbrush. He was watching her.

"Are you following me?" asked Dominic Fontana.

Rosa wondered if it would be unforgivably rude to turn and leave without answering. "I'm here with my uncle," she said instead. "We were invited to dine with His Holiness."

"Master Michelangelo is here?" He lurched up, his movements sending the wooden planks creaking dangerously.

"Cardinal de' Medici had a few private matters to address with him," she said, before Dominic could fall to his death. "Not for a young lady's ears, apparently." Dominic snorted at that. "Is this what you've been working on?"

She padded toward the scaffolding. Through the mishmash of planks, she could make out the shadowed suggestion of a fresco that covered every free inch of chapel wall space. "Impressive."

"You can barely see it. Here." And to her genuine surprise, Dominic moved his meticulously organized paints and brushes aside and patted the scaffolding next to him. "Come on," he said.

She hesitated. She should be using this time to assess the vault stair door, to plot out the chapel or the eyelines or—

"Your clothes won't get mussed," Dominic said. "I promise."

Well, if he was going to goad her. Rosa bunched her skirts in one hand and used the other to haul herself up next to him, ignoring his proffered arm. "As you wish," she heard him mutter as she settled, looking up at the fresco—

Her breath caught in her throat.

Rosa had spent the last few weeks haunting the workshop of the finest (reluctant) fresco painter in the world, but even if she hadn't had the benefit of that immersion, it was her livelihood to be able to pick out quality work from the dross. Taking in the spread of this particular piece . . . words failed.

"Still think it's impressive?" Dominic asked, his tone wry.

Rosa couldn't find it in herself to snap back. It *was* impressive—a sprawling mural in vibrant color and exquisite detail. She was eye level with a man in green, who was preoccupied with wrangling an oversized cat on a leash. The look of exasperation on his painted face was so real that she winced along in sympathy. In fact, every one of the countless figures marching across the walls shared this lifelike quality, so masterfully rendered that she could believe they were on the verge of stepping into the real world.

"It's wonderful," she finally said, tearing her eyes away. Dominic was watching her, his face inscrutable. "You're . . . touching it up?" Rosa would not say it aloud, but from what she had seen, Dominic Fontana's artistic skills were nowhere near those represented here in this chapel.

But maybe Dominic had heard something of that thought in her tone anyway. He turned back to his paints, flushing high across his cheekbones. "Master Gozzoli finished it in 1461," he said. "This fresco is over fifty years old. And with time, it has developed fading and cracks. You can see it here—" His finger hovered over the shoulder of a young boy on a white horse. Behind him was painted a tree in a deep green where, if Rosa looked closely enough, she could pick out a hairline fracture. "So I find them and I fix them."

"How?" Rosa asked.

"More plaster and more paint," he said. Maybe it was the lamplight or maybe it was just the topic, but his eyes were brighter and more engaged than she had ever seen from him. It was impossible to meet that enthusiasm with anything less than a wholehearted smile. "It's just a question of matching the style of the artist, and then matching the materials. Fairly straightforward if you have the right tools, and I have a system for color matching, where I take a small sample back to the workshop and work with my own temporary base to—"

He cut himself off, the brightness abruptly draining from his gaze. Rosa floundered for a moment, wondering when the next words would come. But he was silent, listening intently to the footsteps approaching in the courtyard outside. The closer they got, the tighter his shoulders wound until they were up around his ears.

"Dominic," she said. He didn't react, his eyes fixed on the front door.

But the footsteps passed the chapel without slowing—a servant or a guard going about their business. Dominic's whole body sagged.

"I have a lot of work to do, signorina," he said. His eyes were flat again.

"You can call me Rosa, you know," she said. An olive branch.

But he just picked up his paintbrush and began mixing pigments together on his pallet. *Deep green.* The exact color of the fresco's tree. Rosa sighed. "Don't let me keep you," she muttered, and made sure to shake the scaffolding as much as possible as she clambered down.

Safely back on the ground, Rosa took a moment to re-center herself. *The vault. That* was why she was here. She had not *infiltrated* the *Palazzo Medici* to watch a young artist who could barely draw splash paint all over someone else's work. She could see the door to the vault corridor from here—she would concentrate on that, and on the many *thousands* of gold florins beyond it.

Running one finger lightly over a pew, Rosa paced the circumference of the chapel, plotting toward that closed door. *Ten steps to the scaffolding,* she thought. *Another ten . . . fourteen . . . seventeen . . . to the passage from there . . . so from the chapel doors it would be*—she reached for the doorknob, just to test it—*sixteen steps? Maybe fourteen if she ran*—

"You don't look like your uncle."

She jerked her hand back to her side.

Dominic was still sitting with his back to the rest of the room. His hand moved lightly as he dabbed paint onto the fresco.

"I suppose not," Rosa said. She kept both eyes pinned to Dominic, the vault corridor behind her. If he was going to insist on peppering her with comments, then she would keep him in her sights. Reaching back, she scrabbled for the doorknob. "Is that a bad thing? I don't think I'd wear a beard as well as he does."

"Don't sell yourself short," he said, as she closed her fingers around the knob and gave it a turn.

The door did not so much as shift in its frame. Locked. *Damn. Add another item to the to-do list.*

"You'll make me blush," she said. "But earlier—you never said—for the color matching, you have a system?"

"You don't really want to hear about that," he said, sounding embarrassed.

"How will I know until you tell me?"

Dominic sat back on his heels with a sigh, setting his brush down on his pallet. He slung his legs over the side of the platform, feet dangling over the tiled floor. Rosa paced closer, looking up at him.

"I've been doing it since I was young," he finally said. "My mother taught me."

"She's a painter?"

"The best I've ever known," Dominic said. "And I include your uncle in that. It's—painting—it's always been such a . . . a joy. For her. Every step of the process, it lights her up inside. You can see it in her face and in her fingers. She loves it." Rosa, who was busy being transfixed by a similar spark in Dominic's own face, had an idea of what he meant. "She had me mixing colors for her when I was four years old. She taught me about composition and complexity and light and shadow. Drilled it into my head. It should have been a bore, but . . . I used to trail after her all the time, mimicking every one of her brushstrokes. Every flourish. I wanted to be exactly like her." He paused, his gaze going somewhere deep inside of himself. "I haven't seen her since I was fourteen."

It was suddenly too difficult to maintain eye contact. Rosa leaned her hip against a pew, tracing the engravings with her fingernails. "She must be proud of you," she said.

"She is," Dominic said. "Coming to Florence to work for Master Michelangelo. It's a great honor. And I think—well. There was nothing left for her to teach me. I had the techniques down, but in terms of practical application? It requires something in the way of creativity that I—" He swung his heels against the scaffolding. "I think she hoped Master Michelangelo would be able to guide me in that department. And he has been very generous," he hastened to add. "Setting aside space in his workshop—he did not have to do that for me. I will always be grateful. And he got me this job, which—is rewarding—"

Maybe if he spoke with a little more verve he'd actually be able to convince himself. "It's where he got his start, after all," she said. "With the Medici."

He shot her a sideways look. "Are we starting this again?"

"Not at all," she said. "I wouldn't disrespect my hosts."

"You're mocking me."

"We're just *talking*, Dominic."

His spine was ramrod straight. "I don't see you bothering your uncle like this. How can you needle me about my choices when the same ones got him to where he is today?"

"And how do you think he feels about that?"

He let out all the air in his lungs in an irritated puff, but Rosa could read him like a book here in this chapel. Surrounded by his paints and brushes, far from the pressure of his master's workshop, he was vulnerable. He was a man struggling to measure up to a genius, and he didn't have the tools to so much as *start*. In someone less self-aware, this would curdle into blustering arrogance—maybe that version of Dominic Fontana would stumble into success just because admitting to his weakness would be the same as self-destruction.

But *this* version of Dominic Fontana, razor-wire tight on the edge of a rickety scaffold, *bled* for approval that he was never going to receive. There would be no national acclaim for his inspired works. And because he was not blind to himself, he would never clamor for it. He would simply continue mixing paints for someone else's work in an unseen corner of Michelangelo's workshop until the world moved on, or he did.

"Do you miss her?" Rosa found herself asking. "Your mother?"

"I am where I need to be," Dominic said, recitative.

"There's no shame in missing family."

His eyes sparked again—something more poisonous than delight kindling beneath his dangerous eyelashes. "Easy for you to say," he said. "You're with yours."

The words hit Rosa squarely in the face, jolting her out of the honey-warm cocoon of sandalwood-scented chapel air. She pushed off the pew, standing squarely on both feet. "Don't hold me accountable for your loneliness, apprentice."

"Then don't pry, *signorina*." There was a clatter as Dominic tossed a paintbrush onto the platform next to him. "Lord above. All I want is to finish my work, but everywhere I turn—"

"Excuse me for stepping on your *patronage*—"

"And we're back to this again! You think so low of me for working with the Medici when it is my career on the line—"

"I don't think low of you for—"

"*But you are the one sitting down to dine with them.*"

"A-hem."

Rosa and Dominic both froze, eyes locked on one another. From this distance, she could tell that his knuckles were white where they clutched the edges of the scaffold—to stop himself from falling? To hold himself back from lunging at her? It hardly mattered.

A servant stood in the open chapel door with her hands clasped, carefully not looking at either of them. "Signorina?" she said, apparently to the ceiling. "Your presence is requested in the garden."

"Thank you," Rosa said. She could still feel Dominic's eyes drilling holes between her shoulder blades as she stalked out of the Magi Chapel and into the sunlight.

23

KHALID

"Five!"

Sergeant Bianci's order rang over the dusty stable yard. Khalid brought his sword around to tag against his partner's. Guardsman Ricci sagged under the blow.

"Keep your elbow in," Khalid suggested. "It will steady your blade." He nodded approvingly as Ricci made the adjustments. "Good."

"Two!" shouted Sergeant Bianci. This time, when Khalid's sword met Ricci's, Ricci's blade did not dip. His face split into a triumphant smile.

The days following the riot had seen a souring in the atmosphere of the Medici Guard. Surveillance of the Palazzo's doors and windows had increased. So, too, had the patrols throughout the city—at least two pairs of men in Medici blue were making the rounds at all times. It was a wonder that Khalid's uniform did not bear scorch marks from the glares of the City Guard.

On top of this increased security, the guardsmen were now required to attend sword drills twice a week. Before the riots, this had been an optional exercise. Barely a third of the guard had bothered to attend. Now, the yard behind the Palazzo was filled with sweaty, resentful men swinging swords at one another in half-time every Tuesday and Thursday afternoon.

"You're doing well," Khalid told Ricci. The boy glowed, elated, and squared up for the next sword form.

It did not come. There was a footman at Sergeant Bianci's side, whispering in his ear. The sergeant's face, never far from red, grew redder. He gave a tense nod to the servant and turned back to his men. "Continue. Free drills." Without another word, he hurried past the stables, headed for the front gates.

In his absence, guardsmen either paired up to practice or found some bit of wall to lean against. Khalid circled about Ricci to adjust the young man's footwork. "Better," he said. "Now try again." They squared up—and a heavy hand clapped down on Khalid's shoulder.

It was no surprise when Khalid turned to look into Vieri's face. He had caught the tail end of the nod the footman had directed into the crowd of guards after the sergeant had scuttled away. But just because the sight of Vieri's grin was expected did not mean that it was welcome.

"Stop wasting your time with the children, bin-Halil," Vieri said. There were a few other guardsmen at his back, and they dutifully snickered. "How about a match with an equal?"

Let me know if you see one, snarked a thought in the back of Khalid's mind. It sounded like Giacomo. Khalid did not give it voice. "I do not believe Sergeant Bianci would approve."

"Do you see him? I don't see him." Vieri swung his sword in a capable figure eight. "Come on, bin-Halil. Show us what the golden boy's made of. We're all *dying* to know."

This was not a good idea. Khalid could see it in Vieri's face as easily as he could see the sun in the sky. But he had taken enough of the man's taunts to last a lifetime, and so . . .

"As you wish," Khalid said. He fell into a guard stance, feet planted and sword raised.

Word of the match spread quickly through the stables. By the time Vieri lifted his blade in a rush of attack, a wide circle had been cleared for them. Khalid had plenty of room to sidestep Vieri's swing, ignoring the plume of dust that rose as the sword hit the packed earth.

"Fast on your feet," Vieri said, circling. "That something they teach you in Ferrara?"

Khalid did not respond. He was too busy eyeing the man's stance and his grip. If he rushed Khalid again, it would be an easy thing to target his wrist with the flat of his sword. Khalid could force him to drop his weapon, and then this whole farce would be finished—

Vieri did not rush Khalid again. His blade flashed once, and then twice, quicker than Khalid had anticipated. Khalid brought his own sword up in response, meeting Vieri's attacks in quick succession. Vieri broke away again. His grin had a jagged edge to it.

"Almost had you there," he said. "You look a little ragged. Burning the midnight oil?" Khalid feinted. Vieri skipped back, laughing. "It must be difficult to report to duty every morning when you've got other obligations. Like that friend who came to see you."

Khalid nearly tripped. *Marino.* "Interesting company to keep, bin-Halil," Vieri observed. His eyes were intent. "Very interesting."

In response, Khalid drove forward with a flurry of blows, his sword dancing in quick slashes toward Vieri's arms and legs. The guardsman did not so much block them as dart hastily out of range, nearly running from the onslaught. "Did I strike a nerve there?" he called.

"You seem unable to strike much of anything," Khalid muttered.

It was a mistake. A few of the guards overheard this. Their laughter bloomed and grew around the circle until it surrounded them. Vieri's flush plunged deep purple. He charged, and his sword met Khalid's with a clang, locking at the hilt. "You think I don't know you're up to something?" Vieri hissed through the crossed iron. "You may have won over the sergeant, but he's an idiot." The locked blades swayed as Vieri dropped one hand. "I see right through you."

It took only a moment for Khalid to realize that Vieri was reaching for a dagger. But that was long enough for Vieri to slice it upward toward Khalid's gut. Khalid felt the fabric of his jerkin tear before he was wrenching back. He pressed a hand to his side and was relieved to see that it came away clean.

The crowd was shouting warnings and encouragements. Khalid had a brief and disorienting memory of a warehouse on the Genoa docks. But that confusion fled as Vieri's sword jabbed in again, and Khalid dodged back out of its reach.

This was fine. Khalid had faced off against men with two weapons before, more times than he could count. Vieri was no different. In fact, he might even be a bit easier, given that he was not unpredictably drunk, nor was he cornered, nor did he owe money—

But Khalid had forgotten that Vieri had friends.

It was a trip that got him. Someone had extended a foot from the ring of Medici blue. Khalid was sent sprawling to the ground, the wind knocked from his lungs and his blade jarred from his fingers. A moment later, Vieri was descending on him. Khalid jammed a kick into Vieri's stomach, but still the man came on, blade raised to strike—

"Guardsmen!"

Captain Romano's shout brought the entire stable yard to a standstill. He stalked through the guards like some vengeful god, eyes blazing. Ricci scuttled a few paces behind him, sweat beading his brow. He must have sprinted for the captain.

"Brawling?" Captain Romano demanded. "On duty? What the *hell* is wrong with you?"

Vieri scrambled to his feet, fumbling his dagger back into its sheath. "Captain—"

"The rest of you are dismissed," Captain Romano said. "Vieri. Bin-Halil. With me."

He led them past the kitchens, to the small guardhouse beyond. Khalid followed without protest, his thoughts in an uproar.

Vieri had seen Marino—had seen *Khalid* speaking with Marino. Had he overheard anything? Did he even know who Signore Traverio was? Could he get Khalid removed from the Medici Guard? Could he get him arrested? What did he know?

The questions continued to swirl as Captain Romano ordered Vieri into the guardhouse and flashed a stormy glare at Khalid. "Wait here," he gritted. The door closed behind him. A moment later, the captain's furious "You are a *disgrace* to the Medici Guard—" filtered out into the dusty sunlight, clear as day. Khalid focused on putting his uniform back in order.

It was only when he'd finished straightening his belt that he realized he was not alone.

There was someone watching him from the kitchen door. A woman. She wore a gray silk gown over a bright white chemise, and her chestnut hair was caught up in a black net. She was watching him with wide brown eyes.

Khalid realized with a jolt that he recognized her. This was the woman from the window. The woman Giacomo had risked so much for a glimpse of. And the second Khalid's eyes met hers, she plucked up her skirts and, to Khalid's unending dismay, began to scurry across the yards *toward him*.

Perhaps, Khalid thought as he helplessly watched her draw nearer, it would have been better if he'd allowed Vieri to stab him.

24

ROSA

B y the time Rosa arrived in the Medici gardens, she'd wrangled her temper into check, but she hadn't managed to banish it entirely. She could still smell the sandalwood incense clinging to her clothes and feel Dominic Fontana's injured glare as she emerged onto the manicured grassy lawn.

The garden had not been as lovingly recreated on her blueprints as the Palazzo's interior, which meant that the white marble statues that lined the gravel walkways were an aesthetic surprise. She soaked them in as she passed, willing their cool lines to soothe her. By the time she reached the table at the garden's far end, she had almost regained her equilibrium. *Almost.*

Michelangelo had been settled at Cardinal de' Medici's right hand. But Rosa's attention only glanced over the two men before being inexorably drawn to the third person at the table, a man who gazed out over the garden with a proprietary air that betrayed his identity even before she got a good look at his face.

He was striking in the sense that he was memorable rather than handsome. His eyes—large, deep-set, and dark—looked her over from head to toe as she approached. His mouth was generous, splitting his face widely beneath a strong nose.

Pope Leo X smiled, beneficent and serene. Rosa dropped into a deep curtsy as the angry lightning inside her chest roared back to life.

It will feel like you are traveling back in time. Wasn't that what she'd told Michelangelo in the carriage? Because it wasn't just places that were known by the memories they contained. It was people, too.

"My child?"

Rosa straightened hastily, brushing at her skirts with both hands and hoping that the angry flush on her cheeks would be mistaken for embarrassment. "Forgive me, Your Holiness," she murmured, keeping her gaze on the ground. "I find myself a bit overwhelmed."

"That's quite alright," the Pope said. His voice was smooth and warm, slipping over her skin like honey. She shivered.

"My niece, Your Holiness," Michelangelo said, looking very much as though he'd like to evaporate into the air. "Rosa de' Lombardi."

"You are just as charming as my cousin said you were," the Pope said, holding a hand out to Rosa. She dimpled, bobbing forward to press a quick kiss to the golden ring that hugged one thick finger. "Perhaps even more so."

"Your Holiness is too kind," Rosa said.

"Impossible," the Pope said. "Now sit, sit. The wine is getting cold!"

Rosa made a big show of hurrying to her seat. Despite the Pope's protestations, there was every indication that the three men had already tucked in, the small plates in front of them bearing crusts and crumbs from the trays of pastries and pies in the center of the table. Rosa let herself be served, mulled wine flowing into her cup in a dark river, delicate cakes and savory meats piling on top of one another, forming a mountain of decadence.

"Thank you again for your patience, signorina," Cardinal de' Medici said. Unlike his cousin or Michelangelo, his own plate sat untouched. He sipped lightly at a glass of juice, though if Rosa hadn't known any better, his sour expression would have had her assuming that it was vinegar. "I hope you weren't too bored while you were waiting?"

"Oh no!" Rosa chirped "The Palazzo is so fascinating, I don't think it would be possible to be bored for even one moment!"

"*Charming*," the Pope repeated, nudging at Michelangelo. Michelangelo stared down at the table in front of him.

"I found myself in the most *breathtaking* chapel," Rosa said. "I confess, I have never seen anything like it! That fresco—it is *incredible!*"

The Pope chuckled. "It must run in the family. Your uncle was *obsessed* with that fresco when he was an apprentice here," he said, waving a hand absently behind him. A servant hurried up to fill his empty cup of wine. "Went and studied it every chance he got. If he wasn't at work then we could find him crouching in the chapel like a penitent. But instead of praying to God, he was praying to Master Gozzoli and his paints!"

"That's a bit much, Your Holiness," Cardinal de' Medici remarked calmly, but the Pope just rolled his eyes.

"You remember as well as I do, Giulio," he said. "*Diana. Paula. Carlo.* He had a name for every figure in that painting."

Rosa couldn't imagine the gruff sculptor as an adolescent, much less an adolescent who named the figures in someone else's fresco. "Even the animals?" she asked.

Michelangelo's lips twitched, and for a moment, Rosa thought that he might actually smile. "Yes."

She was going to press him about that later. "I suppose it's fitting," she said, a serious wrinkle in her brow. "*Know well the condition of thy flocks.* Isn't that what the Bible says?"

The Pope's laugh was delighted. "Exactly so!" he exclaimed. "Cleverly put, my child. You have been wasted in the countryside."

"Although the passage does use 'flocks' in the metaphorical sense," Cardinal de' Medici said. "More in line with . . . parishioners. Penitents. Those under your protection."

"Well, those *metaphorical* 'flocks' have tried to make their 'condition' known quite loudly, haven't they?" All trace of humor had vanished from the Pope's voice, replaced drop for drop by pure acid.

Michelangelo shifted, reducing a cake into a small mountain of crumbs, piece by piece. Even the air had stilled at the Pope's snapped remark.

Rosa knew that it was only a matter of seconds before someone changed the topic and the conversation carried on, stilted and abbreviated. They would pretend as though the subject had not been mentioned, which would set the whole meal to festering. And if that happened, then the odds were better than good that Rosa and Michelangelo would be leaving the Palazzo empty-handed, due to nothing more than one man's bad mood.

"Forgive me, Your Holiness," she ventured. "Are you . . . perhaps speaking of the . . . unrest this past week?"

Emotions chased across the Pope's face, one swapping for the other before being replaced by the next. Fury, shame, fear . . . Rosa waited to see which would win out.

Finally, Pope Leo fixed her with a grave frown, rage still burning in his eyes. "I ought not have brought it up in front of a young lady," he said. "But yes, that is what I am referring to."

Rosa shivered. "It was so frightening. I've never seen anything like that."

"And you never will again," the Pope assured her. "We are taking steps to make certain that such activity is heartily discouraged."

There were alarms ringing in Rosa's head. "Discouraged?"

"Your Holiness . . . ," Cardinal de' Medici cautioned, but Pope Leo brushed his cousin aside.

"Don't be such a stickler, Giulio," he said. "The poor girl was scared out of her mind. A little assurance is the least I can offer." He turned back to Rosa. "You say 'know well the condition of thy flocks'.

I am afraid that our flocks have been poisoned. But for every poison, there is an antidote." His smile was comforting. "The security of Florence—and of good, kind people like yourself—is paramount to the Medici family. We will use strength to preserve it, if necessary."

"How?"

"Well, my child, we've done it before. Have you heard of a city called Prato?"

Rosa's mouth was dry, despite the wine. The sandalwood incense clinging to her clothes had transformed into acrid smoke. Somewhere in the back of her head, she could hear screams, the *twang* of bow strings releasing, the rush of the river—

I'll be right behind you.

"No, Your Holiness," she said.

"You would have been young, I suppose. It's not far from here, only an hour's ride. Beautiful place. And unfortunately, a few years ago, it became overrun with treason and dissent. It fell to us—my cousin and the Church—to stamp that rebellion out in order to preserve the peace. That's what we're doing now—we're preparing to preserve the peace in Florence."

Her hands were shaking. Pope Leo hadn't noticed, but Michelangelo was watching her like a hawk. She tucked her hands into her lap. "The same way you did in Prato."

"If necessary." Cardinal de' Medici's words were cold.

"It is in all of our best interest that Florence remains stable," said the Pope. "Many of the noble and merchant families of the region have already made their support known. You are safe here in the city."

Only years of practice kept the smile on Rosa's face. Beneath the surface, her mind was whirling as jigsaw pieces came together.

Romano's ledger. It held the records of the City Guard, each meticulously inscribed line the outlined seams of Florence's protections.

And if a person—or a family—could find the seams, then they would know where to tear to bring the whole thing down. This, paired with the indulgences streaming through the Palazzo gates, bled from the pockets of wealthy men, piling up in the vault beneath the Magi Chapel—

Ten thousand florins. It had been an amorphous concept, something she'd been chasing as a vicious dream. Now Rosa realized it was also enough to pay for an army. An army that would flatten Florence to the ground. And with the City Guard gone, who would stand in their way?

Smoke weighed heavier in her lungs. She couldn't breathe.

"I am relieved to hear it," Rosa somehow managed. Her skin was cold. "I would hate to see any harm come to such a beautiful city. I feel as though every day I see something new!"

The sunlight and Rosa's flattery had worked together to sap Pope Leo of his ill temper. "You are too kind, child. Michelangelo, you must keep her here. She cannot be allowed to return to—whatever mudflat she escaped from."

"Yes, Your Holiness," said Michelangelo. Rosa wondered if he was naming painted animals somewhere in the safe recesses of his own mind.

"In fact," the Pope said, "we will make certain that you never wish to go back home again. After all, what young lady wouldn't have her head turned by a glamorous banquet?"

There it was. The reason that she'd stepped foot in this Palazzo in the first place—the reason that she'd agreed to sit down across from the men who had—

"Banquet?" she asked.

"You haven't mentioned it to her?" Pope Leo asked Michelangelo. There were hidden blades in his tone. "One might think you were pretending this obligation didn't exist."

"It hadn't come up," Michelangelo said, the response of either an idiot or an artist.

"I wouldn't want to be an inconvenience," Rosa interjected, before Michelangelo could cause any serious offense.

"A beautiful woman's presence at a fine party is never an inconvenience," the Pope said, leaning forward to pat her hand.

Rosa found that she was clutching her knife.

"I can think of no greater honor, Your Holiness," she said. "I'm sure it will be an evening no one will ever forget."

25

KHALID

Khalid had never been one to run from confrontation. He would have loved to run from this one.

The woman wouldn't stop moving. He inched back against the guardhouse and kept his gaze fixed in the middle distance. Still she advanced, intent, ignoring all conventions of proper distance.

"Signora," he said, once his shoulders could dig no further into the wall.

She barely blinked. This was another problem, because her eyes drew at him like a sucking current. The rest of her was beautiful, in a way he could objectively appreciate. But her wide brown eyes and thick dark lashes dug at his recollection like a mouse chewing through plaster. They set off fireworks of familiarity, stretching back past the night at the Casa Petrucci. Had he met her before? In Genoa? In Tunis?

He would have stepped around her if he was not chained to this spot by Captain Romano's order. Inside the guardhouse he could still hear the captain's diatribe. He did not want to worsen the situation for himself by disappearing. And even if he had been free to move along, it would have been unforgivably rude to pull away from someone so above him in position.

"Please."

Her voice was low, her accent refined. And there was something familiar about *that* too . . .

He gave in. "Can I be of assistance, signora?"

She gazed up at him, those light brown eyes shifting. She was searching his face. He wished she wouldn't.

"You were outside my window."

He could not help his stuttered inhale. He hadn't realized that she had gotten a good look at him in that alley. Then again, how many Tunisians wore Medici Guard uniforms?

But he could not give in so easily. "You must have me mistaken for someone else."

"You were there," she insisted. This was beyond enough. Khalid stepped smartly aside, putting open air at his back and distance between them.

"I do not know you, signora," he said. Some facet of this woman's familiarity made him want to check his pockets.

"There was another man as well," she said. She was speaking faster now. Her eyes never left him. "Outside the Petrucci house. He wore blue and black and—he would be about nineteen. He had red hair, but it was dyed." She lowered her voice. "You took him away."

Khalid bit back a curse. Giacomo had promised—he had *sworn* that his adventure in that alley would not impact the rest of their plan. Khalid, the fool that he was, had chosen to believe him. And now the consequences of that decision were staring Khalid in the face.

Not only had she seen Giacomo, but she had *recognized* him. And now she had recognized Khalid as well.

"You know him," she breathed. "Do you know where he is?"

"You must have me mistaken for someone else," he said again. But the woman didn't seem to hear him. As Khalid looked on in horror, she dug down the front of her bodice, searching for something. "Signora!" he hissed.

"Here," she said, ignoring him. She produced a piece of paper, which she pressed into Khalid's nerveless hand. "Please take this."

Her eyes were imploring, and the familiarity roared back. But the dizzying déjà vu couldn't be explained by a brief glimpse through a window. He had the impossible thought that he had encountered that expression in those eyes before . . . not long ago . . .

"Give it to him," she said. "He needs to know. I didn't think—I didn't know if he—"

"Signora—" Khalid tried one last time, but broke off as she shook her head.

"I just need to know if Giacomo is safe," she said. "And if he's happy. And if—"

"Giulietta?"

The woman pulled back, head whipping around. The call had come from beyond the kitchens, back toward the Palazzo. In an instant she was gone, her steps quick—she darted around the guardhouse just as two men emerged from the Palazzo into the sunlight.

"There you are," said one of them, middle-aged and bald beneath his plumed cap.

"Caro," Giulietta responded, taking his arm. "How was His Holiness?"

"Impossible," the man grumbled, already guiding her away. *Petrucci*. It could only be him. "Apparently he has more important things to do this afternoon."

"Like breaking bread with *artists*," added his friend.

Giulietta's response was inaudible, sympathetic noises fading into the distance as her husband led her back into the Palazzo. Khalid let out a slow breath, his heart rabbiting beneath his ribs in a way it hadn't even when Vieri had come at him with a knife.

But Khalid did not have a moment to unravel what had just happened. The guardhouse door yanked open and Vieri stomped out. He paused in front of Khalid, mouth opening to spit something poisonous—

"Bin-Halil!"

Vieri's jaw snapped shut at Captain Romano's bellow. He swiveled and marched away.

The captain's lecture was stern but reserved, nowhere near the reaming he had given Vieri. "Guardsman Vieri will be on probation until the banquet next week," he informed Khalid. "If he troubles you again, you will inform me."

"Vieri and I were simply sparring, Captain," Khalid said, eyes fixed over Captain Romano's shoulder. Vieri would certainly blame any punishment he received on Khalid, which would only cause issues down the road.

"I didn't ask your opinion, bin-Halil," Captain Romano bit out. "Vieri is on probation and your ego *will survive* reporting any future infractions." And with that, Khalid was dismissed.

The rest of the afternoon passed in a fevered blur. The letter burned in his belt-pouch, a constant presence in his mind. Through the rest of drills, through his patrol, he could not tear his thoughts away.

If he gave it to Giacomo, was he inviting the other man to hare off on another misadventure? Giacomo had given his word, but what was that worth? And if Giacomo crumbled so spectacularly at the sight of Giulietta Petrucci, what would he do if he read her note?

He would destroy the letter. He would incinerate it, the moment the opportunity presented itself. He would keep things simple and eliminate risk, just as Signore Traverio would want him to do. The decision was made.

So why did the prospect of it turn his stomach?

By evening, a splitting headache was throbbing behind his eyes. Feeling thunderous, Khalid stalked to the guardhouse to report off-duty for the night. Guardsman de' Carlo was there, having evidently already been relieved at the Casa Romano by the furious Vieri. "Headed out?" he asked.

"Mm," Khalid grunted. "Home."

"Get some sleep," de' Carlo advised, paternalistic for someone who was barely sixteen. "Oh, and before I forget—" He produced a packet from some unseen shelf inside the guardhouse and handed it to Khalid. "Someone left this for you."

It was a cylinder of rough brown cloth, tied loosely with two pieces of hemp. Goose bumps prickled the back of Khalid's neck. "Who?" he asked.

De' Carlo just shrugged. "The messenger didn't give a name."

Khalid yanked off the twine and unrolled the cloth. The moment the bundle began to unravel, the unmistakable smell of old fish filled the guardhouse. De' Carlo swore, covering his nose.

The last turn in the cloth unspooled, and something thin and sharp tumbled out. Khalid caught it before it could hit the floor, and held it up to the lamplight.

It was translucent and small, almost unidentifiable. But Khalid had not worked for the Weever of Genoa for three years to not recognize a Weever spine when he saw one.

This was a message from Signore Traverio. *I am watching you*, it said. *I am waiting.*

Don't screw up.

26

GIACOMO

"No, no, no," Sarra said, her cheeks flushed pink in the firelight. "You're not understanding me. It was one-of-a-kind, with all these—what were they, Rosa?"

"Rubies," Rosa said.

"*Rubies*, right, they were all over it. A wrought gold cross covered in rubies. *Ugly as sin, and worth a king's ransom*, that's how Lena described it." Sarra shook her head. "She had it all planned out. She'd been watching that house for *days*. It was going to be perfect. And then she snuck in the window the night of the job and found my father already stuffing it in his bag."

The afternoon before the banquet had seen the whole lot of them piled into the millhouse, the hearth blazing against the late-autumn chill. A few minutes of muddling over the fire, and Giacomo had produced a vat of mulled wine, which he ladled into whatever cups and beakers were passed his way.

They were a few rounds deep now. Agata had claimed the chair closest to the fire, citing old age and brittle bones as usual. Michelangelo hovered a few paces away, one eye trained on the door. If he was not comfortable in their midst by now, Giacomo supposed he would never be, and so he let the man's skittishness go.

Sarra sprawled on her back along one of the kitchen benches, her empty cup dangling from her hand. Rosa was curled up across from her, skirts tucked around her legs. She had barely touched her wine, her gaze unreadable as Sarra rambled.

And Khalid . . .

He'd taken up a post by the door, his arms crossed and his face impassive. It was a version of the man that Giacomo hadn't seen here in Florence, but not an unfamiliar one. This Khalid was the one who lurked in Traverio's shadow back in Genoa, and Giacomo did *not* enjoy meeting him again.

It might not have worried Giacomo as much if this hulking bruiser act was only for the evening—they had a big day ahead of them, and people reacted to stress in different ways. Some chewed their finger-nails. Some, like Sarra, drank too much and lost themselves in rambling digressions. Some, Giacomo supposed, could revert to taciturn menace.

But. Giacomo had not been able to get more than monosyllabic grunts out of Khalid for the last *week*, and truthfully, Rosa hadn't been much better. Both of them had returned from the Palazzo Medici looking like someone had taken their worlds and shaken them like a child's toy. Since then, Rosa had stomped through the last scraps of planning, radiating white-sharp anger through her ever-thinning smile, and even Giacomo was not foolish enough to ask why.

As for Khalid . . . he seemed unable to speak to Giacomo or even look him in the eye. It had, second by second, been driving Giacomo out of his mind. He hadn't realized how much his own tranquility depended on getting a rise out of Khalid, and now that *that* was gone . . .

Giacomo gulped his wine.

"They stared at each other for at *least* a minute. Lena had no idea my father was casing the house, and he didn't know she was either. D'you know she'd pulled a Castillian Blunder *single-handed* to get in there?"

"That's not possible," Giacomo said.

"Not possible to anyone but Lena Cellini."

Rosa set her cup on the table with a tiny *click*. "Sarra."

"It was the beginning of a beautiful partnership, Rosa, don't you want to hear the story?" Sarra teased. "It's your history, too."

Rosa said nothing. Her knuckles were white where they clutched her skirts.

"Well, I think this moment deserves a toast," Giacomo declared, holding out his cup. "It has been the honor of all honors to work alongside you amoral criminals—and Il Divino—these last few weeks, and I would just like to say—"

"It's bad luck to toast before the job is done," Rosa said.

"Is that . . . a saying?" Michelangelo asked.

"It's a thieves' saying," Agata said through a yawn.

"It's a Lena saying," Sarra clarified.

Sarra seemed to be the only person in the millhouse who didn't pick up on the dark cloud rolling off her partner. Giacomo cleared his throat. "Well, I've never let a bit of superstition get in the way of a good time." He raised his cup again and tilted a nod toward Rosa. "To our fearless leader. To us. And to becoming rich beyond our most far-flung dreams."

The sips in response were half-hearted at best, and Giacomo sagged, resigned to the banality of what should have been a glorious moment.

"I should head back into the city," said Michelangelo. His gaze had not stopped flicking between Sarra and Rosa since Sarra had begun rambling.

"I must go as well," said Khalid. "I am on duty at the Palazzo."

Rosa nodded. "I'll see you both tomorrow," she said. Michelangelo thinned his lips and shoved through the front door without further farewell.

Giacomo watched Khalid drape his cloak over his shoulders and thought, *Unacceptable*.

If this really was the final evening of their partnership and they would be parting ways once the job was completed (assuming best possible scenarios and survival and all that), then Giacomo *refused* to be *forced* to bid farewell to this wooden effigy of a man. Something *had* to be done. And if he had to risk verbal or physical evisceration from Khalid then . . . so be it.

Ignoring the stares of Rosa and Agata, Giacomo casually stood, brushed off his knees, and made his way over to Khalid.

"This was a missed opportunity, Signore al-Sarraj," he commented. "We could have told the tale of the start of *our* beautiful partnership. It would have brought the house down." He nudged at Khalid's ribs and tried not to take it too personally when Khalid stepped out of his reach. "Imagine: The Genoan docks at sunrise. An up-and-coming young grifter spots a staggeringly handsome mark striding boldly toward him—"

"I do not have time for this," Khalid said.

"Don't you have any respect for narrative structure?" Giacomo asked. "We're nearing the conclusion of our story, isn't it fitting to revisit the beginning?"

Khalid only grunted and yanked harder at his cloak ties.

This was, abruptly, the limit of what Giacomo could stand. "Won't you even look at me?" he demanded. "If I have done something to offend you, Signore al-Sarraj, I would think you'd have the decency and forthrightness to let me know."

"You know what you have done," Khalid said.

"Is this about—" Giacomo lowered his voice, very aware of Rosa's keen ears. "Is this about the night of the riot? I thought we talked that through."

"*You* talked it through," Khalid said, just as low. "All you do is talk. You talk people in circles until they lose sight of what is real and what you truly mean—" He broke off, anger bright in his dark eyes. "You want to revisit the story of our meeting? Fine. The grifter and the trusting mark. You laid a trap and I fell into it. I helped you and you picked my pocket for it. Have we finished?"

Anger flushed through Giacomo. "I *didn't* pick your pocket. I'd intended to. But I didn't."

Khalid glowered. "Why not?"

"Vice and voice." He shrugged, feeling a little awkward as some of his anger drained away. "I'd been so used to marks trying to out-smart me. Take advantage of me. It had been a pleasure to run circles around them. And then you—you were kind. So I kept my hands to myself."

"You still conned me."

"That's the life, Signore al-Sarraj," Giacomo said with a sheepish grin. "But if I'd followed through on my initial resolve and taken every coin you'd been carrying, do you honestly think Traverio would have let you see the next sunrise?" Khalid was still frowning at him. Giacomo sighed. "I didn't pick your pocket," he repeated. "I never would."

"Because I was kind to you once?"

Giacomo's breath escaped on a quiet laugh. "No, no. It's because— I suppose because I know that, no matter how many times I invite you to, you would never strike me."

Khalid's frown deepened. "What does that have to do with it?"

"You'll figure it out."

Khalid seemed to have lost his words. His jaw worked a few times, soundlessly, and Giacomo took pity on him, plucking the ties of Khalid's cloak from his hands and fastening them himself. "Just think," he said. "In a few hours, you'll be through with this whole getup. Honestly, it's a shame, this color really does wonders for—"

"Can I see you later?"

It must have given Khalid *such* satisfaction, to see Giacomo choke on his own tongue. "See me?" he stammered. "Uh—"

"There are . . . things we must discuss."

Giacomo nodded, trying to catch up. "Discuss . . . later. Not now."

Somewhere behind them, Agata let out a bark of laughter at whatever Sarra had just said. Khalid's gaze stayed steady on Giacomo's face. "There are too many people now."

"Goodness." Giacomo's cheeks were flushed. It must be the wine—it was dizzying him, too. This was *not* how he had expected this conversation to go. "Well. Signore al-Sarraj, you surprise me. So ominous! What could I have possibly done to invite such drama?"

"Later" was all Khalid said.

"You know where to find me," Giacomo croaked.

Khalid cracked the door open. "Good night," he said, and then he was gone.

Later. Giacomo groaned.

This was going to be torture.

27

ROSA

A hush fell over the mill as the evening wore on. Agata was tucked up by the hearth, snoring lightly. Giacomo had long since disappeared, slipping out the door into the brisk night and muttering something Rosa couldn't understand about *later*. And so it was just Sarra and Rosa left, staring into the searing depths of the fire.

"Did you think," Sarra began, "that Khalid and Giacomo would go this long without ripping each other's throats out?"

"Yes," Rosa said. There was a low thrum beneath her skin, one that had been there since she'd sat across the table from the Pope and smiled as he'd described the unthinkable. "That's why I brought them on."

"It's good, I suppose," Sarra said, as blithe as she'd been all evening. "Friendship blooming on the job." Rosa raised an eyebrow. "*Something* blooming, at any rate." Sarra laughed, so abruptly that Agata gave a sleepy snort on her pallet. "Do you remember that apothecary Papa and Lena worked with? Luigi something. With the chin?" *Vannini*, Rosa thought, but did not contribute. "How they were all staked out in that grain silo for days, and he fell head over heels for the farmer's daughter?"

He nearly blew the whole operation by proposing during the getaway, Rosa heard in her mother's laughing voice. Suddenly it was the most important thing in the world that she push herself to her feet. "I don't remember."

"Yes you do," Sarra insisted. "We all went to the wedding. Well, I was only seven, but we were there!"

"It's getting late," Rosa said. "Pietro must be worried about you."

"He's fine," Sarra said. "Come on, you *must* remember. Pietro stole two sips of wine and started dancing on the table. All those trays of castagnaccio—I couldn't look at a chestnut again for months. It was our family's last big wedding—"

"We're. Not. Family."

Sarra's jaw snapped closed, shocked into silence by Rosa's hiss.

Had it been any other evening, Rosa might have taken a moment to gather herself, to calm down. But the weight of the last six weeks—the last five years—*tomorrow night*—pressed down so hard that every feeling she'd had since returning to Florence curdled into vitriolic pellets of anger and frustration, careening out of her like a rifle shot.

"I don't have any family. I'm not looking for any family. I am *looking* for ten thousand gold florins. You and I may have shared some of our childhood. We may have heard the same stories, eaten the same meals. But that does not make us family, and I need you to get that through your head. There's too much at stake here for us to waste time sitting around, playing at being sisters when everything I've worked toward for five years is on the line. That's not why I hired you."

"Hired me." Sarra's face was a blank mask. "Like a maidservant."

"No," said Rosa. "Hired you like a criminal. Like Sarra the Tinkerer. That's who you are, isn't it?"

"It's—I—"

"You're a talented engineer. You know the city. You're hungry for work. That's why I brought you on board. Unless you thought I did it for nostalgia's sake?" Rosa snorted. "Just because you won't tell Pietro about your work—"

"I made a promise—"

"*Doesn't mean that you can slot me in to fill his place.*" Rosa's fingers were aching. She realized that she was clenching her fists. "Our sisterhood is something you have conjured from sentiment in your head.

Pietro is your brother. If you want absolution, you will have to go to him. But you never will. You're too scared of how he will respond, so you hide behind a promise you made to a dead man, who can be neither proud of nor disappointed in you."

The words slapped through the air, sending Sarra rocking back where she sat. The silence that followed was poison; Rosa could see the sickness rising in Sarra's eyes as she stared up at Rosa, disbelieving.

She would be well within her rights to strike Rosa, or at the very least, to walk off the job. Rosa braced herself for both. Instead, Sarra just stood gracefully, disappointment and anger shuttering her gaze.

"Very well," she said, and the reserved maturity in her voice left Rosa, one year her senior, feeling very young and very foolish and very, very out of her depth. "If we are colleagues and nothing more, let's discuss the job. Let's discuss *every part* of the job. Let's discuss Lena."

Rosa's heart plummeted. "What does she have to do with any of this?"

Sarra huffed a bitter laugh. "You must think I'm a fool, to ask me that question. But I'm not. And I can't just continue on pretending as though she doesn't exist. I can't even mention her *name* around you—"

"Who asked you to?" Rosa demanded. The walls were closing in, caging her like a trapped wild animal.

"Then what about the ledger? If I cannot talk about your mother, then surely I can ask about *that*."

"There's nothing to discuss."

"There is. And before you say that it's not my place to push—why would you hire a second who doesn't know the whole picture? You risked our skins to get our hands on some ledger that you won't even show me. What do you get out of keeping this secret?" Rosa struggled to endure Sarra's icy blue glare as it pierced her. "You promised this was just about the money. You promised it wasn't personal."

Rosa said nothing. Because she couldn't answer, not truthfully—not without admitting that she'd been deceiving Sarra from the moment she had walked back into Sarra's life.

But she should have known that silence wasn't all that much better than the truth, because Sarra seemed to look straight into the heart of her. "Papa and Lena never lied to each other," she said.

"Why, because they were *family*?"

"Because they were *partners*!" Sarra's cry burst out of her all at once. She wrangled herself back under control. "I understand. I am not my father. You are not Lena. But if you write her out of existence, then you write yourself out too. She is a part of you, which means that she is a part of this team, and there's nothing you can do to change that."

"She's not here, Sarra."

"You don't have to remind me," Sarra retorted, brushing past Rosa.

"Where do you think you're going?" Rosa challenged, more to have the last word than to actually dig for an answer.

Sarra didn't falter. "Home," she said. "You run this job how you want to run it. I won't push for more. You wouldn't be able to deliver, anyway."

"Good!" Rosa snapped, but Sarra was already striding out the door. It slammed closed behind her. Agata barely stirred.

Rosa fumed. She was furious. She was embarrassed. Who did Sarra think she was, lecturing her? Rosa was not the one who had carved herself in two for years. Rosa was not the one who had been living a *double life*.

It felt good to kick the wall, and then it felt terrible and she worried she'd broken her toe. And *then* it felt even worse because she realized she was throwing a temper tantrum, and *then* she remembered how young and *stupid* she had felt in the face of Sarra's cool anger. And then she felt even more furious at herself and only barely avoided kicking the wall again.

She's not here.

You don't have to remind me.

Rosa's next breath caught in her throat. When she exhaled, it carried a sound.

"Mama."

It was the first time in years she'd allowed herself to think the word, much less say it aloud. Now it zinged against her mouth, skittering down to her heart, bouncing against every tender and bruised part of her along the way.

She couldn't stay here. She needed light. People. Something familiar, comforting—

She went to the Mercato Vecchio.

It didn't take long to find what she was looking for. The stall was as much a fixture of Florence as the city walls. It had weathered mad monks and titanic bankers and even the brief gasps of the Republic. It looked the same as it had when Rosa was small, lacquered with blue and green stripes. The words LAMPREDOTTAIO CARLOTTA were a beacon beckoning Rosa in.

"And how is the best cook in Florence doing tonight, signora?" her mother had asked beneath that sign, more times than Rosa could count. And Rosa had watched Signora Carlotta—barely taller than the counter and with flyaway white hair that could give Agata's a run for its money—smile and laugh and offer Lena an extra serving at no cost, which Lena had always insisted on paying for.

"I may be a thief," she had told Rosa as they cradled their steaming lampredotti, "but it does not do to steal from greatness. Unless you've got a fence lined up."

Rosa reached the window just as the customer ahead of her turned, food in hand—

Just as *Dominic Fontana* turned, food in hand.

"You—" he said, and then, "Why," and then, finally, "How many times can the same person sneak up on me before I have to suspect that the Lord is playing some kind of joke?"

This made her want to smile, damn it. She shook her head. "No jokes tonight," she said. "You have my word."

"What, uh." He shifted the soft roll to his other hand. "What are you doing here?"

"Signora Carlotta is the best cook in Florence," Rosa said, flashing a pale imitation of her mother's smile.

Behind the counter, the old woman snorted. "Flattery will get you nowhere, signorina."

"I've always thought she was the best in the world," Dominic chipped in.

Signora Carlotta blushed. "Stop it, you silly boy."

Rosa shouldered Dominic aside at the window. "Two lampredotti, please," she said. "If the silly boy is finished."

Dominic lingered as Signora Carlotta laid out two rolls and began to ladle stewed tripe onto them. "I'm . . . glad to have seen you," he finally said.

Her fight with Sarra had burned away all capacity for diplomatic words. "Why?"

"I said some . . . unkind things," he said, picking at the crust of his lampredotto. "In the Magi Chapel. You asked about my family, and I reacted badly. I shouldn't have done that."

Signora Carlotta shoved the lampredotti across the counter. Rosa tossed a lire down and picked them up. They weighed heavy in her hands.

How is the best cook in Florence doing tonight?

There was somewhere she had to be.

"Thank you," she told Dominic. "But I shouldn't have pried."

"Can I make it up to you? Something to eat?" He glanced at the lampredotti. "Or drink?"

His eyes were so earnest. The roll in his hand was dripping sauce down his long fingers, but he didn't seem to notice. Rosa watched that drip as it disappeared around his wrist, and then she watched his eyelashes as he blinked and then she watched the pair of Medici Guards patrolling the piazza in perfect step.

"I have to go see someone," she said. "But I wouldn't mind some company."

28

KHALID

"You're quiet," Sergeant Bianci commented. At Khalid's sidelong glance, he shook his head. "Quieter than usual."

"Thinking about tomorrow," said Khalid, which was not a lie.

I've never picked your pocket. I never would.

Guilt had rocketed through Khalid at Giacomo's protest. Of course. He'd *known* that Giacomo hadn't lifted Signore Traverio's money the night they'd met. But it had felt right, in that moment, to accuse him of it.

He was confused. Giacomo confused him. He said all these things and made all these points and assumed that Khalid would understand. *The same reason I know you would never strike me.* What did that *mean*?

He would ask Giacomo later. In the morning. After his patrol.

"This way," Sergeant Bianci said. They were in an older part of Florence, closer to the walls than the city center. Here, buildings and sheds were plastered with anti-Medici bills, so thick that they became background noise. Sergeant Bianci paid them no mind.

He was paying no mind to much of anything, in fact, now that Khalid considered him more closely. His gaze was constantly shifting, scanning the streets with restless attention. They passed a trio of City Guards who glared as they marched by. Sergeant Bianci barely blinked.

"Are you well, Sergeant?" Khalid ventured.

The sergeant's eyes slid to Khalid and then away again. "Well as can be expected."

"Captain Romano must be anxious about the banquet."

"Mm," said Sergeant Bianci.

Perhaps this will just be a quiet patrol, Khalid thought at the same time a crash and a shouted exclamation echoed up ahead. The noise jerked Khalid from his reverie and did the same to Sergeant Bianci beside him.

"There," Khalid said, pointing to a dark space between two buildings. The sergeant nodded and took off at a trot, Khalid on his heels. One after the other, they turned off the main street into a narrow alley.

It was black as pitch. The building walls and the cloud cover did a good job of blocking out the moonlight. Khalid squinted through the dark, searching out the source of the crash. "This is the Medici Guard," he called. "Is anyone injured?"

The only response was the sound of footsteps scraping against stone. "Sergeant, perhaps you should light your lantern," Khalid suggested.

Sergeant Bianci did not reply. But Khalid was becoming keenly aware of a presence at his back. There was someone standing between him and the street beyond.

Slowly, he turned.

"Hello, Yazid," said Vieri.

Then something hard and heavy slammed down on the back of Khalid's head and the world blew out like a candle.

29

SARRA

... just because you won't tell your brother about your work ...

... that does not make us family ...

What did Rosa Cellini know of anything? Sarra had spent weeks absorbing her orders. She'd done the job she'd been hired to do, and for what? The promise of a fool's fortune and the pleasure of being accused of idiotic sentimentality.

And was she wrong? whispered a treacherous voice inside Sarra's head. *You can't pretend you did not expect to be embraced like a sister. Not to yourself.*

Sarra's heels ground into the cobbles as she turned, decisive, onto her street. Soon she would be home. The thought kindled a spark inside her chest. She would see her brother. Someone who wanted her around. He'd tell her of the commissions he'd received and they'd make something to eat and she would be warm.

And lying.

An itch ran down the back of her neck. Sarra brushed it aside as another side effect of her guilty conscience. The outline of the print shop was in sight, looming in the lamplight—

Another itch tickled, this one strong enough to draw goose bumps, and Sarra, with two years of surviving delicate situations under her belt, could not ignore it. This was more than nagging shame—it was the unmistakable prickle of eyes.

She was being watched.

Under the pretense of adjusting her shoe, Sarra paused. She squinted out under her brows as she fussed, taking in the street. There was nothing obviously untoward, at least at first glance. Three men staggered across the road, leaning on one another in the companionable manner of drunks everywhere. A young woman paced outside an open door, lightly jouncing the fussing newborn in her arms.

And in the shadows of the baker's shop, a man slouched against the wall, arms folded across his chest.

He was so still that Sarra wondered if he was asleep on his feet. But the prickling on her neck didn't let up. He was watching her. He had to be. She wished she could see his face to be sure, but between the dark and the low brim of his hat, his features were obscured. She could only make out the smudged tattoos that marched over the backs of his hands, twisting up into the sleeves of his jerkin and disappearing from sight.

They regarded one another for a moment, a standoff in the dozing dark. Then the man's chin dipped in the barest of nods. He pulled his cloak tighter, and set off, slinking into the night.

Sarra shivered again. *Sleep*, she told herself. *You need sleep. You're imagining things.*

The print shop door barely made a sound as she swung it open, thoughts full of the soft bed waiting for her—

A room full of faces snapped up to stare at her. Hands grasped for dagger hilts. If Sarra hadn't been quite so surprised, she might have shouted.

"Shut the door, for Christ's sake—"

That was Pietro's voice, hissing over the heavy silence. He was glaring over the bed of the printing press. All she could do was stare back, mouth hanging open like a fish. "Shut the *door*, Sarra!" her brother repeated.

Dexterity had deserted her. She fumbled the latch shut, brain frantically scrambling to work out what she had just stumbled into.

The print shop was more crowded than it had been since Pietro had opened three years before. She counted six faces including Pietro's, mostly men. The oldest was perhaps in his late fifties. The youngest could not have been older than eight. And they were all staring at her with expressions ranging from anger all the way down to terror.

"You didn't say you'd be having company," Sarra said, turning back to the room.

Pietro just looked at her, stone-faced. "I didn't think you'd be home."

"Mm." The men were clustered around the printing press in a protective phalanx. Sarra paced closer, conscious that they were shifting to block her. She was aware, deep in her gut, that if she looked at whatever was on the printing press bed, she would not like what she saw. She was also aware that she was fairly certain she already knew what it would be. And the shortest of the press's protectors—a *little girl*, for Heaven's sake—couldn't do much to stop her. "You're working late," she observed. Placing a gentle hand on the top of the girl's cap, she leaned over, peering down at the press.

There was a sheet of paper there, freshly stamped. A bill. Sarra reached out, fingertips grasping the edge.

"Sarra" was all Pietro said before she flipped it over.

VIVA LA REPPUBLICA FIORENTINA screamed at her in gigantic, bold print. *Long live the Republic.*

Sarra's blood was ice in her veins as she looked up at her brother. "Pietro," she said. "What have you done?"

30

KHALID

K halid was running.

His robes flapped around his ankles and his sandals skidded against the cobblestones as he took corners too fast, legs pumping and arms flailing for balance. Wind whipped against his cheeks, and he braced himself for a blast of chilly Genoa damp—

But this breeze was warm. It carried an ocean scent that was light and fresh, so unlike the close, fishy stench of the Genoan docks. And that was when Khalid noticed the bright whitewashed walls that surrounded him, the vibrant blue doors. The wind did not feel like Genoa because he was not in Genoa.

He was in Tunis. He was home. And then—

"You're late."

He was tripping over the lintel into his father's textile shop, already waving an apology as he entered. "I know, I know—"

Baba stood near the front, facing down a stack of heavy rugs with worrying determination. "Yusuf and Fatma are in the back with Zeineb," he said. "She's been fussing. All night." Now that he was closer, Khalid could see the dark circles under his father's eyes.

The smell of cinnamon and stewing chicken wafted from the back door, and Khalid raised an eyebrow. "And Fatma is still cooking?"

Baba snorted affectionately. "Try telling that woman anything."

"I'll make sure she hasn't fallen asleep over the fire," Khalid said, and followed his nose through the shop and into the courtyard. It was a wide space, open so the sunlight might warm the glazed blue floor tiles. An oven was built into the side of one wall, glowing with heated coals. Another wall supported a pale awning, under which pillows and futons had been piled . . .

And where, sure enough, Fatma lay fast asleep, with Yusuf at her side and their baby between them. Which meant that the only person attending the bubbling tagine in the oven was a young man with interesting brown eyes that smiled at Khalid's arrival.

"She was the walking dead," he said, nodding toward Fatma. "And your brother wasn't much better. I packed them off before they could burn the shop down."

"Are you certain you can handle this?" Khalid asked, eyeing the simmering pot.

"Of course I can." The man grinned, familiar and mischievous. "Trust me."

For some reason, the words sank heavy in the pit of Khalid's stomach. "Giacomo—" he said, and it sounded like a plea.

Giacomo just laughed and took his hand. "Rise and shine, Yazid," he said.

Khalid frowned at him. "That's not my—"

Something hit Khalid's face, hard enough to set the world spinning. He lolled sideways, rolling his temple against something rough and wooden. His head pounded. His stomach surged. His arm throbbed. His entire body was a lightning storm of pain.

"He's awake."

Khalid was not certain that was true. He could still hear the ocean.

"Get him up."

Khalid was yanked, first to his knees and then to his feet. With no small effort, he winched open his eyes.

It was near–pitch-black. The only light came from a sliver of moon and a scattering of blurry stars that spun lazily above him. He swallowed down his nausea.

He was nowhere near the ocean, Tunisian, Genoan, or otherwise. No, he was in the back of an open cart on the marshy banks of the Arno River. Squinting through rippling pain, Khalid could make out the dense tree line that scooped back from the water, creating a peaceful, secluded inlet. The sight of it rang bells of familiarity in the back of Khalid's mind, but every time he tried to collect his thoughts, they scattered in a thousand dizzy directions.

There were no signs of life. Unless he counted the crossbow digging into his back.

"That's a nasty bruise." Khalid did not have to see the speaker's face to recognize his smug tone. Vieri's hand was heavy and rough on Khalid's shoulder. "Did you piss someone off?"

"Stop messing around." Khalid felt a disappointed twist in his chest as Sergeant Bianci stepped into view. There was no trace of his normal friendly warmth. Now the sergeant's eyes were sullen and dark. His own crossbow dangled loosely from one hand. "Get him down here," he ordered.

"What are you doing?" Khalid's mouth felt full of cotton.

"What a question!" Vieri crowed, jabbing at Khalid until he climbed down onto the riverbank. "After all your plans, you've got the balls to ask us what *we're* doing."

Khalid's right arm jarred when he reached the ground, sending agony through the rest of his body. He only barely caught himself against the cart as the world slipped from under him.

"Sergeant," Khalid said, forcing his lips and tongue to cooperate. "What is this?" Bianci wouldn't meet his eyes. Khalid tried again. "You do not have the authority—"

Vieri snorted. "We *are* the authority. Who else is there? The City Guard? They're on their way out." He jumped lightly down from the cart to loom over Khalid. "A friend of yours paid me a visit. He told me *all* about you."

One of Khalid's hands was numb. The other was a riot of scarlet agony. The ropes around his wrists were too tight. "What?"

"Oh yeah," Vieri said, all glee. "Turns out you've sold us a few lies! We were very surprised to hear it. Bianci especially, since, you know, he was the one who stuck his neck out to get you in the guard in the first place. I think you hurt his feelings."

"I have never lied to you," Khalid lied. "I swear—"

"Oh?" said Vieri. "So the name 'Traverio' doesn't ring any bells? How about Genoa? You ever been to Genoa?"

It was the mention of Signore Traverio's name that jogged his memory. Khalid took another look around him. The Arno was nearly black in the moonlight. A few paces down the shoreline, someone had dragged a large rowboat ashore. There was a canvas draped over it.

Il Rifugio. That was the name of this inlet. A smuggler's landing, one that Signore Traverio's associates had mentioned time and again in their reports. Not that this information did any good to him now.

"I'll take that as a no," Vieri said. "Let's try one last name. You let me know if this sounds familiar." He paced around Khalid, coming face to face with him. "Khalid al-Sarraj."

"Stop messing around," Bianci growled. "Let's get this over with."

"Fine, fine," Vieri grumbled. Grabbing a handful of Khalid's collar, Vieri shoved him down the boggy bank toward the river's edge. Khalid, unsteady as he was, did not resist.

Vieri and Bianci had learned his true identity. And instead of turning him over to Captain Romano and perhaps endangering their own livelihoods, they had decided to take care of the complication themselves. "Here," said Bianci, pointing to a flat rock in a patch of reeds. "Put him here."

"You heard the sergeant," Vieri said. His smile had too many teeth. "On your knees."

Khalid did not go to his knees. "This 'friend'. Was it the same one you spoke of before?"

Bianci was growing paler by the moment. "On your *knees*," he hissed.

"If I am to die," Khalid said, "I would like to know who I have to thank for it."

Vieri rolled his eyes. "Little fella," he said. "Wiry. Tattoos. That answer your question?"

It did more than answer Khalid's question. It turned Khalid's blood to ice. He barely felt the sting as Vieri's crossbow bolt nicked him. "Don't make me ask again."

Khalid obeyed, mind still a swirl of shock. Because if Marino had told Vieri and Bianci about Khalid, what else had he told them? What else did he *know*? Who else was in danger? And did Signore Traverio know this was happening at all?

"My partners will come after you for this," Khalid said, glaring up at the guardsmen.

Vieri snorted, but Bianci looked unsettled. "Very scary," Vieri said. "But we're onto you. Tomorrow, the Palazzo Medici becomes a fortress. Checkpoints, sentries, searches . . . no one's getting in, not even your friends. *If* they survive the night, that is."

"'If'—"

"That's enough," Bianci barked. Vieri shot him a sarcastic salute and stepped back. Suddenly, despite Vieri's insubordination and Bianci's discomfort, they were a united front. Even their faces blurred into a single set of features, regarding Khalid with impassive cruelty.

"Khalid al-Sarraj," Bianci intoned. "You have been found guilty of treason against the Medici family. Hereby you are relieved of your duties and sentenced to death. May God have mercy on you."

"Or not," said Vieri. And as one, the two guards brought their bows to bear.

There was a rushing in Khalid's ears. For a moment, he thought it was the much-loved music of the ocean surf. The ground rolled beneath him, keeping time with the swells of the waves.

And then the panic came. Adrenaline coated his tongue in coppery bitterness, and he realized what he was hearing was not the ocean at all. It was the pounding of his own heart, a racing drumbeat to warn him of the fact that he was about to die. He was about to die and it was his own fault.

His thoughts chittered and shrilled, one after another, chasing through his skull. *You have failed. You are a fool. You tried to save your family and you have doomed them instead. You will die here, hundreds of kilometers from home. No one will ever come looking for you, much less avenge you. You began this foolhardy journey alone, and you will end it alone—*

Why would I never steal from you?

Giacomo—

You'll figure it out.

No. He was not adrift. There was solid rock beneath him, digging into his knees. And more than that, there were people waiting for him—back in a lamplit millhouse further down the Arno, and across the ocean, in a whitewashed house in Tunis. He had not doomed anyone, not yet. He was not alone. And maybe he was not a fool.

"Trust," Giacomo had said. "Trust me."

He would just have to survive long enough to prove it to himself.

The crossbows released, but Khalid was already moving. He rolled to the left, keeping his weight on his good shoulder, before coming up in a low stance. One of the bolts had gone wide—Khalid was not sure whether it was Vieri's shot or Bianci's—but the other clipped his lower ribs, painting his skin with a line of fire. Khalid swayed for a teeth-gritting moment as pain threatened to send him unconscious. But the fog would have to wait until later.

Vieri and Bianci were too busy gaping to react. Khalid took the opportunity to rush Vieri, knocking his crossbow from his hands. In the next moment, he drove his shoulder into Bianci's stomach, bearing the man to the ground. The sergeant, soft from years of wine and women, crumpled into a ball. Khalid darted forward to snatch the man's belt-knife and wasted no time in flipping it around to saw at his bindings—

Which was when a battering ram *slammed* into his side.

Khalid crumpled to one knee. Someone had sucked all the air from the world. He could not breathe and his arm was on fire and something was creaking loose in his chest—

Vieri stepped in front of him, tucking a blackjack into his belt. "It's over," he said. He plucked up his crossbow again, training it on Khalid. "You're going to disappear now, and no one is going to—what are you doing?"

Khalid was pushing himself to his feet. His arm dangled uselessly at his side. There was nowhere to run, not with that crossbow in front of him and the river behind him.

Surprising even himself, Khalid smiled.

"Go to hell," said Vieri, and fired.

Khalid al-Sarraj toppled backward into the Arno River and disappeared.

31

ROSA

It was always a long walk to the northern part of the city, but it felt particularly long tonight, with Dominic trotting at her heels. The bustle of the crowd made the quiet between them louder—unbearably loud, deafening.

Dominic broke first, clearing his throat. "I'm afraid to say anything."

Rosa glanced sideways at him. "Me too."

"I don't want to fight."

"If we fight you could just apologize again."

"I don't want to apologize."

"Then let's not fight."

Dominic muttered something that sounded like "Great start." Rosa chose not to hear it.

"So. Your mother is an artist. You like lampredotto. You're from . . ."

"Chiusi," Dominic said.

"You're a long way from home. Do you miss it?"

His smile was sweet. Rosa wiped the last of the lampredotto grease off her hands with too much focus. "All the time."

"Why don't you go back?"

"I thought I might. When my apprenticeship is over. But now . . . I don't know. What would I do in Chiusi? It's such a tiny town. I'd have to . . . find some cheesemonger willing to take a chance on an ancient apprentice. Spend the rest of my days hawking Pecorino in the marketplace."

"Not painting?"

"No one needs frescoes in Chiusi. Especially not from a mediocre artist."

"I've seen your work. You're not mediocre."

"Ah," Dominic said, "but that's not *my* work. I can copy anybody *else's* work—like that fresco in the Magi Chapel. I can replicate it so well you'd never be able to tell the difference between their brush-strokes and my own. But when the time comes to *create* something?" His shrug was full of effort. "It's no wonder Master Michelangelo despairs of me."

"He despairs of everyone."

"Maybe." He shook his head, an attempt at dislodging the topic to leave it in the street behind them. "What about you? Where are you from?"

She shouldn't have been caught off-guard by the question. She could lie—she *should* lie, she had been lying to him since she'd met him. But something about where she was headed and what was looming on the horizon was making it impossible to come up with the name of a town—any town in the entire world.

She'd been silent too long. Dominic nudged her arm. "Come on. Aside from the fact that Master Michelangelo is your uncle, I don't know anything about you."

"Lampredotto," Rosa managed.

"Lampredotto doesn't count."

"Are you going to the Pope's banquet tomorrow?"

Dominic's eyebrows shot up. "This is your idea of a neutral topic?"

"Dominic, we could argue over the color of the sky."

He grinned. "To be fair, that's the kind of thing you should never bring up to an artist."

Someone laughed at that, and Rosa was surprised to realize that it was her—the sound bubbling up from deep in her chest and twisting out her throat. Dominic's smile widened and he glanced down, pleased with himself.

"I will be there," he said. "The Pope was pleased with my work in the chapel, so I was extended an invitation. I suppose . . . you have something to say about that?"

A million things, in fact. But when she opened her mouth, the only thing that came out was, "We're here."

The Church of Santo Stefano in Pane was not an impressive structure, at least from the outside. It slouched against its neighbors, a relic from another era in a city that was made of relics from other eras. It was difficult to take in the sloping roof, the crumbling pillars, the scuffed mosaics, without comparing it to the gleaming white of Il Duomo, which loomed proudly only a few kilometers away. Rosa had been told by—she'd been told that the church was built on the foundations of a Roman ruin from eons past. It certainly felt that way, steeped in centuries the way that very ancient things were.

Her palms were sweating. She had been putting this off from the moment she'd set foot back in Florence—*too long, too long, sorry, sorry*—

She pushed through the church door, and didn't waste a glance to check that Dominic followed her inside.

For all the chaos of the city streets, time had stopped inside the church. The pews, the altar, the windows—the years bypassed them all, preserving them as they were preserved in Rosa's memory. There was the fresco of the saint with the crossed eyes—there was the chip in the floor she'd definitely had nothing to do with—there was the pew where she'd huddled over her clasped hands, too terrified by ghost stories of Roman centurions to look up—

When she'd visited in the past, the church had been filled with whispering worshippers muttering their prayers to the golden cross that loomed over them. Now, too late in the evening for it to even really be evening anymore, the place was silent.

The door swung closed behind Dominic, and he paused to take in the empty nave. "I thought you said you had to see someone?"

Rosa squared her shoulders. "This way."

Their footsteps boomed against the chilly stone walls as she led him down an aisle. There, just where she remembered it, was a small altar on the left. It was as understated as the rest of the church, but—and perhaps this was just Rosa's imagination—it possessed a certain gravity. A painting hung from the wall, surrounded by sputtering candles and wilting flowers. A man gazed out from the chipped gilded frame; he was young, serious-eyed, his shock of curling hair wild enough to give him a second halo.

Rosa slid into a pew and looked up at him.

"My mother always used to bring me here, whenever we were in Florence," she said. Her words filled the corners of the empty church, echoing in the hush. "Because of him. Saint Stephen. He's probably—he might be one of your master's saints."

"Artists?" Dominic sank down onto the pew next to her.

"Masons."

"If Michelangelo heard you call him a mason—"

"My mother said as long as there was a church named after him nearby, we were never far from home. So every town and every city we traveled through, no matter where we were, we always found the nearest altar to Saint Stephen and lit a candle." Leaning forward, Rosa picked up a guttering candle. "Saint Stephen is also the patron saint of a city called Prato." She touched the flame to the blackened wick of another candle, watching the golden light grow. "You asked me where I'm from. So that's . . . where I'm from."

She felt Dominic go still next to her. "I've heard of Prato."

Rosa's smile was cold. "I'd imagine so. Even in Chiusi."

The Cathedral of Santo Stefano in Prato had been—so like this small church, but so different. When Rosa had been a child, she had thought the place had been conjured up by God himself, since surely it was impossible that a man would have been able to build ceilings as soaring or paint frescoes as glorious . . .

She'd made the mistake of telling her mother this, once. Lena hadn't been angry with her—Lena Cellini was never angry with her daughter. But she had looked uncharacteristically serious as she'd taken Rosa by the shoulders.

"You listen to me," she'd said. "There is nothing so 'impossible' in this world that God has to take it on himself. There are only things that very clever people have not done yet."

Hearing this blasphemy from her mother's mouth had rattled Rosa. But she'd never been able to shake the notion that a place as beautiful as the Cathedral had to be infused with some magic. Even as she traveled at her mother's side learning how the crooked world worked, she had clung to that belief. It was common for her to sneak into the pews after completing a job with Lena—not to pray, but simply to bask, to feel safe, surrounded by something . . . incorruptible.

Which is why she'd hidden there when the army marched in.

"It was five years ago," Rosa said, turning the last lampredotto over in her hands. "In the last days of the Republic. Prato was—it was—"

Quiet. Calm. Too small, sometimes, to Rosa at twelve. *Home.*

Dominic didn't prompt her, but his warmth at her side grew as he leaned closer. "It was invaded," she finished. "The Catalonians. They took the city in less than a day."

There had been warnings, of course. Rosa remembered the old men whispering in the street. Shop windows had shuttered. Mothers had kept their children inside. But so few had *left*. And why would they? They had the might of the Florentine army to protect them.

The wide wings of the Republic would shelter Prato, just as they had promised for almost two decades.

But the Florentine force that had arrived had been a skeleton of the whole. Just enough to ease the guilt of the Republic, which had kept most of its soldiers home to ensure its own protection. And by the time this reality dawned, the Catalonian army had been on their doorstep.

So Rosa had hidden in the Cathedral.

"It wasn't a battle," she said—whether it was to Dominic or to the painted gaze of Saint Stephen, she wasn't sure. "No matter what you heard. The Florentine soldiers—the few there were—died fast. And then so did the rest of the city."

For a few hours, it had seemed as though the Cathedral might actually be the sanctuary she'd believed that it was. The sounds of fighting and dying filtered through the windows, the smell of blood wafted in, the shadows of soldiers marched in silhouette along the street outside. But none of the men were inclined to violate the sanctity of the church. Rosa had huddled with dozens of women and children, doing her best to keep someone's toddler calm and resolutely not thinking that Lena should have come to find her by now.

The peace didn't hold. It was never going to. Rosa was barely surprised when the Cathedral doors burst inward, admitting a flood of soldiers. She had watched in dissociated calm as her babysitting charge was ripped away, as gilded sconces and tapestries had been torn from the walls, as the frescoes that had always whispered God to her had been torched. The high ceilings—such a marvel—rang with screams and cries—

Even now, sitting in a smaller church in a larger city, Rosa could smell the smoke. "They sacked the city," she said. "Burning, raping, murdering. Five thousand dead in one day."

Dominic's voice was hoarse. "But you got out."

She hadn't meant to. But she'd been sneaking into the Cathedral of Saint Stephen for too long not to know a few secret ways out, and while she was lost in her shock, her body had done the thinking for her. In what had felt like the blink of an eye, Rosa found herself standing in an alley off the Piazza del Duomo, struggling to breathe through the billowing smoke.

The screaming and crying had long been silenced, and eerie quiet had descended. The only voices filtered from streets away. Rosa could pick up a scant few words in her limited Catalonian, but the boisterous laughter told her more than a direct translation ever could. Heart pounding, she backed further into the alley, pressing against the wall, feeling the knobs in the stone dig into her spine—

"*Rosa!*"

Only years of training at her mother's side had kept Rosa from jumping out of her skin at the hissed whisper of her own name. Looking up, she'd found a familiar pair of dark eyes—red-rimmed, from smoke or tears—peering down at her from the rooftop.

"Mama?" she'd croaked.

Lena Cellini's smile of relief could have lit the whole world. "Come on, my girl. It's time for us to get moving."

It had been surprisingly easy to avoid the notice of the Catalonian army as Rosa and Lena picked their way across the Prato rooftops. Lena had moved above the chaos like she was out for an evening walk—mother and daughter, taking in the summer night air. Every time Rosa had slipped, she'd been there to keep her from falling. Every time Rosa had hesitated, she'd been there with a smile of encouragement. Buoyed in Lena's wake, it had been almost possible to ignore the carnage playing out below them.

They hadn't stopped moving until they reached the city walls. Lena had dropped to her belly on the last rooftop, inspecting the intimidating limestone with a casual air. Rosa had sprawled next to her, trying to mimic Lena's calm, despite the fact that her heart had been hammering beneath her ribs. "Almost there," her mother had whispered. "Do you hear that?"

Rosa had closed her eyes to listen. It had taken a moment to tune out the din of destruction, but once she'd managed it . . . "The river!"

Lena had grinned. "Are you ready for a swim?"

The descent from the rooftop had been more of a controlled tumble, but Rosa had managed it without breaking any bones. Soon, she'd stood beside her mother at the base of the wall, watching as she deftly hauled herself to the crenelated top. Lena had crouched there, fighting for balance, before turning to lend her a hand—

Rosa would never forget the way her face had paled.

Six soldiers had appeared at the end of the street. They were no longer marching in unison—they were *heightened*, somehow, whether on bloodlust or wine—but they had wasted no time in spotting Lena at the top of the wall. One of them had shouted something that Rosa couldn't understand—

And suddenly the soldiers had been stampeding toward them, all in a rush. Rosa had stood, frozen, unable to do so much as breathe—

"Up, up, up—" she'd heard her mother urge, and muscle memory had her raising her hands mechanically. She'd felt her wrists grasped in Lena's strong grip, and then she had been rising, hauled, until she sprawled across the top of the wall next to her mother.

The shouts of the soldiers had amplified, ringing from all directions. More reinforcements had been on their way. Rosa hadn't been able to tear her eyes from the men closing in below. She hadn't been able to stop herself from noting, sickly, the glint of their crossbows . . . and the figure who strode behind the soldiers at a sedate pace, backlit by the setting sun.

"You have to go, Rosa," Lena had told her. Her words had been muffled. They hadn't wanted to fit into Rosa's ears. "You have to go. Now."

"What—about you?" Rosa had stammered, eyes still fixed on the approaching figure.

"I'll be right behind you," Lena had said. Her face had been serious—more serious than she'd been on the rooftops, more serious even than when she'd lectured Rosa about mankind's ingenuity. "But you have to go."

Rosa wished now that she'd been looking at her mother before she'd fallen—pushed backward into the Bisenzio River. Instead, she had been staring at the street below, and the puzzling figure who had just stepped into a ring of torchlight. It had only been a glimpse, but the light was enough to illuminate the bright red of his clothes—Cardinal's robes—and a face that anyone raised in the shadow of the Florentine Republic would recognize.

It was this that had been etched beneath her eyelids as she hit the water.

The Bisenzio had been rough, swollen by summer rains, but Rosa was a strong swimmer. Breaking the surface of the water, she'd found that she was alone—no sign of Lena. Too scared to call out, she'd gasped for air and peered through the growing dusk back to the city.

Lena had still been crouched atop the wall. But as the current carried Rosa downstream, she saw the silhouette of something that had turned her to ice.

Two crossbow bolts protruded from her mother's chest. She'd clutched at them, in shock or in pain—and as Rosa had watched, a third arrow flicked up from the darkness to bury itself beside the first two.

The wordless sob that had torn from Rosa's throat was barely human. She had struggled against the river, trying to swim back to the city—to her mother—to the wreckage of everything that had raised her—

But Lena's head had turned. Her eyes had found Rosa's, *impossibly*, even in the dark. She had smiled her familiar smile. She had shaken her head—once. And she had toppled forward—off the wall, back into broken and savaged Prato, and out of Rosa's sight.

The pull of that memory was almost as strong as the river's undertow. It took Rosa a long moment to work herself free, breathing deeply against the vivid images, until she found herself sitting once again on the pew in the tiny church, blinking back tears and clutching a greasy lampredotto next to Dominic Fontana.

She angrily swiped at her cheeks. "I shouldn't have gotten out," she told Dominic roughly. "My mother didn't." It annoyed her, the shake in her hand, as she reached out to place the roll in front of Saint Stephen. "She liked Signora Carlotta's recipe too."

"I'm—so sorry, Rosa."

Finally, Rosa allowed herself to face him. He was grim in the wake of her story. Suddenly it was the most important thing on Rosa's long list of priorities that he be made to *understand*.

"Five thousand innocent lives," she repeated. "Do you know why?"

"Could there be a reason for anything like that?"

"Yes. The soldiers who invaded and killed and raided might have been Catalonian. But they were there *because the Medici family recruited them*. I saw him, Dominic. Giuliano de' Medici. Your Pope. When he was still just a Cardinal, he brought the soldiers to Prato. And if you ask him, the reason for that massacre was to 'keep the peace.'" Rosa laughed. "What a joke. The only chaos in Prato was the chaos they created. But do you know what Florence did after Prato was destroyed?"

"They ended the Republic," Dominic said faintly.

"Prato was an example," Rosa bit out. "And it was very clearly received. Florence welcomed the Medici family back with open arms.

No more freedom—just more greed." Her blood was fire in her veins. "For the Medici family and their avarice, Prato burned."

Dominic's eyes were soft and sorry. His lips were the same, parted on a soundless apology. He looked as though he had no words for whatever he wanted to say.

"I—" he said, which was as far as he got before the church door shut with a slam. Rosa twisted in the pew, ready to glare at the intruder—

Alberto Spinelli, the world's worst criminal mastermind, swayed in the aisle. He waved, the green bottle in his fist sloshing wine over the flagstones.

"It's you," he breathed.

The bottom dropped out of Rosa's stomach. *Shit.*

32

SARRA

S arra barely heard the *click* of the door closing behind the last of Pietro's . . . friends? Guests? Co-conspirators? She was too deafened by the panicked ringing in her ears. She couldn't look away from the paper, phrases like "Medici corruption" and "A return to freedom!" stoking her panic higher.

Pietro was still watching her, impassive. It was too much. The sight of the press, the symbol of the life they'd scraped out together, was too much. "Upstairs," she said, strained through her teeth. She stalked to the back of the shop and up the stairs to their rooms.

The paper was still clutched in her hands, and when she reached their kitchen she slammed it on the table. Pietro slipped in after her, and they were alone, two strangers staring at one another in the home they had built together, silence stretching between them. But more than before, the silence was heavy. It carried weight.

It was possible that it carried enough weight to break them.

"I don't understand," she said slowly, "what in God's name you were thinking."

Pietro's lips set in a stubborn line under his beard. "Everything in there is true." He wasn't looking at her. He certainly wasn't looking at the kitchen table, where the ink still stood wet on the crumpled bill. VIVA LA REPPUBLICA FIORENTINA. It might as well have been a suicide note.

She felt like the top of her head was about to pop off. "It's *treason*, Pietro, it doesn't matter if it's *true*. What was your plan? You and that handful of nobodies—some of them are children! And you're using them to take on the entire city?"

"I didn't want Gio and Cat around. But once they found out about us—"

"A couple of *kids* uncovered your seditious society. And you really think this whole thing won't be traced back to you? How many printing presses are there in this city? I bet you can count them on both hands."

"Someone has to stand up to the Medici family."

"And you're doing it with *pamphlets*." A few more pieces clicked together and Sarra reeled. "Lord—the riot. It started when a boy was caught posting *your bills*. *You* started it—"

"Was I supposed to let them make an example of Gio?"

"Did you have to set the city on fire to save him?"

He had the decency to look abashed. "It may have gotten out of control. But people are *angry*. Do you know what's brewing up north? There are those who want to break from the Church entirely—"

"There are always those who want to break from the Church—"

"Not like this. That Medici Pope has us all on a leash of indulgences, and he's leading us right to Hell for the sake of his own power and wealth—"

"This isn't one of your university lectures!" she cried. "You can't go around stoking sedition just because you've been missing theological debates!" He still wasn't looking at her. "Pietro. *Listen to me.*"

His eyes finally snapped up, blazing with frustration and hurt. "No," he said. "I'm done listening. I want to *talk*. Where were you tonight?"

Her shoulders tensed. "I was *working*—"

Pietro barked a bitter laugh. "For the de' Baldis, right—"

"While you were carving a target on your own back for the Medici firing squad."

"Let's not forget *your* target," Pietro shot back. "Or do you think I'm a fool?"

"Of course I don't—"

"You've been treating me like one. Rosa Cellini comes to town, and you're out all hours of the night, wearing my old clothes and keeping secrets? Really, Sarra? Or do I call you the Tinkerer? It's so difficult to remember sometimes."

Speech deserted Sarra. Because he was right, at the foundation of it. All of her flimsy excuses . . . it was insulting to believe she'd fooled him for even a single moment.

Her father had always answered Pietro's questions truthfully. Perhaps part of the reason for this was that the Nepi family was not good at lying.

"I'm frightened for you" is what she finally managed, and damn everything, there were tears pricking at her eyes. She dashed them away. "I'm—I'm just frightened for you."

"Yes, well," he said gruffly. "I'm frightened for you, too."

And then he went to the sideboard and got two cups. A moment later, feeling as though she might fly apart at the seams, Sarra retrieved a bottle of wine and filled them.

They drank.

"How long have you known?" Sarra asked.

He met her eyes over the rim of his wine cup. "I've always known."

"But *how*?"

"How could I not? You'd talked about joining up with Papa and the Cellinis since you learned how to speak. And then—when Papa died and our debts began to mount . . . it didn't take long to hear of Sarra the Tinkerer. It's not difficult arithmetic."

"Why didn't you say something?"

He looked so much like Papa in this light. "And drive you away? Papa was gone and—so was Signora Cellini. And Rosa—we didn't know where she was. I didn't want to lose my sister too. I didn't want us to lose each other." The candlelight reflected in his eyes, brightened by unshed tears. "Why didn't you?"

"I promised Papa," she whispered. "He didn't want you dragged into—all this. Not when you hated it so much." She dabbed at her cheeks with her sleeve. "I'm sorry. I'm really sorry. I didn't mean to break that promise."

"You didn't," Pietro said. "And besides, I never would have asked you to make it in the first place."

"Yes, but—you never liked that Papa was a grifter. You wanted a quiet life. You were leaving the university and all of that politicking. You don't like chaos."

"Don't I?" He tapped the bill, and Sarra managed a tearful laugh. "I was happy with my life as a printer. But I missed the excitement of university. I thought I would be fine without it, but then I scratched that itch and—"

Sarra nodded. "You love it."

Her brother's smile was crooked. "I've missed my sister."

Of all the things, why was *this* what did her in? Sarra's face crumpled. She set her wine on the table before her trembling hands could upset it, a sob shaking her shoulders. "I've—I've missed being a sister."

"Hey now—*shh, shh*—" Pietro nearly toppled his chair as he rushed to her side, wrapping an arm around her. She turned her face into his shoulder and let herself cry, let him pat at her head, let herself be absolved.

"I don't want to be half a person anymore," she told him, when she could muster words without choking on them.

"I don't either," said Pietro. "Family and chaos. Without both, the Nepis are a pair of ghosts."

They sat there for a long moment, as somewhere behind them the fire crackled, waves of warmth suffusing the room. Sarra took a deep breath, feeling her chest loosen for the first time in what must have been years.

"How about Rosa?" Pietro finally asked. "Is she a ghost too?"

Thinking of Rosa stung, but less than it had an hour ago. "I think," Sarra said, "that she will be if she's not careful."

"Is she—in danger?"

Are you? was his unspoken question. She decided to answer it out loud for a change. "I'll come through," she said. "In one piece, even. So will she." A jaw-cracking yawn stopped her from continuing, and Pietro snickered at the sight of her tonsils.

"You better go to bed," he said. "I'll bank the fire. Something tells me you have a big day tomorrow."

"Mm." She drained her wine cup and made her way toward the bedroom, already taking the braids out of her hair. There was a release in her scalp that she hadn't realized she'd needed, an absence of tension she felt deep in her eye sockets.

"Sarra!"

Pietro crashed through the door, his face an ashen mask of blank horror. "What in the world—" she said, before breaking off in a cough. There was a haze in the air, thin but growing steadily thicker. "Is the chimney blocked?" she asked.

"No fire in the hearth," he said. "It's downstairs. The shop—it's the shop—"

Sarra was across the kitchen and to the door in the space between two heartbeats. She barely heard Pietro shouting "No, Sarra—" before she yanked the door open and—

How was it possible? The first floor of their building had become a doorway to hell while they had been shouting at one another in their kitchen. Flames billowed, roaring and crackling and leaving nothing but black char in their wake. Through the blaze, Sarra could make out the shape of the printing press, a shadowy skeleton standing against an inferno. Sturdy as it was, it had not yet crumbled to ash, but as Sarra watched, one of the struts holding the tray in place snapped, sending a shower of red-hot lettered ingots scattering to the ground.

The heat was unimaginable, rolling up the stairs in a solid wall that blew Sarra's hair away from her face. She doubled over, hacking coughs threatening to turn her lungs inside out, eyes streaming in the smoke.

"Here—" Pietro shoved something damp into her hand—a water-soaked rag. She pressed it over her nose and mouth and started down the stairs with some mindless notion to somehow—*somehow*—salvage her brother's livelihood—

With a shower of sparks and a deafening crash, a beam parted ways with the roof and smashed into the stairs just a few steps down from Sarra. She tripped over her skirts, stumbling backward with a yell. Pietro caught her under the arms and hauled her back up the stairs.

Her shoe had just skittered off the top step when the entire staircase collapsed onto the landing below. Sarra and Pietro threw themselves back into their kitchen, scrambling away from the flames that billowed even higher now, licking at the walls, at the doorway, at the ceiling.

With a kick, Sarra slammed the door shut on the fire and shoved herself onto her hands and knees. "Window," she wheezed, grabbing for Pietro's sleeve and dragging him up. "Window."

He nodded, his eyes bloodshot above the rag he'd shoved over his own mouth. Together, they dashed for the small window that looked out over the Oltrarno street below. The flames had drawn a small crowd that was growing with every passing second, onlookers and neighbors who feared for their own homes. The beginnings of a water brigade, stretching from the shop to the Arno, were starting to form, but given the size of the blaze, it would be hours before the fire was extinguished. The remaining bystanders were attempting to contain the spread of the flames.

And in the midst of this commotion were three men, hats pulled low over their eyes, watching the blaze from the shadows of a doorway half a block down.

If Sarra had not spent her life among criminals and crooks, she would never have given them a second glance. But they were too calm, too still amidst the swirling hysteria. And they watched the fire with an almost . . . proprietary air.

One of them sported a mass of twisting tattoos.

The kitchen door toppled inward with a horrible crash, and suddenly there was a lot less floor than there had been a moment ago. The heat of the flames was singeing her hair. There was no more time to waste. "Over here," Sarra rasped, striding to the only other window, which looked out over a narrow, dingy alley. They usually kept it boarded up, a desperate attempt to block out the awful smells that wafted inside during the warm summer months.

At her nod, Pietro began prying at the boards. Soon, there was a space large enough for even Pietro to squeeze through. He cupped his hands into a stirrup and Sarra allowed him to lift her up over the sill. She dangled there for a moment before dropping to the cobbles. Pietro followed a moment later, his landing much less graceful, and she helped him to his feet.

"Get out of sight," she said. "Find somewhere safe to spend the night. I'll find you in the morning."

"Sarra, what—"

She squeezed his arm. "I'll find you," she repeated. "*Go.*"

Pietro nodded, terse, and then she was alone. Feeling her heart throbbing somewhere in her throat, Sarra the Tinkerer took off at a jog, down the alley, away from the print shop window.

Behind her, Sarra Nepi's quiet life burned.

33

ROSA

Alberto wove toward Rosa like a bleary bad dream. "It is you," he said again, loud enough to send his words echoing off the church walls.

Dominic stepped in front of Rosa. "Keep your voice down, man," he said. "Don't you know where you are?"

But Alberto was either too drunk to hear him, or too drunk to care. "You're Sarra's friend."

Rosa frowned with gentle concern. "You have me confused with someone else, signore."

"Rosa. You're *Rosa*. I've been looking for you for *weeks*."

Dominic glanced at Rosa, confused. "Who is this?"

Alberto was getting too close. She rose, straightening her skirts. "I have no idea."

"You're *Rosa*," Alberto insisted again. He really did smell. "It's you. I've been following you since the Mercato Vecchio."

If that was the case then Rosa's senses had truly been blinded this evening—by anticipation, by memory, by Dominic, or by all three together. She placed a gentle hand on Dominic's sleeve. "I believe he's drunk," she whispered. "We'd better leave him to it."

Alberto did not block her path as she approached, but he also didn't stop talking. "I just spent over a month in the city cells," he said. "Because of that job *you* crashed. My whole crew got taken that night, but you—walked away. You *knew*."

There was a confused crease between Dominic's brows that Rosa didn't like. "Knew what?" he asked.

Alberto waggled his fingers. "Knew how it was gonna go," he said.

"She's Saint Nicholas. She knows how it's gonna go. Hey!" Rosa was almost to the door now, escape within reach. *Shut up, shut up.* But Alberto just kept going, louder and louder. "You owe me! You screwed me over and—I don't know how but—you *owe* me. Hey! You hearing me?"

She wasn't. She was closing the door on Alberto and striding across the piazza and putting off looking at Dominic's face for as long as possible.

She'd managed to make it a good distance before Dominic spoke. "Rosa."

She didn't slow. If she kept moving, maybe she might be able to outrun the inevitable. Instead, she flashed him a bright smile—the same one her mother had given her right before she'd pushed Rosa into the Bisenzio. The same one Rosa had worn every day since. "I don't envy that man when the monks find him passed out beneath the cross tomorrow morning."

"Rosa."

"I think there's a tavern in the next piazza, if you're still hungry—" He was looking at her as though he didn't know who she was, but she forged onward, wheedling. "Come on, Dominic. You didn't take that drunk seriously, did you?"

"He knew you."

"I bet he thinks he knows a lot of people."

"He called you Saint Nicholas."

"This is what I'm trying to tell you. He was out of his mind."

"Saint Nicholas is the patron saint of thieves."

Rosa searched inside herself for the core of icy, burning, angry strength that lived between her lungs. She took a breath in and, on the exhale, let it seep through her body, lighting her up, clearing away some of the muddle clogging her head. "Of merchants, too," she said. "What's your point?"

"So you're a merchant?"

She could see every detail of him with frozen clarity—the cracks in his expressionless mask, the doubt and hurt flickering through. "No," she said. "I'm not."

"You're a thief," Dominic said. Rosa just looked at him. He shook his head, his composure fracturing further. "I knew there was something about you—I knew you were—"

"You didn't."

"I know an imitation when I see one," he snapped. "It's my job. And you have *always* been an imitation. Are you even Master Michelangelo's niece?"

"No."

"Does he know? You're . . . scamming him?" He paced away, running a hand through his hair. "No. No, it's the Medici family, isn't it? Of course it is. Is your name even Rosa?"

She realized with a start that her icy strength was flickering. With every heartbeat it withdrew further, retreating back to the core of her. The places it left behind ached and burned, like fingers warming after too long in the winter air.

This was Dominic's fault. He had tricked her into lowering her guard, and now she was standing in this piazza like a *fool*, grasping for calm that was beyond her reach.

"Why would you believe anything I tell you, if I am what you say I am?" she asked, trying not to wince at the wildness in her own voice.

"Tell me anyway."

"My name *is* Rosa. Rosa Cellini."

Dominic laughed. "You're right, I don't believe you."

"I was born in Prato. Everything I told you tonight is true. Everything the Medici family has done—"

"They haven't lied to me."

The thaw had left her vulnerable and cruel. It *hurt*. She wanted to make him hurt too. "They lie to you every day. They invite you to their banquets and promise you fame and riches. Prestige. Patronage. But you said it yourself. You're a mediocre copycat. How far do you think that patronage will take you without the talent to back it up?" She advanced on him. "Do you know what the Pope sees when he looks at you? It's the same thing I see. A connection to your master. An easy target. A mark."

Dominic flinched back. "Why are you doing this?"

"They murdered five thousand men, women, and children. They murdered my mother. They will do the same to everyone in Florence, if it means they can keep their power. They're already gathering funds to buy another army. I will not apologize for myself, Signore Fontana. *You* are the one who keeps running back to them."

Betrayal, anger, frustration, doubt . . . they were all laid bare on Dominic's face in the torchlight. Her own feelings surged in response, a painful mirror, and Rosa channeled the last of her icy strength into keeping her distance.

If he'd taken a single step closer, she would have been done for. But Dominic only bowed. When he straightened, that impassive mask was back in place. "Goodbye, signorina."

The last scraps of ice inside of her steamed and evaporated with every step Dominic Fontana took from her. By the time he was out of sight, she was parboiled, tender and vulnerable. And it was all her own fault.

She fled.

He is a distraction, she thought. *He is a* distraction *and you ran straight toward him. How could you possibly think you had something in common?*

He could turn you in, whispered another insidious voice in her head. *He knows too much.*

This was why she'd kept their circle closed. This was why her life had been her work. This is why she'd left no room for family. Anything beyond that meant disaster. It meant either her work would collapse, or she would. It meant he couldn't—*wouldn't*—understand.

Rosa didn't notice that she'd crossed the city walls until she heard the rush of the river and realized there was lush green grass padding her footsteps. Peering blearily through the night, she found the silhouette of the millhouse at the top of the bank. There was a candle flickering in the window—someone was still awake.

Something in the river sloshed. Rosa stopped dead.

It had not been the lapping of the current. It was too big to be a fish or a bird. Which meant that whatever had made that sound was either an animal or—

She turned around.

There was a body in the river shallows, limbs outflung. Even in the dark, Rosa could make out the dark smears on the clothing. The clothing that she *knew*.

"Khalid?" she whispered.

One bloodshot eye opened. One arm twitched.

In the river, Khalid coughed. "We have a problem."

34

GIACOMO

"Later," Khalid had said. Giacomo had thought this a cruel promise—dragging out some delicious inevitability, forcing Giacomo (who had never been a patient man) to pace the millhouse, listening to Agata's snores and torturously anticipating *later*.

If Giacomo had known what *later* entailed, he would not have been so eager.

It had been Rosa's shouts that summoned him down to the river, where the sight of Khalid—of his bruises, his wounds, his broken bones—had stunned Giacomo wordless. He had silently followed Rosa's orders, and together they had managed to wrangle the man to his feet, half-supporting and half-dragging him up the embankment to the mill. Giacomo had lain Khalid on the kitchen table while Agata—roused by Khalid's groans and Rosa's swears—had busied herself with boiling water or grinding herbs or other witchy tasks.

Giacomo lingered, useless, as Rosa interrogated Khalid about what happened, and then interrogated Agata about the state of his injuries. He stood by as she threw a shawl around her shoulders and dashed off again to find Michelangelo, to track down Sarra, to scrounge out the tattered remnants of their plan and stitch them back together. It was only when Agata began to bark commands—to build up the fire, to fetch bandages, to press Khalid's shoulders down while she splinted his arm—that he could move, purpose piercing through the miasma of shock.

Rosa was right, he thought. *I really shouldn't have given that toast.*

Finally, the flurry of activity subsided, the only evidence of its passing in the rivers of sweat on Khalid's forehead and the trembling muscles of Giacomo's arms. Agata gave the knotted bandage at Khalid's side a pat, tartly informed him that he would not be dying tonight, and turned her stern glare on Giacomo.

"Keep him conscious," she ordered, her voice low. "If he sleeps, he may never wake."

And with that terrifying directive, she bustled back to her workbench.

Giacomo, suddenly aware that Khalid's shoulders were very warm and bare beneath his hands, eased back to put some space between them—and found himself caught in a lightning-fast grip. Khalid's good hand had somehow snagged one of Giacomo's wrists, clamping down hard enough that Giacomo could feel the bones grinding.

"Hah," Giacomo said. "Well. Looks like there's nothing wrong with *that* arm."

"Giacomo," Khalid said. His eyes were half-lidded with pain.

"Shh," Giacomo said, because that seemed to be the thing to do. "Don't speak."

"My arm is broken, not my tongue," Khalid replied, with a flash of irritation that warmed Giacomo. "And you said we could talk later."

"Khalid—"

Khalid's eyes slipped closed, his breath evening, and a shock of panic ran through Giacomo. "Alright, alright!" he exclaimed. "We'll talk! We'll talk about whatever you want!" Khalid opened his eyes again, glimmering up at Giacomo with a spark of mirth through all the pain, and Giacomo sagged over him. "Sadistic man."

"Yes," said Khalid. And then: "You never picked my pocket."

Giacomo laughed, feeling a little manic. "Are you still preoccupied with this, Signore al-Sarraj?"

"You dare me to strike you, even though you crumple in the face of threat—"

"I don't *crumple*."

"Because you know I will not." Khalid's gaze was fuzzy but intent. "I did not understand at first. But I do now."

"You figured it out?" Giacomo asked.

Khalid nodded, muzzily satisfied. "You trust me."

Giacomo's cheeks flamed. "Is that all?"

"No," Khalid said. He lolled his head back. "Look in my bag."

Giacomo wanted to laugh off the request, but there was something in Khalid's dark gaze that brought him up short. Whatever this was, it was important to Khalid, and so he slid out of Khalid's grip and went to rustle through the satchel. It was mostly empty, save for a set of clothes, a few coins, a spare bit of leather thong, and—

"The letter," Khalid confirmed. Giacomo peered at it in the firelight. "It is for you."

Khalid's eyelids were sagging again, and this time Giacomo did not think it was feigned. He hurried back to the man's side, taking care to jostle him a little as he hoisted himself up onto the table beside Khalid. "You're writing me letters now?"

"Not from me," Khalid murmured. "From a woman. A lady."

"An admirer?" He cracked the seal. "Not unexpected, but I've been off my game since coming to Florence and—"

Which was when the words on the paper began to sink in. Giacomo's tongue stilled so quickly he nearly choked on it, all thoughts fleeing his mind.

"Not an admirer," Khalid said.

I mourned you, the letter said.

I loathed myself, the letter said.

Where have you been? Have you been happy? the letter said.

Giacomo felt as though he'd been punched in the gut. He felt ten feet underwater. He felt *insane*. "No," he finally said. "It's—from my mother." He looked up into Khalid's bruised face. "*How* did you get this? How—where did—was she—" Khalid took his wrist again, and *that* situation was becoming *rapidly* untenable. Giacomo needed the world to pause for one moment, just long enough to get a grip on. "Sorry. It's all just a bit of a shock," he eventually continued. "My family is . . . not something I'm in the habit of speaking of."

"You do not have to," said Khalid, and how the *devil* did he manage to deflate Giacomo every time he opened his mouth? Giacomo made a living by talking rings around people, and here came Khalid with his single-sentence potholes, each of which made Giacomo feel as though he had been sent sprawling in the road. "But if you want to, I would not mind listening."

"I know, I know," Giacomo said. "But if I don't keep you awake, then Agata may turn my skull into a goblet, and you're lying there all wounded and heroic, and who am I to resist a stalwart young man?" But something in the air, or in Khalid's eyes, demanded a bit more honesty. "I haven't—it's hard sometimes, to remember who I am, when I am so many people so often. But this"—he waggled the letter—"it's a blueprint. Like the ones Rosa stole. It's . . . *ach*." Frustration bubbled up in his chest. Why was it so difficult to force out the words?

"Your mother sought me out at the Palazzo," Khalid said. "She wanted to speak with you. You sought her as well, in the alley. Do you wish to speak with her?"

Giacomo grimaced. "I haven't seen her in four years."

"That does not answer my question. Why have you not seen her?"

If it had been anyone else, Giacomo would have answered with a flippant lie. But this was Khalid. *Khalid*, who had faced off with Giacomo across piers and alleys all over Genoa. *Khalid*, who had lived in a violent and treacherous world, and who had never become violent or treacherous himself. He was right; Giacomo trusted him. Khalid was, perhaps, his friend.

He only hoped Khalid would still be his friend after he learned the truth.

"Alright," he finally said. "I guess I'll start with the most obvious. You know what people say about me, don't you? They say that I'm a madman. And for all your reticence, Signore al-Sarraj, I imagine that you've done the same. That's fine, I don't hold it against you. Because—you would be correct, it turns out. I am mad. Or I was. Or I was given to believe so.

"The last time I saw my mother," Giacomo said. "My name was Giacomo Petrucci. And I was disappearing."

It hadn't been his choice, which had been ninety percent of the shock in the moment. Giacomo Petrucci was not a boy used to being denied much of anything. In all his fifteen years, things had just appeared to him, if not on a silver platter, then wrapped in a silk scarf or gilded in gold. It was the glory of being the second son of a wealthy family—none of the expectations and all of the riches. Giacomo had reveled in it, unquestioning.

He should have questioned it more. But he had been young and stupid and, after a few groping encounters behind the stables, he had been in love.

"I thought it was magic," he said. "I was obsessed with the theater, you see—and don't you roll your eyes at me. I loved the costumes and the lights and the way that people could be anybody they wanted on that stage. But I also loved the stories. I loved the *love* stories. And it was magic, to realize that maybe people really did feel the way the playwrights said they did." His smile was lopsided. "Pretty intoxicating stuff, when you're fifteen. It went to my head."

"What happened?" asked Khalid.

"We were . . . found out," Giacomo said. "I'd never needed to be careful about anything in my life. But I needed to be careful here and I wasn't. And then I was dragged before my father and the local priest, and I realized just how stupid I had been about so many things. My father didn't know what to do. His son, behaving so sinfully—but Father Bernardo had an idea."

They had called it a hospital, but it was more like a prison, a maze of damp rooms with bars on the windows and chains on the walls—the perfect place to store the mentally unsound, the generally troublesome, or the sinful until they faded from memory. Giacomo Petrucci had watched in horror as his father agreed to the priest's suggestion and, for a sum, signed away his second son. His protests had earned him a set of manacles. His tears had earned him a black eye.

"They didn't let my family see me off," he told Khalid. "No one was supposed to know where I'd gone. But you couldn't sneak anything past my mother. She"—*found me as I was loaded into a wagon, chains on my wrists and bruises blooming*—"she asked me where I was going. What I was doing." Giacomo scoffed. "Father might not have told her the . . . details, but she knew enough. She knew better than to ask those questions and she did it anyway. And I—"

Apparently I am in need of additional schooling, can you imagine? So here I am, off to university like some barrister. *But I'll be back for the Novena. Promise.*

He could still taste the coppery desperation in the back of his throat. "I wanted to plead with her to stop all of—everything. To save me. But she didn't want to hear it. She wanted to be reassured. So I played a part. I lied. *University.*" He spat the word. "A few months later, 'university' was supposedly where I died."

Supposedly. Giacomo Petrucci certainly hadn't made it out of that place. There were still some nights he awoke, soaked with sweat, convinced that he was wasting away in one of the unlit, unwashed cells. On those days he avoided his own reflection, afraid that he would find it emaciated and haunted, the brand they'd pressed into his shoulder festering, his lips bleeding—

"But you did not die." Khalid's voice broke in. "You got out."

"I was lucky. The guards were . . . lax. I escaped."

Because he had been *pretending*, ever since he'd lied to his mother. Pretending that he was someone else. *Anywhere* else. And this had made the priests angry and the guards angry, and then things had gotten worse. Which had only driven him *further* into his dreams, which had—

Anyway. It had been bad. And Giacomo had seen no way out. Not until the bird.

It had been a mustached warbler and it had landed on the high, narrow window of his cell, and the sound of its song had dragged Giacomo down from his thundercloud to land, heavy and broken in his own body.

He'd cried, all day and night. And then he'd figured out what he was going to do about it.

"Grifters are made, not born," Giacomo told Khalid. "I was made in that place." With months of waiting and watching and playing the harmless madman until he had the ability to turn the guards against one another and distract the priests and steal the keys and limp into the night, feeling the fresh air on his bug-bitten, bruised, burned skin for the first time in a year.

"You wondered if I want to talk to my mother, and to be perfectly honest, I don't know. Our final parting was a lie. She wanted it to be a lie. I've often wondered, since then—maybe she never loved me at all." He plucked at the edge of his cuff, absent-minded. "My father would shoot me on sight if I ever returned . . . to his house, so I've not had the chance to ask her. Not until I heard that they might be in Florence."

Khalid cocked his head. "Your lover. Was she sent away as well?"

Giacomo's heart was racing, but he refused to look away. "He," he said, "was a bookbinder's apprentice and an orphan, with no family to disgrace. He lost his position and was forbidden from ever returning to Grosseto."

The silence that followed stretched for a lifetime. Only the flutter of Khalid's eyelashes told Giacomo that he hadn't fallen unconscious. "Did you ever see him again?" he finally asked.

It wasn't the question Giacomo had been expecting. Another pothole. "No," he managed. "But I haven't looked for him. He was kind and lovely and I adored him. And I ruined his life. I don't want to do that to him twice. He doesn't deserve it."

"Perhaps he would like to know that you are alive. He must have mourned your loss."

"I doubt it," Giacomo said wryly. "My attentions toward him were enthusiastic, but they lacked a certain finesse, if you know what I'm saying. I can't imagine there's much for him to pine for, so he's far better off—*ow*, Khalid—"

Because Khalid's hand had tightened around Giacomo's wrist so hard it was nearly unbearable. "No," he said.

"'No'? What do you—"

The millhouse door banged open, admitting a gust of chilled night air as well as Rosa, Michelangelo, and an inexplicably singed Sarra Nepi.

She whistled at the sight of Khalid. "You may have had a worse night even than me."

"Are you alright?" Rosa asked, her sharp eyes flicking over Khalid's patchwork bandages. "Are we all here?"

Khalid still had not released Giacomo's wrist. Now his grip pulsed, just once, in light reassurance. "We are good," he said. "We are here."

35

ROSA

Prato had fallen. Rosa had gone on.

She'd been twelve, scared, alone for the first time. Her first instinct, once she'd crawled from the Bisenzio, had been to find Matteo Nepi, to find Sarra, to shelter with the remnants of her family.

But a spark had ignited in her heart, icy and burning. It dug its roots into her guts and spread into her chest, growing stronger every time she remembered the screams at the Cathedral, the smoke in the air, the silhouette of her mother.

Rage. It had burned cold. It had kept her moving. The Rosa Cellini that emerged from the ruins of Prato had been a creature of calculated frost, fueled by schemes and grifts and revenge. There had been no room for childhood stories or familial compassion; those were warm things, and the moment Rosa thawed, her drive would melt as well. So she only considered her past through a thick pane of ice and did not allow herself to retreat to the Nepis' home to be cared for and mourned with. She had not been a grieving girl. She'd been one of Michelangelo's cold marble statues.

Or perhaps she'd simply been a fool. Because now, looking around at her team—her *friends*—Rosa wondered if her frost had been harsh enough to burn others.

They were a bedraggled mess. Sarra's gown was blotched with ash, her sleeves singed by stray embers. She gulped at a waterskin, her second since she'd pushed through the mill door. Khalid leaned against Giacomo on the long kitchen table, beads of sweat streaking his brow. The player's fine shirt and hose were streaked with Khalid's blood. Agata bore similar evidence of her emergency doctoring. Now she sipped at a steaming tisane, her sharp eyes monitoring her patient for any sign of further distress.

Only Michelangelo remained unstained by the events of the evening. He had still been awake when he'd been summoned, pacing and sketching, unable to sleep. Even now his expression was unmarred, a cultivated blank that could only be born of shock.

"How's your arm?" Rosa asked Khalid.

"Well enough," he lied.

"Agata?" Rosa turned to the old woman, who shrugged.

"Fractured," she said. "But it's a clean break. The ribs are cracked, but they'll heal if he's not too careless with them. He was very lucky."

"He doesn't *look* lucky," Giacomo muttered.

"Can you move your arm?" Sarra asked. Her voice was a smoke-cracked croak.

"I can try—" said Khalid, but Agata cut him off.

"He will not," she said. "It must remain immobile for at *least* three weeks—"

Huddled against the wall, Michelangelo shifted. "The banquet is tomorrow."

"Without Khalid," Giacomo said, voice heavy, "we don't have an in at the Palazzo."

Rosa sank into a chair. "Which is only part of the problem."

"They are increasing security at the Palazzo," Khalid said. "Last-minute measures."

"They're already setting up a guard post at the end of the street," Rosa said. "A checkpoint. I saw it when I went by. Every carriage and wagon will be searched before they are allowed to approach the Palazzo Medici, and they will be searched again as they leave."

"They will be on the lookout for the smallest hint of suspicion," Khalid said. "And authorized to react as they see fit."

"Meaning they're free to kill us," Giacomo said.

"*Encouraged*, sounds like," Sarra said.

"Wonderful."

"More security measures means more men needed," Sarra said, though she didn't sound enthusiastic. "We might be able to slip someone else inside with all the new hands—"

Agata shook her head. "If I can't get my tools past the checkpoint, then no number of undercover guards will—"

"We can—figure something out—" Sarra said.

"We *don't have time*," Michelangelo growled.

"And if we're sloppy," Giacomo said, "we'll end up with blades through our chests—"

Rosa listened to this at a distance, the voices whirling about her, threads of muffled panic. They were frustrated and, after the dangers of the evening, they were afraid. Rosa was too. The situation closed in around her, walling her off, suffocating. She searched inside for that spark of rage, the thing that had fueled her for five years. If she could reach it, then maybe she could fight through this paralyzing stupor—

But it had faded. And all that was left in its wake was—

"Quiet."

Rosa's voice was low, but it carried to every corner of the mill-house. She listened to it expand, pushing the panicked babble aside until all that was left was ringing silence, space enough for her thoughts to move freely.

And they *were* moving. They were trotting—racing—sprinting. One idea sparked against another, and then the next, a waterfall that spilled all the way to the Palazzo Medici.

Her friends were watching her; Rosa could feel it, even though she did not look up. "Weeks ago," she said, "I stood in front of you and I said that in return for taking on the most powerful men in Florence, you would walk away with riches beyond your wildest dreams." Slowly, she raised her head. "I lied."

Sarra's face was unchanged, solemn beneath the soot, and once Rosa had met her gaze she found she could not look away. "The money isn't the reward," she admitted to Sarra, and to the room at large. "Or—it's not the whole reward. It's not why we're doing this. It's not why . . . I've been doing this."

Sarra shifted, dipping her chin in a tiny nod. Rosa was released. She sought out Michelangelo, still tucked against the wall as though it might shield him. "Master Michelangelo," she said. "Your *David* statue. What is he thinking?"

The artist blinked at her. "It's a statue. It's not thinking anything."

"You put your blood and sweat into it. That's what you told me. And that's enough to bring anything to life. So what is he thinking?"

Michelangelo's shoulders hunched. "I suppose . . . he's frightened about what he's going to do. He's worried that he won't be enough. Won't be strong enough."

"Is that all?" Rosa asked.

"He's frightened. And . . . determined."

"Which is why he does it anyway."

"Yes. But that's just a story—"

"You're right, Master Michelangelo," Rosa said. "But it's good to remember stories. We are not noble shepherds like David. We're thieves. But that doesn't mean we can't be like David and do something right. Hurling this rock at the Medici is the right thing to do, because the alternative is allowing them to grind this city into the dust, just like they've done before."

"It is a nice speech," Khalid said. "But the banquet starts in eighteen hours. And our plan is in tatters."

"Nothing is impossible. There are only things that very clever people haven't done yet."

The words sliced into Rosa, and she looked, startled, into Agata de Rosso's sharp eyes. "That's what your mother used to say," Agata said. Rosa nodded dumbly. "You're young," said Agata. "To me, five years ago was yesterday. It was yesterday that the Medici razed the Republic, and it was yesterday when they murdered Prato." Rosa could only watch as the old woman reached out a hand. "It was yesterday when I heard what happened to your mother." Agata brushed Rosa's cheek, her fingers dry and warm. "It's never been just about the money for me either, Rosa."

Another shovel of sand landed on the dying embers of Rosa's rage. "Nothing is impossible," Rosa repeated. Emotion grated through her voice. "I still believe that. Lena—my mother couldn't stand in the way of the Medici's greed, but—we can. We're very clever people, I think. We can do this."

"*How?*" Giacomo's voice was hollow.

Rosa drew a shaky breath. "Have you ever run a game of Find the Lady?"

- PART III -

36

DOMINIC

D ominic was sulking.

He would own up to it, as unflattering as it was. Because the alternative was to admit that, actually, he was licking his wounds like an injured dog. And hadn't his pride taken enough blows this evening without adding *that* to the count? He certainly thought so. And so he slouched on a pew in front of the Magi fresco in the candle-gilded dark and sulked.

A mediocre copycat.

He sloshed the words around, drowning them with her venom. He turned them over and over, a masochistic urge, waiting for them to sting against the bruised edges of his hurt feelings.

But the hurt didn't come. Not from that insult at least. What had chased Dominic into this chapel in the middle of the night was not the disparagement of his talents. That arrow had long since been blunted, both by the remarks of others and by his own critical eye.

It was the rest of it that was the issue. The whole evening. Finding Rosa—or whatever her name *really* was—in the Mercato Vecchio. Hearing the catch in her voice as she whispered into the church gloom. Watching the spark in her eyes turn from imploring to injured just before he turned his back on her.

He shouldn't feel this terrible. After all, wasn't *she* the one who had lied to *him*?

The issue was this: As a creator of mimics, Dominic knew a false copy when he saw one. He had spotted the edges of Rosa's mask from the moment they'd met. But that mask had evaporated this evening in front of Santo Stefano's painting. Everything she'd told him—about Prato, and her mother, and the Medici . . .

What was he supposed to do if she'd been telling the truth?

"If you are seeking guidance," said a voice, "you're looking in the wrong direction. The altar is behind you."

The Pope was standing in the door, wrapped in a dressing gown. Guilt and shame slammed into Dominic at the sight. He surged to his feet. "Your Holiness," he stammered, "I apologize—"

"It's quite alright," the Pope said, waving off Dominic's apology. He glided down the aisle, his slippers sliding across the tiled floor. "I find myself similarly in need of respite this evening. Sleep always eludes me on the nights I need it the most. You should have seen me before my Papal coronation. I was a *wreck*." He levied a raised eyebrow at Dominic. "Though I do wonder that my guards let you in so late."

"It's not their fault," Dominic said. "I told them I had forgotten some supplies after I took down the scaffolding. They shouldn't get in trouble for—"

"So noble, child," His Holiness laughed, sinking into a pew across from Dominic. "Never mind. As long as guests aren't ranging free through the Palazzo tomorrow, that's fine. I will have to make sure Romano tells his men to . . . *corral* the herds."

"Corral . . . ," Dominic echoed.

"In light of the recent *unrest*," the Pope sneered the word, "I think it's best to keep people to the gardens, don't you?"

"Yes, of course," Dominic agreed. He wondered whether Rosa was aware of this, and then he berated himself for wondering. What did he care if a thief's plans were ruined? What difference did it make to him?

His Holiness did not seem to have noticed Dominic's internal struggle. He was studying the fresco with an appreciative interest. "This is remarkable," he murmured.

Dominic ducked his head. "Thank you, Your Holiness."

"The faces, especially—they are more alive than I have seen in years. You have done your master proud, Signore Fontana. Though he may not be vocal about it."

Dominic had never made Michelangelo Buonorroti proud in his life, and he was keenly aware of it. But it would not do to correct the Pope. "Thank you, Your Holiness," he said again.

Perhaps he didn't do a good job at disguising his thoughts because the Pope just chuckled. "Ah, never mind Michelangelo," he said. "He's always been *impossible* to please, even when we were boys. What you have done here is marvelous. I would go so far as to call it extraordinary."

They lie to you every day.

Dominic wanted more than anything to believe what His Holiness was saying. But he had spent his entire life in the company of great artists. He knew extraordinary work, and his contributions to Master Gozzoli's original did not meet that bar.

"I'm just a painter, Your Holiness," he said, keeping his eyes pinned to the flagstones.

This was not what the Pope wished to hear, evidently. "Your modesty does you credit," he said, a little colder this time. "But do not let it overwhelm your achievement. You could do great things. Just as Michelangelo did before you."

How far do you think that patronage will take you without the talent to back it up? "I am no Michelangelo, Your Holiness."

He could see the eye roll that the Pope was holding back. "That's not what I see," His Holiness said, as though from an infinite well of patience. "This work speaks to that. And this is what you were able to accomplish on your own! Imagine what you might be able to produce working side by side with your master!"

It was almost exactly what Rosa had hissed at him, her magnetic dark eyes radiating hurt and anger. *A connection to your master,* she'd said. *A mark.*

Somehow he'd gotten . . . muddled. The last few months, wandering through the halls of this rich and powerful family had clouded his mind. He'd felt the Medici eye on him and started to think . . . *maybe.*

His gaze sliced sideways, toward the tips of the Pope's house slippers. They were as fine as any shoes Dominic could hope to own. "That would be a dream, Your Holiness."

"It would just be the fulfillment of your talent. And there is always room in our family for talent. Here"—the Pope pointed to the fresco—"do you know the secret of this piece?"

Dominic had spent countless hours of his life poring over the fresco centimeter by centimeter, and yet: "I'm afraid not."

"To the casual observer, it appears to be just another depiction of the procession of the Magi," His Holiness said. "But there is a deeper meaning. Every person in this procession is a friend of the Medici family. My father, Lorenzo"—he stabbed his finger out at a mounted figure in gold—"and that's the old Duke of Milan there. The Sforzas are buried in there somewhere. Among the rabble. And on and on." He fixed Dominic with the full force of his attention, pinning him in place. "What you have spent the last weeks restoring is a record of the most powerful men in Tuscany. Those who have been the shepherds of its prosperity. Its sculptors, to put it in terms you are most familiar with. Without them, Florence would have fallen into anarchy long ago."

Five thousand men, women, and children, Dominic thought, and, *They will do the same to Florence.*

The Pope smiled. "Perhaps you were not wrong to seek counsel from this fresco after all. Who knows? The next young artist to restore it may wind up painting your face among the rest. The Medici are always eager to sponsor talent, after all."

For a moment, Dominic thought his ears were playing tricks on him. "Forgive my assumption, Your Holiness, but are you offering—"

"My family's patronage. I think you and your master make quite the matched set."

"Because of my talent." Dominic's tongue was heavy in his mouth.

The Pope's expression turned stern. "I am not given to over-flattery, Signore Fontana."

"Of course. Of course! This is very generous, Your Holiness."

"Mm," he agreed, rising. "We will speak more tomorrow. You will do quite well with the Medici. You and your master both."

If Dominic bowed low enough he wouldn't have to worry about whatever his face was doing, so that's what he did, bending nearly double until the *shush*ing of the Pope's embroidered dressing gown had faded and the chapel door was shut once again. Dominic was left alone with the fresco—and the hordes of Medici allies depicted therein.

He could have informed the Pope of whatever Rosa was planning, he realized with a start. Why hadn't that crossed his mind in the moment?

Five thousand men, women, and children. And unless he was mistaken, it seemed as though Rosa was maybe going to do something about that.

But was it worth throwing away the certainty and legacy of a Medici patronage on a grifter's *maybe*? Who was to say that Rosa was good on her word? And who was to say that she'd even be able to succeed? The Pope had said *corralling*, and what if that was an obstacle Rosa hadn't predicted?

He knew who he needed to talk to. He did not want to talk to them. Luckily, it was so late that any conversations would have to wait until the morning. And in the meantime . . .

His fingertips itched.

Feeling more settled, Dominic shoved to his feet and pushed out the chapel doors. If he started now, then the ink would be dry by morning.

He had his own *maybe* to conquer.

37

KHALID

Instinct directed Khalid back to the Vite Contorto pub. There was no guarantee that Traverio would be holed up there again. But if Khalid's hunch about who had burned the Nepi print shop was correct, then Traverio's men would want the chance to blow off some steam.

The pub was full to bursting when he pushed inside. He was not sure how many of these drunken revelers were working for Traverio, but he could spot Marino at least, at the bar ordering another round. It only took him another moment to find Traverio in the same corner, tankard in hand. Khalid fought back the urge to sag with relief. Agata had done a fair job of patching him up, but he was not certain if he would have been able to chase all over Florence looking for the man without keeling over. And he did not want to give Vieri the satisfaction of having killed him.

Tucking his splinted arm against his side, Khalid strode through the crowd.

"Signore Traverio!" he called, loud enough to be heard over the throng. Traverio turned to him with a broad smile. Behind him, Khalid could see Marino spot him over the rim of his tankard. All blood instantly drained from his face. Another theory confirmed; Khalid would bet good money that Traverio had no idea that Marino had been in contact with the Medici Guards.

"My boy!" Traverio said, greeting him with open arms. "So good to see you!" He looked Khalid up and down. "You look like absolute hell."

"I'm here on business," Khalid said.

"Always so serious. Come join me in my little corner. Come, come."

Doing his best to disguise the pain still rocketing through him, Khalid sank onto the empty bench. It would do no good to be seen as weak by anyone in this pub, not while he had only one arm at his disposal.

"You're about to keel over," Traverio said. Marino appeared at his elbow, a tankard in hand. Traverio took it but didn't drink. "Better tell me about this business of yours before you do."

"You already know," Khalid said.

"Ah yes," said Traverio, a sly gleam shining in his icy eyes. "You could call that a statement of intent. In case you'd forgotten what was at stake if you renege on your end of our agreement." He sucked his teeth with a *tsk*. "Who knew print shops were so flammable? All that wood and paper—don't tell me that's what happened to you? You weren't anywhere near that shop when it went up—"

"I wasn't," confirmed Khalid, not looking at Marino.

"Good, wonderful. You're no good to anybody if you're embers. But Signorina Sarra had to learn—you do not do underhanded business in my territory without consequences."

Khalid's ribs sent a stab of pain up his side and he didn't bother fighting down a wince. "The gold," he said once the radiating pain had subsided. "I can get it to you. Tomorrow."

Traverio's eyebrows shot skyward. "*Tomorrow*," he repeated. "I didn't realize all it took to hone your focus was a bit of arson."

Khalid thought about the burn marks and soot streaks on Sarra's clothes and shook his head. "It's not that. It's all *this*." He gestured at his bandages, at his face, at his torn clothes, at *everything*. "I have reached my limit, Signore Traverio. These people expect too much from me, and when things fall apart, I am the one who bears the consequences."

Out of the corner of his eye, he saw Marino stiffen.

"You will betray their trust?" Traverio asked.

Sarra grinning at him over the table in Genoa. Agata patting his cheek. Rosa's even gaze inviting his thoughts. Giacomo smiling, his hand in Khalid's, his laugh—

Every opportunity he had dreamed of in leaving Tunis—everything he had been fooled out of in Genoa—he had found here in Florence. But—

"A thief who trusts is not a thief," Khalid said. "He is a fool. And what I plan to take from them was never theirs to begin with. I will get you the gold. It will be boxed up for you. It will be set up on a wagon. I will even make sure to provide the horses. All you need to do is be where I tell you when I tell you, and the money is yours."

A long beat stretched between them as Traverio's eyes flicked over Khalid's face. Khalid didn't know what he was looking for, but there was no dishonesty in him. He simply sat, enduring the inspection, awaiting the judgment.

It could have been ten seconds. It could have been ten years. "If that's the case," he finally said, "then your father's debt is safe." Traverio's smile was a lightning crack—bright and stunning. "It's good to have you back, Khalid."

Khalid nodded. "Please believe me when I say, signore—I would not want to work for anyone else."

38

GIACOMO

"Where's Khalid?"

The millhouse—what Giacomo could see of it from his nest of blankets—was empty save for Agata, who was packing vials and packets into her tool kit with focused precision. She glanced over at him, unimpressed. "I thought you would sleep 'til Judgment Day."

This did not answer Giacomo's question. He shoved off his pallet, wrenching shoes onto his feet. "Where is he?"

"I'm too old for this," Agata muttered, but when she saw his pleading face, she heaved a sigh. "Outside," she told him. "Don't be stupid."

Giacomo was already halfway to the door. "No promises, my queen."

True to Agata's word, Khalid was outside, and the sight of him leaning against the low river wall did nothing for Giacomo's heart rate. He had his green jerkin unbuckled over a clean linen shirt, and if Giacomo had not been looking for the pained stiffness in his shoulders, he would not have known that the man had come millimeters away from death the night before.

He was not prepared for the shuttering of Khalid's face as he approached. "You are awake."

All panicked haste fled Giacomo, replaced by an apprehension he was not sure he had ever felt before. He slung a leg over the wall, keeping his distance. "We have enough to tackle today without my dozing. How are you feeling?"

"Mm." Not an answer, but Giacomo let it slide.

"How are you feeling about *today*?" he asked, a different question in a similar outfit.

Khalid huffed a breath. "Terrified," he said, and Giacomo couldn't help but laugh.

"I will never get over the way you will just say anything, Signore al-Sarraj. Any other man would bluster and deny. You are an experience. My foolish heart can't take it."

"Khalid," said Khalid.

"Huh?" Giacomo blinked. Agata had said not to be stupid and he was letting her down.

"You called me Khalid last night." Then: "Do you need me?"

"Uh," Giacomo managed.

"You were looking for me," Khalid said. "Just now."

He had to know what he was doing. He *had* to. "I . . . was," Giacomo said. Surely there had been a reason for it beyond blind panic.

"Was it . . . perhaps because I will need to change my appearance?" Khalid asked, insultingly prompting. "For the delivery? And I will need the help of an expert?"

Giacomo glared at him. "You are insufferable," he informed Khalid. "Wait here."

It was a short dash inside to grab his disguise kit, but Agata's knowing and exasperated look made it seem eons longer. When he emerged again, Khalid was sitting on the wall, his broken arm tucked against his side. Giacomo caught the edge of Khalid's tight wince before he spotted Giacomo and smoothed it over.

Biting back his concern, Giacomo made his way over and set the kit down at his feet.

"We won't have time for anything elaborate," he said, sorting through the depths of the bag. Scraps of fabric, wigs in every color, tins of glue—they sifted through his fingers, appearing and disappearing in rapid succession. "But that's alright. It should be alright. It *will* be alright. Ninety percent of this is just changing your silhouette anyway, so." He sat back on his heels, chewing his lip. "Maybe there's someone else who can do this part."

"Giacomo."

"You're right. You're right! Ninety percent!" With a fit of frantic energy, he yanked out two fistfuls of woolen scarves and turned back to scrutinize Khalid. "As for the other ten . . . I've got just the thing. But it's important that you . . . don't . . . move . . ."

Like every good grifter, Giacomo kept a set of makeup pots in his kit, which could be mixed to create the illusion of bruises, scars, gashes, or even unblemished, unbroken skin. These were what Giacomo produced now, unstoppering them and setting to work.

He could feel Khalid's eyes on him as he focused, his gaze intense in the way it always was and always had been. "Lire for your thoughts, signore?" he asked.

"I would worry about you."

Giacomo met Khalid's intent stare. "Last night," Khalid said. "You said—your lover would not worry about where you went. But I would worry."

The makeup brush froze in Giacomo's fingers. "Don't—don't be cruel, Khalid."

"I am not being cruel. I am speaking from experience." Khalid's shoulders sank in a sigh. "Your mother's letter—I told myself I would burn it. I worried that if I passed it along, you might do something . . . foolish."

"I promised that I wouldn't."

"You did not see yourself that evening outside the Casa Petrucci. I scarcely recognized you. You were no longer . . . *there*. I would not see you that way again. Not if I could help it."

"So why didn't you burn it?"

"Trust" was all Khalid said. *Pothole.*

"Well. *Khalid.*" Giacomo let out a slow breath. "Close your eyes, please." Khalid complied, and Giacomo was released from the man's obscenely intent gaze. With gentle strokes, he began the process of covering the evidence of Khalid's misadventure, bruises disappearing beneath the paint.

"Hm," Khalid hummed, contemplative. "How are *you* feeling about today?"

Khalid's tone—his inflection—so perfectly mimicked Giacomo's a moment earlier that it startled a laugh from him. He resigned himself to touch-ups. "If *you* are terrified, there is absolutely no hope for us mere mortals. I am absolutely *shitting* myself, Lord above—the uniform I can do. Playacting as a guard? I just block out two-thirds of my brain and run on the remainder. *March. Stand. Frown.* Easy. But the last bit—"

"What is the last bit?"

"The bit that landed you in the river last night."

It took Khalid only a moment to puzzle this out. "The fighting."

"The fighting," Giacomo echoed. "I have spent, oh, roughly every moment of my nineteen years becoming the world's preeminent expert in distracting prospective pugilists from their violent goals—or, failing that, in ensuring that I'm very far away from the fists when they start flying. *Evasion.* That's always been my watchword. That's how I stay in control. But as you saw that night—"

"Evasion does not always work," Khalid supplied.

"No." If there was a tremor in his hands as he dabbed at Khalid's face, Khalid was kind enough not to mention it. "And when I feel the exits close, it's as if I'm right back in that hospital. Helpless. With Father Bernardo breathing over my shoulder. It's—" He drew back with a sigh, lowering his brush. "No matter. It is what it is. You will play me and I will play you and—we'll walk away from this city with several thousand florins in our pockets."

A muscle under Khalid's eye jumped. "Are you finished?"

"Yes. Oh, with your face? Yes." Khalid opened his eyes as Giacomo admired his work. "Good as new," he said. "You'd never know you were at death's door twelve hours ago. But the disguise is only part of it, you understand? The rest—you remember what I told you?"

"Vice and voice. I remember," said Khalid. There was a flash of something in those dark eyes—regret or concern—and then it was gone. "You are a better teacher than you know."

Some emotion was crawling up Giacomo's throat, trying to strangle him. "You'll be careful, won't you?" he asked.

Khalid was very close. "I have to leave for the Palazzo soon," he said. "But we have enough time."

Giacomo's heart was beating so *loud*, surely Khalid heard it. "We do?"

"Yes," Khalid said. "Because it is my turn to be the teacher. And your lesson starts now."

39

SARRA

It had been a near thing, but the immolation of Nepi Printing had not, in the end, taken the rest of the Oltrarno along with it. In the watery dawn light, evidence of the neighborhood's efforts to preserve their homes and businesses was everywhere—upturned buckets and damp blankets, puddles of water and a single, splintered ladder.

Only the print shop's easternmost wall still stood. The rest had been reduced to charred wooden beams and crumbling plaster. The roof was gone, terra-cotta shingles heaped in shattered piles on the ground. Plumes of smoke wafted delicately—Sarra watched these black clouds drift toward the sky and disperse into flakes of ash, which coated everything in a layer of gray grime.

Pietro's heavy footsteps were even louder in the carbonized debris of their home. He stomped around the remnants of the chimney, streaked with soot from head to toe. "Good news," he said. "That ugly blanket from Aunt Sofia is gone."

"Small blessings."

"*You* say small." He hesitated. "I'm guessing the press is . . ."

Sarra looked down at the pile of what could only generously be called timbers. The framework of the printing press had been hefty, and so the *suggestion* of it still stood, a skeleton of the machine it had been. But the bed was split in three places, and the press itself was a mess of sooty metal. A few letter blocks had somehow been spared the worst of the flames—these lay scattered among the rubble, the occasional glimmering treasure for anyone who cared enough to find them. But on the whole . . .

"It's gone," she said. The words choked her throat as much as the ash.

Pietro took this with the same stony resolve he took most things, his great shoulders heaving in a single sigh. "Well," he said. "That is disappointing."

"There's that old cooper near San Frediano," she said, a little desperately. "He's looking for someone to let his workshop, now that he can't take on so many customers. We could set up there—it would give us somewhere to start building the new press—"

Pietro wrapped an arm around her shoulders, pulling her into a hug, and it was then that she realized that her vision was starting to swim. She closed her eyes and felt something inside of her give way.

"I'm sorry," she whispered. "For the press. For Papa. For everything."

He stepped back so that she could see his face. "Sarra. I've had a grifter for a sister, for a father, and for a godmother," he said, and to his credit, his exasperation was more affectionate than stinging. "Even if Papa was concerned about dragging me into that world, that boat sailed a few decades ago." Pietro's mouth twisted a little with old sadness. "You know how Signora Cellini's death frightened him. He wanted us to be safe. If he could have wrapped us in wool and tucked us up on a shelf, he would have done it. But he knew you were bound for this life, so your promise was the next-best option." He tugged at the end of one of her braids. "At the end of the day, though, he just wanted you to be happy. He'd understand."

She wasn't used to hearing Pietro say so much in a stretch. "What about you? And the print shop?" she asked. "Don't you get to be happy?"

Pietro gave her a crooked smile. "Listen. When all this is done—"

"Tonight."

"Tonight, Christ above. We'll leave Florence. We'll go wherever your work takes you. But we'll do it together."

Had the ground turned to quicksand? Sarra felt as though she was flailing. "But the press—and your work here—"

"Florence is not the only city questioning the Pope. I can write from anywhere." His sigh was world-weary. "I was never a very good printer anyway. What's that smile for?"

Her grin deepened. "I haven't heard you this settled on something in years."

Pietro rolled his eyes. "Brat."

The sun was starting to climb in the sky—Sarra could feel it warming her back. "I have to go," she said, and braced herself to hear him ask *where*?

But he just gave her shoulder a squeeze and stepped back, shoving his hands into his belt. "Rob them blind," he told her.

Sarra shouldered her pack. "You can count on that."

It was different this time, making her way to the millhouse. There was nothing more that she was running from—no lies, no guilt— only things that she was running toward. The future seemed, suddenly, a great deal brighter ...

Provided she could make it through the next twenty-four hours in one piece.

There seemed to be some sort of grappling match between Giacomo and Khalid when Sarra arrived. Giacomo was doing his best to subdue Khalid who, even one-armed, was more than capable of resisting the stringy player. Sarra sidestepped them and did not ask questions.

Rosa was alone in the millhouse when Sarra pushed through the door. Sarra paused, the memories of their fight fresh in her memory. They hadn't had a chance to talk about it, between Khalid's injuries and the print shop and the plan, and now ...

Rosa was standing over her pallet with her arms clutched tight around her middle. Sarra peered around her, at whatever had her so wound up.

It was a gown, draped heavy and luxurious across Rosa's quilt. Deep blue velvet caught hints of gold and red from the hearth fire. The silver of the sleeves was complemented by the matching embroidery that ran along the seams, and by the ribbons that tied them to the overgown. It was the sort of gown that any girl would dream of.

Rosa was frowning at it.

"What did that dress ever do to you?" Sarra asked, slinging her pack onto the worktable.

Rosa sighed, brushing a strand of hair back from her face. "Do you think it's too much?"

"I mean, it's not something *I* would ever wear." When Rosa just chewed her lip, Sarra realized that quips were not going to land in this precise moment. "It's beautiful."

"I don't want to draw too much attention to myself."

"You also don't want *no* attention, right?" The lip-chewing increased. Sarra rolled her eyes, grabbing up the tangled mass of thin rope she'd left piled on the stool and beginning to wrap it in a tight coil. "I'm a tinkerer, Rosa. I'm no lady. I can't tell you the dress code for a banquet with the Pope."

"But what if it's all wrong?" Rosa seemed to be presenting this question to the universe at large. "What if this whole job falls apart because of my *dress*?"

Sarra was starting to realize that they were talking about more than their plan here. "You had that gown made, right?" she asked.

Rosa nodded. "Yes."

"Then it'll be perfect." That got Rosa's attention, her gaze flying up to meet Sarra's. Sarra was surprised at the depth of uncertain worry there, but perhaps she shouldn't have been. For all of Rosa's bravado the night before, they were facing an incredible task. "You know this job. You've weighed the pros and cons. And that includes the amount of . . . dots?" She squinted at the cuffs. "What are those?"

"Rosettes," Rosa replied absently.

"Well, you decided this gown should have them, so I'd bet this gown should have them."

Another nod from Rosa, this time a little faster. "Yes," she said. "You're right."

"Were you ever going to put it on?"

That got her an exasperated sigh, but it shook Rosa out of whatever rut she'd stumbled into. She grabbed up the gown and began the arduous process of maneuvering into it, wrangling yards of velvet and voluminous lengths of chemise with incremental success.

Sarra did not offer to help. She kept her attention focused on the neat coil of rope in her hands, which she tied shut and placed into her pack. Next, she picked up her crossbow and ran it through its checks, testing each dial and each knob with an artificer's expertise.

"Pietro sends his best wishes," she said.

"Oh?" said Rosa from somewhere in the gown's depths, too careful.

"He said that we should take every last copper we can from the Medici." The sight dial was sticking, just a little. "It turns out he is no great supporter of theirs. *Viva la Repubblica.*"

"Oh *no.*"

"Oh yes." Sarra dug the oil from her pack and stole a pipette from Agata's workbench, carefully avoiding the row of Agata Specials glinting in the sunlight. "He knows about the Tinkerer. It's . . . good. I'm glad."

Rosa's face emerged in the dress's collar, a wild-haired turtle in a shell of blue velvet. "You told him?"

"I didn't have to," Sarra said. "But also, I did have to. Yes. I told him."

"I—that's good. I'm glad. And I—I owe you an apology, I mean, I shouldn't have—" Rosa's words tumbled over one another in a rush. "I said horrible things and—hang it all, can you help me with this?"

She had somehow gotten an arm in the gap between the bodice and the sleeve, the bunching of her chemise wedging her in place. Sarra stowed her crossbow and bustled over, taking hold of Rosa's elbow and maneuvering her into place.

Rosa stood and let herself be maneuvered, a stark contrast to the stiff and unyielding girl Sarra had been dealing with for the last few weeks. "Sarra—" she began, and stopped. Sarra did not prompt her. If Rosa had something to say, she would have to do so under her own power.

"It—was a lie," Rosa finally continued. "To say you are not my family. I lied. I've avoided you for five years *because* you are my family. After Prato and"—her breath caught—"and Mama, all I wanted was revenge. But when I thought about coming back to you, your father, your brother—that desire would flicker. Give way to . . . wider things, future things. Things I didn't think I had room for. So I told myself that my family was gone and I didn't come home. And when you told me I wasn't alone, I lashed out. But that's not an excuse. You are Sarra the Tinkerer. You're also—my sister, if you'd like. I am glad to know both."

Sarra untwisted some of the sleeve ties, laying the ribbons flat against Rosa's shoulder. The other girl's gaze was heavy on the top of her head. "I was scared," Sarra finally said, "of how Pietro would respond when I told him about the Tinkerer, so I didn't. You were right about that. But keeping the truth from him wasn't kind."

"Wasn't he angry when he found out?"

Sarra snorted. "Well, yes. So was I. But not because of this job or his bills or any of that." She plucked at Rosa's chemise, pulling the fabric through the ribbons in even puffs. "The secret was the thing that was hurtful," she said. "Both ways. It was hurting me and it was hurting him."

"And you're glad it's out." Sarra could see Rosa's brain whirring, picking apart her words in search of something.

Sarra took a breath. "If we shut each other out, then we evaporate. 'We'—our family. *Us*. It evaporates. Does that make sense?" Rosa didn't say anything, but there was emotion swimming in her eyes. "Anger passes," Sarra said. "All the dark stuff. It passes. But only if you give it an escape. And then there's an afterward."

Rosa was not, as a rule, a person who was easy to read, but this morning appeared to be the exception. Irritation and hope, grief and happiness—they crashed across her face in waves, leaving behind a girl who looked simultaneously five and thirty-five, innocent and life-hardened. "I wish they were here," she whispered, so softly that her lips barely moved. "Either of them. Both of them."

Giving Rosa's sleeve one final pat, Sarra stepped back. "Me too," she said. Then, because they could not face the day with such heaviness in their hearts, she grinned. "But I don't think my father would pull off this gown quite as well as you."

The corners of Rosa's mouth twitched, a battle against a smile that was ultimately lost when she laughed. The hollowed-out Rosa was swept out to sea, replaced by the girl who was seventeen and ready to outsmart the whole world. "I got you something," she said, once she'd gotten herself under control. A few covert swipes of her fingers removed any trace of tears. Sarra focused her attentions back on packing her gear and allowed Rosa her plausible deniability.

"Why?" was Sarra's ungrateful answer.

"Don't get used to it." Rosa was digging in a worn chest at the foot of her pallet. Her gown, still unlaced down the front over her chemise, pooled around her in a sea of blue velvet. "I just thought it might help out today."

She turned back to Sarra. In her hands was a stack of deep green and gray cloth. "I had Signora Tommasi put them together when she was working on Rosa de' Lombardi's gowns," Rosa said. "I had to guess at your measurements, but—" She shrugged. "Would you take these? I'd like to get myself put together before the boys come in and get a show."

The cloth proved to be a doublet and hose in a thick wool, and a fine linen shirt to go underneath. They were sturdy and handsome, and just the right size.

"Thank you," Sarra said, and meant it.

Rosa pulled a face. "Stop thanking me, you're making me uncomfortable."

"Won't happen again."

"One more thing?" Sarra looked up from her beautiful new uniform to find Rosa holding her ledger. She presented it to Sarra. "As we're partners . . . it's past time we talked this through," she said. "Though I should warn you—it's not entirely about the money."

Sarra opened it. A skim of the first page had her letting out a low whistle. "You don't say. I can think of quite a few people who would love to get their hands on this."

"Will you ensure that they do?"

"Of course," Sarra said. But there was something tugging at the corner of her mind when she glanced up, something that glinted further into focus with every passing second.

"You've got an idea," Rosa said. She was studying Sarra and Sarra's faraway expression with that Lena Cellini scrutiny.

"I've got . . . the beginnings of one," Sarra said. "To put this ledger to its fullest use. I just have to ask Pietro if he's up for it."

40

ROSA

Fearsome energy beat dissonance to the well-sprung rocking of the carriage. It tugged at her limbs and heart, so unlike the frozen fire she'd lived with for so long that she didn't quite know what to do with it. This energy was present. Immediate. *Real*.

Rosa ground her forehead against the carriage wall and willed her racing mind to slow.

Understandable. It was *understandable* that she felt this way. The plan she had taken years to craft had been turned on its side in the span of a few hours and, yes, perhaps she should have accounted for such hiccups, but Khalid hadn't *died*, and they still had enough material to move ahead.

Still, it was galling to be made to scramble when she had proceeded with such deliberation in the past. Rosa Cellini had spent the majority of her seventeen years happily parting people from their money. She had loved it and embraced it—manipulation and sleight of hand had come as naturally to her as breathing. Lying was second nature—she had never lingered on her falsehoods, never regretted them. Each lie had been in the service of a greater goal, one she was closing in on even now.

But.

Do you know what Pope Leo sees when he looks at you? The same thing I see. An easy target.

It was far from the worst thing she'd told someone. But she kept *hearing* herself. Her voice rattled around in her skull, turning the words into a head-splitting refrain.

And Rosa had a sinking feeling that she knew why.

Something blooming, Sarra had said, just before the night had started its slide into hell. Rosa pushed back against the memory. She was not Giacomo—not the type to get moony over someone while she was working.

However. At the end of the day, Rosa had blown herself wide open for Dominic Fontana. She had admitted things she hadn't been able to speak of to people she'd known her entire life. And after all that, he had repaid her by recoiling.

An easy target, she had called him, hurt and reeling and trying to convince herself. But when all was said and done, the grumpy little painter from Chiusi had somehow worked his way under her skin and snagged there. Not a target. Something else.

If you give it an escape, Sarra had said, *then there's an afterward*. But what could be "afterward" with Dominic Fontana?

Rosa was saved from answering this because the carriage was swaying to a stop and she was stepping onto the cobbles in front of Michelangelo's workshop. The building was unnaturally quiet, particularly for midafternoon. Gathering her skirts up, she pulled open one of the double doors.

The artists and apprentices who usually clogged the space had been given the day off, so Rosa had a clear sightline all the way to Michelangelo's back corner. Shadows danced against the sheets, lit by the afternoon sunlight, and the faint sound of male voices echoed toward her.

One was too irritated to be anything but Michelangelo's. The other belonged to Dominic.

She should go. She didn't know how Dominic would react to seeing her, and even if he didn't call the guard then he might just throw a tantrum, which would still be a headache.

She crept closer.

"Pageantry and nonsense," Michelangelo was grumbling. Through a gap in the sheets, she could see him messing with his embroidered jerkin, shoulders tense and uncomfortable.

The partition sheet billowed as Dominic swirled a cloak, settling it across his master's shoulders. "Of course, Master Michelangelo," he said, sounding as wrung-out as Rosa felt.

Michelangelo cast an assessing look at his apprentice. "Didn't stop you from dressing up." It was a particular skill of his to turn a casual observation into an insult, and Rosa flinched on Dominic's behalf. Dominic's doublet and hose were of a handsome rich burgundy, and there was no trace of marble dust or paint in sight—a marked upgrade to his daily attire.

But Dominic's only reaction to Michelangelo's snide comment was to duck his head in acknowledgment. "Yes, Master Michelangelo," he agreed dutifully.

Michelangelo snatched the clasps of his cloak away from his apprentice. "Stop echoing. If I wanted to talk to myself, I'd shout into a canal. What's going on in that thick head of yours? You've been denser than usual all day."

The silence that stretched between the two artists was leaden and long. "Rosa is not your niece," Dominic finally said.

Michelangelo's fingers stilled. "No."

Dominic's head dipped in another dissociative nod. "She's . . ."

"She's a blasted clever woman, is what she is," Michelangelo snapped, springing back to life and making short work of his cloak. "And she's possibly the devil incarnate."

Rosa tried not to take offense at this, which was all the easier because her attention was pinned so completely on Dominic. The young apprentice was listening, running some unknown calculation in his head. "But you trust her," he said.

Michelangelo shrugged. "For all her—for all of that. Her heart is in the right place."

She expected some pushback from Dominic—she wouldn't have blamed him if he'd attempted to drag his master back to the light. But he just looked the older man square in the eye with an assurance Rosa had never seen from him.

"The Medici offered me their patronage," he said. Rosa's heart dropped into her stomach.

Michelangelo turned his gaze again to the mirror, bypassing Dominic. "Lucrative."

"Yes."

"In some respects," Michelangelo amended, and to Rosa's surprise, Dominic nodded.

"Not in others," he said.

Michelangelo snorted. "That's for damn certain."

"Should I take it?"

"You're asking me, Fontana?"

"Yes."

In the mirror, Michelangelo's eyes shifted—just a few centimeters, but far enough to lock with Rosa's. She held his gaze, watching as he plucked up a hat with a fluffy feather erupting from the brim and settled it on his head. His curls bloomed from the bottom, puffing out in a halo. "I sold my soul decades ago," he said, so soft that Rosa could barely hear him. "But your life is your own. I can't tell you what to do with it. You'll have to make your own mistakes." Then, a bit louder, "Hand me that boot brush. My carriage will be here any moment."

Taking her cue, Rosa slipped back toward the door on silent feet. When she stepped into the cool November sunshine, the smell of marble dust was in her nose and Dominic Fontana's contemplative expression was on her mind. She turned her face into the breeze and breathed it in.

Something blooming.

And maybe, Rosa thought, that wasn't such a bad thing after all.

41

KHALID

I t was past midday by the time Khalid maneuvered his wagon onto Via de' Pucci, one block from the Palazzo Medici's gates. Florentines and tourists crammed every thoroughfare from the Palazzo down to the Piazza del Duomo. They elbowed and jostled one another, jockeying for a glimpse of one of the visiting nobles or even the Pope himself.

The only reason this throng was not beating down the Palazzo's front door was the checkpoint that had been established at the end of the street. True to Vieri's boast, no traffic flowed into or out of the Palazzo Medici without a thorough search. Khalid watched, inching closer, as a deliveryman was subjected to examination by a pair of guards in Medici blue. They went over his wagon centimeter by centimeter, opening crates to rifle through layers of table linens, before finally waving him on.

Khalid drove his mule forward and held his breath as the guards turned their attention to him. He resisted the urge to scratch at his cheek where Giacomo had laid the pigments on the thickest, concealing the plum-purple bruising under his eye. It felt unnatural, greasy and uncomfortable—but even Khalid had to admit, after a glimpse at his reflection in the water basin, that Giacomo did good work.

Still, he kept his chin buried in his overlarge scarf as he drew the mule to a halt, his face shadowed by the wide brim of his hat. The two guards on duty were relatively new hires, not men he had much interacted with. The shorter of them hailed him first. "Delivery?"

Vice and voice. "Yes, signore," he said, his voice deferential. "From Master Bartolini."

The guard—Agosti, Khalid thought he was called—stared blankly. "Bartolini?"

"He's the vintner," his partner piped up from the other side of the wagon. He was already peering beneath the vehicle to check the underside of the wagon bed.

Agosti's eyes shone. "Oh *right*," he said, a great deal more interested than he had been a moment ago. He held out a hand. "Receipt."

"Right away, signore." Khalid produced the document Rosa had put together. It listed the number of barrels, the time of their ordering, the date of delivery, and the vintner's name. Agosti made a show of reading it. He was holding the paper upside down.

The wagon bed dipped. The other guard had clambered aboard. He was poking about the casks with a proprietary air. In the street behind him, Khalid glimpsed a slender figure in Medici blue slip out from the crowd and stride toward them. He kept the approaching man in his peripheral vision, but most of his attention was pinned, helpful and obsequious, to Agosti and the receipt.

"Seems to be in order," Agosti said. "Bartolini's been paid in full?"

"Yes, signore."

The guard in the wagon gave a significant cough. Agosti caught his eye. A smile spread across his face.

Some people want to feel smart, Giacomo had said. It was not an observation Khalid would have made six weeks ago. Perhaps he ought to feel unsettled. Instead, he realized he was fighting a smile.

"Except," said Agosti, who was squinting at the receipt in a mockery of consternation, "it looks as if . . . but this can't be right . . ."

"Signore?"

"The count is off." Agosti flourished the receipt. "Bartolini forgot a cask."

The figure in blue was almost level with them now, his strides carrying him past the checkpoint with authoritative momentum. *He* was not stopped and searched by Agosti and his partner. His uniform marked him as a Medici Guardsman, same as them.

"We counted very carefully, signore," Khalid insisted.

The back of his bench creaked as the guard in the wagon leaned over Khalid's shoulder. "You don't seem to follow," he said. "Your master. Forgot. A cask."

The approaching guardsman threw a casual salute in Agosti's direction. Agosti absently returned it. His attention was fixed on Khalid.

Some people want to feel powerful.

Khalid bobbed his head in a cowed affirmative. "Of course," he said. "You're absolutely right, signori. Here—" He clambered off the wagon and scuttled to the back, where the barrels were lashed to the sides. With his good hand, he freed a cask and patted the lid. "My oversight."

He stood back as the guards wrangled the cask down and rolled it into the guardhouse. Then, with a smug grin, Agosti was handing the receipt back to Khalid and waving him through.

The new Medici Guard was at the Palazzo's front gates. His eyes met Khalid's for only a split second. But there was no mistaking the flash of gleeful approval on Giacomo's face, even from this distance. Then he was gone, vanished into the Palazzo Medici.

There was a coal glowing in the depths of Khalid's stomach. He barely felt the pain in his arm as he hauled himself back into the driver's seat. Then, with a snap of the reins, he urged his mule forward— toward a blazing sun that glittered like Medici gold.

42

SARRA

It had been difficult enough, shouldering through the throng near the city walls to deliver Rosa's ledger to its intended recipients. Making her way into the Cathedral of Santa Maria del Fiore, just blocks from the Palazzo Medici, had been nearly impossible, the crowds were so thick. Truly, the only good thing about the overwhelming press outside was that it meant there were so few people *inside*, and once Sarra finally managed to shove into the cool stone sanctuary of the Cathedral, she felt as though a physical pressure had been lifted from her shoulders. She breathed deeply, inhaling incense and prayerful silence and exhaling the noise and chaos of the Piazza's cheering onlookers.

It was not Sarra's first time inside of Florence's celebrated Duomo, but she took a moment to get her bearings anyway. As ever, the dizzying frescoes that ringed the interior of the domed roof were a marvel of art and design, and the soaring ceilings brought a marveling smile to her lips. A few priests busied themselves near the front of the nave, unaffected by the revelry just beyond the double doors. The pews were occupied as well, a handful of worshippers with their heads bowed, casting their prayers up toward the heavens.

Maybe they were onto something.

There was a basin of holy water at the end of the aisle. Feeling a bit foolish, she dipped her fingers into it before sketching out the sign of the cross.

She didn't close her eyes to pray. It would have been false

deference, a hollow apology. And she was going into today with her eyes open. She might as well pray with her eyes open too.

I won't ask for help. She arrowed her words toward the crucifix at the front of the nave, and the tortured, blessed man affixed to it. *I won't even ask to preserve my own safety.*

Water dripped from her fingertips. What was she *doing*? Praying to God for a chance to pull one over on his mouthpiece—if God really was listening, then maybe she shouldn't call his attention.

But still.

We're good people, Lord. She shoved the weight of conviction behind the thought. *That man—that* mark—*is not. All I ask is that you don't interfere. We'll take it from there.*

Slightly confrontational, but her point had been conveyed. She nodded to the crucifix, wiped her fingers on her hose, and made her way around the edge of the nave to the staircase.

In her past visits, Sarra had never taken on this staircase, and for good reason. The walls were so narrow that the edges of her pack brushed both at once, and the stairs went on *forever*, up and up and up, winding dauntlessly around the edges of Il Duomo. The occasional slitted window allowed the Piazza's cheers to resonate through the stairwell, ringing in Sarra's ears like tolling bells. She didn't spare the crowd a glance; she would get ample opportunity soon enough. What she did study were the frescoes, so much closer from up here, the painted figures taunting her with their even faces and calm eyes.

She glared at a cherub. The cherub smiled benignly back. Sarra kept climbing.

Her legs were burning by the time she reached the top, but there wasn't any time to catch her breath, much less take a rest. She panted to a stop at the final window, which opened over the western side of Il Duomo, where the crowds spilling onto the streets were not nearly as dense. All eyes were pinned to the Palazzo Medici, which meant that nobody was paying any mind to the impassive facade of Il Duomo.

It also meant that nobody noticed as Sarra Nepi leaned out the small window with her modified crossbow in hand, took careful aim at the Cathedral's cupola above her, and fired.

Her arrow ripped through the air, trailing a thin length of rope—an invention of her own. The head was hooked and blunt, designed to anchor to surfaces rather than to pierce flesh, but she hadn't had as much time to test it out over the last few weeks as she might have liked . . .

The end of the rope, still tied to the crossbow, shuddered and sagged. The arrow had caught on the cupola. With careful hands, she tugged, testing the give lightly at first, then harder.

It held.

For now, Sarra thought, and then indulged in a wry grin. She tucked her crossbow into her pack. Then, grabbing the rope with both hands, Sarra swung out the window. Her feet braced on the sill, a final escape back to solid ground—

And then she began to climb.

43

GIACOMO

We counted very carefully, signore.

Giacomo bit back a smile as he marched through the first-floor corridors of the Palazzo Medici, keeping careful distance between himself and any other guards who crossed his path. He hadn't given Khalid enough credit, perhaps, but he really didn't think that could be blamed *entirely* on him because the man had written off what Giacomo did for a living as *distasteful* up until . . . yesterday? So how was Giacomo supposed to have predicted that, once he'd given himself permission, Khalid would be a natural performer?

He did survive six weeks in the Medici Guard, he thought. *And then he wound up in the river.* They canceled each other out, those two facts. Maybe Giacomo should stop marveling about Khalid al-Sarraj before he wound up in the river himself.

Between bouts in their hurried training session, Khalid had laid out Giacomo's path through the Palazzo, one least populated by prying eyes. Giacomo had listened with half an ear as he struggled to escape Khalid's grapple for the millionth time, his muscles protesting the *hideous* exertion he was putting them through, but he was a professional and it was *professional* to remember things like schematics and routes and escape plans and so he had. Now his feet, scraping awkwardly in his borrowed boots, carried him confidently to the servants' stairwell that Khalid had specified, and he started to climb.

They had done their best with the waterlogged wad of cloth

that had been Khalid's guard uniform, but there hadn't been time for proper tailoring. A few hours drying in front of the hearth and some hasty stitches to repair the pummeling-and-Arno-induced tears had resulted in a suit of clothes that passed basic muster, provided that nobody noticed how many times the sleeves were turned up or how the belt had required the addition of a new hole to cinch the hose shut. As long as things went according to plan, that would not become an issue. *Should* not become an issue.

There was a lot hanging on that "should." It made Giacomo sweat.

He turned off the staircase on the top floor. Where the first story was overrun with servants and footmen and guards now, all tripping over one another in their banquet tasks, the third was for the family only. Only higher-ranking guardsmen or those with special dispensation were allowed in these halls. Which meant he would have to be very quiet, very quick, and very lucky.

First right...

Giacomo kept his footsteps steady and strong as he set off across the carpet, his eyes fixed somewhere in the middle distance. Furtiveness would only invite scrutiny. He took the right at the end of the corridor without poking his head around the corner first, just as a patrolling guard would, and corralled his sigh of relief when he found the stretch of corridor empty.

Sixth on the left...

It was a sunny hall, lined on both sides by windows. The ones on the right overlooked the courtyard, which was rapidly transforming from a gorgeous architectural masterpiece into a gorgeous architectural masterpiece with *gilding* under the oversight of several stern-faced upper-level servants. The windows on the left boasted a slightly less picturesque view, framing snapshots of the city street, the nearby Cathedral of Santa Maria del Fiore, and the mob of Florentine onlookers.

Somewhere out of sight a door opened, and someone spilled hurriedly into the hall. Giacomo caught the echo of raised male voices before the door slammed shut again. A moment later, a teenage girl in a servant's uniform skittered around the corner, her face slack and pale and her eyes pinned to the floor. Giacomo squared his shoulders as she hurried past, an empty silver pitcher clutched in her hands, but the girl didn't give him so much as a glance. In another moment she was gone, padding down the servants' staircase, and Giacomo was once again alone.

Well. *That* was unnecessarily exhilarating. Giacomo had every faith that he'd be able to charm his way past a servant girl, but that didn't mean he had the *time* to do it, and especially not the time to do it *right*.

A fumble in his doublet produced the scarlet scarf he had stashed there earlier, and then Giacomo wasted another few seconds figuring out how to unlatch the leaded glass window. The rusted hinges *shrieked* as he pushed the pane outward, but nobody materialized to tell him off or run him through, so Giacomo went ahead and hung the scarf over the ledge. It flapped in the stiff wind, and Giacomo was graced with a vision of this entire endeavor being gutted because a scarf had up and blown away, so he grabbed the edge of the cloth and worked it into the gap between the windowpane and the ledge, jamming it in as hard as he could—

"What is the meaning of this?"

Giacomo turned.

Cardinal Giulio de' Medici filled the hallway quite impressively for such a slender man, making up for the narrowness of his shoulders with the venom in his eyes. This gaze now raked Giacomo from crown to toes, poisoning and burning and pinning him in place.

There was no running. The Cardinal needed only to shout—Giacomo would be full of crossbow bolts and Medici steel before he even made it to the front gates. All he could do was drop into a bow, absorb the blazing ferocity of the man's glare, and *pray* as somewhere above Florence, Sarra attempted the impossible.

Hopefully—*hopefully*—it would be enough.

44

SARRA

The cheers of the crowd were audible but subdued up here. Instead of the cushioned, echoey silencing of the Cathedral walls, it was as though someone had taken the swelling of voices and scattered them like marbles on a sheet of granite, flattening and dispersing them across the hundreds of meters that separated Sarra from the ground.

The fact that she had the space for thoughts like these while she made her slow and steady way up the side of Il Duomo was either the best or the worst thing about this entire undertaking. On the positive side, they kept her from sparing a glance downward. On the negative side, they kept her occupied *with* thoughts of the faraway ground, which was not productive.

The *chunk-chunk* of the toes of her boots lodging into the cracks between roofing tiles seemed very loud, even against the wind. She decided to concentrate on that instead, and on the burn in her shoulders and biceps as she hauled herself toward the cupola, hand over hand.

Chunk-chunk. Maybe she should have spared a prayer for her own safety after all, but . . . it was too late now.

Chunk-chunk. Had her father ever undertaken a task as foolhardy as this one? Perhaps this is why he never gave in to her begging for stories. If Sarra had known he was spending his time away at impossible altitudes, she would never have slept a wink.

Chunk-chunk. Maybe Pietro had a point, with all his worrying.
Chunk-chu—

Her foot met crumbling stone, and then empty air. She had enough time to gasp "Shit—!"

And then she was *falling*, slipping down the side of Il Duomo in a shower of moldy brickwork. The lurch of gravity yanked the rope from her fingers, and suddenly she was holding nothing but thin and empty air, and the shouts of the crowd below seemed much closer and more overwhelming than they had a moment ago.

She scrambled at the roof tiles, desperate for any handhold, scrabbling for the rope. But the roof was smooth and Sarra was plummeting like a stone and the rope had caught the breeze and was dancing out of her grasp—

And then *back into it again*.

It was as though one moment the only thing she could catch hold of was wind, and the next that same wind had plucked up the rope and deposited it directly into Sarra's hands. She grasped tight, feeling the wrench in her shoulders as her body shocked to a halt and then swung and swung.

It had all happened so fast. She had fallen maybe a meter and a half. The cupola was still near, assuming she could get her paralyzed muscles to obey her brain and carry her there.

Our Father who art in Heaven, she thought, riding the edge of hysteria. And kicking out with her boots, she sunk her toes into the ridge between tiles. *Chunk-chunk.*

Her brush with death solidly behind her (beneath her? Sarra shied away from that phrasing), it was a simple matter to clamber the final meters to the unfinished cupola. She hauled herself onto the small platform and allowed herself a minute to sprawl on her belly, hugging the stones and ignoring the wind as it whipped tendrils of her hair out of their braids.

"Next time," she muttered, "I'll wear the pretty dress and Rosa can do this part."

It was with great reluctance that she shoved to her knees and dug her crossbow back out of her pack, mostly because *this* was the point at which she could no longer ignore the cobblestones. Florence was sprawled across the landscape below, colorful and hazy with distance, and from here she could see all the way past the city walls to the green rolling hills beyond.

It was a beautiful view. Sarra resented it.

The stock of her crossbow was a reassuring weight in her hands as she loaded the next bolt. This was also an arrow that she had created for this job, trailing yet another length of cord. It seemed to thrum in the notch, dreaming of flight as she opened the driver from her belt-kit and peered through the scope.

The Palazzo Medici swam into hazy focus, and Sarra had a brief moment of déjà vu. It hadn't been so many weeks ago that she'd been sitting on another rooftop, peering at the Palazzo through this same scope.

Third floor . . . third floor . . . cogs clicked and whirred as she scanned along the line of windows, driver twisting the dials as she kept things in focus. *Yes—*

There, dangling from the sill of the last window in line, was a tiny scrap of red cloth. There was some slight movement in the shadowed hall inside, but that was most likely just Giacomo pacing as he waited on her.

Better not keep him waiting.

Sarra stowed her belt-kit, steadied the crossbow against her shoulder, let out a slow breath—

And let her finger find the trigger.

45

GIACOMO

E ven bent double in a forelock-scraping bow, Giacomo could feel Cardinal de' Medici's icy glare boring into the top of his head.

Damn, he observed to himself, quickly followed by *damn*, and then by *damn*.

"Explain yourself, Guardsman," the Cardinal demanded. Giacomo, tired of watching the man's shoes, straightened and fixed his gaze at a point on the wall just behind the Cardinal's shoulder.

The point on the wall where Sarra's crossbow bolt would *very soon* be buried. Unless, of course, she bypassed the wall and went straight through the Cardinal.

Damn.

"I gave you a command, Guardsman," Cardinal de' Medici snapped. "This floor is restricted to the family and to personal servants. I don't believe you fall into either category."

"No, Your Eminence," Giacomo stuttered. "I know that, Your Eminence."

"Then *why* are you *here*."

Something glinted in the corner of Giacomo's eye—a metallic sparkle near Il Duomo's cupola. Whatever limited time he had was rapidly running out.

"Captain Romano's orders, Your Eminence," he explained to the brickwork behind the Cardinal. "It's part of the heightened security measures."

Cardinal de' Medici's cold eyes narrowed. "I wasn't aware those were to extend past the ground floor."

"Yes, Your Eminence."

"Was—is there a *need* for this?"

Unless Giacomo had suddenly become completely terrible at his job—that was a flicker of *fear* sparking in the frozen plateau of the Cardinal's face. "Most likely not, Your Eminence," Giacomo said, bland and recitative, a grunt regurgitating instructions. "But there've been reports that have . . . in-cen-ti-vized Captain Romano to increase the safeguards around the Medici family. Uh. Which means you, Your Eminence."

"What reports."

Giacomo fidgeted, partly for the show of it and partly so he could get another glimpse out the window. There was no further sign of movement at the top of Il Duomo, but that could mean anything ranging from *Sarra is about to make a skewer out of a Cardinal of the Church* to *Sarra is now a pancake on the cobblestones.* "Captain Romano said I was to keep quiet about them, Your Eminence."

"They're *my* reports, Guardsman," Cardinal de' Medici said. "I paid for them. I pay for you too. *What is going on.*"

"Of course. Of course. Ah." He inched closer, as close as he dared. "You see, Your Eminence, there is a . . . concern about some of the banquet guests. It's only a murmuring!" Giacomo hastened to add. "This is why Captain Romano didn't want to worry you. But. In light of the . . . recent unrest in the city, there is a suspicion that the . . . disruptors are being . . . well. Funded."

"Funded," Cardinal de' Medici echoed from a great distance. "And Captain Romano believes that benefactor . . . may be at the Palazzo tonight?"

"It's only a hunch!" Giacomo exclaimed. "But . . . yes. There is a chance." He cocked his head. "Are you quite well, Your Eminence?"

In fact, the Cardinal looked gray, and his voice, when he next spoke, came out in a rasp. "I—" he said, but that was about all it seemed he could muster, because he was whirling and stalking back toward the door the servant girl had emerged from without another word.

The scarlet robes had barely disappeared from view when something zipped past Giacomo's nose with a sharp *fwip!* and hit the wall. He hopped back, just far enough to take in the crossbow bolt buried in the plaster *right* where the Cardinal's head had been. A thin length of rope trailed from the end of the bolt, extending from the plaster out the sixth window and disappearing up into the sky.

Not a pancake, then, he thought.

Working quickly, Giacomo severed the rope and tied it to a wall sconce. Four tugs on the rope were the signal, and then all there was to do was to focus on not having a heart attack and channel whatever energy was left over after *that* on listening as hard as he could for signs that the Cardinal or any other damned Medici had decided to make this corridor their business. Then—

Something was buzzing.

Giacomo cocked, listening harder. Was there a bee? Had a bee survived the first freeze of winter and found its way into the Palazzo? Was Giacomo going to have to face off with a *bee* on top of everything else?

But no, small blessings abounded—the buzzing was coming from the line itself, which vibrated just enough to hum in Giacomo's ears—vibrated because there was something sliding along it, heading straight for the Palazzo window.

Giacomo braced himself as the object grew nearer, an indistinguishable speck solidifying into the familiar shape of Agata de Rosso's brown leather kit. It flew through the window at a terrifying speed, and Giacomo just barely managed to stop it before it smashed into the far wall. The impact stung his palms, and he spared a brief moment of horror for the chemicals inside, but when he failed to explode, he quickly untethered the line, freed the bag, and gave the rope one final tug. It snaked back out the window a moment later, pulled by Sarra's unseen hands. Then, with a quick yank to liberate the incriminating crossbow bolt, Giacomo clutched the bag to his chest and made for the stairs. His next task could afford no delays.

He found what he was looking for in the shadow of the Palazzo kitchens, hidden under a pile of splintered furniture and broken barrels. A few moments of shifting revealed hinged doors set into the earth.

It appeared to be nothing more than a root cellar—but Giacomo, who had seen the blueprints of the Palazzo Medici, who had *studied* them—knew quite different. He lifted one of the doors and descended.

The first thing he noticed was how close and damp the air was down here. He lit a torch to ward away some of the chill—and nearly dropped it in surprise.

The walls were not the rough-hewn stone or packed earth that one might expect from a cellar. Someone had applied a coat of plaster— plaster that had been covered in light sketches of people, of things, of places, of mechanical contraptions Giacomo could not even *begin* to understand. Each drawing was formed from soft, purposeful strokes that breathed unexpected life into the rutted plaster, and Giacomo was only stopped from tracing the fluttering wings of a sparrow by the fact that both his hands were occupied.

There was no question that these could be the designs of anyone but Master Leonardo da Vinci. And it was this realization that redirected Giacomo to the task at hand. With great reluctance, he turned his gaze away from the wall and toward the splintered plank at the far end of the cellar. It came away with a quick yank, and suddenly Giacomo was staring at a mass of iron cogs and wheels and levers and . . . spikes.

This was the underside of the Magi Chapel corridor—the traps that promised pain and mutilation to any unaware trespasser who would try for the Medici vault. And it was completely beyond Giacomo's realm of comprehension.

Fortunately, that didn't much matter. He opened Agata's kit.

"You must listen to me carefully," Agata had told him, the lines of her face smoothed into somber granite. The contents of her tool kit had been laid out on the kitchen table, powders and potions and bundles of herbs arrayed in neat lines. Giacomo had been mesmerized by the vial of blue liquid—it had been *bubbling*. "Sweetcake. Giacomo!"

Giacomo had torn his gaze up to meet hers. "My attention is ever yours, my queen."

"None of that," she'd said, with a sharp pinch to the back of his hand. "This is important. You cannot sweet-talk or charm anything on this table. The only way we get through this is if you heed me right now. If you don't, then either you will end up in a coffin, or Rosa will. Do you understand?"

Giacomo had taken a stab at a laugh, though his mouth had gone suddenly very dry. "Of course, of course. How hard could it be?"

Her eyes hadn't faltered, and Giacomo had experienced a searing and physical comprehension of her reputation as a formidable witch. "Do you. Understand."

He'd nodded. And then the quizzing had begun.

He heard her words in his head now as he sorted through the bag, fingers gingerly brushing across glass tubes and cloth-wrapped bundles, searching, searching . . .

Aqua fortis, she had called it. And then she had called it *spirit of niter*. And *then* she had told him that he'd better watch his fingers with it if he didn't want them rotting off, which was why when he found it lodged at the bottom of the bag, cushioned in a bundle of old rags, his hands trembled as he drew it out, unwrapped it, and held it up—*not too close*, Agata hissed in his ear—to the torchlight.

It wasn't much to look at. It could be a vial of water. But Giacomo knew better than anyone that appearances were nothing to build certainty on.

"If this aqua fortis is so powerful," he'd said to Agata, "then why not simply douse the traps and be done with it?"

"Do I put on a false beard and tell you how to do your job?" she'd asked him, her hands a blur of motion as she'd picked through the objects on the table. "Signore da Vinci designed in *iron*. You might as well slap a suit of armor over the contraption." She held a few things up for his inspection. "This requires something with a bit more . . . innovation."

Giacomo pulled her selections out now—a candle, a length of twine, and a jar of water—and wondered if he'd been tricked into conducting some witchy ritual.

"Spirit of niter is touchy," Agata had said. "It doesn't get along with other compounds. On its own it's perfectly fine, but introduce the wrong element and things become . . . unstable."

The woman had a talent for understatement because what Giacomo came to understand was that he had been sent here, into this glorified root cellar, to set off what was essentially a bomb. But because *that* wasn't *ridiculous* enough, he could not simply dump water into aqua fortis and watch da Vinci's work disintegrate—no, no, no, *apparently* something-something-chemical fog-something-something-*suffocation* meant that he would have to set up the detonation on a delay to avoid *dying* where he *stood*.

"Which makes *perfect* sense," he muttered to himself as he tilted the jar of water at an angle and anchored it there with the length of twine. "Because if there is one thing that Giacomo san Giacomo is known for far and wide, it is feats of mechanical engineering."

The candle was next, set underneath the twine. Then, with the gentlest of touches, Giacomo lifted the aqua fortis and positioned it just beneath the descending trajectory of the water jar. Or at least, where he *hoped* the water jar would fall.

He was sweating by the time he sat back on his heels, the close air of the cellar clinging at his temples and collar. Still, despite the budding terror and anxiety, he spared a glance at Master da Vinci's sketches, which still flickered warmly in the light of his torch.

"Terribly sorry about this," he told them. They didn't answer.

Then, with a strike of his flint, Giacomo lit the candle . . . and ran.

46

ROSA

I f the Palazzo Medici had impressed Rosa on the first visit, the second left her stunned. What was already gorgeous and opulent had been somehow embellished to impress the guests who glided past, their eyes wide and wondering.

The increased security only cast the Palazzo's wealth in starker relief. Rosa and Michelangelo's carriage had been searched twice on their way to the front gates—once at the end of the block and again at the doors. Inside the Palazzo, guards marched through the courtyard at regular intervals, and Rosa could catch glimpses of more uniforms moving beyond the upper-level windows. As far as she could tell, the only stirring of trouble had come from the merchant couple in the carriage behind theirs, who had not been pleased by the indignity of the checkpoints. The wife was even now making her dissatisfaction known to her husband as they made their way through the courtyard, heedless of his shushing.

In a glittering procession, they emerged into the gardens, and for a moment, Rosa had the nonsensical idea that she'd been transported to some ancient fairyland; someone had gone to great lengths to light small candles among the shrubbery and statues. They glimmered and winked in the shadows, bathing the gardens in an ethereal glow. Where there were no candles, there were garlands of glass beads and bright flowers and ribbons, which picked up the light and reflected it back in blues and greens and reds and yellows. Even Michelangelo, perennially unimpressed by the world at large, took in a surprised breath at what the garden had become.

"Well, if it isn't Il Divino!" The string quartet in the corner was no match for the booming voice that greeted them as they stepped onto the white gravel path. The Pope beamed from the high-backed chair at the center of a long banquet table, Cardinal de' Medici at his right hand. Smaller tables had all been set up in neat lines, covered in Medici blue linens where the Pope's was covered in white.

"Your Holiness," Michelangelo grumbled.

"Your Holiness," Rosa echoed, dipping a curtsy. "I am without words. This is a marvel."

"Yes, it is nice, isn't it?" The Pope flapped a hand at his surroundings. "Just wait 'til you try the food. The cooks have outdone themselves, from what I hear. Come, come—latecomers will just have to reckon with the consequences of their own tardiness if we start without them."

Beside him, Cardinal de' Medici inclined his head in a shallow nod of acknowledgment. "Please," he said, gesturing toward the seats on the other side of the Pope.

Michelangelo muttered something as they followed a footman to their seats. "What was that?" she whispered.

"*Display*," he hissed. "This is a *display*."

Of course it was. The Medici were keen on making a favorable impression on the wealthy families they'd gathered here, and what was more impressive than showing they had the most famous artist in the country at their beck and call?

"Now you know how your statues feel," Rosa whispered, and caught the edge of his glare as they slid into their seats.

From the head table, Rosa had a view of the entire garden, across the other tables where guests glittered in the candlelight, bedecked in outfits worth enough to buy out the whole of the Mercato Vecchio.

All fell silent the instant the Pope raised his hands, the fairy lights glinting off his rings. "Thank you all," he declaimed. "I cannot put into words how much your presence means to us. It pleases God to know that there are such pious people in Tuscany, some of whom have traveled far to be here. And with that in mind, I have prepared this meal as a token of my gratitude. If you will join me?" He clasped his hands. "In Nomine Patris, et Filii, et Spiritus Sancti . . ."

The recitation wound through the night, and Tuscany's blue bloods bowed their heads to hear it. But among their number, there was one who was not deep in prayer.

Dominic Fontana sat at one of the nearest tables, his eyes fixed on Rosa.

What did he see? Rosa the heartless thief? Rosa the grieving daughter? Something else? Michelangelo had told Dominic that Rosa's intentions were good. Had he believed his master?

His lips parted. Would he say something *here*? Before all these people? Was he—?

He spoke, and it was with the voice of a hundred, all rolling together as one peal of thunder to rumble the word "Amen" so loudly that it rang off the marble statues. Rosa had lost the end of the Pope's prayer in her distraction, and now there were servants bustling from the archway behind the head table, carrying tray after steaming tray. She avoided Michelangelo's confused glance and slid back into the warm embrace of Rosa de' Lombardi, who had never been emotionally befuddled by any artist's apprentice, and who had never encountered a meal like this in all her years on this earth.

"Oh *my*," she breathed, as a roasted pheasant was settled in front of the Pope. This was swiftly flanked by a tureen of rich broth topped with aromatic herbs, and a plate of fluffy white bread. A young servant slipped in at her side to fill her wine goblet from a brimming pitcher.

"Tuck in, tuck in!" urged the Pope, whose plate was already piled high. "It's called a feast for a reason!"

The evening devolved into a haze as servants ducked in and out, ensuring every table was groaning under the heavy platters. Michelangelo buried his nerves in his plate, eating with a voracity that belied his wiry frame. Rosa could not bring herself to follow suit. The show of it all—the *display*, as Michelangelo had called it—had soured something in her stomach. She picked at her food, taking bites only when she felt eyes on her.

She only allowed herself a glance at Dominic with every other course. Dominic, however, exhibited no such restraint. Every time she looked up from her plate she found him staring straight at her, his own food untouched.

"Well now, brother!" The Pope was smirking as he leaned into Michelangelo, his goblet dangling from his fingers. "I had never thought you much of a Cupid."

Michelangelo froze, a slab of roast hanging from his knife. "What?"

The Pope's goblet swayed, first toward Rosa and then, vaguely, toward Dominic. "Don't tell me you've missed the *looks*."

Rosa did not have to fake her blush. "I'm afraid Your Holiness is mistaken—"

"I may be a man of God, but I'm not *blind*, my child," the Pope said with an indulgent chuckle. "And poor young Fontana looks positively *bereft*. I must council you—whatever sleight he has dealt you, find it in your heart to forgive him."

"He is poised to become a very wealthy artist indeed." Cardinal de' Medici sawed sedately at a sliver of pheasant as he spoke.

Her sour stomach curdled solid. "Is that so?"

"I believe he is the next gem in the Medici family legacy," the Pope said, pitched loudly enough to reach any listening ears.

Dominic's eyes were drills in the side of Rosa's head. "How intriguing."

Cardinal de' Medici's knife had frozen in his hand. He was staring out across the gardens, his cold eyes narrowing. "Your Holiness," he murmured.

Rosa tried to follow the direction of his gaze, but it landed somewhere on a knot of merchants with no particular purpose. Whatever the Cardinal saw, though, it had his grip tightening on his knife.

She didn't have time for this. With a delicate cough, Rosa dabbed at the corners of her lips. "Would you excuse me for just one moment, Your Holiness?"

The Pope laughed. "Yes, go! Make up! I know how you young lovers are!"

Rising, Rosa bussed a kiss across Michelangelo's cheek. "Make sure he doesn't leave the table," she whispered, with a significant glance back to the glowering Cardinal. "No matter what happens." Then with another curtsy, she bustled back toward the courtyard.

The Medici could gossip all they wanted. It wouldn't stop her from burning them down.

47

GIACOMO

Giacomo was crossing the busy kitchen, halfway to the rendez-vous, when everything went to hell.

"Guardsman!"

If Giacomo walked quickly and with enough purpose, then maybe reality would twist so the person shouting would not, in fact, be shouting at *him*. He could make it to the Magi Chapel and Rosa would be there and they could smoothly and competently rob these Medici bastards and nothing would go wrong ever again.

"Guardsman! Halt!"

Then again, it was a fine line to walk between plausible deafness and blowing-the-whole-operation-by-getting-collared-for-insubordination. This, it seemed, was going to require the use of his ears, so he ground to a halt and let the scullery maid behind him curse as she had to dodge.

It was another guard who had flagged him down, and as Giacomo watched the blue uniform approach, his stomach twisted in a split second of worry that he would somehow *know*, or that the Cardinal had raised the alarm, or *something*.

"All guards are to report to the gardens immediately," said the guard, whose eyes were slightly wild above his impressive beard.

Something was wrong. Something Rosa hadn't foreseen was warp-ing their plan out of shape, and if guards were being summoned then the warping was happening right in front of the Medici. That was one half of the catastrophic conclusion coming into focus in Giacomo's mind. The other half was the ticking clock on the Magi Chapel. He was already running late for the rendezvous, and if he was any later . . .

"Gardens," Guardsman Beard snapped. "*Now.*"

Which was not the sort of order Giacomo could argue his way out of, at least not without wasting time that neither he nor this guard had available, and so he followed in the man's wake.

Maybe this is good, he reasoned. *If I'm on the scene—whatever's happening, I can steer it—or at least buy us some time, and then Rosa will still have a chance to crack the vault—*

There was an edge of hysteria to it. An infusion of hysteria. His thoughts were *drowned* in hysteria, and it was all he could do to keep a straight face as Guardsman Beard shoved the garden door open and marched out onto the lawn.

It was the subdued atmosphere that struck Giacomo first. Lively chatter and even a little shouting were only to be expected from a banquet lubricated by bottomless vats of wine. But the voices that filtered past the topiaries and the statues were muted and *reeking* of tension, and Giacomo felt a shiver sparkle down his spine as he padded in Guardsman Beard's footsteps.

". . . *Unseemly,*" someone was muttering, too loud to be quiet and too slurred to be sober. As Giacomo passed a gap between topiaries, he caught a flash of movement—a merchant clad from head to toe in mustard yellow, who was gesturing with his wine goblet as though it was a magician's staff. "It's *unseemly,*" the merchant said, even louder this time, twisting sideways as his wife made a grab for his drink.

"Lower your voice," she hissed.

The merchant would not be settled, and his goblet swerved in another figure eight. "It's no way for a man of God to behave."

Guardsman Beard took a sharp corner around a looming piece of statuary, and suddenly Giacomo had an unimpeded view of the entire garden. His first instinct was to seek out the long, well-appointed banquet table where the Pope, Cardinal de' Medici, and Il Divino were all seated. Between the decorations and the food, it should have made a jubilant picture.

But Cardinal de' Medici was frowning. Pope Leo was glowering. Even Il Divino was affected, his shoulders hunched around his ears as he poked at his plate.

The chair next to him was empty.

Guardsman Beard made a beeline for Captain Romano, who stood at attention behind the Medici cousins. The captain's sour face was even more sour than usual, and he glared out over the banquet tables with acid in his eyes.

". . . wasn't enough for them to own our city," the merchant was declaring. "They had to own the church, too!"

The Pope's voice was tight as a harpsichord wire as he gritted, "Captain Romano."

"He's just a drunk," Michelangelo murmured to the Pope.

Maybe that would have made a difference if the merchant hadn't at the same time abandoned any pretense at volume control and shouted, "We were better off as a Republic!"

"I will handle this, Your Holiness," Romano told the Medici, but his assurances fell on deaf ears. Both scions were glaring in the direction of the belligerent merchant and did not appear to be hearing anything but the drumbeat of mindless rage.

"There have been reports," Cardinal de' Medici gritted out between his teeth, "that the sponsor of this city's insurrectionists is in attendance here tonight."

Giacomo kept his gaze pinned straight ahead.

"He would dare come here?" the Pope hissed. The beacon of his ire swiveled to Romano. "You would allow him inside our home?"

"I will handle this," Captain Romano repeated, bowing as he shuffled back a few steps. Then his hand was clamping down on

Guardsman Beard's shoulder. "*Discreetly*," he whispered. "We do not want to cause any more of a scene."

Giacomo personally thought that ship had sailed, considering that everyone in the garden was gaping openly between the sozzled merchant and the head table, and that the Medici themselves looked on the verge of ordering a mass execution.

But the guardsmen did not have the chance to act before another guest surged to his feet. "You bite your tongue before I have my men rip it from your head!"

The bottom plummeted out of Giacomo's stomach. Of course. Of *course* his father would jump to the defense of the most powerful family in Florence. Of *course* he would not miss the opportunity to lick a pair of Medici boots. Haze crept at the edges of Giacomo's mind—the same fog that had taken him at the gambling house and compelled him to wander out into a riot. He was helpless to do more than gawk at the Petrucci patriarch and at the faces flanking him, because if Signore Petrucci was in attendance, then the odds were better than good . . .

The haze was only thickening, so when Captain Romano said, "*Deal with him*," it took Giacomo a moment to realize that the order was meant for *him*.

Giacomo could slip away. The atmosphere was slanting from "party" and toward "mob," and he could melt into the chaos on the pretense of following the captain's command and then disappear. It was risky and his absence would *definitely* be noticed, but at least he wouldn't have to *fight* anyone. Or, worse yet, let anyone else fight *him*.

The thing was, though, that Rosa's chair was empty, which meant that *some part* of this foolish plan was still rolling along. There was still a chance they could pull it off. And Giacomo did *not* want to be the one who blew that chance.

He strode toward the merchant and the crowd parted around him.

This was because he was doing his best to channel a very *specific* version of Khalid—the one Khalid had retreated into this last week, the one Giacomo *disliked. Muscles. Frown. Traverio's clenched fist.*

Giacomo could nail the frown, at least. One out of three wasn't bad.

"You are speaking against the *Pope*," Petrucci—*Father*—was saying. "You will be damned for what you say!"

"The *Pope* is using our city to line his family's pockets!" the merchant said, and Giacomo felt a pang of sympathy for the man, as poor as his timing was. He wasn't *wrong*.

"He's not wrong." Giacomo briefly lived in the panicked reality where he had uttered his thoughts aloud, but the speaker was a young man in a green-and-brown jerkin cut high in the distinctly daring Florentine style.

Petrucci gaped, and Giacomo savored the sight through the growing haze. "You *dare!*"

"The Medici are *not* my overlords!" the merchant roared back, and then Giacomo was at his side, carefully angling himself to keep his back to the red-faced Petrucci patriarch.

"Signore," he said. "Perhaps this would be better continued elsewhere."

"I've seen the bills," the young dandy said. "The Medici Pope holds our souls ransom in exchange for *coin*."

"You question the will of God?" Petrucci bellowed, his eyes cutting to the table at the end of the garden where the Pope sat, still as a statue.

"The Medici are not God, they are *bankers*," the merchant spat.

At a loss for options, Giacomo laid a hand on the merchant's arm. "I must insist—"

He had hoped the gesture would be placating, but the merchant lurched out of his grasp and swung to face him, his blurry eyes flicking over his uniform. "*You* insist?" His breath was potent enough to send Giacomo reeling. "*You*? A lackey? A puppet?"

"A marionette!" the dandy chimed in, delighted. "And who is pulling your strings?"

Guardsman Beard loomed at the dandy's shoulder. "Take your leave," he bit out.

"You're all marionettes!" the dandy said, gathering up his cloak and shaking a finger toward the gardens at large. He seemed to be the sort of person to light on a metaphor and then stick with it, for better or worse. "All of you!"

"*Now,*" rumbled Guardsman Beard, and the dandy was marching along the banquet tables, his nose in the air. Guests' heads swiveled as he passed, some on the verge of cheering while others looked as though they'd like to disappear into the ground.

"You as well, signore," Giacomo said to the merchant, still watching the dandy's tailored back as it flounced toward the Palazzo's front gates. "It's time for you to—"

"Watch out!"

The warning must have had a direct line to Giacomo's brain because he was flailing sideways in a wild tangle of limbs, skidding just out of reach as the merchant's drunken punch whiffed through the air next to his ear, and then—

That voice. That *voice*.

Giacomo whirled and—yes, that—that was his mother, half-risen from her seat just beside Petrucci's empty one.

She looked at him. He looked at her.

Neither of them looked at the merchant until his second punch collided with Giacomo's eye socket.

48

ROSA

She was still on schedule, but only barely. Rosa slipped into the courtyard's deep shadows, padding along the walkway. There was no sign of a guard patrol, but that was only a matter of time. Still, Rosa kept her pace steady, refusing to cave to the hammering beat of her heart that urged her to move faster, to break into a sprint—

Which was the only reason she was able to avoid crashing into the footman who stepped into her path from the corner staircase.

Her slippers skidded on the flagstones. "Signore!" she exclaimed. "Please excuse me—"

The footman didn't snap at her to *watch where you're going* only because that would have been *highly* improper and most likely grounds for a beating. "Guests are to remain in the gardens," he informed her instead. "Tours of the Palazzo are not available at this time."

Giacomo must be at the chapel by now. "Oh dear," Rosa fluttered. "I was on my way back from the garderobe. I must have gotten turned around."

It was a swing calculated to embarrass, but the footman had either the thickest face Rosa had ever encountered, or he was so accustomed to dealing with outlandish things within the Palazzo walls that he barely batted an eye. "The gardens are behind you, signorina. I am sure you have been missed."

Which left Rosa with three possible options. She could return to the banquet and avoid raising further suspicion. She would be stuck fielding the comments of both Medici scions until she could come up with another excuse to leave the table, which would be difficult to do without raising any eyebrows or worries as to the state of her digestive health, and by which point their window of opportunity may have closed.

She could insist to the footman that she had further business to attend inside the Palazzo, which would put him on the alert and attract the attention of the guards.

She could attempt to subdue the footman by force, which was a laughable notion she dismissed out of hand. In her entire life, the largest thing she'd ever had any success in "subduing" was the raccoon behind their house in Prato, and even then, the raccoon had nearly come out on top.

Three options, all spinning through her head in the span of a split second, picked up and discarded in turn. *No* and *no* and *no*—

"There you are!"

Dominic strode up the walkway as though he owned it, his burgundy doublet and hose black in the spare lamplight. "I told you to wait for me," he scolded. "Luca, thank you for tracking her down."

The footman's manner had softened upon Dominic's greeting, and he bobbed a bow. "It's the captain's orders, Signore Fontana," he said. "No guests allowed into the Palazzo without authorization from the family." His grimace was apologetic. "Including yourself, I'm afraid."

"Of course, of course," Dominic said. "When you say authorization, would this do?"

The paper in his hands was sturdy and thick, the edge weighed down by a red wax seal. Luca the footman took it, a degree of surprise registering in his eyes as he scanned the scribbled writing.

Dominic plucked up Rosa's hand, giving her fingers a warning squeeze before she could pull away. "As you see," he said, "His Holiness granted me special dispensation to show Signorina de' Lombardi my work in the chapel." The wink he leveled at Luca made it clear that his "work" was not his painting.

"I've been so looking forward to seeing it," Rosa said. "Though Uncle Michelangelo warned me that it might not be as impressive as Signore Fontana promised."

Luca swallowed, fumbling as he rolled the paper up and handed it back to Dominic. "Of course. Whatever you need." He was already sidling around them.

Dominic clapped him on the shoulder as he went. "You're a good friend, Luca," he said. "Don't let them work you too hard!" The footman's snort said *not likely*, and then he was stomping toward the garden archway, leaving Dominic and Rosa alone in the courtyard.

What stretched between them was not exactly silence, given the distant laughter and chatter of the banquet, but it was as weighty as silence. Dominic was *looking* at her, focused and intense, the same way he had looked at her outside the Church of Santo Stefano the night before. It occurred to Rosa that she was having a hard time breathing, and that this was likely Dominic's fault. She ripped her hand out of his and then, after a moment's consideration, yanked the paper out of his grip and unfurled it.

Her heart sank. She had spent the better part of five years studying whatever scraps of the Medici family had come her way, and what she was looking at was unmistakably the signature of Pope Leo X, underscored by the heavy, official seal of the Papal Office. By the authorization of His Holiness, the paper decreed, the painter Dominic Fontana had the freedom to accompany Rosa de' Lombardi anywhere in the Palazzo she wished to go.

"You didn't," Rosa hissed. "You *told* the Pope?"

"*Told* him? No, Rosa—I put this together last night."

She stared at him. "Last night. You just . . . 'put this together.'"

He shrugged, looking a little helpless. "I heard about the new restrictions and . . . I thought there was a chance it could help you. Just in case."

Just in case. He had *thrown together* one of the best bits of forgery she had ever seen, *just in case.* "I . . ."

He straightened his shoulders, reaching for a bit of dignity. "You could say thank you."

"I could have handled it." Was he standing closer now? She stepped back, tripping on the hem of her skirt in her haste to put some space between them. "I have to—" she started, but there was no way to finish that sentence, not out in the open. Instead, she turned and marched to the Magi Chapel.

The doors eased closed behind them, shut by Dominic's gentle hands. The chapel was dark and empty, with no sign of Giacomo. Rosa busied herself with hunting down a candle.

"Go back to the banquet," she told Dominic, her voice low. "Go back."

He didn't move. "I'm going to decline their patronage," he said. Rosa didn't allow herself to react to that, picking up the candlestick and pacing a lap of the room. "Rosa, did you hear me? I'm going to turn the Medici down."

Rosa squared her shoulders and faced him, the length of the central aisle stretching between them. "Fantastic. Good job."

"Is that all?"

"I don't know what you want me to say. You may turn down the Devil, or however you want to see it, but I'm still—a thief, wasn't it?"

"And a grifter, too." His eyes were pinned on her. All that artistic focus and intensity and she wondered how she had *ever* deluded herself into thinking that she'd fooled him. Dominic Fontana had seen through her the second they'd met, had known her for a fake as soon as she'd smiled at him in Michelangelo's workshop.

"Right, how could I forget? So what are you still doing here? You don't know me."

He blinked. "I know you like teasing me," he said. "I know you like feeling clever. I know you loved your family. I know you're trying to take the Medici down a few pegs. And"—he dipped his chin, ceding something—"I know the Medici family is dangerous. I know enough."

Something flipped over in the pit of her stomach. "What do you want, Dominic?"

The corner of his mouth ticked up in the glimmer of a smile. "Whatever you're up to. I want to help."

49

GIACOMO

"Ave Maria, gratia plena, Dominus tecum."

The cold had cored him so deeply that it had replaced his bones. He was made of it, a frozen man, a skeleton of ice.

"Benedicta tu in mulieribus, et benedictus fructus ventris tui, Iesus."

His fingertips were so pale they were blue. He traced them along the worn wooden beads of the rosary out of memory rather than sensation. He couldn't feel a thing.

"Sancta Maria, Mater Dei."

Yes, he was a frozen man, deadened to feeling.

"Ora pro nobis peccatoribus, nunc, et in hora mortis nostrae."

Except for the jagged line of fire that ran from his jaw down to his clavicle.

"Amen."

"Again."

Father Bernardo was unmoving on his stool. The riding crop dangled at his side, a promise that had been fulfilled four times since they had begun their work three hours before.

The wooden bead slipped over his finger. "Ave Maria, gratia plena . . ."

The blow hit him out of nowhere, flinging him to the stone floor. He lay there, breath knocked from his lungs, a deep ache setting into his ribs beneath the brighter burn of agony. His numbed fingers scrabbled at his side, seeking to—what? Hold himself together? Giacomo Petrucci had been torn to shreds months ago.

"You think God cannot tell when you are going through the motions?" Father Bernardo stepped into Giacomo's field of vision. "You are a sinner.

Your prayers hold little enough weight as it is. You must be guided." The *riding crop was gripped tight in his fist. "I will guide you. To Heaven."*

Giacomo didn't need to look to know that the priest was raising the crop. He curled onto his side, shielding his face. This would anger Father Bernardo, but so did everything else.

Squeezing his eyes closed, he waited for the blow to fall.

"I would not see you that way again."

In the protective shell of his own arms, Giacomo blinked. Those words hadn't come from Father Bernardo. They certainly hadn't come from himself.

"Not if I can help it."

It wasn't real. It wasn't real. *That frozen hell—it was behind him. He was out, he had gotten out, he had gotten* himself *out, and now—*

Now he was standing in the gardens of the Palazzo Medici with a drunk merchant weaving in place before him and the Pope scowling in the background.

And his face. *Lord.* His face *hurt.*

"Had enough?" There were still shades of Father Bernardo in the merchant's voice. That nightmare was still alive in the back of Giacomo's mind, but it wasn't drowning him.

"This is your last chance, signore," Giacomo said, unearthing bravado from several layers of panic. "If you do not leave, then you will be arrested and tried for treason."

What had the Medici put in their wine, that this merchant would think to respond by charging Giacomo? What potion of misplaced bravery? Giacomo wondered if Agata had such a thing in her stores, and then he wondered if he could steal some for himself because the man was grabbing at Giacomo with his big, meaty hands and Giacomo was bracing himself for the tidal wave of panicked memory to pull him under—

It didn't come. The man's fingers were vises around Giacomo's arms, but the swell of nausea did not rise, and Giacomo did not feel the phantom blow of the riding crop against his skin or the hiss of the brand against his shoulder. It was . . . unexpected. *Thrilling*. Giacomo *laughed*, a single huff of exhilaration that only the merchant caught.

"You're laughing at me?"

Somewhere behind him there were guards shouting—Captain Romano and Guardsman Beard were ordering guests back, circling the merchant, preparing to pull him away. But Giacomo had Khalid in his ear now, and in his head and in his eyes, looking soft under the early-morning sun, his voice as calm and steady and strong as his hands.

"If helplessness is what gives you trouble," he had told Giacomo just that morning, "then you must not let anyone tell you that you are not in control. Not even yourself."

Giacomo's gaze had been drawn, inevitably, to Khalid's good hand, which was in the process of clenching into a fist. At the sight, Giacomo's stomach sank. "I can't—" he began, and stopped, and began again. "I'm no good at the hitting part. I remember too well what it's like on the other end."

"I do not want you to *hit*," Khalid had replied. "I want you to learn what to do when the time again comes that you are cornered with *other people* who want to hit *you*."

He'd said it like it was inevitable, which Giacomo found rude, but he'd been distracted from voicing his irritation by the wry quirk of Khalid's eyebrow. "Well?" Giacomo had prompted, with an eyebrow-waggle of his own. "Don't leave me in suspense."

"The first part is easy." Khalid had tapped his fist lightly against Giacomo's shoulder. "You make certain that they underestimate you."

Giacomo had nodded, once. "I can do that."

They hadn't had much time to practice—certainly not enough for the motions to become second nature to Giacomo the way they were to Khalid. But it had been only one move, and Khalid had drilled him on it for an hour before they had parted ways, and Giacomo had always had an elephant's memory where Khalid al-Sarraj was concerned, so . . .

"Loop your arm beneath his," Khalid had directed, so that was what Giacomo did now, snaking his left arm under the staggering merchant's armpit and drawing his hand up behind the man's back. "Grab his shoulder and step your foot back." Giacomo did this too, digging his fingers into the man's doublet and pivoting sideways to plant his right foot in the grass. "Then you just let him drop." Instruction and action were tethered—as soon as Khalid's words rippled through his memory, he was pulling the merchant forward, stepping around him to drop him to his knees, winching the man's arm high in the air behind his back.

"Then what do I do with him?" Giacomo had asked the first time they stepped through the motions. He'd had Khalid's good arm bent gingerly in the air, terrified of hurting him.

Khalid had smiled up at him over his shoulder. "He's helpless." *You're not.* "You can do anything you want."

"You *bastard*," snarled the merchant, who was not as charming as Khalid, and Giacomo discovered that what he wanted to do was press the man's arm to the side until he shut up.

"That's more like it," he said. He was panting, which was embarrassing because Giacomo's victory had more to do with the merchant's inebriation than Giacomo's competence.

Still, the display had met Captain Romano's approval, at least. "Excellent work, Guardsman," he said, striding up with Guardsman Beard.

Giacomo straightened as well as he could with his knee dug into the merchant's back. "Thank you, Captain."

"Take him," the captain ordered, and a moment later the merchant was hauled upright.

"I can deliver him to the City Guard," offered Giacomo, who had no such intentions and was, in fact, planning on sprinting to catch up with Rosa, wherever the *hell* she was.

"No need," Captain Romano said as Guardsman Beard dragged the merchant away. He was already swiveling back to the banquet's head table. "You're with me."

Again. *Again.* Really, it was no wonder that Khalid had risen in the guardsmen ranks so quickly because *apparently* they handed out approval to *anybody* and didn't care at all if that person had *very important other obligations.* Battling a scream, Giacomo trotted to keep up with Captain Romano's long-legged stride.

The guests had been placated (at least inasmuch as they had all returned to their seats), but the atmosphere remained subdued. Petrucci, of course, was re-ensconced in his chair looking self-satisfied. And Mama—*Mama*—was perched in the next seat, gaze rooted to the tabletop.

She had recognized him—for the second time now, even in disguise, and maybe that was a sign that Giacomo was slipping. Was she wondering what he was doing here? Was she angry that he had not responded to her letter? *What was she thinking?*

If the mood was tense in the gardens, then it was downright *poisonous* near the head table. The Pope was *still* glaring at the spot where Giacomo had subdued the merchant, and guests and servants alike were subtly changing course to keep out of his line of sight. Cardinal de' Medici's lips had thinned so much that they almost disappeared, and his pale face was sallow with rage. Il Divino had given up the pretense of eating and was staring up at the heavens.

"Tell them to get out," the Pope gritted to his cousin. "All of them."

"It really is not to be borne," the Cardinal said, turning a matching glare over the gardens.

If the Pope ended the banquet, their plan would evaporate. This whole evening was rapidly slipping out of alignment, they were done for, they were drowning—

"If you cut the night short," said Il Divino, "will that not be seen as weakness?"

As one, the heads of Giovanni and Giuliano de' Medici swiveled toward the artist. He shrugged. "Forgive me for presuming, but it seems to me that you'd be showing that the rabble have control over you. In your own home."

This was punctuated by a careless sip of wine. Giacomo bit back a smile. Who knew six weeks in the company of thieves could have such a wonderfully corrupting influence on a man?

Cardinal de' Medici frowned. "He has a point, Your Holiness."

Giacomo was sure the Pope would disagree. But after a tense few seconds, he leaned back in his chair. "Very well," he said. A lesser man would have crossed his arms.

"Excellent decision, Your Holiness," Michelangelo said.

"It would have been a shame to cancel the fireworks," Cardinal de' Medici allowed.

"Very true," Michelangelo agreed. "I hear it will be a devil of a show."

50

DOMINIC

Something's wrong.

Rosa had not stopped pacing since the doors of the chapel had shut behind them, her hands twisted in the blue velvet of her skirts as she made yet another lap around the small room. She had not said as much aloud, but it was written in every line of her body, every step of her slipper on the tiled mosaic floor.

Dominic watched her from his refuge against the fresco, leaning against the painted figures as though they might lend him strength. He had not dared to move since they had reached their détente, but he was keenly aware that the night was only growing shorter the longer they lingered here.

He steeled his nerves. "Rosa?"

Rosa's pace stumbled, just a fraction, and she glanced over at him for the first time in what felt like forever. Her eyes were wide, and in their dark depths, Dominic could see the decision click into place. "Giacomo's late," she said. "We'll have to go without him." And without another word, she bent double and lifted her skirts.

The galvanization that had filled him at her first words fled Dominic immediately, and he pressed himself back against the wall, looking anywhere but at Rosa and the bright white of her exposed chemise. "What—" *Was it hot in here?* "Why are you—what are you doing?"

She had the *temerity* to *roll her eyes at him*! "Make yourself useful," she said, pointing toward the chapel doors. "Keep watch."

Fighting down a brilliant blush, Dominic sidled past her, painfully careful not to get too close to her exposed undergarments. Despite his carefully averted gaze, he still caught the edge of Rosa gripping the hem of her chemise in her teeth and giving the garment a wrench. Stitches popped, and a moment later, something small and metallic jingled to the floor.

"Dominic? I'm decent," she said, singsong, and Dominic glared back at her over his shoulder. She had scooped up a few pieces of iron, and even though the chapel light was dim, Dominic could still tell that they were thin and strangely shaped . . .

"Lockpicks?" he asked.

Rosa spun them in her fingers. "It's one thing for the Medici Guards to search their guests' carriages for anything suspicious. But no noble family would survive the scandal of ordering *servicemen* to lay hands on the underthings of a *lady*."

"What lady?" Dominic deadpanned. It startled a delighted smile out of Rosa, miles from the carefully constructed one she had levied at him before. It sent the temperature of the chapel ratcheting up a few more degrees. He loosened the collar of his doublet.

Rosa, for her part, did not seem to notice. She moved to the door set into the chapel's far wall, the one that had always been locked as long as Dominic had worked here. *Click* went the long metal hook as she slid it into the keyhole, followed by another *click* as the pick joined it. Her tongue caught between her teeth as she worked them together, feeling for pins until—

The third and final *click* was much louder, and with a twist of the doorknob, the door was swinging open on well-oiled hinges.

"How did you do that?" Dominic asked, a little awed.

Rosa stood back with a satisfied nod. "My mother wasn't teaching me to paint," she said. "Come on."

A dark, narrow passage stretched out from the newly open door, wide flagstones disappearing into nothing. Dominic could spot the outline of an unlit torch a few steps in, and he started to trot forward, ready to grab it up to light their way—

Rosa's grip on his arm was iron. "Don't."

"Why?"

"We don't know if it's safe yet."

Dominic slowly took a step back. "How will we know if it's safe?"

"Giacomo will tell us if he disabled the trap."

"But Giacomo's not here."

Rosa nodded, slowly and dreadfully. She took a deep breath. "Are you a praying man?"

Dominic glanced back at the fresco he'd poured months into, in the chapel of the man he was about to rob. "Right now?" he said, a little hysterically. "Yes."

Rosa stepped forward.

Beneath her, the flagstones shifted. Dominic clenched his teeth, bracing for—detonation? Screams? A lightning bolt from the heavens?

Nothing happened. The flagstone held under her weight.

"*Christ*," Rosa hissed, gulping in air. There was sweat standing out on her forehead, but the smirk she flung back toward Dominic was confident. "Coming?"

With a roll of his eyes, he followed.

Knowing that, wherever Giacomo was, he'd been successful, did not do *much* to alleviate the tension as Rosa and Dominic made their way along. Every few paces, a flagstone would emit a threatening creak and Dominic would go through seven stages of panic in a split second. To counteract this, he retrieved the torch and lit it. The passage was much less intimidating now that they could see where to put their feet.

"You're not a mark," Rosa suddenly said, apropos of nothing.

Dominic paused. "Oh?" he finally said. "Was that . . . supposed to be an apology?"

"No," she shot back. They had rounded a bend in the corridor, and now a wider hallway stretched before them, long and straight, the walls pinching toward one another in the gloom. Dominic couldn't be certain, but he thought the floor beneath them was slanting slightly downward. He kept close on Rosa's heels as she plodded into the dark, holding his torch aloft like a righteous sword.

"I apologized for what I said," Dominic offered.

Rosa's eyebrow twitched. "No, you didn't."

Hadn't he? "I said I wanted to help you and that I understood you and—"

"Mhm."

Fine. But— "In my defense, you did lie to me."

"Yes." She gave him a shy smile. How was it warm down in this dungeon as well? "Sorry about that."

"Uh—" he stammered. "Thanks. And—sorry I called you all those things."

"They were true. Are true." She sighed, loud in the darkness. "I have to ask. Dominic. The writ from the Pope?"

"Yes?"

"How? The seal—the signature—they looked just like the real thing."

How? He'd had months to roam the Palazzo Medici, and during that time, so much of the family and their details had seeped into his bones. Putting all that knowledge—the size of the Papal seal, the color of the wax, the character of the handwriting—had been just like copying a Botticelli figure into Dominic's own work. It had been like replicating a color from the fresco. It had been *easy.*

"It's nothing special," Dominic said, because there was no time to explore any of that. "Just—what did you call it? A mishmash of other men's art?"

The vault loomed out of the darkness with the abruptness of a living thing, stopping her from pressing for more specifics. One moment they were staring into the void and the next, the void was in possession of hinges.

"You see that?" Rosa asked, pointing to the double-lock set into the door. Her other hand dug into her belt-pouch, producing a set of keys. "Here—"

She nearly fumbled the keys as a scream split the air, blood-curdling and ear-splitting, even muffled as it was by a thousand tons of limestone. It was unearthly, unnaturally loud, deafening enough to be heard all the way in the Palazzo vaults, the shriek of a dying phoenix—

It ended in a distant *pop*.

"Was that a rifle?" Dominic asked, heart racing. "What the hell *was* that?"

"Fireworks," Rosa said over another searing *pop*. "We're running out of time—"

At her direction, Dominic slid one of the keys into the lock on his side of the door as she did the same on her side. "Together on three," she told him, and their keys turned in unison, spurred on by the volley of multicolored explosions. Then, with a small nudge, the door was swinging inward and—

They stepped into the Magi vault.

Upon first glance, it was depressingly unimpressive. Dominic had expected to be greeted with overwhelming opulence and splendor— ornate tapestries, perhaps, or piles of jewels. Instead, stacks of rolled canvas and heavy boxes cluttered the floor, lending the air of a storage closet rather than a trove of treasures.

But Rosa only had eyes for the room's centerpiece: a massive slab of stone that lay flush to the floor, solid and unmovable.

Dominic gaped at her. "*That?*" he asked. She didn't credit him with a response, striding closer to get a better look at the edges of the stone, feeling the places where it met the floor. "You must be joking," he said. "It will take a miracle to lift that thing."

She turned to him, a triumphant flush rising in her cheeks. "Luckily," she said, "I never leave home without one."

51

KHALID

"By the time we're through tonight," Sarra whispered, "I think we'll have poisoned every guard in Florence."

They were standing inside the guardhouse where Khalid had only hours ago been forced to relinquish a wine cask. That cask stood now, tapped and open, in the corner. Wine dripped from the tap into a slop bucket, a sporadic percussion. The smell of it filled the small space.

The guards were there as well. But unlike the cask, they weren't standing.

"This won't hurt them," Agata had explained that morning, handing Khalid a vial of some colorless liquid. "Well. It won't hurt them beyond a nasty hangover."

"What is it?" Giacomo had asked, leaning close to study the concoction.

"Never you mind," Agata had snapped, tart as always. "But I wouldn't get too close. You mix that with wine and a drop will lay you out for a good hour."

"What about a cup?" asked Khalid. He had spent the last month and a half in the company of guards. He had never known them to stop at a drop.

Agata had just smiled her gummy smile. "If they rouse before the next sunset they'll be lucky."

The old witch was true to her word. Khalid had watched the checkpoint from several streets down once the delivery had been completed. The moment the influx of guests had ceased and the banquet had begun in earnest, there had been a loud series of thumps as the cask was tapped. Then fifteen minutes of boozy laughter. Then silence. And now, none of the drugged guards so much as twitched, even when Sarra and Khalid stripped the slighter one of his uniform. This went to Sarra, who changed her own doublet and hose out for those of Medici blue. Khalid, meanwhile, produced a horse blanket from his pack and tucked it, one-handed, over the unconscious men. Between the nighttime shadows, the thin moonlight, and the hypnotizing fireworks bursting overhead, it would take a keen-eyed passerby to notice something amiss.

By the time this was finished, Sarra was tucking her braids up underneath her cap. "Good?" she asked. He nodded. She was tall enough to pass muster, at least at a glance. "Good," she repeated, leaning out the guardhouse door to squint at the front gates. "Coast is clear," she whispered. "I don't see any patrols."

"None?" Khalid frowned. He had foregone the other guard's uniform out of fear that it would make him more recognizable to men inside the Palazzo. Instead, he wore the homespun brown shirt and loose hose of an ostler under a long, patched jerkin. The effect was of a shapeless burlap sack, but Giacomo had told Khalid to change his silhouette, and so . . .

"No sense in pulling back now." Sarra clapped him on the back. "Good luck."

For a moment, Khalid was back in Flora's tavern on the Genoa docks. *I want to offer you a way out*, Sarra had told him, confident in her borrowed clothes. She'd shown him the road to Florence, and he had taken it, unaware of what, exactly, was waiting at that road's end.

Who knew print shops were so flammable?

"I am sorry," Khalid whispered. Then, before she could respond, he was slipping out of the guardhouse and toward the Palazzo Medici.

It was an eerie journey. All other sound faded against the deafening cracks of the fireworks, which echoed against the Palazzo walls.

And still, Khalid saw no sign of the Medici Guards. By the time he rounded the rear of the building, the hair on his neck was standing on end. He crept to the rightmost window, half-certain that it would open to reveal Captain Romano, or an entire squadron of guardsmen, or the Pope himself.

But there was no movement through the glass. And the window, when he jiggled the frame, swung outward without a squeak. There his blessings stopped. It was no easy task to haul himself over the sill with one arm bound to his side. By the time his feet were planted on the richly lacquered floorboards inside, sweat was standing out on his forehead.

He was in a small study, well away from the banquet. The room was richly appointed but impersonal. From what Khalid understood, it was rarely used by anyone but guests of the Medici family who required somewhere to work. *And,* said a voice that sounded a bit like Giacomo, *thieves and criminals looking to make a killing.*

Khalid took a step toward the door and had to catch himself on the wall as the world swayed. His arm was a firebrand of pain, and every movement stoked the flames higher. He shoved through the wall of agony, getting his feet underneath him again.

Sarra had been right. There was no sense in balking at this point, not when faltering could throw off the whole operation.

Trust, he thought. *Trust them. Trust your team.*

And, wiping his forehead on his sleeve, he started for the wine cellar.

52

ROSA

" I 'm beginning to detect a pattern," Dominic said. He held the garment that had been the skirt of Rosa's chemise at arm's length, pinched between his fingertips.

"We work with what we have," Rosa retorted, working at the weave of her snood with two hands. "Are you going to stare at it all night?"

The apprentice blushed a brilliant red and gave the chemise a deft yank. With a series of small pops, the cloth parted—not in the jagged tear of something ripped haphazardly, but in a neat line. Dominic was left holding a length of evenly trimmed cloth, rough and sturdy canvas rather than the traditional linen or muslin. He laid it atop the stone slab with overzealous care, eyeing it as though it might at any moment transform into an adder and attack him.

"This is what you were sewing at Master Michelangelo's workshop?" he asked, giving the chemise another yank. Rosa listened to the sound of tearing with relief; the durable fabric had not been comfortable next to her skin.

"Maybe." One of her hair ornaments, a pretty, gilded piece of metal set deep in her curls, came free, and she tossed it onto the stone with the cloth strips. It landed with a heavy clatter for something so delicate. Immediately Rosa started loosening its twin, which was fixed to the other side of her head.

"This is one of those 'my mother didn't teach me to paint' things, isn't it," he said, fingers flying deftly now as he reduced the rest of her chemise to strips.

"Hand me one of those?" she asked. The second hair ornament slipped from her curls, worked through the netting of her snood until it lay heavy and solid in her palm.

Unlike the newfangled Henlein lock or the mechanized traps on the stairs, the vault slab was devilish due to its intractable simplicity. It had cost Sarra, Agata, and Rosa several late nights bending their heads over the problem.

Corrosives. Explosives. Lubricants. They had batted ideas and inventions back and forth for *days*, traced in diagrams and outlined in half-finished sentences using whatever dishes and scraps had been abandoned on the kitchen table.

"It's simply too big," Agata had finally griped, sinking back at her workbench. "We can't move it."

"*Mm*," Rosa had said, but she had been watching Sarra. The tinkerer's gaze had gone distant, staring into the depths of the lantern's flame.

"No," Sarra had said slowly. "Not if you move it right."

Simply. That had become their watchword. The stone block was simple. Getting it into position in the first place must have been simple. And removing it . . . that would be simple too.

The rough iron handles hammered into the sides of the stone were utilitarian, numerous enough so that a squad of guards might be able to shift the rock from its cradle.

Rosa did not have a squad of guards. What she *did* have was the makings of a rudimentary—but effective—pulley system.

Canvas straps woven together formed one long, sturdy rope. One of Rosa's hair ornaments, which might have looked like filigreed finery but was, in fact, iron heavy enough to give her a headache, was snapped to the rope's end and hurled over the exposed rafter, hooking the rope on the other side and circling the beam in a snug embrace. The second hair ornament joined its twin on the rafter a few meters away, dangling free. Then Rosa was working the canvas rope through one of the stone's handles and threading it up through the empty hair ornament, leaving it loose on the other side.

This hanging length of rope she passed to Dominic. "When I say pull," she said, "*pull.*"

He looked from the rope to the rafter to the stone slab and then to her. She braced herself for skepticism—to reassure him that she knew what she was doing or to be ordered to explain.

"Where should I stand?" he said.

She blinked. "Nearer the door."

He took a few steps in that direction. "Are you ready?"

"Are you?"

Dominic smiled. And then his arms were bunching, straining, *steeling* as he hauled, casting the rope over his shoulder like a dockworker. It went taut, a line of force running from Dominic to the rafter, to the slab, and then up again. For a moment, nothing happened. The stone stayed settled in its cradle, just as impossible as it promised on first glance.

Then something grated.

The stone was shifting, rising bit by bit into the air, dragged upward by Sarra's ingenuity and Dominic's effort. A gap appeared underneath—millimeters, then centimeters, then more—

From overhead came a groan, a wooden, organic sound, but Rosa was too fixated on the widening dark that yawned beneath the slab to hear it as anything more than background noise. "That's enough," she called, and Dominic paused, sweat beading on his forehead. Grabbing the rope dangling beneath his fists, Rosa tied it to the door's handle in a quick knot. "Good." Dominic let his hands fall away, shaking out his fingers and, after a single creak, the canvas rope held.

The gap beneath the slab was about two feet wide, big enough to slip through without a squeeze. This is what she did, holding her breath as she scrabbled under the looming lip of stone and dropping herself into the pit below. Any hopes of a controlled descent quickly evaporated—the walls were too slick for that, her feet slipping against mold. She landed on her hands and knees, wincing as her shin crunched against something knobby and unyielding.

Sitting back on her heels, Rosa took in her surroundings. The air was damp and stifled down here, choked with dirt and mildew and the weight of a hundred years without sun. The light from the vault above only illuminated a sliver of the ground . . .

A sliver of the ground that *glittered*.

"Rosa?" Dominic sounded winded. A moment later his face appeared in the gap, sweaty and worried. "Everything alright?"

Rosa loosened the ties of the woven sack that had broken her fall and peered inside.

Piles of buttery gold gleamed back at her. The sins of an entire city. An entire *country*. And deep within Rosa, underneath her breastbone, that spark of icy fire roared back to life.

"Mary, mother of Christ," breathed Dominic. Above him, the rafter gave another creak.

They had to move. "Here," Rosa said, heaving the gold to him. He caught it awkwardly and slung it behind him, turning back just in time to catch the next sack Rosa flung his way.

Come on, my girl. Lena Cellini's voice was in Rosa's ear, cold where it had always been so warm. She sped up at her mother's urging, heaving bags up to Dominic almost too fast for him to catch. It was easy now, despite the weight of each sack, her strength fueled by the frozen wildfire raging in her lungs. She could smell smoke. Beneath her eyelids, Prato was burning.

The next toss smacked against Dominic's chest, bowling him backward. "Rosa, slow down," he said, but she didn't have the breath to answer him. She was already reaching for the next sack, for that savage delight that filled her with every penny she robbed from the Medici. *Go*, her mother whispered, arrows jutting from her chest. *I'll be right behind you.*

Thunk. The sack landed on the flagstones beside Dominic as, overhead, the rafter gave another creak. Dominic glanced up, eyes worried. "Is that all?"

"Almost," Rosa panted. "Only a few more."

There was another creak, and the stone slab dipped, the gap shrinking just enough to be noticeable. "Rosa!" Dominic called.

She held a bag up to him. "Here."

Dominic reached for her hand instead. "Forget the money, grab onto me."

"The *money* is why we're here!"

"It's not why *I'm* here!"

"Dominic! Take the gold!" The slab dipped again, a little further this time.

"You'll be crushed!"

With a frustrated huff, Rosa heaved the gold up toward the empty space. But it was too heavy—it caught against the lip of the pit and toppled back down, opening as it fell, showering the pit floor with gold florins.

Time slowed. Rosa watched the coins spin to a halt, Dominic's shout echoing above her.

How can you say you've gotten your revenge if you haven't gutted the Medici to their core? hissed the voice of her mother. *How can you say you've avenged* me?

But that wasn't really Lena talking. It was that frozen shard of grief and anger. And why shouldn't she listen to it? It had gotten her this far, after all.

In the gap above, Dominic's face was a terrified mask. And, unbidden, another voice whispered through Rosa's thoughts.

If we shut each other out . . . we evaporate.

Yes, grief and anger had gotten her this far. But the Prato Rosa had known was dead. So was Mama. And she did not need to join them.

Rosa grabbed Dominic's hands.

And then she was rising, finding footholds in the city walls—no, no, it was the sides of the pit—helping Dominic along as the rafter above groaned and splintered and *split*—

They sprawled onto the vault floor just as one of Rosa's hair ornaments *pinged* free and sent the stone slab slamming back into its cradle. The almighty boom it made as it landed flooded the small vault, driving Dominic and Rosa's hands over their ears until the echoes finally faded into nothing.

She had landed on her belly, her skirts tangling about her legs. She kicked her feet free, twisting to find that Dominic had tumbled onto his back, on a pile of coins that spilled out beneath him like a halo. He looked up at her with wide eyes.

"Ow," he said.

The giggles came out of nowhere, frothing up from her stomach. She dropped her forehead into her hands, her shoulders heaving, energy boiling away like so much steam. A moment later, Dominic's laughter joined hers, just as loud and unhinged.

They were still wiping away tears when the vault door opened. Dominic choked, laughter lodging in his throat, struggling to sit up while the coins beneath him shifted and gave way. Rosa shoved herself to her knees a beat behind, fighting down giggles and forcing herself to look up at Khalid and the wine casks that filled the doorway.

Khalid's brow furrowed. "What did I miss?"

53

KHALID

The stable yard breathed with life, packed as it was with coaches and carriages. The drivers had left just enough space between them to stop the horses from panicking. Even so, there was barely enough room for a man to slip through without his shoulders scraping against walls of finely lacquered wood.

Khalid did his best, but his progress was all the more complicated by the handcart dragging behind him, and the two casks that were lashed to it. He threaded through the space at an angle, leery of startling the horses or thumping against any of the carriages.

Reaching the end of the line, Khalid peered into the open yard beyond. A small fire had been kindled in a weathered old barrel outside the stables. Drivers and stable hands were gathered around it, passing bottles and playing cards, voices raised in congenial tipsiness. None of them were paying much mind to their charges, but if Khalid emerged, he would surely be spotted.

There was still not one single guardsman in sight. Even the Pope's gilded, glorious carriage had been unguarded. This might have been some comfort, except—

"Where is Giacomo?" he had asked Rosa in the Magi Chapel. They had made quick work of the Medici coin, loading it by the sackful into the barrels.

Rosa had shaken her head. "There's been no sign of him. Nothing."

"I will look for him," Khalid had told Rosa, already moving toward the door. "I can be back in just a moment—"

But she'd caught his sleeve, a gentle tug that stopped him cold. "Khalid," she had murmured. It had not been unkind. "We both know there's too much riding on this right now." She'd given his sleeve another tug, supportive rather than quelling. "You trust him, don't you? Trust he can take care of himself."

He had nodded, eventually, and trundled the cart out of the chapel and toward the stables. He would see Giacomo again, at the end of this. For now, Khalid had a job to do.

There was a shout from the barrel fire, followed by a chorus of groans and laughter. The drivers were standing. Some were making rude gestures at the retreating back of a Medici footman. Others were taking final swigs from their flasks before stowing them away. Then, a swarm dispersing, they began their staggered ways toward the carriages.

Khalid slunk back, his mind whirring. It was early for the banquet to be breaking up, but there was no sense in worrying over that. He needed to get to cover, and quickly. If he was caught out in the open, there would be no saving their plan.

The carriage buried furthest in the stable yard was a tall coach, squeezed in on both sides. It would be enough to hide him from the eyes of the ostlers and the drivers . . . if he could make it there in time.

He would have to.

And with a wrench that set his injured arm screaming, Khalid wheeled the cart around—and bolted.

54

DOMINIC

Dominic frowned at the single remaining cask as the Magi Chapel doors shut behind Khalid. "I could have carried this one."

"This money isn't going with Khalid," Rosa said. "It's for something else."

"I don't—" Dominic stopped himself. Rosa seemed to take particular delight in keeping him in the dark, and Dominic would not rob her of her fun—not if it was the only alternative to the rage that had nearly drowned her in the vault. He could still see flickers of that cold anger in her face, though they were softer now. He would do what he could not to rekindle them. "Very well," he said. "Then—are *we* getting the cask out of here?"

"Oh yes."

He waited for her to elaborate, but when no further explanation was forthcoming, he rolled his eyes. If she would not tell him how to help, then he would figure it out himself. With quick fingers, he began to pull at the fastenings of his jerkin.

He took some savage pleasure in watching her nearly choke on her own tongue. "What are you *doing*?"

"Please, signorina. As though I haven't become intimately acquainted with your underthings this evening—"

"Stop, stop, stop—" She grabbed for his hands.

"Everyone on the other side of that door thinks we disappeared into this chapel for a very specific reason. 'Unimpressive,' wasn't it? Don't think I've forgotten that." He didn't pull away when she wrapped her fingers around his, stilling his movements. "Shouldn't we make it look like they're right?"

"That's . . . actually clever," she said.

"Am I thinking like a grifter?"

"Like a forger. But I need you to listen to me now." She squeezed his fingers. "I don't know what I would have done if you hadn't been here tonight. But if you go now, back to the banquet—you'll be able to keep hold of your livelihood. Your life." Her dark eyes flicked between his. "Dominic," she whispered. "It's not too late for you. Go back."

"Back to my life," he echoed. She nodded. "My life as an artist's mediocre apprentice? That life?"

True smiles could only be startled out of Rosa, but he was getting the hang of it. The corners of her mouth tugged upward before she could conquer her expression. "Well—"

"I'm turning down the Medici. I made my choice. And not to offend you, Rosa, but I saw you back in that vault. If this gets dangerous—*more* dangerous—then you might need someone there to pull you out." He shrugged, one shoulder sloping up and then back down. "You don't have to do this alone."

Her gaze grew more intent as she studied his face. Whatever she was seeking, she must have found. "Very well," she said, finally letting his hands drop. "If you want to throw your life away, I can't stop you. But do me a favor? Stop undressing."

"If you insist," he said. "What's the plan?"

Rosa pulled both chapel doors open at once.

A Medici Guard stumbled to a halt just outside. He stared from Rosa and Dominic to the cask to the open passage door and back to Rosa and Dominic, slack-jawed.

"Shit" was all Dominic had time to mutter before the guard opened his mouth, and his cry echoed throughout the courtyard, bouncing from windows and columns and tiled floors.

"Thief!" the Palazzo bellowed. "Thief!"

55

ROSA

Rosa hit the grass hard enough to send her swaying on her knees, fighting for balance against the grips of the guards. Dominic followed, wincing at the impact, and the wine cask crashed down half a moment later, rattling on the lawn beside them.

The Pope stared down at them. He was as still as one of his treasured statues, and as pale as one, too. Both of his hands gripped the arms of his magnificent carved chair. He had barely moved since Rosa and Dominic had been brought in, marched along the rows of tables at sword-point, and now that Rosa had enjoyed ample time to study the apoplectic rictus of his expression, she concluded that it was a subject fit for Michelangelo himself.

Speaking of whom, Il Divino was watching the proceedings with the wretched expression of a man experiencing severe gastric distress or apoplexy or perhaps both at the same time.

"They were discovered in the Magi Chapel, Your Holiness," Captain Romano explained, before lowering his voice so that only those close by might hear. "The vault door was open. The vault . . . appears to be empty."

"Empty," His Holiness said. At his side, Cardinal de' Medici was simmering. "The cask?" Romano said nothing. "Open it."

The captain glanced about with apprehension, demonstrating a coolness of head that quite impressed Rosa. "Your Holiness," he murmured. "If I may be bold, might I suggest doing this away from . . . prying eyes?"

Truly, Rosa thought that *prying eyes* was underselling the situation.

Because while, yes, the crowd in the garden had thinned a bit since Rosa had first made her departure, there were still a number of occupied seats at the banquet tables—seats that were unlikely to empty further, given this irresistible entertainment.

The Pope seemed to realize this as well, an ember sparking within him enough to draw his attention to the gardens at large. "Perhaps," he acquiesced. Rosa's stomach flipped over. Whatever was to happen to her and Dominic here in the middle of this crowd would surely be one thousand times worse in the evil privacy of the Medici dungeons.

"We will do no such thing."

Cardinal de' Medici was on his feet, both fists planted on the table. He glared down at Romano, at Rosa and Dominic, and at the cask, eyes burning with fury and color high in his sallow cheeks. "We are not the ones trespassing on the property of our hosts. We are not the ones *stealing*. What have the Medici done to be ashamed of?"

This last was directed at the gawking onlookers, the men and women who had gathered to be wined and dined and entertained by the Medici family.

"Your Eminence—" Romano began, but the Cardinal was past listening to his inferiors.

"I had been warned of the presence of seditionists here this evening," he proclaimed. "I had been informed they were seeking *funding* for their treasonous acts. But I did not believe that they would go so far in their desperation as to take from the Church."

Who had been spinning such stories to the Medici? But Rosa's question was answered almost as soon as it was asked, as a flicker of movement behind the Pope drew her eye. A guard, his uniform a bit too big, was fidgeting in the shadows of an oversized topiary. *Giacomo.* He might not have made it to the Magi Chapel, but he had evidently been busy enough here in the gardens.

But Cardinal de' Medici did not notice Rosa's momentary distraction. He was seeing nothing but red. *"Open. The cask,"* he ordered, leaning forward with a venomous glare.

This was enough to smother the spark of common sense smoldering inside of the Pope, and at his nod, Captain Romano sent the cask toppling onto the grass.

The top popped off, unleashing a stunning river of gold.

The gardens went silent.

"What," the Pope said, "do you have to say for yourself?"

His question was directed at Dominic rather than Rosa, to her small chagrin. "Your Holiness," Dominic stammered, "this is all a misunderstanding. We were—we were in the chapel because—Signorina de' Lombardi asked to see the fresco, and so—"

"I should have known your motives were sinful," spat the Pope. "A mediocre artist, obsessed with that *awful* painting—you couldn't be anything but a grifter. And now it turns out you were—you were—"

"Robbing Florence of its place in Heaven," supplied Cardinal de' Medici.

"What have you done with my money?" the Pope hissed, rounding the table.

"Your Holiness!"

There was a commotion growing near the kitchen entrance, a roiling turmoil of servants and guardsmen that finally parted to expel a trio of guards—

As well as Khalid al-Sarraj.

He limped ahead of his captors, his arm clutched to his side and his face gray with pain. One guard with a particularly smug face shoved Khalid to his knees only a few paces from Rosa, and she could see Khalid's gaze fuzz and go out of focus as he fought the urge to pass out. Beside the topiary behind the high table, Giacomo's silhouette

stiffened and straightened, anxiety radiating off every square centimeter at the sight of Khalid's distress.

"Rosa . . . ," Dominic muttered, but Rosa just grabbed his hand
and squeezed it. *Quiet now.*

"Bin-Halil?" Romano rumbled. "Vieri? What is this?"

"We discovered him near the stables," Vieri said. "Skulking around
with these—" There was a *thunk* as the guards tilted a handcart on its
side, offloading a few wooden casks identical to the one spilling liquid sunshine next to Rosa.

"Captain." Cardinal de' Medici was watching Romano, sharp and
incisive, though it wouldn't have taken a great intellect to read the
dread on the captain's face. "Do you know this man?"

Now steady on the ground, Khalid's stare was level and calm and
fixed on nothing in particular. He might have been on an afternoon
stroll, for all the concern that showed on his face.

"He is Yazid bin-Halil," Romano said, slowly, as though he very
much did not wish to. "A member of the Medici Guard."

"If I may, Captain," Vieri cut in, "the man you call bin-Halil is actually a *criminal* named Khalid al-Sarraj—an enforcer employed by the
Genoan gangster Giuseppe Traverio."

For a split second, Khalid's gaze flicked to meet Rosa's, just long
enough for her to twitch her eyebrow at him. But she was not the only
person reacting to Vieri's revelation here in these gardens. Romano's
forehead creased as he squinted at Vieri. "How do you know that?"

"Your Holiness," Michelangelo cut in, "my niece is just a naive girl—"

"Your niece has *deluded you.* She is a con woman." The Pope turned
back to Rosa. "Answer truthfully," he commanded. "Why were you
working with these two men?"

Two men. So he did not suspect the collusion of his family's most
lauded artist. A small weight lifted from Rosa's shoulders even as she

summoned tears to her eyes, blinking up at the Pope through a weepy haze. "I'm sorry, Your Holiness, but you're mistaken—"

"I am *never* mistaken," the Pope cut her off, his voice rising. He paced toward the cluster of kneeling prisoners. "I expected something like this. The people of this city are so predictable. So entitled. You thought you could walk into the greatest house in Florence and just *take my money*?"

The murmurs among the guests had started up again and amplified with that declaration. *My money*. Twice now, he had said it. This was not the sentiment of a godly man—it was that of a banker.

"Well, you have overreached yourself," His Holiness continued, deaf to the growing dissent. "You know now that it is impossible to cross the Medici family and get away with it." He was still directing most of his vitriol at Dominic, whose grip on Rosa's hand was growing bone-crushing.

"And *you*." The Pope wheeled on Rosa, who shrank into Dominic's side, still playing the timid country girl. "After everything your uncle has done for you—this is how you repay him?"

"How *could* you?" Michelangelo's voice rasped, wrought with heartache and betrayal. It was a performance for the ages, and if there had been any lingering Medici suspicions of his involvement, they would surely be dismissed by the devastation in his face.

And with his safety secured, it was time for Rosa's own performance to take a turn. Her tears evaporated in an instant, her fearful mien igniting like a candle's flame. Gone was any trace of flinching terror. "You were too *blind*, Uncle," she snapped, so sharply that Michelangelo flinched back from the words. "You must have seen the way this family hoards wealth. They are a den of greedy dragons. This gold they've *extorted* from Florence is not to *save souls*. It's to enforce their authority, *by any means*—"

"Silence!" the Pope roared. The pallor in his cheeks had long been suffused with apoplectic scarlet. He held out his hand to Vieri. "Your sword."

A rumble of unease swept through the remaining guests. But this was not enough to stop His Holiness in his tracks. "Give me your damned sword, Guardsman!" The command jolted Vieri, who handed it over. "You have broken into my house," the Pope declaimed, pacing toward the wine casks—

Toward *Khalid*.

Rosa tensed. She'd wanted to push the Medici, but had she pushed them too far? She could see some of that stoic tranquility draining out of Khalid's eyes. There was no sign of Giacomo—the shadow of the topiary was empty. She didn't know where he'd gone or whether he was even still watching.

And still, the Pope continued his advance. "You have stolen money from the Lord God Almighty. You have committed treason of the highest order." His grip was remarkably sure on the hilt. "And you will be punished."

The sword was—it was lifting—swinging up, over Khalid's head and Rosa was bracing, readying to do the unthinkable, to *rush the Pope*, anything to save Khalid—but she was too late, and the blade was coming down, falling in a savage blow on—

The *wine cask*.

Khalid flinched aside as Vieri's sword jammed into the top of the barrel, splintering the sturdy wood in half. Again, the Pope raised the blade and *again* he brought it down, chopping at the lid as a woodsman chops firewood. "*No one*," he hissed, "*steals from the Medici.*"

The cask collapsed in on itself, shuddering to pieces under the onslaught, the decimated lid rolling from the body of the barrel like a decapitated head. The Pope kicked the wooden staves apart with the toe of his brocaded slipper, the sword dangling freely from his hand.

Then, all at once, the energy left him. He froze on the spot, death-still. And as Rosa, leaning against Dominic to calm her racing heart, got a better look, she could see why.

There was nothing glimmering amidst the shards and splinters. Not one gold florin winked up at them.

The cask was completely empty.

56

SARRA

"What the devil is taking so long?" The voice inside the carriage was petulant, and Sarra didn't bother responding. The uniform she wore fit her well enough, but no disguise could lower her voice. She settled for sharing an eye roll with the driver, and thumping the side of the carriage twice, the universal sign for *all clear*. The driver tipped his cap, and a moment later, the carriage and its irritable occupants were trundling down the street.

There were no carriages rolling up to take its place—the flow of guests departing the banquet had slowed, at least for the moment—and Sarra allowed herself a quick breath of relief before turning back to the *real* task at hand. With a pained grimace, she grabbed the heavy woven sack off the guardhouse floor and hauled it across to the checkpoint's opposite door.

Khalid's wagon was right where she had left it, parked in the Palazzo's inbound lane, the mule occupied with an overstuffed feed bag. He didn't so much as flick an ear as Sarra eased her burden aboard, doing her best to muffle the promising *clink* of metal on metal within. She nestled the sack among dozens of its fellows and, working quickly, lashed the pile to the wagon bed. To her critical eye, they looked innocuous enough. *They could be full of potatoes*, she thought, a little hysterical. *Or maybe turnips.*

They clinked again as she jumped back down. She did her best to ignore it. *Just keep it together*, she told herself. *We're close. We're so close, and then we'll be done with this job, and with Florence, and with the whole Medici family . . .*

But if they were close, then shouldn't there be another carriage rolling out toward the guardhouse now? And if they were close, then shouldn't Sarra have seen signs of guardsmen patrolling the Palazzo in the hour she'd been posted here?

Gritting her teeth against dread, Sarra stalked around the wagon to the driver's bench. The mule blinked at her as she grabbed for the reins, lips blurring in an aggravated huff.

Sarra blinked back. There was something different here, something *off*, something she was missing . . .

Someone had removed the feed bag.

"Thank you for doing the hard part."

Sarra whirled just as two figures stepped into the light. The one on the left was wiry and small and covered in tattoos, familiar in a way Sarra couldn't quite place.

The one on the right she had no trouble placing at all. "Traverio," she breathed. Her palms were sweating.

He bobbed an ironic bow. "Signorina Tinkerer."

"What are you doing?"

"Taking what's owed to me."

Sarra's eyes narrowed. "I don't owe you anything."

"Khalid feels differently," he said, and suddenly there was a hand on her back. The tattooed henchman had flanked her while she'd been watching Traverio's approach.

He had fewer teeth than even Agata, and smelled a little like woodsmoke. And when he smiled, she remembered where she had seen him. He had been in the street outside the print shop. Watching it. Watching her. Right before everything burned.

"You," she said.

His smile widened. "Oops."

"Tell the Cellini girl thanks from us," Traverio said.

Then—a sharp pain across the side of Sarra's head.

Then—nothing at all.

57

GIACOMO

The Pope stared. So did Cardinal de' Medici. Actually, once Giacomo had managed to tear his gaze away from Khalid (who was, mercifully, *not* bleeding out on the flagstones), he could pick out the individual dumbstruck expressions on Michelangelo, the entire host of Palazzo Guards, and every single guest. Even Fontana, the young artist, stared, his jaw hanging slack and wide. "Empty?" he said, louder than he had doubtless intended.

Giacomo shrank further back into the shadows behind one of the Medici's immaculate marble statues, and reached for his belt-pouch.

His Holiness pointed to the other cask, his finger shaking with fury. "That one. Get it open."

The choked rage had Captain Romano springing into action. Unsheathing his own sword, he pried open the lid of the cask and looked inside.

He didn't need to speak a word. His ashen face said enough.

The Pope wheeled on Rosa and Fontana, thunder rumbling in his voice. "Where is it?"

Rosa raised both hands, palms up. Empty. "Gone."

"Where. Is the money." He was stalking toward them now, Vieri's sword dangling from his hand, and his glare was pinned on Fontana. This was all *rather* escalated, and Giacomo's pulse, which had not flagged since he'd watched Khalid face down a flailing blade two seconds ago, ratcheted up another notch.

"I honestly don't know," said Fontana.

The slap was unexpected. It connected hard enough to echo off the walls, and sent the apprentice's head snapping sideways, blood trickling from a thin cut high on his cheek. It appeared that His Holiness's rings were useful for more than just decoration, and Rosa's yelp sounded just as real as Fontana's shocked gasp.

But that was not the only effect of the blow. An affronted susurrus was rippling through the crowd. At his table, Giacomo's father watched the scene with obvious interest and, Giacomo was intrigued to note, Giulietta seemed to have extricated her arm from her husband's grasp.

But none of this was of any import to the Pope. "*Where is my gold?*" he hissed right into Fontana's face, and for a moment, Giacomo was sure that the two of them would be run through right there and left to die in the middle of the beautiful, manicured Medici gardens.

He'd had about enough of this. As a player, Giacomo knew when it was time to close the curtain, and he could feel it in his gut that the moment for such a finale was at hand. He scrabbled in his belt-pouch, fingers closing around something cool and smooth, ready for the final bows—if only he could get some confirmation from Rosa . . .

"Your Holiness," Captain Romano said, ever the voice of reason. "I assure you, we have taken precautions against situations like this. Our guards have been searching every carriage and cart in and out of the Palazzo. The gold cannot have gone far."

"Are you so certain?" Rosa asked. The savage spark in her eye blazed higher in the face of the Medici's fury. "When was the last time you sent someone to check on those guards?"

Cardinal de' Medici's gaze had gone inward. "The carriages," he breathed. "They put the gold on the carriages. Isn't that right?"

Rosa met his eyes, unflinching.

The Cardinal looked as though he would quite like to swear. "Captain!" he barked. "Send men to the checkpoint!" As Romano hastened to comply, Giacomo tucked himself even further into the shadows. He had been roped into service too many times this evening to allow it to happen again.

"I will kill you," the Pope remarked to Rosa, almost conversational. "You will not leave this place alive."

Rosa *tsked*. "Not a very holy sentiment, *Signore de' Medici*," she said, matching his casual tone. "And I don't believe I'm the only person who thinks that."

For the first time, the Pope looked around, shaken out of his fog of fury. His perusal of the gardens took in the assembled nobles and merchants—and the nervous glances and disapproving mutters spreading in a web between them. And in his momentary distraction, Rosa's gaze shot sideways, meeting Giacomo's with pinpoint precision, even hidden as he was.

The sight of his penitents' shaken faith only heightened the Pope's rage, and he whirled back to Captain Romano and the Cardinal, thrusting a finger toward the three kneeling captives.

"I want their heads," he barked at Romano.

"Your Holiness," Romano protested, eyeing the crowd with a healthy mistrust.

But Cardinal de' Medici was already nodding grimly. "You'll have them."

Which was when Rosa's chin dipped in a near-imperceptible nod. *Time to draw the curtain.* And Giacomo san Giacomo had never been content to deliver a finale without a flourish.

One smooth step took him out onto the grass, just outside the ring of torchlight. And then his arm was flinging out, unleashing something small and glittering that arced away from his fingers. He saw Rosa launch herself sideways into Fontana, sending them both sprawling—saw Khalid dive headfirst onto the lawn—

The twin glass vials—an Agata Special—tinkled as they made contact with the smooth white flank of one of the gorgeous marble statues. Giacomo flung his arms over his head and covered his ears and then—

58

KHALID

Khalid was flat on his back when he opened his eyes. There was damp grass soaking the back of his shirt. His ears were ringing. He opened his mouth to ask what was going on and choked on a lungful of acrid smoke.

Giacomo's worried face swam into view above him. He was shaking Khalid's shoulder—his *bad* shoulder. Khalid groaned, and Giacomo scrambled backward, his lips moving around an apology. He wasn't whispering, Khalid realized. The ringing in his ears was just too loud for him to hear anything else.

Khalid pushed himself to his knees, giving Giacomo a shaky wave. *I'm alright.*

The same could not be said for the gardens. Guards and statuary lay scattered about the lawn like discarded puppets. From what he could tell, through all the smoke and debris, people were beginning to moan and twitch as they regained their senses. No one *appeared* to be dead, but Khalid was not about to go around checking pulses.

Michelangelo was blinking dazedly at the head table. He looked rattled, but no worse for wear, and gave Khalid a brief nod as their eyes met. Rosa and Fontana were already back on their feet. They were having a muttered conversation over, of all things, the stirring body of the Pope. With one last glance down at His Holiness, Rosa allowed the apprentice to pull her toward the kitchen doors.

"Khalid? Khalid!"

The ringing was fading. Khalid could make out the edges of

Giacomo's voice. He smiled woozily into the player's face. "You are alright."

"I'm always alright. Are *you* alright?"

A ridiculous question, Khalid thought, even though his arm hurt quite a lot. He grabbed the player's hand, allowing himself to be hauled upright. "We must get clear," he said. "We do not have much time."

This was when Khalid noticed that Vieri was sprawled on the ground at his feet.

The guardsman must have taken a chunk of statuary to the forehead. There was a bruise the size of an orange blossoming over one eye. He moaned as Khalid moved closer. When Khalid's shadow fell across his face, Vieri's eyes blinked open. As soon as he realized what he was looking at, fear swamped his face.

His sword was unclaimed, a meter from Vieri's hand. The Pope must have lost his grip on it during the blast. Khalid picked it up.

It would be easy to bring it down on Vieri. To kill him the way that he had tried to kill Khalid. To strike like Traverio would order him to. He glanced back to Giacomo and found the other man watching him, level and calm. He would not flinch from Khalid if he did this. Giacomo would understand.

But staring down at Vieri's sallow, fearful face, something stayed Khalid's hand. Not mercy. The furthest thing from mercy. Khalid's hand was stayed by . . . a better idea.

He allowed his smile to turn wolfish. *Vice and voice.*

"Marino thanks you," he said, and that was it.

A breeze washed his face, light and teasing, as he followed Rosa and Fontana out of the courtyard. Maybe it was the echo of the blast or the promise of triumph, but Khalid could have sworn he heard the wind whisper.

Home.

59

GIACOMO

The chaos in the Palazzo, when it had receded, had done so quickly. In one moment, the gardens had been a blast zone of dazed and disoriented bodies, and in the next, the Medici scions were being rushed to safety while Captain Romano barked furious orders.

Giacomo had given Vieri five minutes until he got himself together enough to approach the captain. He had shown up inside of four, anger tremoring behind his helpful veneer. "They're headed to Il Rifugio," he'd said. "It's a smuggler's inlet just outside the city walls. I heard bin-Halil mention it to the girl."

Romano's frown had deepened. "You *heard* this?" he'd asked, incredulous, which had been fair because the tinny ringing had only just begun to fade from Giacomo's ears and Vieri had been standing even closer to the blast.

But with Medici outrage burning at his back, Romano'd had no choice but to follow the lead he'd been given. The horses had been readied, all guards not nursing shrapnel injuries had mounted up, the company had made to ride out—

And had stalled in the stable yard.

The reason was embarrassingly mundane. The explosion had sent both horses and drivers bolting, which meant that many of the guests' carriages had been stranded directly in the guards' path.

"Shift these!" Romano ordered, and Giacomo rushed to comply, scrambling off his horse and jogging to the nearest carriage. It was no effort to move, not with six other men pushing together, and the guards were able to clear the drive in a manner of minutes.

The wheels had only just stopped moving when an unfortunately familiar voice bellowed from the Palazzo entry. "Captain Romano!"

Romano did not seem unfamiliar with it either. His eyes fluttered briefly shut in defeated resignation before wheeling his mount to face Signore Petrucci. Giacomo's father was storming out into the stable yard at full steam, heedless of the swarm of armed guards.

"Stand aside, signore," the captain intoned. "I have no time for this tonight."

"You have no time for much of anything," Petrucci retorted. "And neither do the Medici! Too wound up in their enemies to spare a moment for those who would be their friends."

"Guardsmen, mount up," Romano ordered, ignoring Petrucci. Giacomo stepped back from the carriage, his hands skimming the lacquered wood—

And pinning there, gripped in place.

He looked up. The carriage window, which he had thought to be empty and dark, was now filled with Giulietta Petrucci.

She held his hand, so tight that her knuckles were white. It hurt, but he couldn't bring himself to care, not when she was near enough that he could make out the lines around her soft brown eyes, the silver in her chestnut hair.

Somewhere, Giacomo's father was still ranting. "Three times I have come to the palazzo for an audience and three times I have been ignored, slighted, and now *assaulted*—"

It was background noise. The only thing that mattered was his mother's face and the fact that she knew him, even in this ill-fitting uniform and low light.

"Giacomo," she whispered. The sound of her voice wrapped about him like an embrace.

There were tears on her cheeks. Suddenly Giacomo was seeing her as he had that final night. There had been tears on her cheeks then, too, as she'd clutched her shawl about herself and asked *What are you doing?* despite the fact that, in her heart, she'd *known*—

His heart was racing.

"*Mama*," he whispered, a plea. *Don't make me lie. Don't make me pretend. Not to you. Not for you.*

She nodded, a smile touching the corners of her lips. Releasing the death grip she had on his hand, she reached out to run her fingers lightly along his cheek.

"Be clever," she said. Not *be good* or *be safe* or a querulous, terrified question. A single tear splashed onto the wood of the carriage window, but no more than that, and it did not wash away her smile. Giacomo gave her fingers a squeeze of acknowledgment and stepped back, allowing her hand to drop away.

There were no goodbyes. Petrucci was stalking toward the carriage, leaving a clench-jawed Captain Romano in his wake, and Giacomo swept out of his path with a deferential bow. Perhaps if his father had been more observant, he would have noticed his second son standing within arm's reach, but he had never made it a habit to notice Giacomo before and he was not about to start now. A moment later, Giacomo was mounted up and trotting at the rear of the Medici contingent, forcing their way through the Florence streets.

He pulled his whirling thoughts together with a wrench of effort. He would process later—he would *have* to, because he knew that the second he began picking through those emotions, he would have a complete and total nervous breakdown and for *now* he really needed to focus on keeping up with the other guards and not losing his seat.

"This way!" shouted Vieri from the head of the company, pointing down the wide street that led to the eastern city gate, and the thunder of hooves on cobbles grew louder as the guards urged their horses on. Shopkeepers, vendors, and revelers all surged out of the way with shouted curses and insults, their discarded belongings mulched beneath the relentless stampede.

The Torre della Zecca was lined, as ever, with red-uniformed City Guards, and Giacomo could see Captain Romano bracing himself for a confrontation as the company thundered up. But strangely enough, they were waved past with barely a scowl, the City Guardsmen lining the gate in neat formation as horse after horse passed beneath the looming tower. Giacomo, the last of the Medici Guards, could feel their eyes burning into his back as he urged his mount faster into the night.

It was only a short ride to Il Rifugio, and Giacomo heard their quarry before he saw it, a waterlogged cry of distress echoing across the river. "Captain!" he called. Romano nodded, signaling the rest of the troop, and the guards slowed to a trot as they rounded a bend in the path, a wide stretch of empty dirt road unspooling before them.

From the left came the sound of the Arno's rushing waters, perfectly ordinary this close to Florence. But the river was blocked from view by a thick stand of greenery, which snarled and tangled around itself for two dozen solid meters. The average traveler might not take this for anything more than another bit of road. Florence's less reputable element, on the other hand, might see it as a prime opportunity for a bit of criminal activity.

Unfortunately for the less reputable element, the tree cover did not do much if, say, your boat was simultaneously sinking and falling into several pieces, and you yourself were not a strong swimmer. At least, this is what the two men struggling in the current were discovering.

"Halt!" Romano ordered as the river swept them past the tree line. "Get them out!"

A few of the guards dismounted to comply, wading out into the

Arno to grab the two men and drag them to the riverbank. There they lay, beached, gasping, and thoroughly bedraggled.

One was scrawny, with corded muscles standing out in lean ropes beneath his sun-leathered skin. He was occupied with vomiting river water and so Giacomo instead looked at the other man, a portly fellow in finer clothes, who was already pushing himself to his knees.

Traverio. Giacomo would know him out of a thousand, the way that anyone who passed through Genoa might. But more than that, he would know the man who had kept so tight a grasp on Khalid that he had nearly driven the life out of him. In all Giacomo's years of crossing paths with Khalid, his orbit growing tighter and tighter, he had never actually seen Traverio, because to do so would have been to ask for trouble. Now that he had the opportunity, he decided that he very much did not like the man's face.

"Get up," Romano barked.

"There's no need for that, Captain," Traverio told him, smooth despite the indignity of his appearance. "We're just a couple of unlucky fishermen who caught a bad current."

"I have never seen a fisherman who dresses so well," Giacomo muttered, loud enough for Romano to overhear, and watched the captain's mouth thin in an unhappy line.

"Search them," he ordered, and the guards jumped to comply. Traverio bore this indignity with a politician's smile, as a few more Medici Guardsmen dismounted, either to help or to get a better view of the proceedings. Giacomo did the same. He was near the back of the company, a wall of men and horses between him and the riverbank, and if Giacomo knew anything about humanity in general and guardsmen in particular, then he knew that nobody would be prying their focus away from the strange fake fisherman and his retching friend until they stopped being so perversely entertaining.

It was when the scrawny smuggler was hauled upright that things grew *really* interesting. The moment the moonlight hit his face, Vieri took *complete* leave of his senses, transforming into a man-shaped mass of choking rage. What was even *more* interesting was the fact that the smuggler had caught sight of Vieri as well and had undergone a similar—if not identical—transformation.

"You *bastard*—" shouted the smuggler at the same time Vieri yelled "You piece of *shit*—" and then Vieri was launching himself off his horse toward the smuggler, quite prepared to strangle the man to death.

"Guardsman!" Romano reprimanded, but the situation had never been in his hands to begin with and now it was spiraling completely out of control. The entire company watched as Vieri collided with the smuggler and the two men toppled into the river shallows, exchanging blows and curses in equal measure. "Double-crossing son of a bitch" was a phrase used liberally by the both of them, interspersed with "Brought them here—" from the smuggler and "Working with al-Sarraj the *whole time*—" from Vieri.

Giacomo took that as his cue. The captain was shouting, Traverio was being shoved into manacles, and a few Medici Guardsmen were doing their best to separate the brawling pair and getting nothing but elbows to the face for their troubles. It was chaos and it was beautiful and it was the perfect time for Giacomo to slip into the tall fields on the far side of the road.

Behind him, guardsmen shucked their boots and waded into the river, combing the muddy riverbed in search of the missing coins. The splashing and shouting faded with distance, but Giacomo stayed just within earshot until he heard what he'd been waiting all night to hear.

"What the hell is *this*? Printing blocks?" It was the bellow of a Medici captain at the absolute end of his rope. "Where are the coins? Where the *hell* is the money?!"

60

THE DAVID

For the second time in as many months, Cat followed the carriage.

She was doing a pretty good job of it, she thought. She'd been on its tail ever since it had turned out of the Palazzo Medici, and nobody was paying her any mind. Probably she was getting better at being sneaky. After what had happened, with Gio and with the bills, they'd both gotten a lot sneakier. Also, she wasn't carrying a ball of shit this time, which helped.

The carriage was moving faster than it had before, with no bubble of Medici Guards around to protect it. This was because they'd gotten the sack. At least, that's what Gio had said early that morning, when they'd watched all those men walk away from the Palazzo with sad faces and no more uniforms. Cat believed Gio about this because she could hear the shouting from inside the building. "That's the Pope," Gio had told her, his eyes wide, as the shouter yelled a series of very bad words.

Now there was only one guard left, a man with dark circles under his eyes who smelled a lot like smoke. *Captain Romano.* Everyone in the city knew him. He kept pace with the fancy carriage on horseback, and Cat bobbed in his wake.

"Every bag we pulled from the river was just the same," the captain was saying. He sounded like he wanted to be somewhere else, or maybe just to take a nap. "Filled with letter blocks from a printing press. The thieves must have switched them—"

There was a *thud* and then a bunch of clinking from inside the carriage, like someone had thrown a lot of small, heavy things. "You *let* the thieves switch them," hissed a voice—the shouter. The *Pope.*

Cat almost tripped over a loose cobblestone. "Oh no, don't you dare *flinch* from me, Giulio, you bear as much responsibility for this fiasco as the idiot captain."

"Yes, Your Holiness," intoned another, flatter voice inside the carriage.

"And what the *devil* is taking so long?" complained the Pope.

The devil that was taking so long was the Piazza della Signoria. Once again, the fancy carriage and the fancy men inside it had proven themselves to be very silly indeed. Because the Piazza was absolutely *packed* with people—not just Florentines, but those who had come to town for the banquet, and those who had come to stare at the people who had come for the banquet. And the carriage was stuck right in the middle of it all.

"We ordered these streets cleared," said the flat voice.

"Yes, Your Eminence," Captain Romano said. He was talking slow and careful, like Cat did when she was worried about annoying the printer. "However, without the men to back that order up, enforcing it has been . . . difficult."

"I hate this damned city," the Pope grumbled.

"Have you not recruited the City Guard?" the flat voice asked.

"I have attempted to do so," Captain Romano said, even more slowly. "But they are . . . frustratingly reluctant to cooperate."

The captain continued placating the men as Cat slowed. The carriage was almost to the center of the Piazza now, surrounded by people on all sides. Which meant it was time for Cat to play her part.

She took a deep breath.

"*Viva la Repubblica!*" It took Cat a moment to recognize her own voice. She sounded almost . . . grown-up. "*Viva la Repubblica!*" she yelled again, and this time she wasn't alone. The chant was growing, blooming throughout the Piazza. It spiraled in intensity and in volume. "*Viva la Repubblica!*"

The crowd surged, pulsing around the carriage. For a moment, Cat lost sight of it. But along with the surge, Cat heard an almighty *thump*. And when the crowd ebbed, she could see that the carriage was rocking on its wheels.

"Christ!" came a shout from inside, woozy with jolting as someone slammed against the opposite door. *Thump. Thump.* The carriage pitched with blow after blow. At the front, the driver was shoved from his bench, disappearing into the crowd below.

The curtain flicked open, and the Pope's pale face stared out at the crowd. His head jostled with the motion of the carriage. He looked very frightened. "Romano!" he shouted, but Captain Romano had been separated from the carriage by dozens of shouting Florentines. And in the middle of the throng, his eyes landed on Cat.

It might have been ego talking, but Cat thought there was a spark of recognition in the Pope's eyes. Cat stuck her tongue out at him.

"To me!" Captain Romano bellowed. "Guardsmen! To me!"

He was calling to a cluster of men in red—the City Guard. They lingered at the edges of the mob. To Cat's eye, they looked like they were trying not to laugh. And they *definitely* didn't look as though they were about to rush in and help out.

"Will you shirk your duties like this?" Captain Romano demanded. "How can you just *stand* there while this carriage is threatened?"

"It's a Medici carriage, isn't it?" said one of the men. "Not our problem."

"Of course it's your *problem*," Captain Romano roared. "It's a public piazza!"

"Oh, now he cares about jurisdiction," commented the second guard.

"Where is Captain Santini?" the Medici captain demanded. "He will hear of this—"

"He's not our captain anymore," interjected the first guard. "Not since he's been selling us off to *you*."

His companion brandished some sort of book in the air. "Look familiar, Romano?"

Captain Romano went faintly green. "How did you get that?"

"Why would I tell *you*?"

"Santini won't be back in the city anytime soon," said the second guard. "Not if he knows what's good for him." He looked back over Captain Romano's shoulder. "Looks like your master's making his exit. You better heel before he decides to put you down."

The besieged driver had managed to claw his way back onto the front bench, the climbing protesters falling back for him. Now the carriage was finally making some headway, finding a path through the quelling crowd. With a last grimace, Captain Romano prodded his horse into a trot as the Medici cleared the final rings of chaos and burst out onto the Via Porta Rossa.

In the Piazza della Signoria, the mob cleared almost as quickly as it had formed. The deafening chants subsided as soon as the Pope's carriage was out of sight.

A small vegetable cart trundled past, making good time despite the hubbub. As they passed Cat, the short driver pushed their hat back— just far enough for Cat to get a glimpse of one twinkling dark eye.

The eye winked. Then something was arcing through the air, landing in Cat's hands with a jingle. Cat inspected her prize. It was a purple velvet purse, filled with the unmistakable shifting weight of gold florins. There was a cross embroidered on it.

By the time Cat looked up again, the cart and its driver had been swallowed by the crowd.

Cat pocketed the purse, whistling to herself. Gio would *die* of envy. And tonight, they could eat ciambelle until they were sick.

It was going to be a good winter.

61

KHALID

The getaway from the Palazzo Medici had been clean—as clean as the escape from an explosion in the Pope's house could be. Khalid had found Rosa and the young painter as soon as they had hit open air. "Take Dominic," she had said, and Khalid suddenly had a very shellshocked charge trailing him through the city gates while Rosa disappeared into the crowd on her own.

Neither of them had said a word until they reached the millhouse, where the sight of Sarra lying pale and still on a pallet under Agata's formidable care had been a nasty surprise. Dominic and Khalid had been shooed away to await whatever outcome the night would bring. The painter had taken up shelter against the millhouse. Khalid had taken his rug down to the river, lost himself in the Subh prayer, and then sat still and silent until the first rays of early sunshine began to warm his face.

He didn't open his eyes at the sound of nearing hoofbeats. He didn't open them at the twitters of morning birdsong. He didn't open them as a gust of icy wind rushed past, biting through his clothes and chilling his fingers, or as a looming silhouette approached, close enough to block out the watery sunlight.

"You're smiling."

Khalid was reasonably certain that he was not smiling. The night's exhilaration was fading rapidly. In its wake was a bone-deep exhaustion, topped off by the growing ache as his various injuries let him know that they were not to be forgotten. His arm hurt. His ribs hurt. His cheeks hurt.

He hadn't done anything to his cheeks. His cheeks should not hurt.

Khalid realized that he was, in fact, smiling.

He opened his eyes.

Giacomo was leaning against the riverbank wall. He still wore Khalid's old Medici Guard uniform. In the early-morning light, touches of gold and amber were picked out in his hair. He was watching the water, profile turned so that Khalid could not see the growing bruise streaking his left temple.

"It was a good job," Khalid said. He stood, pacing to Giacomo's side.

"Yeah?" There was a manic tinge in Giacomo's voice. "Which part was your favorite? Where you almost died? Where Sarra almost died? Where I blew us all up?"

"Traverio?"

Giacomo smirked. "As you planned. If he's lucky, he'll spend his life rotting in a Florentine prison. If he's unlucky, His Holiness will get his hands on him. Either way, the Weever of Genoa's reign of terror is at an end."

Khalid nodded. "That. That's my favorite part of the job."

He had shown the weever spine to Rosa in the millhouse the night before. His brush with death had still been sparking on his mind, as had Giacomo's whispered confessions. It had left him feeling . . . inspired. Truthful. Trusting, for the first time in many years.

Rosa had inspected the spine for a full minute, and then studied Khalid's face with the same level of focus. "I should have told you sooner," he had said, as the weight of her scrutiny grew.

"I understand why you didn't," she'd said. "It can feel safer to go it alone. And with your family on the line—"

"And your lives."

She'd drawn up at that, a little flushed. "Well. I'm actually kind of flattered." With delicate fingertips, she'd folded the cloth closed and slid the whole package back across the table to Khalid. "What do you make of this?"

"It is a threat," he'd replied, a little taken aback by the obviousness of the question.

"What else?" she'd asked. When he'd just looked at her, unsure how to respond, she'd given him a supportive smile. "This isn't a trap. I'm just curious how you see this. You know Traverio better than the rest of us. You also know the day-to-day workings of the Palazzo better than the rest of us. So how do those things link together?"

He'd taken a moment to consider. "I think . . . ," he'd said slowly, "that Traverio is being careless. To leave such a thing at the front gates of the Palazzo Medici in broad daylight? It is a bold move, but it is also a foolish one." He had traced the outline of the spine through the kerchief, feeling the shape. "I think that the more he ties himself to our job, the more he ties himself to us." Khalid had looked up at Rosa, into her approving dark gaze. "Which means we can use those ties to drag him wherever we please."

"It may be dangerous," Rosa had cautioned him. "It will definitely be difficult."

"To be rid of Traverio for good?" Khalid had replied. "Nothing is too difficult."

A few close calls with edged weapons later and Khalid still would not take any of it back. Especially not with Giacomo's impressed stare on him, warmer than even the sunlight. "You played him like a fiddle," Giacomo marveled.

"Vice and voice," Khalid said. "I learned only from the best."

Comfortable silence stretched between them. There were ducks on the water. Khalid's smile widened as he watched them, bobbing together and then apart and then together again, carried downstream by the current. A few months ago, he would have resented those ducks and their freedom. Now, he could appreciate them.

"What now?" he asked Giacomo.

"I'm not sure yet," Giacomo said. "Lord knows none of us can stay in Florence after last night. The open road calls and I am helpless but to answer, etcetera, etcetera, so, you know. Anywhere and everywhere."

"Will your family be looking for you?"

"I don't think so," Giacomo said, an edge to his voice. "They never have before. And even if they do, I'm good at not being who people think I am."

"Yes," Khalid agreed. The ducks were almost to the bend in the river now, paddling out of sight. "But I am glad to know you when you are you."

Beside him, Giacomo rocked as though he had taken a blow. "Signore al-Sarraj, you cannot simply come out and *say* such things," he said, familiar and teasing. "You'll stop my heart. I'll fall down dead in my tracks and that will be on you. Aren't you worried that I'll go getting all sorts of ideas? You would *not* approve of—"

"Then you do not know me as well as you think."

Giacomo was staring at him. Khalid could see it out of the corner of his eye. "Khalid."

"Giacomo." He twisted to meet Giacomo's stunned gaze.

Giacomo studied his face for a long moment, eyes flicking as they catalogued every feature. He let out a breathy laugh. "You should smile more," he said. "It suits you."

Reaching out, Khalid brushed his fingers along Giacomo's bruise. He didn't miss how the other man's breath caught in his throat. "You should get in more fights," he said. "It suits you."

"You," Giacomo said, "are a flirt, it turns out."

"Is it working?"

"For God's sake," Giacomo said, and then he was kissing Khalid, leaning up with one hand on Khalid's chest. Khalid did his best to help out, injured as he was, twining the fingers of his good hand with Giacomo's and trailing his lips across Giacomo's cheek to his bruised temple and then back to his mouth again.

They were both short of breath when they parted, staring at one another with wide eyes. Khalid could feel himself beaming—his cheeks would be in agony for *days*, he was sure of it. He welcomed it. Anything to help him remember this moment.

"I take it back," Giacomo murmured into the centimeters between them. "You're not allowed to smile, I won't have it. It's devastating. I'm going to drop dead."

"You said that already."

"Then it is *doubly true*, you should know better than to doubt me—"

"Don't drop dead."

"Fine. *Fine*." Giacomo let out a sigh. His lips were a little redder than they had been a few minutes before. Khalid congratulated himself for this. "Are we absolutely *certain* we have to leave right at this moment?" Giacomo said. "Surely the Medici will grant us a reprieve if I explain to them that I need an immediate repeat performance of you and *that*. Probably an encore. Definitely an encore." He blinked, a little dazed. "Khalid, I want an encore."

"I—" Khalid began, and stopped.

Because they were standing on a path together. He could see that now. It stretched backward to a dawn-touched alley in Genoa, and forward to something that looked a little like a dead end.

Giacomo had not looked for the boy he had loved in Grosseto. For shame or for fear or for hurt, he had let the world carry him away. Khalid did not want to be like that boy. But unless their path changed, the dead end would take them both.

"Come to Tunis."

The words were an impulse, but one Khalid did not bother to check. Giacomo's eyes shot wide at their utterance. "Are you serious?" He sounded unsteady.

"Yes."

"You—you would want me in your city?"

"I want you with me."

Giacomo swayed theatrically, but his eyes were bright. "Remember what I told you about stopping my heart?"

"You do not want to come?"

"Of course I do." Giacomo made a grab for Khalid's hand, holding it in both of his. "I just want to make certain you know what you're getting into. I can be a lot, I've been told. Some people even say I'm mad."

"I want an encore too."

Giacomo blinked at him again. He seemed to be struggling to digest what Khalid was saying. "How do you keep *doing* that?" he muttered.

"Doing—"

"With the potholes, it's—"

It was Khalid's turn to kiss him, leaning over to press his lips to Giacomo's. Their first embrace had been a dam breaking, a flood of adrenaline and acknowledgment and desire. This one was softer. Khalid thought it felt like a promise.

"Yes," Giacomo said when they parted. His eyes were still closed.

Khalid's heart double-thumped in his chest. "Yes?"

"Yes, yes, I'll come." Giacomo cracked his eyelids open, peering at Khalid with an edge of irritation. "Now I know you kiss like that, I can't really leave you alone, can I? Ifriqiya." He cocked his head. "It sounds nice."

The path they stood on was unending, and it led far, far away from Genoa. The Lanterna di Genova was nothing more than a nightmare and the sunlight was on Khalid's face and soon he would see his brother. And Giacomo's hand was warm in his.

He smiled. Beside him, Giacomo made an affronted, wounded sound.

"It will be."

62

DOMINIC

Dominic did not sleep. Perhaps he would never sleep again. He doubted, sometime around dawn, that he had ever slept even once in his life. How could he, when he could not remember a time his heart was not rabbiting in his chest and his cheek was not stinging every time he opened his mouth?

Michelangelo pressed a bottle of wine into his hand. Dominic drank. They watched the sun rise over the Arno river.

It had still been dark when Master Michelangelo stomped up, plaster dust coating his graying curls. He had taken up a post beside Dominic, wrapping his cloak around himself, and stared out over the horizon. Dominic had attempted to do the same, but the welling panic in his throat was making that increasingly difficult with every strangled breath. And if the bottle of wine now sloshing in his hand was any indication, he wasn't doing a great job at hiding it.

"The Pope slapped me," he said, apropos of nothing. Michelangelo snorted.

"Almost as good as absolution. Depending on how you take it." Michelangelo plucked the bottle from Dominic's fingers and took a swig. "Didn't expect you'd make it here. There's a middle ground between denying a family's patronage and committing treason, you know."

"It didn't feel like it at the time," Dominic said. He tried to imagine a reality in which he'd taken another path this evening—left Rosa to manage on her own or turned her in to the Medici Guards. Both left a sour taste in his mouth. "It doesn't feel like it now."

"Hm," Michelangelo said. It was the same hum that, for years, had sent Dominic shrinking inside his own skin—the one that said, very clearly, *you will never be good enough*. Now, though, Dominic simply reached for the wine and took a swig. He and Michelangelo stared out over the river.

It was the older man who spoke first, to Dominic's surprise. "Do you know what you'll do now?"

An image flashed through Dominic's mind: Rosa's face as she inspected the Papal writ he'd created. "No," he said, unsure whether or not he was lying.

"Hm," Michelangelo said again. That shrinking impulse did not come. "Well. The Lord has seen fit to punish my involvement in this caper by sending a fresco my way. I'm off to Rome by midday." Silence stretched between them. "I might have use for an apprentice."

The past twelve hours had been brimming with unbelievable things, and somehow this was the thing that shocked Dominic the most. He stared at the artist, who kept his own eyes pinned on the skyline. "Master Michelangelo—"

Approaching hoofbeats saved him from figuring out how to end that sentence, and Dominic barely dodged the mill door as it flew open. A woozy Sarra stumbled out, just as two vegetable wagons rounded the bend, each pulled by a pair of plodding mules and guided by a driver in a wide straw hat.

"Go easy, girl—" scolded Signora de Rosso, chasing Sarra out of the mill. But Sarra was already moving, unsteady legs turning her dash into more of a controlled stagger. "Pietro!" she called. Dominic shoved to his feet to follow, ready to catch the girl if she fell flat on her face.

This was unnecessary because in the next instant, the taller of the two drivers was leaping down from his bench to catch Sarra's shoulder as she pitched forward, hauling her back to balance on her own feet. A bearded face beamed from beneath the broad brim of his hat. "Don't say you were *worried* about me."

"Shut up." Sarra punched at his arm. "Are you alright?"

"I could ask you the same question." He patted at the lump beneath her copper hair, and she swatted him dizzily away. "Though I know Sarra the Tinkerer doesn't get taken out so easily."

A huddle was starting to gather around the carts. Signora de Rosso arrived, already fussing over Sarra, and Michelangelo followed. Behind Pietro, Dominic spotted Khalid and Giacomo hiking up from the riverbank.

"Signore?" The second cart's driver held out a small hand to Dominic. He took it, stepping back to allow the woman to descend—and then paused as a familiar thrill ran through his fingers.

Rosa Cellini doffed her hat and winked a dark eye at him before jumping down onto the grass. She didn't let go of his hand.

"What a fine morning!" Giacomo declared. "What an unparalleled and exquisite day this is turning out to be!"

"Not so loud, please," Sarra said, rubbing her head.

Dominic did not miss the concerned glance Rosa shot Sarra. Neither, it seemed, did Signora de Rosso. "She'll be alright," the apothecary said. "Just needs a day or two of rest."

"None of us counted on Traverio clocking you like that," Rosa said. It sounded like an apology.

"He got the wagon," Sarra said. It sounded like an acceptance.

Giacomo *tsk*ed. "And after all the trouble you went through to load it."

The morning's panic threatened to make a return. "Someone—someone took the money?" Dominic asked.

"Don't say 'took,'" Sarra said, feeling the knot on her skull. "'Took' is such a soft word. And anyway—"

"The talk is that he was caught by the river," said Khalid. "*In* the river."

"His boat . . . ," Dominic said, studying Rosa's face. This news should be crushing, yet the only thing he saw in her expression was fiery satisfaction. "It sank?"

"Straight to the bottom of the Arno," Giacomo chipped in. "Apparently, despite Captain Romano's best efforts, not one single coin has been recovered. And the captain's request to divert more men to the search was met with the gentle reminder that the Medici jurisdiction is contained to the Palazzo." He nudged Khalid's side. "I'll bet you anything that didn't go over well at *all*."

"Anything?" Khalid nudged Giacomo back. "You already owe me ten percent of your take."

"If the money is lost, then what take is there?" Dominic asked. Perhaps he was beginning to catch his companions' insanity, but he felt as though he was the audience to a play, watching as the players spun their tale to its conclusion. By their words, this should be a moment of true devastation, and yet a current of bright amusement ran through the circle.

"Signore Fontana is worried that we've failed," Sarra told Rosa gravely. At her side, Pietro gave a low chuckle.

"There, there, signore." Giacomo sidled around to pet Dominic's hair soothingly. "There will be other massive fortunes . . . other chances to risk life and limb . . ."

"Giacomo," Rosa chided, but Dominic did not swat Giacomo's hand away. He was too busy watching a budding smile spread across Rosa's face, bright as the rising sun.

"Your disappointment is understandable," Rosa told him, circling to the back of the vegetable cart. Burlap sacks of onions and carrots sank the wagon bed heavy on its axles. *Too heavy.* "To go through years of planning and come out on the other side empty-handed? I can't imagine a more disappointing conclusion to this entire affair. Thank Heavens, then, that when Traverio bashed poor Sarra's head in and stole the wagon . . . that was *all* he was stealing."

"Not 'all'," Pietro said. "He took what was left of my press as well."

Dominic's gaze cut to Sarra. "So when his boat went down in the river—"

"People will just leave their boats anywhere," the girl commented.

"Uncovered. Obvious," Khalid added.

"Susceptible to the elements and to . . . rats. Rot. Augers and drills and chisels." Sarra shrugged. "Sometimes you wouldn't even notice the damage until you're already on the water."

"What happened to the gold?" Dominic asked.

Rosa leaned a hip against the vegetable cart. "It never made it out of the Palazzo."

"You're telling me it's still inside?"

Her smile was wicked. "What do you think?"

He could see the seams now, where her plan had come together. "I think it's in these carts. But I don't know how."

"Sarra?" Rosa held a hand out, and Sarra pressed a belt-knife into it. "Everybody ready?"

Michelangelo huffed. "Get on with it."

"As Il Divino requests." And with a flourish, Rosa brought the knife down.

It was not the first time Dominic had seen the wealth of Florence spill out onto the ground. He'd been treated to that sight twice in the last twelve hours. But watching the waterfall of gold as it tumbled from the tear in the burlap and out onto the grassy bank of the Arno was different. It promised something—for everyone standing, speechless, around the humble vegetable carts, yes, but also for the city that loomed on the horizon.

Funds enough to buy another army, Rosa had said. A country's ransom.

Not anymore.

Giacomo was the first to recover the power of speech. "How about that."

"Oh my," Sarra murmured.

"*Damn*," Signora de Rosso swore.

Dominic plucked up a florin and held it to the light. He was impressed that his hand only shook a little. "Do I have to ask?"

"You probably haven't heard, but there was a grave incident in the Piazza della Signoria this morning," Rosa informed Dominic, abruptly very serious. "A crowd of protesters mobbed the Pope's carriage. Very loud. Very intense."

"Those protesters," Pietro chipped in. "They are so excitable."

"From what I understand, they swarmed His Holiness's carriage for over ten minutes," Giacomo said. "The Medici might have managed to keep them back, had they not fired a good portion of their guard in a fit of temper—"

"And the City Guard might have been more inclined to help, had they not recently been slipped a ledger of a very sensitive nature," Sarra said.

"A ledger containing evidence that the Medici Guard was scheming to usurp the City's power," Khalid added.

"A terrible betrayal, yes, yes," Rosa said. "All this is to say, the delay in the Piazza della Signoria would have been an inconvenience on the best of days, but this morning . . . there was precious cargo onboard."

The florin slipped from Dominic's fingers. "No."

"To get *this much gold* out of the Palazzo in one trip? You can't do that with just some ordinary wagon. Actually, there aren't many things at all that could transport it without issue. You'd need—what was it again, Sarra?"

"The Pope's own carriage."

"That's—that's impossible." If Dominic had a shred of sense, he would steal one of these horses and flee for the hills.

"That's what we told her but, well." Giacomo pointed at the gleaming vegetable cart.

"Those rioters had their hands all *over* the Papal carriage," Sarra said. "Who knows what they might have made away with? There could have been *anything* stashed in the driver's bench. Hypothetically, of course."

"You didn't."

Rosa's eyes were wide. "*I* didn't."

Khalid raised his good arm. "I did."

"So all that—in the gardens—"

"All that in the gardens," Rosa agreed.

Dominic wheeled back, staring at the sky, at the carts, at the river. The curtain was descending. The players were taking their final bows, and the pieces were finally clicking into place. "This wasn't about the money."

Sarra lifted her chin. "Not *only* about the money."

"There's not a nobleman or a banker in all of Florence who won't think twice about cozying up with the Medici now," Rosa said. "Not after the display the Pope and his cousin put on. They've lost their wealthy supporters. They've cut ties with the City Guard. They've delivered the payroll for their army right to us. They're done."

"How did—how did you know they would do it? Break like that?" He shook his head, clearing out fog.

"Find the Lady," Sarra said.

Rosa nodded. "Any grifter can make a few coins winning a single hand. If you want to score big, you make sure your mark wins those first few rounds . . . but you keep the pressure mounting. And then, once they're feeling like they're in control, on top of the world, with a sure victory—one that *matters*—in front of them—"

"You let them destroy their own reputations in front of Florence's elite."

Rosa shrugged. "I mean, I was speaking in general, but . . . you get the gist."

Find the Lady. Dominic had taken many foolish chances in his own life—moving to Florence, apprenticing himself to a man who hated his craft, throwing in with a dark-eyed grifter on a whim—and this girl had risked the future of a city on a *card game.* He should be horrified, aghast, maybe even a little righteously angry—

He didn't realize that every eye was on him until Michelangelo swatted him across the back of the head. "Well?" the artist demanded.

And Dominic burst into laughter.

"I can't believe"—he said, gulping for air—"you *gambled* on—the Pope himself—"

Rosa watched him laugh, her smile softening as a pink flush rose in her cheeks. "Well, of course," she said. "After all, nobody ever looks to the priest."

63

ROSA

Scraps of Sarra's projects and the remnants of Agata's experiments; straw pallets and the last of their food; it was all swept into packs and bundled away in the blink of an eye. They had spent six weeks turning the mill into their home. It took less than six minutes to wipe away any trace that they'd ever been there at all.

Michelangelo and Dominic were the last to linger, huddled near the ever-grinding millstone. They were absorbed in an exchange of clipped, taut sentences too quiet to make out. Fighting down the temptation to eavesdrop, Rosa gave them a wide berth as she shouldered her bag and stepped out into the sunlight.

She found her team in the process of saddling their horses. Agata was resting against a tumbled-down section of wooden fencing, watching with a smug smile as Pietro fell over himself to ready one of the mules for her. "I love a strong young man with manners," she commented to Rosa as Rosa grew closer, and cackled as Pietro's fingers slipped on the mule's tack.

"Manners?" Sarra chipped in. "Obviously you've never shared a meal with him."

"Which one of us snorts while they chew?" Pietro asked.

"That was *one time*," Sarra shot back, and the conversation quickly devolved into familial bickering as Agata cackled gleefully on the sidelines. Rosa reached reflexively for that inner shard of ice and resolve, to steel herself against the warmth—

And stopped. *None of that, now.* The time for frozen rage was over. And wouldn't it be nice to get a taste of spring?

"All clear in there?" Sarra asked, nodding to the millhouse.

"Almost," Rosa responded. "The artist and his apprentice are having a talk."

"I can't believe you got Il Divino into this." Pietro shook his head. "Of all people."

"We're a very enticing employment prospect," Sarra said. "Even you threw in your lot with us. Even *Signore Fontana*—"

"Don't start," Rosa groaned. "Wait until I've had a full night of sleep first."

"He seems like a nice young man," Pietro remarked, giving the harness a tug. "Capable."

"Talented, as well," Sarra added, nodding sagely. "We approve."

"There's nothing to approve of," Rosa informed them.

"Sure, of course," Sarra said. "At least you're not the worst among us." She jerked her thumb toward the pair of horses a few meters away. Khalid and Giacomo stood back-to-back in between, saddling them. If there was space between their shoulder blades, Rosa couldn't see it.

"Something blooming?" she asked.

Sarra snorted. "Something bloomed."

Rosa cleared her throat. "A moment, signori?" she chirped, and grinned at the way that Giacomo's and Khalid's heads whipped around in unison. "I won't insult you with thanks. You'll be riding out of here with more thanks than you can carry. But it has been a pleasure to work with all of you. If you ever want to do it again . . . come find me."

"Oh, but everything will seem like such small stakes after this," Giacomo said. "I've been spoiled. From now on, I will only go after kings, sultans, and emperors."

"We will have to start planning soon, then," Khalid remarked, and Giacomo looked up at him with eyes that shone with delight.

"Signore al-Sarraj, such *machinations*!" he exclaimed.

Sarra groaned. "I can't take much more of this." She squeezed Rosa's shoulder. "It was good work."

"Worthy of our parents?"

"Are you joking?" Sarra said. "We just robbed the *Pope*. They'd be horrified."

"Hm," Rosa hummed. "I suppose it was a little flashy."

Agata was the first to peel away, accepting the mule's reins from Pietro with a pat to the cheek that lingered just long enough to warrant an eye roll from Sarra. Unlike the rest of them, she would not be leaving Florence in the wake of the job. Her apothecary was still standing, she reminded them (and Rosa did not miss Sarra's wince at that comment), and no one at the Palazzo had any reason to know she was involved in the night's events.

"Don't wait six years to come see me again," she instructed Rosa, "or I'll have something to say about it."

"I still have that bassetta debt to pay, after all," Rosa said, and endured a dry, smoky kiss on the forehead.

Khalid and Giacomo were already mounting up. "Khalid has been kind enough to extend an invitation to Tunis!" Giacomo said. "I think a little sun will be *just* the thing this winter."

Khalid smiled, small and pleased. "We are not finished yet" was all he said.

Rosa laughed. "Safe travels, then," she said.

"Safe travels," Khalid replied. He prodded his horse into a trot, taking off so quickly that Giacomo was forced to yelp his goodbye to Rosa at a canter, racing to catch up.

There were still her own belongings to pack. Rosa busied herself with this, letting Pietro and Sarra's bickering and laughter soothe the pang of watching her friends ride away from her.

She was just fastening the last buckles on her horse's tack when someone behind her cleared his throat. Rosa turned to find Michelangelo scowling at her, Dominic standing—not at his shoulder, in the manner of a polite and attentive apprentice, but planted at his side.

"I suppose this is goodbye," Michelangelo said with no preamble.

"But, *Uncle*—" Rosa whined, and thrilled at his huff of derision.

"No more of that," he said. "I've had enough for one lifetime. Farewell, signorina." To her surprise, he dropped into a low, courtly bow. "I pray that I never see you again."

She pressed one of his rough hands in both of hers. "I hope your prayers are answered."

Michelangelo nodded, a curt jerk of his head. Then he was swiveling on his heel and making for the river.

"You're not going with him?" Rosa asked Dominic.

Dominic shrugged. He was still wearing his banquet finery, a strange picture against the rustic backdrop of the millhouse. "Master Michelangelo invited me to accompany him to Rome," he said. "He has need of an apprentice fresco painter, evidently."

"Oh." Rosa forced a smile onto her face. "I'm sure it will be a very lucrative adventure."

"I told him that my path lies elsewhere."

Someone behind Rosa gave a loud snort. Rosa tossed a glare over her shoulder in time to see Pietro shoving his sister onto the cart's bench and clucking the mule into a trudge.

Rosa winced. "I have to—"

"No, of course—"

"We can't stick around."

He nodded. "I understand."

They looked at each other. The Nepis' cart rolled onto the road.

Dominic was the first one to break. "That looks like a good path, actually."

The breath in Rosa's lungs was cool and sweet. "You think? It's a bit rocky." She took a few steps in the cart's wake, not bothering to fight her smile as Dominic kept pace next to her.

"Well," he said. "What can you do about that?"

"Is he coming along?" Sarra called. Pietro's shoulders were shaking with laughter. But Rosa could not bring herself to be angry, not when Dominic was smiling.

"Where are we going first?" he asked, by way of an answer.

"I was thinking Chiusi for a spell," she said, enjoying the soft joy that spread over his face. "After that, who knows? Provided you don't wish to stay and become a cheesemonger."

"You sound like you have something in mind."

Rosa hummed thoughtfully. "Perhaps," she mused, but what she meant was, *You are an unimpressive painter and a jaw-dropping mimic. And what she really meant was, How would you feel about applying that knack to an . . . alternative field?*

"It would be nice. To travel with you" was what she finally said. She could sense Sarra's smirk. She chose to ignore it as Dominic's shoulder bumped hers, light and teasing. It felt like a thank-you. *An afterward*, she thought, nonsensical and happy.

And then, because she would always be herself, she added, "Are your talents limited to frescoes and Papal orders?"

"I'm not sure," Dominic said. "Do you want to find out?"

ACKNOWLEDGMENTS

This book, like a million others, was born in the terrified, empty hours of a global pandemic. But also, it was born several years before that, in the FinalDraft pages of a screenplay. And prior to *that*, it was born on the streets of Florence, in the brain of a clueless tourist who'd gotten lost looking for the Uffizi while on vacation with her parents.

Which is to say, there are a lot of people who've had a hand in getting this piece of heavy-on-the-fiction historical fiction out into the world. I'd better start naming names fast or we'll be here all night. So, thank you . . .

To Holly West, my editor and the universe's preeminent Rosa/ Dominic fan. Your insightful ideas are a joy, and this book wouldn't be half of what it is without them (or you!); to Dillon West, Jon Reyes, and Cyrus McGoldrick, for such thoughtful notes; to Meg Sayre and Bailie Rosenlund, for this gorgeous cover; to Dawn Ryan and Kim Waymer, for getting *Medici Heist* onto shelves; and to the rest of the team at Mac Kids who made this project possible!

To John Cusick, my agent, who saw my tortured manuscript in his inbox and, out of the kindness of his heart, thought, *yes*. You're an absolute legend, and I'm lucky you're in my corner. And thank you to Melissa White, Madeline Shellhouse, and Chiara Panzeri in Folio Lit's Foreign Rights department, for bringing this book further across the world than I had ever dreamed.

To Kim Yau, Matt Horwitz, Chelsea Benson, and Dave Brown, my Echo Lake team, for opening the door to this brave new world of publishing, and to Alex Kohner and Mitchell Ostrove, my lawyers, for having my back.

Thank you to anyone who has ever read a version of this over the last few years. My writer's group—Matt, Mike, Des, Tara, and Brad; my beautiful Alpacas—Kirsten, Nina, Charlotte, Rachel K, and Walls; Rachel P; Delaney; Lauren; and last but *definitely* not least, thank you to Meghan, whose enthusiasm over the in-process snippets I sent over are the reason I saw this thing through to the end.

Finally, thank you to my family. Mom and Dad—you've never let me doubt that I could achieve my foolhardy creative goals. I have always felt your love and support, and I couldn't have done this without you. Willa—you've been letting me tell you stories since forever, and this one's for you, too. There are both soldiers and shoulders in it. And, Nick—you knew I was always moving forward, even when I felt like I was running in place. Thank you for being my biggest fan.